THRUST
OF THE
STILETTO

DARRELL ZUERCHER

Black Rose Writing | Texas

ISBN: 978-1-68433-385-1
PUBLISHED BY BLACK ROSE WRITING
www.blackrosewriting.com

Printed in the United States of America
Suggested Retail Price (SRP) $19.95

Thrust of the Stiletto is printed in Calluna

ACKNOWLEDGMENTS

I would like to thank my wife, Kelley, for her unwavering support in this effort, and my most devoted friend, R. Mark Colborn, for his positive, critical eye and honesty regarding early drafts.

In addition, I would also like to thank several others who took time to talk with a fledgling author at various conventions and help me address specific issues: Adam Baldwin, Adrian Pasdar, Carole Barrowman, David B. Coe, Lou Diamond Phillips, Timothy Zahn, Todd McCaffery, and Wallace Shawn.

THRUST
OF THE
STILETTO

CHAPTER 1

Black.

Comfortable. Predictable. Controlled.

Roland surrounded himself with it, reveling in its constancy. Slipping into black was better than getting caught, or so the less cautious had led him to believe.

Eyes open or closed—it made no difference. Roland settled back into the lone cockpit chair. It's black, genuine animal hide held him, without inviting him to sleep. He waited, knowing which monitors would illuminate first.

He checked his chronometer and verified his next meal to be in two hours. *Plenty of time.*

Melanie played Mozart.

The periodic changes in the viewscreens hardly registered through his closed eyelids. Little activity went unnoticed; less went unexpected.

"Melanie?"

"Yes, Roland?" Melanie always called him "Roland."

The interface software never seems to point her to anything else. I could modify the randomizer to include a few more nicknames. I could lower the ratio of "Roland" to allow more conversational addresses. Not now, though. "Roland" must suffice, for the time being.

"Any signs of pursuit?" he asked.

"No, Roland. But I am detecting non-standard patrol patterns."

"So, they are still looking for me."

"It appears so."

I can't say I am surprised. Even based on a general description of my ship, they would assume I could not achieve hyperspace once I cleared the asteroid field. Of course, they could be looking for signs I did not navigate the asteroid field but crashed into one of its residents instead. Either way, they should give up soon. Perhaps not soon enough, though.

"How did they detect us when we left the surface?" he asked.

"Is it relevant at this point?" Melanie responded.

"I think it is. Especially since we are still vulnerable to them."

"Our current situation, though similar, is not equivalent to the previous situation. Therefore, the benefit from evaluating our planetary departure is insufficient for applying the necessary resources to conduct the evaluation."

"You see no benefit from determining what mistakes were made?"

"I see insufficient benefit, compared to the resource expenditure. I already informed Jackson of all variables for which he did not account in his calculations. When we exit this asteroid belt, and when we next exit the planet's surface, those variables will be accounted for."

"OK. Fine."

I need to revisit her deductive programming. She is designed to make recommendations, but not make excuses and evade questions. I must have introduced a bug with my last system upgrade. I don't have the energy to deal with it now, though.

"Once our target leaves Dorean airspace when we leave the asteroid's perimeter, what are the chances of avoiding detection?" he asked.

"Using standard countermeasures, we will have a seventy-three percent probability to avoid detection. This probability varies per the proximity of the patrolling vessels."

"Of course. What is the minimum distance to maintain the probability?"

"Twenty-three point one-six kilometers."

Roland smiled. *Anyone who can fly should be able to see us at that range.* "Melanie, when plotting the trajectory for contact, maintain a minimum distance of twenty-five kilometers from any patrolling craft," he directed. "I lost them once. I would rather they not find me again—not now."

"I will pass the information on to Jackson when he is ready to begin his calculations."

"Thank you."

* * *

"No need to worry, Kor. Reginald is the best pilot I know." Abenor glanced from the viewscreen as he picked up his tea.

"I appreciate your assurances, Abenor, but I have a lot riding on this agreement—including a great many future opportunities—and am trying to make sure everything goes well," Kor replied.

"I understand completely. I have my own reputation on the line, Kor. I would not risk that on anyone but the best. I have no reservations in doing so when it comes to Reginald."

"Well, if you are comfortable with him, I can take some confidence from that."

"Absolutely, Kor. I would only trust Reginald with something this important, so relax. He will not let you down."

"Very well, Abenor. I will be in touch when this is over. I hope we can do much more business in the future."

"I look forward to it," Abenor replied, closing the communication session.

* * *

Roland was fatigued. The meal was sufficient for his nutritional needs—they all were—but some tasted better than others. The ones from Bantadam were among the most enjoyable. They strived to move beyond "sufficient" almost too "succulent". Almost. *Simple but tasty. Still, something spicier would have been nice, but I have no more Bantadam options. I will need to return for more if I have a good enough reason to go there.*

The escape and evasion from the Dorean patrol crafts had taken its toll on Roland's nerves. This was his latest of numerous visits to the Dorean planet, but the patrols had changed their pattern since his previous one. These patrol pilots were good. Although he had stayed out of their weapons' ranges, Roland had not been able to shake them loose. At least his ship had not made the escape more difficult. The streamlined shape of the *Stiletto* sliced through Dorea's thick atmosphere with little additional drain on the normal-space drive, leaving plenty to navigate through the wider—but more threatening—space between the asteroids.

One thing Jackson accounted for in his calculations—one thing Roland had programmed him for—was the assumption that the patrol pilots pursued, rather than anticipated. Thus far, every encounter with patrol pilots had proven the assumption true. He had always escaped.

Granted, there was not a lot to keep a patrol pilot's attention, especially here. So little traffic left this planet. The costs for launching any kind of planetary assault would cripple most planets, so there was very little threat from off-world ships, even if invasion were not prohibited by the empire.

Typically, patrol pilots were those beyond their prime, so they were relegated to planetary patrol duty. It kept them flying, which no pilot wants to give up, and it did allow for the occasional orbital rescue. It almost never required anticipation or pursuit. Almost never.

Patrol pilots would not follow a ship into an asteroid field, even one as easy as the Dorea system possessed. Money provides limited motivation. And patrol vessels were never designed to pursue through those fields. Roland knew all the habits of planetary patrols. Dorea patrols were skilled and tenacious despite their age, but they were limited in their scope. *It's nice to know they are still somewhat predictable, even if they improved their tactics.*

Even with the changes in their pilots' skill and tactics, their patrol ships were still too clumsy, being designed for atmospheric and near orbit security for the primary planets. Their sensors lacked the necessary sensitivity to separate the *Stiletto* from its hiding place. Their ships lacked the tight navigation required to negotiate an asteroid field. His did not. He used his ship's strength against their ships' weakness. *And now I am here, waiting for my ride.* As long as the *Stiletto* stayed hidden behind this asteroid, his situation would remain calm. But he was going to get very busy. He asked, "How much longer?"

"Estimated time of arrival is two hours, fourteen minutes," Melanie replied. "I suspect the patrol pattern will return to normal before then. Their existing pattern has been ongoing now for the ninety-four minutes since we cut main power. Previous measurements would stipulate such alterations do not exceed three hours."

"Understood. Still, make sure Jackson calculates for both patterns," Roland replied, rising from his chair. He went to his bunk, near the *Stiletto's* center. Beyond it was the small galley in which he prepared and ate his meals. Aft was his toileting facility and storage, and cargo holds.

Lying down, Roland said, "Melanie, drop the volume by half, and wake me in ninety minutes."

"Should I end this music, and start something softer and slower, like Brahms or *Sounds of the Sea*? It may be more suitable for sleeping."

"No, Melanie. Mozart is fine."

"Very well." Mozart faded more into the background as Roland lay down on his bunk. "Good night, Roland," Melanie said.

Roland, again.

* * *

His image filled the viewscreen. Kor Daga had heard of Mr. Corius's existence but have never spoken to him.

"I realize this is something new for you, Mr. Daga. From your previous successes and the discretion with which you achieved them, I am supremely confident you are the right person for this situation."

"I thank you. I aim for success, and do not accept anything less," Kor replied. "It is no less true for this."

"I am glad to hear it. There is a lot riding on this, for both of us. It is imperative this delivery be on time."

"I assure you it will be. My contact has many reliable transporters available, and he has assured me the one he has in mind is the best, and the most discreet."

"I hope his judgment is as sound as your faith in him. Success in this means more and better opportunities, for you and for me. I, myself, am excited at the prospect. I hope you are, too."

"Indeed. I will make sure..." Kor began, but the screen abruptly went blank. "...it is done with the utmost speed and discretion," he finished after a brief, startled pause.

CHAPTER 2

"Damn it! He locked me out of that, too." Vardri made sure she did not convey her frustration visibly. The glass walls did well to keep sound filtered, but not sight. She did not know whom she could trust now.

She watched the last of the file encryption. *I waited to get this project for almost a year, but I did not plan for this.* She gazed out over the city through one of her windows until the beep from her console told her to go to the next step.

Vardri opened a new message to her mother, writing some thoughtful, but harmless, drivel about her day. *I don't know if he has started monitoring my outbound communication. I must take the chance this makes it through if he is.* She attached copies of some of the pictures she had displayed around her office. They provided some glimpses into the world beyond her metal and glass walls. They showed her in some of the more exotic locations around Dorea.

I hope I live long enough to add to these pictures.

Some movement outside her office drew her attention from her correspondence. She glanced up, faked a brief smile as she exchanged a glance with Tarin who was approaching her door, and then returned to her message. As she finished sending the message, Tarin knocked on the door.

"Come in, Tarin."

The uniformed man strode in, pushing the door behind him. He waited for the door to close before speaking. "Congratulations, Ms. Alarius, on the successful completion of this effort."

"It's still too early for congratulations, Commander. Your crew will still need to field-test RECON before we can claim such a victory."

"A mere formality. You have overseen this project from the beginning. All the initial tests have been completed. I do not expect any new issues to be discovered tomorrow. I am confident the RECON will be successful in the field test. So, I thought we could celebrate tonight. My officers and I would like to invite you and your chief engineer out to celebrate in style tonight. I'll pick you both up here at 1800 hours."

"Tarin, I realize you are eager to proceed with getting this deployed to the fleet, but I have seen too many projects—including military projects like this—halted because something showed up in field tests. I think celebrating is premature."

"Nonsense. Tonight, I will send a car to pick you and your engineer..."

"Beranon," Vardri interrupted, "His name is Beranon."

"Yes. Beranon. The driver will pick you and Beranon up this evening, and we will meet at the Esoterica for dinner and cocktails. Tomorrow, after the formality of field testing is completed, we will throw a party here for everyone who was involved in this work."

"I should go home first. I am not dressed for a party."

"Nonsense. We will be in uniform, so your work attire will be sufficient."

Damn.

"I should see if Beranon has a previous engagement with his family before we can commit to anything. Perhaps after you return from your test tomorrow..."

"More nonsense. Whatever he has planned can be rescheduled in favor of celebrating something so momentous. I will pick you both up at 1800, and I won't take 'No' for an answer."

"Your offer is very generous, Tarin, but I cannot go anywhere this evening," Vardri stated. "I have to..."

"No, you don't, Vardri," Tarin interrupted with a broad grin. "You work too hard. Anything you have left undone can wait until tomorrow."

Vardri considered her options. She had no weapon with which she could overpower Tarin. Even if she did, she had no visible justification for doing so. He had not attacked her nor even threatened her. As far as everyone here could tell, she would be attacking someone without provocation. She could run from the office, but he would put a "no travel" alert on her, leaving her stuck on the planet where he could hunt her down at his leisure.

"Perhaps you're right, Tarin," she responded, mustering a smile she hoped did not look forced.

"Of course, I am," Tarin beamed. As he approached the door, he announced, "My car will arrive promptly at 1800 hours. Be ready for a fabulous evening."

"Thank you again. I will let Beranon know," she said to his retreating back.

She punched in the code for Beranon's office.

"Yes, Vardri? How can I..."

"I need to see you now."

"As soon as..."

"Now, Beranon." After waiting a couple seconds, she added, "Please."

"Very well, Vardri. I'm on my way."

"Thank you."

* * *

Black.

Despite the food and fatigue, Roland was restless. Sleep evaded his pursuit. He tried changing positions. He tried willing himself to sleep. He tried some relaxation techniques he had learned from one expert or another's writings. They failed to bring about the desired effect. Sleep then left him altogether.

The *Stiletto's* interior was spartan. The blackness of the interior walls was broken by active computer viewscreens and keypads. Inactive monitors provided grayness dark enough to be described as a "light black." The active screens were Roland's world. They were his entertainment, his history, his library, his respite.

Roland sought out those screens and returned to his cockpit chair. He checked the viewscreens and retraced his steps.

There was nothing unusual in the customs files or registered flight paths. The hotel reservations confirmed the crew count. I shouldn't be surprised. After all, this is a standard freighter, carrying...something or other.

Its cargo was not important. Its destination was. Roland needed a ride.

He was proud of his vessel. Though he had never invited anyone else on board, he imagined the looks on faces he had seen in his viewscreens. In her current state, the *Stiletto* was the best Interceptor-class ship in space. Built on the long-range fighter chassis but with structural modifications allowing for atmospheric flight, she was small, sleek, and beyond the bleeding edge. Her sensors were well beyond the best money could buy. They would not be available to other pilots for at least six months. By then, he would have already researched and acquired the next prototype system. The normal-

8

space propulsion system aboard the *Stiletto* would typically be used to power ships two classes larger. Her computer processing speed performed calculations faster than many planetary mainframes. Her aft-shielding could withstand a direct hit from any Destroyer-class military vessel.

The *Stiletto* had no weapons, though. There was no need for any. She possessed no long-range travel capability, either—at least, not on her own. She had an emergency hyperdrive, with a spherical bubble. But Roland made use of other vessels' hyperdrives as the need arose. He smiled. After this trip, his ship would be even better. Ricna had the new **R**apid **E**nergy **CON**version prototype. RECON.

Three prototypes were already part of the *Stiletto*. Another six first-generation systems had become part of her. Sure, Roland had sacrificed some armoring and shielding to make room for them, but the *Stiletto* needed enough shielding to handle space debris. She did not require armor at all. No one ever had anything to fire upon—thus far, anyway. *At some point, I will run into something I did not anticipate. Until then, I need to prepare for everything I can anticipate, which includes being on the wrong end of a weapon.*

After the RECON, though, he would be willing to offer them a target. *I have a little business to complete first.*

* * *

Get off the planet, she said. OK. Fine.

I'll take care of the travel arrangements, but you need to leave now, she said. The gate to the spaceport was more crowded than Beranon would have liked. *So many people. How many of them are looking for me?*

Don't look at the guards. He glanced away from a pair of them as he passed by. *Don't look like you are not looking at the guards. I need another drink.*

Beranon entered the line leading to one of the check-in kiosks. *Wait a minute. She said she had booked us into the freight terminal.* He looked around for a sign to direct him there. Nothing.

Noting two guards paying him too much attention, Beranon exited the line and joined a small group of people who were moving away from the guards. Looking behind him, he confirmed the guards had not followed him.

OK, where is the freight terminal? He turned toward the baggage claim area. *Maybe it's in a different part of the port.* He found an information access terminal and located a map showing the freight terminal due south from the main terminal building, but outside the pedestrian areas. *Now what?*

Beranon continued to, and through, the baggage claim area and exited the terminal. He pushed an indicator to show he needed transportation. *So, Vardri, once I get off this planet, what do I do? Go home? No. If she is right, I don't want them near my home.*

A car approached, with an autonomous driver. *I hope they have not programmed these to detain passengers.*

"May I have your desired destination, please?" the driver asked, in a not-too- disturbing electronic voice.

"The freight terminal," Beranon replied.

"Very well, sir. Please engage your security restraint."

Beranon strapped himself in. *I could use another drink. I have had too much already for me to drive myself, but not enough to get rid of this dread. Maybe she is being overly cautious and paranoid. I can't access things I used to be able to, but it's nothing I needed to complete the job. And, all he has in mind is picking us up for dinner tonight. Why is she so certain he would kill us?*

Beranon looked out of the window as the fence around the spaceport went by and slowed.

"Why are we stopping?" he asked the driver.

"I have been instructed to stop, sir."

"But there is no signal here, nor an intersection. The terminal is on up."

"I have been instructed to stop, sir."

Perhaps she is not paranoid. Beranon unstrapped himself and opened the door.

"Please, sir, you must remain in your harness until we reach your destination."

Not a chance, he thought, slamming the door behind him as he ran toward the freight terminal.

CHAPTER 3

Black.

The sunless side of the asteroid monopolized his window. His sensors and the backlit edge of the asteroid suggested the universe beyond. The lighted viewscreens separated the blackness of Roland's surroundings from the blackness outside the ship. On Roland's command, the sensors displayed the shipping lane through which the freighter, *I.S.S. Surrogate*, would pass on its way from Dorea to Erkarth.

The Dorea system had the best asteroid field. Large asteroids, easy to hide behind, were plentiful. Small asteroids, faster and harder to dodge, were not. Roland's experience with the Dorean asteroids had never included the threat of collision while the *Stiletto* was hiding. In other systems, he had been forced to relocate to avoid several moving asteroids as they bounced off the one he was hiding behind. Still, he found asteroid fields to be the safest place to wait for his next transportation provider.

Jackson can handle even the smallest and fastest asteroids when plotting a "tag." The Stiletto's *astronavigation is unparalleled, of course. The best.* Still, Dorea's asteroids made "tagging" much easier. And now, they served a secondary purpose: to provide cover for the *Stiletto* from the Dorean patrol craft. With Melanie's data about the patrol patterns, Jackson would calculate a trajectory to keep the ship out of visual range for as long as possible without jeopardizing the tag. *Hopefully, none of the pilots will deviate from those patterns.* Roland shrugged. *They never have. As a group, they can change patterns, but as individuals, they never vary from them.*

He glanced at the system chronometer. *Forty-two minutes. Then the chase will begin, if they notice my ship.* Roland punched in the commands for displaying the schematics of the *Surrogate.*

Melanie is not scheduled to reappear for eighteen minutes. There is no need to activate her for this. Roland called up his research files with a few touches to the viewscreens. The screens blazed with technical readouts of the *Surrogate*: her exterior, interior, computer systems, access hatches, cargo manifests, and crew and passenger lists—although passengers aboard freighters were little more than cryogenic cargo.

"She sure is an old mother," Roland whispered to no one. He permitted a smile for the humor in his observation: an old *Surrogate* mother. Melanie never responded to his jokes. As human as he had tried to make her interface, he had never been successful at programming humor.

Roland studied the exterior hull of the *Surrogate*. He examined the prominent clusters of the *Stiletto's* anticipated host. With his own vessel possessing a token hyperdrive, he prevailed upon other vessels for long-range transportation. Hyperdrives were large, temperamental, and served but one function: to move a ship from one point to another. Roland had sacrificed the *Stiletto's* independence for other functions. His drive was reserved for emergencies. This was transportation.

Cross-referencing the most secure landing sites with the easiest access to the computer system, Roland confirmed his planned nest.

Behind the cargo hatch, but not quite atop the hyperdrive. That should place me well within the bubble's perimeter.

The *Surrogate* had the standard elliptical hyperspace bubble. Although the older ships still had a spherical bubble, Roland had gotten used to the improved bubble a while ago. So much so, he had no immediate plans to upgrade his own.

Hyperspace technology had always been about speed and distance. Even with the fastest ships, normal space travel was limited. By the time a ship left a solar system, several years had passed. Travel between systems would take generations to complete. But the discovery of hyperspace—and the ability to enter and navigate hyperspace—made travel to other solar systems plausible.

From the beginning, success in hyperspace was achieved by enclosing the vessel in normal space. After learning how to insert a ship into hyperspace, other methods of propulsion failed. The earliest vessels, with their pilots, were lost. The physical laws in normal space were understood. But, even hundreds of years later, hyperspace was largely a mystery. Normal space vessels still could not negotiate hyperspace. Successful travel required ships be encased in normal space in order to move through hyperspace, or, more accurately, to return from hyperspace.

Even though hyperspace existed alongside normal space, the two were incompatible. Normal space inserted into hyperspace acted like an air bubble in water—the hyperspace pushed it out as quickly as possible. This relationship between hyperspace and normal space was exploited. The trick was learning to control which way the hyperspace pushed normal space out. Once a ship was inserted into hyperspace, the hyperspace tried to "spit out" the normal space surrounding the ship, taking the enclosed ship with it. The hyperdrives opened the insertion point into hyperspace at a precise angle. This angle, with the velocity of the ship, when entering the insertion point, determined the distance traveled. The drives also kept the surrounding bubble of normal space from fragmenting from around the ship.

As people started to better understand the physical laws governing hyperspace, they found the elliptical bubble was more efficient. The issue was not how much normal space was present in hyperspace. None was compatible. As long as the bubble enclosed the ship, the process worked. So, they trimmed back the silhouette of the normal space bubble around the ship. This reduction in the volume of normal space carried through hyperspace decreased the amount of energy required to keep the bubble intact. It also lengthened the distance traveled before emerging into normal space. By trimming the bubble, less normal space was dragged with the ship. The principle remained the same: normal space was "spit out" of hyperspace. But now, with less normal space, the ship stayed in hyperspace longer, covering more distance between each insertion.

But the smaller silhouette also meant there were fewer landing sites available to the *Stiletto*. With the spherical bubble, he could place his ship anywhere on his target ship—aft to stern. The bubble left plenty of clearance for a ship the size of the *Stiletto*. With the elliptical bubble, it was the middle third of the target that was now available to him. Within the middle third, Roland located his targeted landing site, so his ship was near the highest point of the ellipse.

As with most space-worthy vessels, the hull had the densest collection of computer connections available on the ship. The *Stiletto's* Lamprey would be able to link into those connections without any trouble. The power to the normal-space drive would then be skimmed to replenish his own ship's reserves. The freighter would never miss it since the amount skimmed would be well within the acceptable tolerances of such an inefficient design. The trick would be getting around the drive before it was engaged for the hyperspace leg of the Erkarth run. But, this was a freighter—a civilian freighter.

"Roland?"

"Yes, Melanie?"

"I could have gotten that for you."

"I know you could, but I did not want to disturb you. Could you get Jackson for me, please? I will need him in a few minutes."

"Sure, Roland. I will see you later."

* * *

Beranon had almost completed the form. *I must use my real name, or the biometric verification will draw too much attention.* Next of kin. *Sorry, honey, but if she is right, I cannot have them look for you to get to me.* He typed "Vardri Alarius" in the form. He identified as unmarried, also.

He then made his way through the corridors to the small passenger section. *I realize this is not first class, Vardri, but I could use a few more comfort features.* He glanced out of a window as he approached his berth. The car he had abandoned was now surrounded by military vehicles with flashing lights. *I guess she was telling the truth. Thank you,* he said to her as he passed her berth, already filling with cryogenic gas. *I'll buy you a drink when we get to Erkarth.* He climbed in and waited for the anesthesia to be administered. *Don't worry, honey, I would never take you and the kids on vacation this way.*

* * *

"Sir?" Roland got Jackson's voice from an old Western movie. It was the voice of some telegraph operator delivering a message to one of the "bad guys." Roland chuckled. He always thought of himself as one of the "bad guys." But in Roland's movie, this bad guy always won.

"Jackson, E.T.A. is twelve minutes. Prepare for engagement." Roland ordered. He had programmed Jackson for efficiency, not civility. Melanie provided conversation. With Jackson, speedy execution of his orders was paramount. Strip out the personality code—leave the executables.

"Roger that, sir." The *Surrogate's* schematics disappeared from the viewscreens, save for those of the exterior hull. Scrolling lines of calculations displayed to Roland's left, while the planned route of the *Surrogate* appeared before his chair. Roland watched the projected paths of the significant asteroids light up another viewscreen. He moved his eyes to the scrolling lines a moment before they paused, switching to a different set of calculations. He smiled as, again, his timing was accurate.

Roland noted the *Surrogate's* planned trajectory. The asteroids' orbital paths were overlaid onto the *Surrogate's*. Then the projected flight paths of each of the Dorea patrol craft appeared on Jackson's viewscreen.

"Jackson, why are the patrol craft routes so large and indistinct?"

"I do not have sufficient data to identify the most common variances to their established pattern, sir. I am calculating all of the potential outcomes, based on possible modifications to each pilot's pattern."

"Understood. Can you track just those pilots who will be on this side of the planet when we exit the asteroid field?"

"Recalculating, sir."

"For those tracked pilots, trend their pattern over the past hour and base your projections exclusively on their trends."

"Very well, sir," Jackson responded, and the remaining patrol routes came into sharper focus. "I must caution you such a constraint will lessen the accuracy of my calculations by almost three percent."

"I can live with that, Jackson."

One by one, the paths of the asteroids disappeared until the path for his current hiding place was displayed with his planned transporter's. The trajectories did not intersect. The shipping channels from a planet maintained a safe distance from asteroid pathways. Still, it was close enough to hide the *Stiletto* from those seeking her. He hoped.

Six minutes. Close enough.

Roland disliked waiting too long between Jackson's plotting and the actual execution of those plots. He played the future encounter over in his mind.

Thrust enough to cross behind the freighter at an acceptable distance. Some pilots were more paranoid than others where space debris was concerned. Freighter pilots fell to the other side. A stray asteroid should cause no undue alarm on board, as long as it was small and slow. Collisions with such free-floating asteroids were not uncommon, and the shielding prevented any serious impact. But the shielding would not extend to the rear unless the ship is in combat. The armor will take care of any incidental collision to the rear. The pilots did keep their eye on the larger asteroids, though, preferring to stay out of their path. *Cut the engines just before sensor contact. The* Surrogate's *sensors have close to our range, but they lack our sensitivity and required much more power.*

No unusual delays were reported from planet-side, so the Surrogate *should not be late. These ships are never early.*

As the freighter appeared upon his ship's sensors, Roland checked the chronometer. On time, as expected.

Roland watched the freighter lumber across his window as he ignited the *Stiletto's* thrusters enough to separate the ship from the asteroid. As he slid into position behind the *Surrogate.* Jackson displayed the energy signature from the freighter's normal-space drive, targeting the optimum location for. Roland verified Jackson's projected thrust parameters while the ship glided into the planned location, and then brought his own normal-space drive to life. The edge of the asteroid glowed more and more as the *Stiletto* moved away from its surface. The green reflection of Dorea's atmosphere came into view. Clouds covered most of the planet, although the surface was habitable. Technology helped in eliminating the more dangerous gases in the lower atmosphere, but the upper atmosphere was left untouched. So, most of the space research had to take place in high orbit, although nowhere close to the asteroids.

Roland smiled again at the thought of some first-year astronavigation student tracking an asteroid fragment as it never reappeared from the *Surrogate's* vector. He would see the fragment break off from a larger asteroid, angle into the heat signature of the *Surrogate's* engine, and vanish.

I wonder how many hours he will search Dorea's orbit for such a fragment before giving up? This kid will say, 'Interesting. I have never seen an asteroid do that before. I should find it again so I can check it out."

Roland shook his head.

It would be a mistake. If it were me, the first question I would ask is, 'What would disappear like that? Sure, it came from an asteroid belt, but it does not act like an asteroid.' Start with the observable, and then speculate. Do not assume the source if the behavior does not support the assumption.

Roland eased the normal-space drive up to Jackson's recommended level. The distance between the *Stiletto* and the *Surrogate* closed. "Melanie, is there any pursuit?"

"No, Roland. No patrol craft are responding to our approach."

"Thank you." *Now, up and over the hyperdrive. Slow down to match velocity, and...*

"Tag." Roland smiled triumphantly. "Fine work, Jackson. Establish lockdown and get Spectre."

"Roger that, sir."

CHAPTER 4

"How is it looking, Reg?" a baritone voice asked. James Reginald Fischer was an imaginary friend from Roland's childhood—an alias. Reginald had come in handy on those occasions when interaction with other people or computer systems was required. Roland had even created an entire, fictitious biography for him.

Spectre called him "Reg"—never "Roland." Spectre contacted other computer systems. Roland made sure no outside contacts had any chance of identifying him as Roland Marcel—all they could find would be "Reg."

"Clean and tight, Spectre. No surprises."

"Right." Spectre had also been programmed with a less formal communication style. Sentence fragments were not unusual, although none of the programming included colloquialisms or contractions. The rules were too lengthy to program; the variances opened the possibility for misinterpretation. "I am establishing contact with target."

Roland hummed as the video viewscreens blanked out. After a couple of bars of Franz Liszt's *Hungarian Rhapsody No. 2*, the center viewscreen jumped to life, displaying line after line of code. "First baby step," he sighed. Roland stretched back into his chair, closed his eyes, and hummed more of Liszt.

Putting the finishing touches on the *Rhapsody* with a flurry of waving arms, Roland opened his eyes, sat up, and faced the now brightly-lit panel of video viewscreens. *Let's see if there is anything here I need to know.* Touching the cool, pseudo-glass surface of the most central viewscreen, which had a visual interpretation of the ship's system health status, Roland announced, "Manifest." The video blinked and changed its output to show Roland the contents of the cargo holds. The system health output switched to a previously blank monitor.

One by one, Roland touched the surrounding screens, with the ship's manifest viewscreen front and center. With each touch of his fingers to the screen, he announced another system: "Outbound communication," "Inbound communication," "Energy transfer," "Passenger files," "Life support status." Each announcement altered the output on the appropriate viewscreen, as his computer routed the content to the desired monitor.

Roland glanced at the energy transfer viewscreen and smiled. *Hardly even into the yellow.* Glancing at each monitor in turn, he made quick calculations. *Spectre will siphon enough fuel from the freighter to replenish the* Stiletto *within the hour.*

The outbound communication screen shows routine flight statistics. The same with the inbound.

Confirmed seven minutes to hyperdrive ignition and three minutes from there to hyperspace itself.

"Spectre," he announced, "Increase energy transfer ration to one hundred and ten percent. They seem to be on a tight schedule."

"Sure thing, Reg. Tee plus ten percent."

The change in the fuel intake viewscreen was not noticeable unless one were looking for it. Roland did notice. He always noticed. Still, the rate of intake would cut too close to the ignition of the hyperdrive. "Pack it in, Spectre. They are starting up."

"Roger that, Reg. Energy transfer complete in twelve seconds. Complete or abort?"

"Go ahead and top it off, Spectre." Twelve seconds. *I will still have one hundred sixty-two seconds before the hyperdrive engaged. We will be invisible to them well before then.* Most of these ships did not monitor energy seepage until the drive was near engagement. He would have almost a full minute of downtime before they even checked. *Smooth sailing all the way to Erkarth.*

* * *

"Is it done?" Tarin asked.

"We were able to complete one of them, sir, but not both," his executive officer replied. "The ship is powering its hyperdrive now, so there is no time to sabotage the manager's chamber."

"Well, if anyone could cause us trouble, it would be the engineer."

* * *

Black.

Hyperspace was dull. There were no flashing lights. No stars streamed past. There was no sensation of movement at all. The Erkarth run was scheduled to last twenty-one hours. Twenty-one hours of black, perhaps interrupted by brief periods of starlight. The elliptical bubbles still required multiple insertions between planetary systems.

Roland thought of sleep, postponing his inquiry into the *Surrogate's* contents. These were prime moments for rest. Scant few were these moments outside hyperspace. *What needs to be done has already been done. Everything else can wait.*

"Melanie?"

"Yes, Roland?"

"Wake me in eight hours."

"Yes, Roland. Sleep well."

There was one monitor in his sleeping bunk. Roland used it exclusively for entertainment. Anything requiring a warning would be relayed audibly by Melanie.

* * *

Beranon felt the anesthesia begin to take effect. *This should be interesting.* He had never traveled using cryogenics because his company always paid for more comfortable modes. Beranon did know several people who had traveled in this manner, so he had researched the process. He had also looked into the survival processes the *Surrogate* employed. The ensured a much lower mortality rate than the fifteen percent standard. They did lack options for passengers to eat prior to the cryogenic travel. *I will be hungrier than I like when I wake up. Not enough time. Everything else is in order, though.*

Tense from the new experience, Beranon found himself fighting against the anesthesia. *Calm yourself. Breathe. Breathe. In a minute or so, you will be safely waking up on Erkarth.* He could feel himself losing ground against sleep. *Fifteen percent.*

* * *

Black.

I would have thought there would be more dreams out here.

Roland woke early, by forty-six minutes. Returning to his cockpit chair, he called for the passenger listing. Some freighters booked small numbers of passengers for less money than more conventional passenger transport vessels. The accommodations fell far short of ideal, and misfortunes befell the passenger liners more often.

"Let me see. Who do we have in storage today?" Roland asked.

"Seventeen cryogenic capsules activated, Roland." Melanie replied, "An additional three are registered as empty."

"Thank you, Melanie. Let me see who they are."

The list displayed. Roland read the seventeen names and their planets of origin. "Scrollin', scrollin', scrollin'," he sang with half a smile as he moved down the list.

"Do you realize your particular phrasing mimics an ancient illustration of entertainment?" Melanie stated, "This particular example centered on a primitive time during the western expansion in the old United States. It is rather coincidental..."

"Yes, I know the reference to the television show, Melanie." Roland sighed. *I cannot program for humor.* He had tried for months. Now, he accepted his comedy had an audience of one.

Fifteen-passenger files showed Roland the typical cryogenic passenger; inquisitive, but without sufficient means for traditional space flight. With fifteen out of every hundred cryogenic passengers dying because of the system shock, cryogenic cargo was not the preferred travel mode for those with other options.

The other two passenger files required further investigation. A man and a woman who did not fit the typical cryo-passenger profile: Beranon Santar and Vardri Alarius. These were passengers with other options.

Beranon Santar listed his origin as Bantadam. *So, what part do you play in hyperspace engineering?* As home of hyperspace technology, Bantadam was industrial and very wealthy, which is why even their extended-shelf-life, ready-to-eat meals were of such high quality. Everyone had a part of the industry and in its resulting wealth. Bantadam was a small, peripheral planet, not known for its interstellar travelers. For people who made interplanetary travel possible, they seldom took advantage of it. When they did, they typically traveled exclusively in the most luxurious accommodations.

Yet, here he was.

Roland shook his head. "All right, Melanie, let me look at this man."

The central viewscreen showed him a man in his mid-thirties. "What are you doing here?" he asked the image. *People do not include Erkarth on a trip to Bantadam.*

"Melanie, who is this man?"

"According to his passenger biography file, Beranon Santar is a Regional Manager of Research and Development for Bantadam Technical Conglomerate. He is unmarried and thirty-four years of age."

Roland got up. He took a few steps away from the cockpit console. He turned to face the viewscreen showing Beranon's face. "Melanie?"

"Yes, Roland?"

"Observation: This Beranon guy is in an unexpected location. His purpose for being here is unknown."

"According to his biographical information, he is vacationing," Melanie responded." However, I am unable to locate any personal items. My data shows most vacationing individuals bringing some items with them."

"Noted," he responded before continuing, "Observation: Beranon looks unkempt and tense. I would expect him to look more relaxed on a vacation."

"Observation noted. I detect a high level of capillary activity in his eyes, consistent with one symptom of inebriation or sleep deprivation."

"'Bloodshot' eyes?" Roland looked again. "They do look 'bloodshot.'" *If he has been drinking, it would explain his appearance.*

"Observation: Beranon's position sounds well paid," Roland continued.

Observation noted. The median household income rates in the top thirty percent of Imperial planets."

"Query: Why is he selecting a vacation involving cryogenic transport? The scenery does not change. There is a mortality rate of fifteen percent. One would expect a wealthy, unmarried man to travel in a more, shall we say, socially promising manner."

"The data I have would support multiple, more preferred methods for people in his demographic, Roland. Query and arguments noted."

Roland returned to the console, leaned back in his chair and locked his fingers together behind his head. "So, we have this guy buying a trip away from home as a piece of human cargo. If he is on vacation, then the destination must mean more than the journey. It indicates this trip is transportation.

"Speculation: he is headed somewhere, rather than vacationing. Most vacationers would book a cruise ship, not cryogenic transportation aboard a freighter. They would want to watch the stars. Beranon will not know anything until he is thawed. And there is a fifteen percent chance he will not survive the thawing process. Yet, he listed his trip as a vacation. Why? Why cryo?"

Roland rose and paced behind the cockpit chair. "You are out of place here, Mr. Santar. What is the reason? Why are you here? Why this ship?" Roland stopped. *Why, indeed?*

Glancing at the other viewscreens, he again noted all readings about the *Surrogate* were normal. Nothing required his immediate attention.

"Maybe this was the best he could get," Roland asserted.

Melanie responded after a moment, "No ships were scheduled to leave Dorea within the forty-eight hours prior to the *Surrogate's* departure. Three ships are scheduled to leave Dorea within two weeks of the *Surrogate's* departure."

"Three ships, eh?" Roland muttered.

"Yes. The freighter *Mammoth* is departing in two days, and two passenger liners, *Miss Alearia,* and *Galina's Pride* are refueling there in eight days."

"So, our friend Beranon caught the first stagecoach out of town."

"I cannot accurately respond to your statement, Roland. If you refer to the same western expansion to which you alluded..."

Roland sighed and shook his head. "Forget it, Melanie. I was not talking to you, anyway." The instrument readings were still within normal tolerances. He looked out of his window, into hyperspace. Black.

Roland nodded once, turned, and resumed his pacing. *Beranon is in a hurry. Why the rush? Why not wait eight more days for much more luxurious transportation? Why must he leave now?*

Speculation: Beranon Santar is rushing to get somewhere; most logically, to Bantadam. What is waiting for him, and why does it require such an immediate response? "Melanie, what is the next run between Erkarth and Bantadam?"

"The earliest run is a freighter, *Colossus*, which runs from Erkarth to Lachelax. From there a tourist transport, *Aradinda*, cruises from Lachelax to Bantadam. There are two other options, but they are not scheduled to arrive until three days after the Lachelax transport. Do you want to hear them as well?"

"No. They must not be upgraded to elliptical hyperdrives, yet," Roland speculated, "Okay, Melanie, how long do we have between our arrival and departure for the Lachelax option? We have to go there anyway."

"Estimated Time of Departure for Lachelax is Arrival plus twelve hours, forty- two minutes, thirteen seconds."

Tight, but manageable. Roland checked the *Stiletto's* chronometer. "We still have a few days before the delivery is due, but since we are headed to Lachelax anyway, we may as well enhance the reputation. But, I do not want to go through another episode like Dorea." Roland sat down. "What is the E.T.D. from Lachelax to Bantadam?"

"Estimated Time for Departure is Arrival plus seventeen hours, twenty minutes, forty-three seconds."

"Okay. Get Jackson working on the tags."

"Will do. One moment, Roland."

Roland, again.

"Melanie, show me this Vardri Alarius."

"Very well, Roland. I will close the file on Beranon Santar and open the file on Vardri Alarius."

CHAPTER 5

Roland turned his head to the left side of the cockpit console until her image on the viewscreen came into the edge of his vision. Upon seeing her, Roland twisted in the chair, turning until it was facing the same way as his eyes. Her eyes—icy blue and piercing—grabbed his and resolved to hold onto them. Roland forced his eyes to look to her hair, pulled taut around her face and tied in the back. *How long is her hair?*

Roland remembered a girl from his childhood who had hair like Vardri's: long and straight, with the color of optical cable. *What is she up to now?* He thought back to the long conversations about his triumphs over the challenges of each improvement and modification to his parents' household environment. *I wonder if she remembers me.*

What was her name, again?

I wonder what she was like in person.

"Roland," Melanie interrupted, "Jackson has completed the calculations for the tag to Lachelax."

Jolted from his reverie, Roland replied, "Um, fine. Fine, Melanie, remind me at Departure minus thirty minutes."

"Very well, Roland."

Roland turned his attention back to Vardri Alarius. *Is an eighty-five percent chance of a better life worth more than a one hundred percent chance of simple existence? She could afford to spend much more money on another flight. She must be saving up for the start of her better life.* "Melanie, who is she?"

"According to her passenger biography file, Vardri Alarius is a Project Test Manager for the Defense Division of Dorea Space and Hyperspace. She is unmarried, and thirty-one years of age," Melanie responded.

"So, she is a project overseer for a company specializing in governmental and military contracts," Roland observed.

He turned his chair away from the monitors. *Is Vardri going to something? If so, why not choose a more comfortable, and safer, path? Surely, she could have waited for the passenger liners to refuel. Of course, they may not be headed in the direction she wants to go.*

Was Vardri running from something? If so, was this a mode to throw her pursuers off the trail? Well, if the Surrogate *was the sole ship on the schedule for four days, it would not be difficult to track her as far as the* Surrogate.

"Well, Dorea is not in political turmoil now. Their president is not scheduled for replacement for two years." Roland leaned back in his chair. "The military is not involved in any border conflicts or civil war. It has been peaceful in Dorea for over three decades."

"What if someone is chasing her? Should I be concerned?" he asked himself aloud. "I doubt it. There is no direct connection between the two of us unless they have traced her here and are pursuing the ship or have someone waiting on Erkarth.

"Just in case, I had better make a hasty withdrawal after we exit hyperspace. No one is going to catch me by surprise. It would be a simple process to ambush a ship like the *Surrogate*. With such lax security, ships like these are easy pickings for anyone with a mind to take them."

"I will have Jackson expedite physical separation upon our arrival."

"Oh, yeah, thank you, Melanie," Roland responded.

After detaching from his host, Roland scanned the surrounding orbits but found no indications of an ambush. *I guess Vardri Alarius eluded her pursuers, or she was well on her way to her better life.* All the company he had was orbital debris. Perhaps the occasional satellite worked. Mostly it looked like junk. Erkarth was not at the forefront of orbital housekeeping. They had not even been capable of interplanetary travel for more than ten years. They seemed to be content on their little, blue-green planet.

"Melanie, are there any signs of discovery?" He hated being discovered against his wishes. Dorea had done it. Fortunately, his newest ECM acquisition performed admirably in its first field test. The phantom transponder signatures and sensor displays it created of the *Stiletto* attracted the planetary defense systems. His modified prototype normal-space drive also generated a reduced heat signature. The missiles designed to lock onto the heat signatures from normal space drives failed to lock onto the *Stiletto*. Roland smiled. *With the RECON system integrated, the* Stiletto *will be visible only to certain weapon systems, as it becomes necessary.*

"I detect no patrol vessels on intercept routes, Roland. Nor have I noted any communication regarding Vardri Alarius, nor any derivation of her name or initials."

"Thanks, Melanie."

Industrial planets were popular with space travelers. They were an easy stopover for repairs. The raw materials were available, though finished parts were hard to find. The more complicated the part, the more difficult it was to find it. Most in need of a finished part could get it fabricated, but it took some time. With enough resources, you could get such parts fabricated faster, but most preferred the longer, cheaper process.

"Jackson, is there any danger from the debris?"

"No, sir," the tenor voice replied, "Our current orbit clears most of the satellites, and the rest are too scattered for our concern. I am continuing to track all debris, though. I will update you if the status changes."

Roland smiled at the prototype sensor array he had installed. Jackson could track every particle of space debris, its size, orbit and velocity, and its potential for damaging the *Stiletto*. The calculation rate was staggering. *Of course, it should be. The whole method for completing the computations was revolutionary.* When Roland heard about it, he had to have it. What he did not have was the money and time to develop it himself. He also did not have the time to wait for mass production. What he did have was the ability and determination to retrieve the single, existing model. "Thanks, Jackson. Get me Spectre, will you?"

"Roger that, sir."

"What do you need, Reg?" Spectre's baritone filled the cockpit.

"Spectre, was Vardri set to debark here, or is she continuing on?"

"I will check into it, Reg."

"Thanks."

"Oh, and Spectre?"

"Yeah, Reg?"

"Is there anything interesting about this planet?"

"I will check, Reg."

"One more thing. Check the scanning frequencies and see if anyone is sweeping this debris. I do not want to get caught up here by some hot shot scanner tech."

"I will keep an eye out, Reg."

Roland prepared another meal as he waited on Spectre's reports. The available time allowed him to genuinely savor the meal, unlike the appreciation of the one he had made while waiting for the *Surrogate*. He sniffed. Unfortunately, the quality of the meal itself would not allow for savoring. *At least, it is nourishment.* He finished the last of the faux wine he had opened several days before. *This is no time for intoxicants, no matter how well they improved the dish. I need my full faculties now. I will be heading back to Bantadam, and I can acquire more of their premium meals. Those are worth savoring.*

After eating, he went back to the hold to confirm his cargo was still secure. His next stop would require a planet-side landing, which could get rough. With the case securely fastened, he returned to the cockpit and leaned back in his chair.

After four more hours had passed, Spectre's voice returned, waking Roland from an unintentional nap. "Reg, Vardri Alarius is registered on twelve departing vessels over the next three months. None of those departures are extended beyond their initial destination."

"So, she is either very indecisive, or she does not want someone following her," Roland responded.

"I would suspect the latter, Reg. She does not seem to be the indecisive type, from what I know from her file."

Spectre continued, "As for interesting items concerning this planet, Erkarth is not developing any new technologies in the fields of hyperspace engineering, propulsion, or navigation. It is not developing new theories in Electronic Countermeasures, data storage, or access. All current technological pursuits on Erkarth have been developed on other planets."

"Unfortunate. There is nothing to interest me here."

"The *Stiletto* was not detected by planet-side scanners. I have intercepted no communication on the planet concerning the *Stiletto*, or any unidentified ship of our general description. I have also detected no orbital sweeps of the debris."

"Well, at least you gave me one piece of good news. Thanks, Spectre."

Roland checked the chronometer. "Well, we will check into Vardri's itinerary later. Right now, I have a drop to make. How are you doing on the first tag, Jackson?"

"Calculated and ready to execute. The freighter, *I. S. S. Colossus*, will be our escort. She will be arriving in approximately three minutes..."

"Twenty-seven seconds," Roland completed the sentence with Jackson. "Yes, I am aware of their timetable. Initiate the tag."

"Roger that, sir. E.T.A. for Lachelax is Departure plus seventy-one hours, nineteen seconds."

"Noted, Jackson. Thanks."

"Reg, our power signature has attracted some attention from the planet. They are in the process of altering some of the working satellites to scan our area. I am powering down unnecessary systems and changing our trajectory, so we drift out of their area of concern. We should be out of the area before their satellites are repositioned."

"Very well, Spectre."

CHAPTER 6

Black.

Black was Roland's color for business. He had always worn black well. His wardrobe now favored black, especially with the new acquisitions. All the best fashions, and the newest trends originated on Tridar. The Tridaran suits he received for his delivery to Dorea were most impressive. Although they did conform to the latest fashion trends, they would also work well in more traditional circles. With the lightweight fabric and smooth texture, they felt as comfortable as they looked powerful. They indirectly communicated what he would verbalize to his clients: James Reginald Fischer III was the greatest smuggler in the galaxy.

"Always impress." Roland repeated his mantra, "Always impress." He held one of the suits to his chest and looked into the mirror, "And this will definitely impress. When I get to Lachelax, they will think the emperor himself was talking to them." With his black hair freshly cut short, and his sharp facial features, Roland gave an imposing first impression. "Brown or black? Brown or black? I think this occasion calls for black. Melanie? Prepare for black."

"Very well, Roland."

Roland stroked his chin and turned his head side-to-side, surveying the results of his facial hair removal. Stubble was unprofessional, but none showed thus far. They guaranteed their results for five years. If the first three were any indication, they were true to their word.

"Ready, Roland."

Roland, again. He laid the suit on his bunk and stepped toward a panel on one wall. The panel glowed for a moment, and then Roland backed away, blinking. He picked up the suit again and looked at his newly tinted eyes. He smiled and returned his suit to his closet.

Roland had orbited this planet numerous times. The pinkish tint to the atmosphere was unusual among the habitable planets, but he seldom paid atmospheric composition any attention. For him, Lachelax was little more than a transit stop, where he had occasional business dealings with a long-time associate. Being such a popular stop for interstellar travelers, though not very special for Roland, he had his choice of transport vessels for tagging. Now, though, he had business to conduct.

"Spectre, check out these coordinates. Are they hot?"

"I will check them out, Reg."

Jackson charted the registered flight path for the *Aradinda*. She was a passenger liner of modest stature. *She was named for some president's mistress, I bet.* These ships were comfortable, without being flashy. First class travel aboard ships such as the *Aradinda* was not as elegant as the name implied. Still, such a passenger aboard her would have few real complaints. *But the outbound ship will have to wait. For now, it is time for work.*

"The landing zone is clear, Reg."

"Thanks, Spectre."

Roland went back to his sleeping area. Opening his closet, he returned to his new suits. Holding the suits to his chest, he looked in the full-length mirror again. He alternated each suit to the front. "Too relaxed," he said as he laid one of them onto his bunk. "This is business. I need to look the part." He hung the selected suit on a wall-mounted post and returned the "relaxed" suit into his closet.

Removing his piloting jumpsuit, he folded it and replaced it at the foot of his bunk. After a quick shower, he slid the Tridaran pants on. He put on a synthetic plant-fiber undershirt, then he wrapped the formal shirt around him, buttoning it bottom to top. Silver-toned cuff links were next. Then came the tie—red, with a black abstract design. One of his business ties, he had a dozen with a similar theme.

Roland inserted himself into the jacket. He buttoned the top button of the jacket and made sure the pants' seams, creases, and cuffs were still crisp. The suit was very light, and it was easy for him to move around. He tried out a few standing poses to see how the suit would respond to the movement of his body.

Satisfied with his attire, Roland checked his hair and face in the mirror. After clipping a few stray hairs that would not behave at the suggestion of a comb, Roland returned to his cockpit and stood behind his chair. *I still have a few minutes, and I do not want to wrinkle the suit. Now would not be a good time.*

"Melanie?" Roland called.

"Yes, Roland?"

"Access the Lachelax law enforcement network. Are there any outstanding warrants or active searches for Abenor?"

"One moment."

Roland whistled part of a Dorean string concerto as he adjusted the way his jacket lined up on his left shoulder.

"There are no outstanding warrants with a reference to 'Abenor'."

"Thank you, Melanie." After combing his hair again, he checked each side of his profile. Satisfied, he returned to his cockpit chair. "Contact Abenor, please."

"Will do, Roland."

Roland shook his head and frowned. *I have got to change her programming.*

"Roland, I have Abenor. Shall I display?"

He sat down and straightened the front of his suit. He checked his reflection from one of his monitors and straightened his tie. He said, "Give me the cargo manifest of the *Surrogate* here," tapping the center viewscreen, "Wait five seconds, then connect me with Abenor."

The viewscreen lit up with lists of items, descriptions, and volumes. Roland assumed an authoritative posture and scanned over part of the listing, waiting to be interrupted by Abenor. On cue, he was.

Well, Abenor, It has been a while. I wonder how well you are doing these days. After a long and fruitful business acquaintance, Roland came closer to trusting Abenor than he did to trusting anyone else. The relationship was one of length, rather than intimacy. Intimacy in business places one in a weaker position. Abenor knew it. Roland knew it.

"Reggie, I'm so glad to hear from you," Abenor's grinning face filled the adjacent monitor.

Roland waited for a full second before turning to face Abenor. *You must have spent years practicing your smile, and it still looks like it was pasted onto your face.* "Abenor," he said, "Are you ready for delivery?"

"Business, as always; no time for pleasantries?" Abenor said, shaking his head. Then he walked away and sat behind a large and ornate desk. "You should lighten up, Reggie. I do not know whether you are running toward something or running from something, but you do not strike me as a happy man."

"Abenor, when I have completed this transaction and received my payment, then I can afford to be happy. Now, I am busy. As for my motivations, they do not concern you."

"I understand, Reggie. I, too, am a busy man. But I do take time to enjoy life. You should do the same." He lifted a glass of some dark liquid, sniffed it, and sipped from the glass. Abenor then smiled. "After all, we never can predict the future, now can we? We may as well enjoy the present."

Roland realized he was thirsty, but this was a time for water. Seeing the glass in Abenor's hand reminded him to never indulge in intoxicants when conducting business. They also put you into a position of weakness. The perception suffers. Decisions are flawed under their influence. *Abenor, you should know better.*

Roland turned to face Abenor's image squarely. "Abenor, as much as I would enjoy conversation regarding the meaning of life and other petty matters with you, I have a timetable with little flexibility. Can we begin?"

"If you wish, Mr. Fischer. I trust you are able to make delivery now." Setting his glass down on the desk, he continued, "Have you located your landing site? I could make a couple of recommendations."

"Thank you, but I do have my site selected. I am transmitting the coordinates with code four." The latest public encryption standard was still two generations behind the *Stiletto's* system. Roland calculated his code was safe for another eight months.

"Coordinates have been received and plotted. I will meet you in thirty minutes. Agreed?"

"Agreed." Roland terminated the connection. "Jackson, prepare for a planetary landing at these coordinates."

"Roger that, sir."

"Plot the course, Jackson, I will fly her myself."

"Roger that, sir. Trajectory plotted."

"Any noteworthy variables?" *The last thing I need is a sudden wind shift.*

"No, sir. I have bypassed all threatening weather systems. You will also be clear of all localized airborne traffic."

"Good work, Jackson. What is the E.T.A.?"

"Seventeen minutes, thirty-one seconds."

"Thank you, Jackson. Get me Spectre, will you?"

"Yes, sir. Right away, sir."

Roland glanced at the mapped trajectory displayed to his left. The selected landing zone was some distance away from any heavy population.

Well, security should not be an issue, but I don't want any surprises. I will have Spectre check things out before I commit.

"What do you need, Reg?"

"Spectre, is there any communication traffic I need to pay attention to?"

"I will check."

Roland leaned back. *No one should be waiting for me. No one ever has, but you never know. There is always a first time.*

Spectre's response was not surprising. "Nothing significant on the secured civilian or military channels. Should I check intelligence channels, as well?"

"No. If the government were after me, there would still be something on one of the other channels."

Roland eased the *Stiletto* into a shallow descent, entering the planet's atmosphere with hardly a vibration. Versatility. Few true spaceships could enter a planet's atmosphere. The aerodynamics were all wrong. But he had designed the *Stiletto* to handle planetary atmospheres like summer homes.

Roland glided the *Stiletto* around the landing zone. Seeing one vessel in the clearing, he asked, "Spectre, do you detect anyone unusual down there?" He scanned the surrounding vegetation. Lachelax had some of the few large carnivorous plants still growing wild. They blended in with the other large, green foliage, but had a distinctly different impact on the animal life wandering too near. Those included intelligent beings, like those who might report Roland's presence to the authorities. One reason this site had been selected was the lack of chance encounters with passers-by. The vegetation would secure them from any accidental visitors, without the risks of technology-based means.

"No, Reg, only Abenor's atmospheric cruiser. I detect no other transponders."

"Thank you." Roland brought his ship down like a feather on the surface of a pond. "When they load the payment, scan it for foreign items. I do not want anything unexpected."

"Will do, Reg."

Roland reached over his panel and entered a code. A small portion of the *Stiletto's* hull withdrew to allow access to the ship's cargo hold. He watched as two of Abenor's men approached. The men carried a large, flat box between them. Roland smiled, anticipating the results of the new data system it held. The men carried the box around to the front of the ship.

Roland watched through his window as they set the box on the ground.

Abenor asked, "Have they arrived yet?"

"I can see them. They are waiting for you, I believe." Roland turned to look back at Abenor's face on the viewscreen.

"Shall we adjourn to the outside to finalize the transaction?" Abenor asked.

"It has not been so long ago, Abenor. As I recall, our last visit was not under the most ideal circumstances. I think I will stay aboard, in case another hasty exit is called for."

"Yes, of course." Abenor shrugged. "I understand your hesitation, but I've made up for it this time. I have checked over the payment myself. Nevertheless, if you want to handle things from the ship, so be it. I will do the same, then. There will be no more surprises from my end."

"I would expect nothing less from you," Roland said, tipping his head. "I had expected you to have done it the last time, too; however, you..."

"Can't you let bygones be bygones, Reggie? What's done is done. I have brought you something special—flew it in from Solicul, for you."

"You? You did something 'special' for me?" Roland asked in mock surprise, "Abenor, really. I..."

"Wait until I open it. You'll see. It is more than what you requested as payment for this delivery. This is not the ordinary first-generation data storage system I promised; it is the next prototype system. What do you think about it?"

"Abenor, you know I do not appreciate changes. However, if this is what you say it is, I am willing to make an exception in your case. Open it up."

Abenor pressed a control and spoke a series of digits toward another part of his console. Roland saw one of the men through his window as he reached down and entered something on the box's keypad. The light on the keypad changed from red to green, and the man lifted the hinged lid on the box.

Roland looked at the assortment of electronics and switches laid out inside the form-fitting container. Roland had not been searching for a new data system, but Abenor had promised him a superior system to what the *Stiletto* possessed. And this system was even a step beyond what Abenor had promised. "I am not going to ask where you got it, but is it clean?"

"Reggie, I'm hurt. Would I give you anything which could be traced? I suspect someone has determined the system is missing, but I doubt they will be able to identify the thief. I left enough of a trail to encourage them to investigate it as a catastrophic failure, resulting in destruction of the prototype."

"Well, so far nothing you have given me has been traced, but I do cover my tracks well."

"Yes, you do, Reggie. Even I cannot find out much about you. But I know enough to know you deliver as promised, every time; which brings me to another point." Abenor spoke away from Roland's viewscreen again, and the men outside the *Stiletto* closed the lid on the box. After the light reverted to red, they lifted the box and walked around to the open cargo door. They set the box inside the hold, withdrawing another case from within.

"They have withdrawn from the ship," Melanie displayed on another viewscreen.

"And that would be...?" Roland anticipated Abenor's response as he closed the cargo door.

"I have this associate who requires swift transportation of some sensitive material," Abenor said, "I have mentioned to him I may know of someone who may be willing to provide the service, for a price."

"I may, at that," Roland suggested, "What is the destination?"

"Darahir."

"Hmmm. Darahir is not a common destination. Why Darahir?"

"Reggie, why there? Why here? Why anywhere? I do not ask such questions any more than I answer them. Come, now. Do I give you a meeting with him or not?" Abenor asked.

"Very well," Roland replied, "What harm can there be in meeting with him? But, if it goes sour, I am holding you responsible. You vouch for him."

Abenor bowed, "I would not have it any other way." Roland announced, "I will send the meeting location to you in twenty minutes. Set the meeting up for one hour after that. No later."

"I eagerly await your coordinates. Thank you for considering this offer, Reggie. I will notify him of the schedule. I bid swift journeys to you, Mr. Fischer."

Roland did not respond as he terminated the connection.

CHAPTER 7

Roland punched in a series of parameters to maximize his security, as he always did when meeting a new client. Three different possible destinations displayed on the planetary map. Roland studied them a couple of minutes as he monitored Jackson's completion of the pre-flight checklist.

"Spectre, check out these coordinates. Are any of them hot?"

"I will check them out, Reg."

"Jackson, when you are finished with pre-flight, get us back into orbit."

"Roger that, sir. E.T.A. for departure is two minutes, nine seconds."

"Fine, Jackson."

"Reg, there is a local festival at LZ-One. The other two are quiet."

"A festival? Great." He sat back in his chair. "Crowds always bring too many witnesses, with too many questions."

Shaking his head, he sat back up and checked the coordinates for the other two landing zones. "All right, then. LZ-Two gives us the better trajectory to meet with the *Aradinda*, if Abenor's associate is on time."

"All systems check out, sir. We are ready for departure."

"Very well, Jackson. Plot the trajectory."

Roland watched as a single green line worked its way from a mass of red and yellow lines of atmospheric traffic. "Trajectory plotted, sir."

"Right. I will take it from here."

"Roger that, sir."

Roland eased the controls back and lifted the *Stiletto* into the sky. He maneuvered his ship along the plotted path his computer laid before him. Breaking through the atmosphere, he guided the *Stiletto* in behind an orbiting satellite and brought her into a matching orbit.

"Spectre, check for detection."

"Sure thing, Reg." After a short pause, "No detection noted."

"Thanks, Spectre. Melanie, open a link to Abenor and give him the coordinates for LZ-Two."

"Will do, Roland."

Roland, again. He shook his head. "Jackson, plot the course to LZ-Two and give me the E.T.A."

"Roger that, sir. One moment." Another green line fought its way from among many red and yellow lines until it became isolated from them. "Trajectory plotted. E.T.A. is Departure plus eighteen minutes, forty-two seconds."

"Got it." Roland got up and went to the cargo hold. *Great. Just what I need! Thanks, Abenor. All my work—all my research and planning—gone. Now I have to rethink the whole installation because you did something "special" for me. Sure, the physical differences seem to be minimal, but what about the functionality? The rewiring and reprogramming I have to do— what about all my rework?*

He punched in a series of numbers on a keypad, and the interior cargo door slid open. He pulled the box out of the cargo hold and entered Abenor's code into the keypad. The light changed from red to green. He opened the lid of the box. The aroma of synthetic packing material and worked metal greeted him.

Roland examined the contents. The installation should not be affected by the change in systems. He had removed enough armor from the front of the *Stiletto* to accommodate the anticipated data storage system. This one was no larger. The control panel may require some modification in order to fit the prepared location, but he could manage it with no foreseeable problem. Still, the change was not anticipated.

Still, if the new system is as good as Abenor claimed, the rework may be worth the time. But, the timing sure is inconvenient. I am THIS CLOSE to getting RECON, and now I must rethink data storage all over again. Roland closed the box and replaced it within the cargo hold. *No. Now is not the time. My current system will last me until I get RECON installed.* Entering another code on his keypad, he watched the cargo door slide into place. *This will wait for another day.*

* * *

"The hyperdrive unit seems to be powering up within specification, Commander."

Tarin nodded at the news but did not smile. "Very well. Power it down and have the team run complete diagnostics on it."

"Sir. Yes, sir," was the response as the engineer returned to his viewscreen. He motioned to his Executive Officer, Major Rosmar. "With me," he announced as he strode from the ship's bridge.

Tarin was silent until the two arrived at his quarters. He then turned and stated, "I think we need to deal with Ms. Alarius. She was clever enough to go off, and it took us too long to track her to the freighter. The engineer is done, but I would feel less apprehensive knowing she was done, too."

"Understood, sir. I will see to it."

"I want you to make certain this package is ready for delivery, but any resources you do not require for it can be applied to Ms. Alarius."

"Yes, sir."

"Dismissed."

After a quick salute, the major exited Tarin's quarters.

"It's too bad about her, though. I tried not to, but I started to like her. She was good," he confessed to himself.

* * *

Roland turned. Twenty minutes from now, he would be meeting a client for the first time—based on nothing more than Abenor's recommendation. *What if it's a trap? What if...no, I don't think Abenor would. At least, not intentionally. We have been working together for too long. I think I would know if he were setting me up. Besides, years ago, someone else had recommended Abenor. Her recommendation worked out well. Abenor has proven to be a worthy client.*

"Jackson, start plotting our exit route from the landing zone. I want it ready, in case this Daga person tries something." Roland sat back into the cockpit chair and took the controls of the *Stiletto*. The sensors showed no other ships in the vicinity, so he eased his vessel from behind the satellite and assumed the path Jackson displayed. Eighteen uneventful minutes passed. Roland arrived at the designated coordinates and circled the area. "Have you detected any company, Spectre?"

"I have detected no one, Reg, except for the ship on the ground."

"Good. It must be Abenor's contact. Melanie? I want to talk to him."

"All right, Roland."

He smirked and tilted his head as he checked his appearance on one of his monitors.

"Roland, I have Kor Daga awaiting you."

He straightened himself in his chair. "Let me see him."

"Mr. Fischer, you have come recommended. It is an honor to meet you today," the tenor voice claimed.

Roland nodded at the image of the middle-aged man. Seeing no hint of congeniality, Roland offered none. "Mr. Daga, I trust my credentials are satisfactory."

"Were they otherwise, Abenor would not have arranged this meeting. You are, in most opinions I have gathered, exceptional; in all, respected."

Roland tipped his head in response. *I doubt you have obtained enough opinions to form a qualified assessment. But I understand showmanship.* He waited.

"As you may know, my situation involves sensitive material and a small window of opportunity. I am willing to pay for your expedition of this delivery."

"I understand your urgency and will comply with your timetable, within reason."

"Of course. The situation requires delivery of this cargo within seventy-two hours. After that, it becomes worthless, and I am out a great deal of money and respect," Kor paused, waiting for the effect to register with Roland. Roland knew it, but held on to what the entertainment industry had taught him was his "poker face." Kor Daga continued, "As you know, respect is much more difficult to acquire than is money."

"Agreed. Did Abenor discuss the terms of payment?"

"He did. However, due to the urgency of this delivery, all I can offer you today is money. Perhaps, in the future, I can pay you in a more suitable currency. For now, however, I am willing to transfer funds to any account of your choosing. I will pay fair market value for the hardware you tend to request. In addition, I will pay you an extra fifty-percent for the remote destination, as well as another one-hundred-percent market value for expedience. Fair enough?"

You are working hard to show more understanding than you possess. How can you put a "fair market value" on something not yet on the market?

"Mr. Daga, in my..."

"Please, Mr. Fischer, call me Kor. People I do not trust refer to me as Mr. Daga."

"Thank you, Kor. As I was saying, in my line of work, there is no 'fair' offer; there is the 'reasonable' offer. This qualifies. I will accept your terms. There are times when money is a suitable payment method. Transfer half the funds now, to this account," Roland said, transmitting a long sequence of characters. "When the time comes, verify delivery, and then transfer the remaining balance." He pressed a series of numbers into his keypad and watched for the confirmation the exterior cargo door had opened.

"Place the cargo in the hold, there, and I will take care of the rest once the transfer has been verified."

"It is acceptable. I will contact you when the cargo has been transferred." The monitor became black.

Roland watched as Kor carried a small box from his ship to the *Stiletto*. *Curious. Such a small package for such a large fee. Oh, well. It is his money.*

Roland called up his bank account, opened under anonymity, and verified the agreed upon funds had been received. When Kor had placed the package in the cargo hold, Roland closed the cargo door and waited for him the clear the flight area. He then eased his ship into the sky. "Jackson, show me the flight path." The green line displayed after a moment and Roland guided the *Stiletto* gracefully upward.

CHAPTER 8

Roland checked the chronometer again. The *Aradinda* was still over four hours away. He put away his eating utensils after disposing of the refuse from his meal. *OK. I am down to six weeks of food. Plenty until I get to Bantadam. I should also empty the trash while I'm there.*

He returned to the cockpit. *Something is still bothering me about these people.* "Melanie? Help me out with this."

"With what, Roland?"

"Observation: Beranon and Vardri both work with hyperspace technology," he stated.

"Observation noted," she responded.

"Melanie, are there any other common items with these two files?" he asked.

"There are no other immediate connections between the two passengers."

"What do you mean? 'No immediate connections?'"

"Beranon Santar lists his 'Next of Kin' as Vardri Alarius, but she did not reciprocate. There was also an announcement referencing a Dr. Radam Nortolis resigning from Dorea Space and Hyperspace eight months ago, and beginning employment at Bantadam Technology Conglomerate, the same company working with Vardri's employer on Dorea."

"Did this doctor work with Vardri?"

"There is no reference to any additional connection with Vardri Alarius."

Hmmm, curious. It could be coincidental. But why list her as 'Next of Kin'? Distant cousins? Another coincidence? "Is there anything else, Melanie?"

"No, Roland, there is nothing else."

"All right, then. The current speculation is this: Beranon is trying to get someplace in a big hurry. Does his file show any reason for his haste?"

"No, the sole reference to Bantadam in his file identifies it as his planet of origin.' The only other reference to a potential destination is Erkarth."

"Understood," Roland replied as he rose and walked the length of the ship, considering the situation. Returning, he said, "Well, if there is no more information available, we will require some additional resources. Jackson?"

"Yes, sir?"

"I need you to access the international network for Bantadam and get me everything on Beranon Santar or the Bantadam Technology Conglomerate. Will you have time before the *Aradinda* departs?"

"I will see to it, sir."

"Be careful, Jackson. I do not want to attract any attention. Use Spectre if you must. Melanie, display our passenger files, then go to the background and let them work. Alert me when they have something."

"Of course, Roland."

Roland looked at both of his puzzling passengers. Vardri displayed her professional demeanor, visible even on the low-end equipment the *Surrogate* used for "human freight." Beranon, on the other hand, looked like one of those guys you step around when passing them on the street.

Roland chuckled. *I would never pass him on the street. He would never catch me in such a public place.* "Well, Mr. Santar, let us say you are on vacation. Did you lose all your money? Is that why you are here in cryo? I guess even the upper crust can get carried away, when..."

"Roland, Jackson has the information you requested," Melanie announced, interrupting him.

"Great! Clear these viewscreens and show me the data."

Roland dug into the file Jackson had compiled. He found a great deal of useless details and procedural jargon. *Well, he is thorough.*

Roland fought through the words he did not use often, requesting Melanie's help when it was needed. He could not be sure, but it seemed the Bantadam Technology Conglomerate owned most of the planet. Their facilities were in every major city on each continent, and many of the smaller cities had some level of representation. Beranon's position placed him in the southern continent. Roland scanned the personnel directory for the southern continent and located Beranon in the Bacado facilities, reporting to a Dr. Radam Nortolis, Chief Technology Officer, Planetary Operations. Nortolis maintained an office in Bacado but seemed to operate primarily from the main headquarters in Ogand.

Roland sat back into his chair, took in a deep breath, and let it out—slow and controlled. "This could take a little while. Even the best computers cannot do everything at the same time." Standing up, he stated to himself, "I think I will let the experts organize the information a little better, while I catch up on some reading."

"Melanie?"

"Yes, Roland?" came the response, a few seconds later.

"Alert me in two hours, and structure Jackson's file into a more readable format. I cannot wade through all his data."

"Very well, Roland."

* * *

"Sir, we have a problem." The technician approached and then shifted his stance as he spoke.

"What kind of a problem?" The foreman responded.

"One of the passengers has gone negative," the technician said. "Negative? How?"

"We are investigating, sir. One of the other technicians was returning from his break, and he noticed some discoloration on the observation glass."

"There was no alarm?"

"None, sir." The technician hesitated, and then continued, "In fact, sir, the system still shows normal conditions."

"I think this is a far cry from 'normal conditions.'"

"Exactly, sir. This does not make sense. We are investigating the system itself to see if other passengers are in danger. Nothing has been identified, yet."

"Very well. We will notify next of kin when we exit hyperspace."

"No, sir. We must wait until we reach Erkarth. The listed 'Next of Kin' is another passenger."

* * *

Roland, again. And again. "Roland?" Melanie called for the third time. Roland realized it was the third time after he became alert enough to count.

Roland closed the idle reader and rubbed his eyes. "Okay, I am awake."

"Very well."

Returning to his cockpit, Roland sat down. "Melanie, show me the distillation of Jackson's file." The central viewscreen showed him several major headings. After selecting "Personal Data," he watched the screen fill with additional headings. *You've got to be kidding me. Still, it is better than unformatted data.*

Scanning the list of headings, "Family" caught Roland's attention. "This should be short for an unmarried 'techno-geek.'" He selected the "Family" heading. *So, he is a liar.*

Beranon's wife and son are still on Bantadam. Are you deserting them? Why? If you are on a vacation, you would take them. You would depart from Bantadam, rather than Dorea, too.

So, you are thirty-four years old, and you have been married to Meghan for thirteen years. Your son—Beranon, the younger—is twelve years old. But your Surrogate *file lists you as "Unmarried." Hmmm. Why were you aboard the* Surrogate, *lying about your marital status?*

"Melanie?"

"Yes, Roland?"

"Are there any entries for a Meghan Santar or the younger Beranon Santar, other than this one?"

"No, Roland. There was this singular entry."

Okay, Beranon Santar, if you were not taking the family with you on your "vacation," did you send them on a different route? "Melanie, were there any other passenger-capable ships departing Bantadam within two weeks of the *Surrogate's* departure?"

"I will take a look."

Her reply came a moment later. "Roland, there were two passenger liners departing Bantadam within the past fourteen days: *Prince Ebamir* and *I.P.S. Nadorn.*"

"Scan the passenger listings for any references to 'Santar.'"

"Okay, Roland. One moment, please."

Roland sighed and waited.

"No matches."

Where to now? Let me see if there is something else here. Maybe something will point me in the right direction. He returned to the main headings and selected "Corporate Projects."

The green and gold "Research and Development" logo filled the top portion of the monitor. *A bit plain for R & D, I would think,* Roland observed. He checked the departmental listing below the logo and selected the "Hyperspace Navigation" department. The basics of their current projects were made clear after the first few paragraphs. *They are working on the ability to modify a ship's route while in hyperspace. If I were using my own drive, this could be interesting; however...* he trailed off while selecting the "Electronic Countermeasures (ECM)" department.

As he read through many pages of specifications and models, he learned the company had begun developing a prototype component that would intercept and reroute a scanning signal, basically rendering the ship invisible. The *Stiletto* was equipped with a first-generation refraction system, which would send the scanning signal into several random directions. To most systems, the ship would be invisible, but the most sophisticated systems could triangulate, given enough time. Roland smiled. He never gave them enough time. Still, this prototype would allow the *Stiletto* to sneak up on a ship without any concern for detection. Even better. *I will definitely come back for this!* He entered the timeline for production and testing and saved the critical data about the ECM component in a separate file.

Giddily, Roland exited the ECM department and scanned the list for other interesting features. He stopped on the "RECON" department. *What is Bantadam doing with the RECON system? Ricna had not even released it for production yet.*

Further reading showed Beranon was overseeing a chip design to integrate the RECON system for use with a hyperdrive. *I was thinking the same thing.* Roland smiled and checked the progress of the project. "I don't know about this design, though. Let me look at the details."

Roland reviewed drawings, requirements, specifications, and personal notes. *He is assuming a great many things here. If this is his prototype, then his testing has to be rigorous. In a perfect setting, I can see this working. But he is limiting it to one type of energy conversion. Sure, it's a broad spectrum, but...I'll need to go through this when I have more time.* "The design is risky, but it might work. Maybe I should tip them about their energy conversion being better optimized," he said, leaning over the keypad. "No, let them figure it out on their own. I did."

Roland checked the timetable for Beranon's project. "Hey, this was scheduled for alpha-testing on Dorea three days ago." He scanned for the project personnel on Dorea but found no familiar names.

"Roland, Spectre has located a new internal record. It states Beranon Santar died in his cryogenic chamber."

"Died? He was not scheduled to be revived until we got to Erkarth. People don't die in stasis; they die coming out of stasis."

"The record claims a system malfunction led to a chemical imbalance, which was fatal."

"Don't they use safeguards?"

"According to system documentation, there are strict controls regarding the chemistry used in cryogenic travel. In addition, there are audible and visual alarms that activate when any change in client health exceeds acceptable thresholds. The *Surrogate* does possess a much lower mortality rate than the industry norm."

"But none of those safeguards kept Beranon from dying. Unfortunate. "Have Spectre store the file. I may want to look at it later. I am always apprehensive about the thought of cryogenic travel."

"Understandable. Fortunately, you need no such accommodations."

"Fortunate, indeed, Melanie."

CHAPTER 9

"Observation: Beranon and Vardri were involved in a project together," Roland stated, as he got up from his bunk and walked to his small galley.

"Observation noted," was Melanie's response.

Pulling out another, adequate meal, he continued, "Observation: Beranon and Vardri were together aboard the *Surrogate*."

"Observation noted."

"Observation: The *Surrogate* was leaving the site of the project test."

"Observation noted."

Roland paused, setting the meal on a counter. He returned to the cockpit and looked at the bank of viewscreens displaying Beranon's and Vardri's images. "Why? What is the connection?"

"I cannot speculate on the reasons for these actions."

Shaking his head and returning to his meal, Roland chuckled, "I know, Melanie. I am trying to think."

"I understand."

After preparing the meal for heating, and setting it aside, Roland returned to his discourse with the computer system. "Observation: Beranon lied about his family situation. Speculation: He was attempting to sever his connection with Bantadam. I guess anything is possible," he conceded, "But why leave his family on the planet, then?"

Roland opened the cargo hold, briefly noting the small black box secured to one side and retrieved a small bag of one of the food staples of the known galaxy: rice. He had several variations from which to select. He settled on a brown version. *This should help alleviate some of the boredom of this meal. Once I'm done with Kor's job, I will offload this basic stuff, and buy all my supplies from Bantadam.* Satisfied with his selection, he turned and checked Kor's cargo. It was still well-secured. Roland then returned to the galley and closed the cargo door.

The meal was ready to heat as he returned with a portion of the rice, and he added the rice, some additional spices, and the rest of the meal into the quick-cooker. Roland could have installed a higher-end model, but he enjoyed the level of manual preparation this model required. As the meal heated, he leaned back against an adjacent counter where he activated a new monitor and resumed his investigation.

So, what role did Vardri play in Beranon's departure? She is a beautiful woman, so he could be having an affair with her. It would explain his listing himself as 'Unmarried' in his bio file. Roland shook his head. *If they were running off together, they would not choose this mode.* He walked back to the cockpit and leaned on the back of his chair. He looked over the data displayed on the viewscreens.

Why would two people from different planets be leaving like this? Surely, the results of the test were not bad enough for this. I would be surprised if they had all the data analyzed in three days. A few moments passed, with no additional insight from the displayed information.

The tone from the quick-cooker alerted Roland, and he stood and turned to retrieve his meal. *If they were not running off together, and they had not been forced out professionally....No one would terminate an employee, then force them to risk a fatal exit from the planet. Even the most vicious companies I know of—* "OW!" Roland snatched his hand back from the cooker. "Damn it! Stupid!" He reached for an insulating glove. "You get your mind away from the task at hand, and you do some stupid things."

Using the glove, he removed his meal from the cooker, and he set it on a counter. After removing the glove, he surveyed his hand. *Well, it does not look serious, but I must be more careful. If you get distracted, you get careless, then...* Roland stopped and turned his head to the cockpit. Walking to his chair, he looked at Beranon's image again.

"Melanie, under what circumstances do people get inebriated?"

"My data indicates the following circumstances: celebration, social communion, addiction, and stress. These account for eighty-three percent of all documented cases of inebriation."

"Speculation: Beranon was inebriated when booking passage aboard the *Surrogate*. He could be under-slept or has awakened from a nap, but I will start with him being drunk."

"Speculation noted, Roland."

Taking his seat, he added, "In a reduced capacity, he made a mistake in his personal bio file."

"Speculation amended."

"Query: What mistake did he make? Did he forget about his family, or did he forget to omit his employer?"

"Query noted, I cannot respond to your query, Roland. The data is insufficient to provide a definitive answer."

"Very well, Melanie. I offer to you the likelier of the two is he forgot to omit his employer. This was due to a distraction.

"Speculation: The distraction driving him to this careless error also led to the stress causing his inebriation. How does that sound?"

"Speculation noted. I can find no data to counter your speculation, but there is insufficient data to confirm it."

"Understood, Melanie. If my speculation is correct, what would cause such a level of stress and distraction in three days?" Roland sat for a few moments. "You said Vardri worked for a defense company, right Melanie?"

"Correct, Roland. Vardri Alarius is a Project Test Manager for the Defense Division of Dorea Space and Hyperspace."

"So, if she and Beranon were working on the same project, it would relate to the Defense Division."

"A logical conclusion."

"I wonder if all of her projects are completed in less than three days. Most of the military projects I come across take weeks or months for testing to be completed. What makes this one so special?"

Roland propped his elbows on his armrests and interwove his fingers in front of his face. "Observation: Beranon is working on an application for a prototype system—the RECON."

"Observation noted."

"How many prototype systems have been installed requiring three or fewer days of testing?"

After a moment or two, Melanie responded, "I find no records of a prototype system installation with three or fewer days of field testing."

"I thought not. Observation: The Project Test Manager and a design engineer for a prototype component installation test are leaving the scene before the testing is completed."

"Observation noted, although there is an element of speculation in your statement."

"I am aware, Melanie, but it is the most sensible interpretation to me." He sat until the aroma reminded him of a previous obligation. "My food!" he exclaimed, bolting up from his chair. Sprinting to his galley, he said, "I hope it is still hot."

Remembering his previous experience, Roland retrieved the insulated glove and laid his food out onto a plate. He decided against sitting at his normal table, which would require a press of a button to drop it from the wall. Instead, he took the meal back to the cockpit. He placed it on a flat area he designed into his console for such occasions. He sat and ate as he contemplated his current puzzle: *Why would two key members of a test team leave the planet without completing the test?*

"Something had to spook them, Melanie," Roland said between bites.

"Do you mean they were frightened?"

"Yes. They must be running away from something scary. It's more than a localized disaster, or they would not leave the planet. We heard no news of a global catastrophe on Dorea. It must be some type of personal issue. But one involving both individuals. Beranon was scared enough he felt he needed to hide his family, but he was also scared enough he still identified his employer.

"What could scare him so much?"

CHAPTER 10

Black.

Kor's box was small, seamless, and black. The one opening was made for a physical key to be inserted into an internal locking mechanism. *It is a rather quaint mode of transportation, using a physical lock to secure a plain box.* Roland wondered what it contained, but he did not seek to satisfy his curiosity. The less he knew about what he transported, the easier he could sleep. At one time, he had determined to avoid transporting drugs. Practically, though, the inspection of the cargo was too difficult. He found it easier to transport cargo without questions or concerns. *But what is so important about this box? If it is so important, why secure it in such an archaic manner?*

Roland withdrew his attention from the box and closed the interior cargo door. Returning to the cockpit, he announced, "Okay, Jackson, map out our trajectory. We need to pick a path to our next host." His central viewscreen lit up with the ascending trajectory of the *Aradinda* in green. Red lines from the neighboring satellite orbits tangled with the green, as if they were weeds attacking an untended garden. The *Stiletto's* yellow intercept route was laid over the red lines, adjusting to make way for some space trash going its own way. Roland considered the distance from the last layer of orbital refuse to his intercept point with the *Aradinda*. Close, but not uncomfortably so.

Engaging the *Stiletto's* thrusters, he slid his ship out from the remnants of Erkarth's numerous space expeditions.

The *Aradinda* garnered a greater and greater portion of the front window. A large vessel, though by no means majestic, the *Aradinda* nonetheless presented herself like a debutante. Roland smiled. "Jackson, get us into position."

"Roger that, sir."

Roland sat back in his chair, permitting himself a sigh of contentment. As Jackson maneuvered, Roland returned to the mystery in the personnel files. He looked at the two faces, again. "Observation: Beranon and Vardri were working on a project together."

"Observation noted," Melanie stated.

"Fact: They left Dorea in an abnormal manner for people of their station."

"It is an unusual manner for people with means, but among my history files are many examples..."

"Melanie, I understand eccentricities. Call this an 'Observation,' then."

"Yes, Roland. Observation noted."

"Thank you. Speculation: They left Dorea under duress."

"The speculation does agree with the facts and observations noted thus far."

"Thank you for the support, Melanie. Allow me to continue. Fact: Beranon listed himself as unmarried when he has a wife and son on Bantadam."

"Fact noted."

"Speculation: Beranon is running from something or someone he fears, for himself and his family. Alternative speculation: Beranon fears the use of his family as leverage against him. In either case, he would attempt to sever visible connections with his family." Roland shook his head. *People complicate things. Give me computers any day.*

Roland got up from his chair and paced. *Beranon was running. It is logical to assume Vardri was running, too. Why would they be running from a politically stable, relatively wealthy planet? What would make Beranon lie about his family? Anyone powerful enough to make him run away could trace his identity back to his family. It does not make sense. If his picture is any indication, he is drunk; he also could be panicked.*

But Vardri looks professional. Is she less afraid? She would not be pursuing Beranon. No one chases someone using cryo. It is too risky. What was it, then?

"Melanie, scan the file for items related to, or contradictory to, my stated facts, observations, and speculations. Categorize them according to degree of relevance. Store the results. I will get to them later. Close this file for now."

"Yes, Roland."

Stretching out on his bunk, Roland tried to remember a little, golden-haired girl, but his memory seemed less clear now. Roland fell asleep.

"The *Aradinda* is approaching, Roland. Contact in twenty-one minutes."

"Thank you, Melanie." Roland stood up and walked toward the back of the *Stiletto*, thinking. But his mind was not on the approaching passenger liner. *Beranon, Beranon, why were you running? What had you so spooked you took a fifteen percent chance of never waking up? Why leave your wife and son?* Roland could think of no reason. *You worked with Vardri. Was this an affair? Then why take a chance one or both of you would not survive? If I had ever wanted to take a romantic trip, this is not the way I would go.*

Roland turned his thoughts to Vardri as he turned to walk back to the cockpit. *Who are you? Where are you going? Why are you going?* Roland imagined Vardri at home. *What kind of place did she live in? White. Stone and wood, perhaps, if they were available still.* He imagined himself at the end of the white stone hallway, watching Vardri closing the distance between them. Vardri's black dress enhancing Roland's imagined shape, with her blond hair tossed over her left shoulder; approaching, drawing a small smile and...

"Contact established, sir." came Jackson's pronouncement.

"Damn it!" Roland exclaimed as he slammed himself into the cockpit chair and spun it to face the viewscreens. *I got sloppy—again,* he thought, *Lazy and sloppy. I never let Jackson do this alone. It is a good thing this one is a bargain liner, not some diplomatic scout ship.*

Collecting himself again, he remarked, "Good work, Jackson. Establish lockdown and get Spectre."

"Roger that, sir."

Roland concentrated on the viewscreens as Spectre initiated his insertion into the *Aradinda's* computer system. Four minutes later, the sky went blank as the *Aradinda* engaged her hyperdrive. *That was cutting it a little too close.*

Roland was looking at the new passenger listings. Spectre had not informed him of any unusual findings in quite a while. Roland had been a bit surprised the hyperdrive was just two models below standard. *Someone must be breaking into a new market. Typically, these cheap transports lag four or five models behind those used by high-class luxury ships, not to mention the declassified military models.*

His attention was drawn, again, to the images of Beranon and Vardri. *If you are as scared as you look, Beranon, you must be fleeing something life-threatening. But, what can cause you to risk a fifteen percent chance of death to escape it? Why would it not concern anyone else?*

Roland got up and walked toward the back. He turned and paused. *A military test is abandoned by civilian personnel three days after its scheduled start. Could there be a rogue? Was someone trying to sabotage the test? Was someone threatening the civilians? It makes some sense, although it is a guess.*

"Still, it would explain a great deal," he stated, returning to his chair. "Melanie?"

"Yes, Roland?"

"Speculation: Beranon and Vardri are both fleeing some rogue military person or persons. The threat is severe enough to force them to leave the planet abruptly. It is also severe enough one person seeks to isolate himself from his family, but he is scared enough he forgets about his employer. Does the data support or contradict this speculation?"

"The data does not contradict your hypothesis. However, the data is inconclusive."

"Understood, Melanie. When Spectre is finished..." Roland's head snapped to his front window as the stars made a sudden appearance. "Talk to me, Spectre. What is going on?"

"Nothing out of the ordinary, Reg."

"I received no information our destination had been reached. It is too early for reentry into normal space."

"We are not at our destination, nor have we reentered normal space."

"Not reentered normal space;" I'm LOOKING at normal space.

"Give me a system check, Spectre."

"All systems are normal. The oxygen level is steady; Power systems functional; Hyperdrive within operating parameters."

"Operating parameters?" Roland ran through a mental checklist. Something was definitely wrong here. *We are not in hyperspace, but Spectre detects the hyperdrive functioning as designed.*

Conclusion: Spectre is wrong. Roland trusted his eyes to provide an image that was an accurate representation of the universe. His eyes presented a star-laden representation of normal space, not the blackness and void of hyperspace.

Speculation: Spectre is malfunctioning. "Spectre, suspend investigation of *Aradinda*, and perform self-analysis."

"All systems are performing within design specifications."

Speculation rejected.

Speculation: The Aradinda *is malfunctioning. Yet, Spectre had detected no anomalies within the computer system running the ship.*

Speculation rejected.

Speculation: The Stiletto *has been detected. If the information the computer is displaying is incorrect, and the computer system providing the information was performing according to design, the most plausible reason for the inaccurate information is deliberate subterfuge.*

"Spectre, begin emergency withdrawal!"

"Terminating connections."

"Come on, Spectre." Roland clenched his teeth as he read the viewscreens. Spectre had gone deep into the *Aradinda's* system. Now he had to retrace his steps to assure a clean break.

Four metallic thuds over his head dropped Roland back into his chair. Magnetic boots.

Speculation confirmed.

CHAPTER 11

Gray.

Gray dominated his eyes. The walls; the door; the bunk; the jumpsuit—they all blended in a monotone chorus of gray.

Roland paced from the small bed to the back wall. He stopped, turned around, and paced back to the bunk. *Since when was Bantadam a destination for the rich and famous? How could I know they had such a level of security aboard what should be a standard transport vessel?* Shaking his head, he sat on the bunk.

Now I am stuck here, wallowing in gray. They take my new suit, and stick me with... Roland threw his hands out to his side, *With this.* He stood and surveyed the front of his jumpsuit. *That was a great suit. Brand new, even. You take it away from me, and give me this... What is this...thing?*

The gray door slid upward to allow the gray uniform to enter. It was a deeper shade of gray than were the walls. Another uniform stood outside the door, waiting. Roland dropped his arms to his side and moved back to the rear of his cell, trying to give the illusion of striding, instead of slinking.

Gray.

The food on the tray the uniform gave him may not be classified as gray. The different courses lack enough individuality to avoid the grayness of their surroundings. Even the metallic utensils with which he was to eat had lost their luster, taking on the duller sheen of gray.

How did I get into this situation? Sure, I was surprised by the level of security on this vessel. Still, mine is by far the superior ship.

I am the best at eluding capture.

My sensors can detect a radiation signature and identify its source long before anyone else would even notice an anomaly against the endless backdrop of the universe. My data analysis is faster than anyone else's. My computer system is well beyond the complexity of this vessel's computer.

And yet here I am. Confined to this space. It may be a quarter the size of my berthing area on my ship, but it lacks all of its comforts...and control.

His domain now consisted of a single room and a small bed with a light blanket. Gray. On one wall was a panel that opened when he needed to relieve himself. The towel provided him seemed dingy, rather than dirty. *Perhaps it is the light.* Ambient lighting, bright enough to read by, came from recessed sources along the top of his cell. Then there was the door.

At times, this door would slide up and away from Roland to allow a uniform to enter, carrying another assortment of colorless and tasteless nutrition, while another uniform waited outside. Roland figured the food would keep him alive but render him docile through sheer boredom. After the uniform exited, the door would slide back down until its magnetic locks sealed again.

This time the uniform brought nothing. It did not deliver. It did not exit. It stood far enough into the cell to allow the door to close. Its eyes followed Roland as he moved to the rear of the cell—a mouse to this watchful eagle.

The uniform spoke as it walked to the side of the cell. "James Reginald Fischer, the Third. Funny thing. No one seems to have heard of you."

Roland stopped. He leaned his back against the wall farthest from the door. "I am not surprised. I prefer a low profile. I try not to draw attention to myself."

"So, it seems." The uniform turned to face Roland. "However, it also seems to be too low a profile to be genuine."

The uniform withdrew a small data viewer from its pocket. "Let's see," it said, looking at the small device. "Mr. Fischer was born thirty-seven years ago in Cutaus, on Ogarius. He appears on different planets, but he calls none 'home.' There isn't even a record of a James Reginald Fischer II on Ogarius. An oversight on your part, I would think.

"Mr. Fischer, I have been investigating people for a couple of decades, and I have gathered information on people using aliases before." The uniform lifted its face to meet Roland's. "I will do so again, rest assured. No matter how clever the person is, he cannot hide from all prying eyes. However a person tries to hide, someone, somewhere, knows something. I always find the person."

Roland smiled. "Perhaps you already found out all there is to find about me."

"That's one possibility," The uniform turned and took a couple of steps before turning again to face Roland. "But it's doubtful. You see, even the records left by people through the normal course of their lives are absent from yours. I find it a bit odd. No one goes through life without purchasing, renting, vacationing, getting an education, or crossing the law at all."

"I am paranoid and very careful about covering my tracks. You never know if some corporation is tracking you for market research, or some psycho is stalking you."

"Even so, you have records of birth, but no education. I find residency records, but no rental or ownership records. You use no credit, yet you pilot a ship." The uniform had closed the distance and now stood uncomfortably close to Roland. "Now, you can either be honest with me about your identity and your reason for being here, or you can wait until we dock at Bantadam and I can get the information from you using more...persuasive, and less comfortable methods."

Roland cleared his throat and shifted his feet. He looked away from the uniform's eyes and to the wall. Gray.

The uniform turned for the doorway. "Very well. I do not give up. If you will not provide me the information I require, I will track your identity through the ship you pilot. It is still attached to our vessel. We'll see if you hid your ship as well as you hid yourself. I suspect the ship will have some interesting revelations for me."

Turning, the uniform continued, "Unless..." He smiled, "You assume I cannot access your ship, Mr. Fischer."

"What makes you think so?"

"You did not put on your poker face soon enough. I have seen your expression numerous times before. You can be certain of this, Mr. Fischer: Many tools are at my disposal for accessing ships. Some are gentler than others. I will access your ship; I will trace your ship; and, I will track you through your ship. Or, you can skip to the end of the process."

The uniform turned to face Roland. It waited a moment. "I see. Very well, Mr. Fischer. We will talk again later." The uniform tapped twice on the cell door. It opened, and the uniform exited into the corridor.

"Wait," Roland called to the uniform. It turned and reentered the room. Roland looked at the tag displayed on the front. It read "Zemadin". "How?"

"Can you be more specific?"

"Mr. Zemadin, how did you catch me? Did I spike a system? Did I land too hard? What gave me away?"

"It was nothing. One of our technical trainees detected an asteroid anomaly. He asked if he could look into it."

"I see." Roland turned away. Someone had asked the right question.

"Is there anything else, Mr. Fischer?" The uniform waited for a few moments, let out a short grunt, turned and withdrew.

Roland paced at the back of his cell. *My ship? Some lunatic uniform is going into my ship? It's mine...that uniform has no right.* Roland saw it sitting in his cockpit chair, fingering his controls, looking at his files. *Why am I getting so worked up? He can't get into my ship. Melanie is programmed so I alone can access her. Of source, if someone were with me, she would allow them entry. But, on his own, no way.* Roland leaned back on the bed, folding his arms behind his head.

But what if he does? Roland shot up and swung his legs back over the side of the bed as he threw the image of pried and cut access panels from his mind. Standing up, he paced the confines of his cell. *Sure, he was ship security. I am an anomaly in his controlled environment. But he would become the same on my ship. If he does not want me* here, *why should he be allowed* there?

And the systems. This guy does not look qualified to check out the Stiletto. *What if he breaks one of the component systems? Some are unique, prototypes—there will be no way to fix any of them quickly. I would need to limp to the nearest service facility possessing the tools necessary to deal with advanced systems plus the understanding to ask no questions.*

What about those places where I got the systems in the first place? What happens if the uniform tracks the system back to the manufacturer? What happens then? "Oh, it's fine, we don't need it now. Go ahead and keep it." Ha!

Roland stopped his pacing. *Kor Daga.* He checked his arm from where the *Aradinda* security had removed his chronometer. *He said he required delivery in seventy-two hours. How long has it been?* Roland resumed pacing.

I must get out of here. This place is bad, but I am certain Bantadam is worse, in this situation. I do not like the sound of the interrogation the uniform will put me through. Kor Daga may be looking for me, and...and, what? What, then? I do not know. I have to get back to the Stiletto. *Then I can do something. I can handle Kor Daga, but not from here. I must get back to my ship.*

What if I fail? What happens to me if I get caught? Can it be worse than this? Roland paused his pacing, considering the answer to his question.

I've got to risk it. Beranon risked it. Vardri risked it. I am far more talented in this area than they are. If they could escape, then I can escape.

But, Beranon failed. What if she failed, too?

Frustrated, Roland went back to his cot, laid down, and thought. *If I keep this up, I will never make it. They will find me still thinking about the possibilities when we dock. No. I will not resign myself to passive spectating as my future is handed to me. I need to get out of here. But how?*

The ceiling was unbroken. There was no access. He sat up and looked around his cell. The air was circulated through several small vents on the walls. They were far too small to crawl through. Roland found no floor venting and no venting in the drop-down panel. There was the door—one door—with magnetic locks.

Roland lay back down. *How can I get through a magnetic lock? How does anyone get through a magnetic lock? Interrupt the circuit. But how do I interrupt it? There are two ways—from the inside, and from the outside. But there is no panel on this side. So, the door needs to open, and then I need to keep it from closing.*

The door opened when the uniform came in to deliver food. There was always another uniform in the hallway. One on the inside, and one on the outside. Overpowering one would leave the other to sound the alarm. So, I interrupt it after the uniform leaves the room, but before the door seals. Not a lot of time.

Roland looked around his cell. *What do I have to work with? It must be small, to avoid detection.* He scoured his cell but found no adequate tool. Everything in his cell was attached to something else. So, he would need to import. Roland sat down and closed his eyes. He mentally checked out all of the contents brought to him with his meals. He found what he was looking for.

One item he did see was a single surveillance camera mounted on the back wall of his cell. Judging from the model number, this ship had not upgraded its security systems for quite some time. *I have seen better camera systems on old freighters. What are they spending their money on? With a camera like this, the monitoring room must be something to see.*

Roland sat down on the edge of his bunk, looked at the wall of security camera viewscreens he was imagining, and blankly stared as he imagined the security officer on duty was doing. Then he smiled. *This ship was not equipped for securing real criminals. Still, if I disable the camera, even the most bored operator would notice. I would not make it ten meters.*

Well, if I cannot blank out the camera, I need to risk the escape within view of the security officer. Maybe he will not be looking at this screen when the time comes. The guards are a different matter. Since I don't know what they do after they leave here, I will have to improvise. I don't like to improvise. Too many variables. Still, the other option is just a quick breath of corridor air.

What he needed now was the food. *I need one uniform to walk through the door and deliver some food.* Not that he was hungry. Not that he enjoyed the offered morsels. He needed the utensils. Anticipating his next meal, Roland shifted his cot to the wall opposite the security camera, and next to the door.

I still cannot determine how frequent my meal deliveries are. Since they took my chronometer, I have no way to track time. Even if I could see the outside the ship, there is no point of reference. If I were to venture a guess, I would estimate between four and six hours. I suppose that will suffice.

Since he had kept a spoon from one such tray, Roland waited a comfortable distance from the door. He waited for the next uniform to enter. He waited for the uniform to set the tray down on his small table. He waited for the uniform to turn and leave. He waited until he finished consuming the bare nutrition given him. He almost savored it—the last meal of a confined man.

After consuming the proffered nutrition, Roland checked his appearance in the gray-framed mirror—metal, not glass. He straightened his prisoner-tagged jumpsuit. He ran his fingers through his hair since they took his comb. He polished his shoes with a portion of his gray blanket. He paced around his cell. He sat. He paced...again. He sat...again. He tried to sleep, but the thought of freedom would not permit it. He waited for his next meal.

CHAPTER 12

As the door opened to allow entry to another uniform, Roland sat on his cot. The second uniform waited outside. The first uniform delivered the usual tray of nutrients and withdrew to join the other uniform in the corridor. As the uniforms turned down the hallway, Roland grabbed the spoon and sprang up on top of the bed. Timing his leap from the bed, he shoved the handle of the spoon into the top gap as the sliding door closed. The door encountered the spoon and sprang back away from the wall, taking the spoon with it. Roland lunged and caught the spoon just above the corridor floor. He stepped back into the cell and peeked to see if his attempt was noticed.

As the two uniforms made their way down the corridor, one did notice.

Great. Roland turned and took two quick steps in the other direction. Hoping his timing was correct, he turned again and charged the uniform. They met at the doorway when Roland lowered his shoulder and directed the oncoming uniform through the doorway, where he caught the end of the bed. Stumbling but not falling, he came back toward Roland.

The other uniform got to Roland first. Roland stepped toward the door while grabbing the front of the uniform, dropping the spoon. He twisted himself until the uniform was between himself and the cell door.

He let go and slapped the panel to close the door. The door slid shut again. The lock sealed.

Roland laughed as he retrieved the spoon. *You have to love these magnetic locks. If something gets it the way, then they run back home with their tail between their legs.* With a smile, Roland took his first deliberate breath of freedom—at least, limited freedom, for now. "I guess security personnel are not trained to hold anybody who wants to get out," Roland muttered. "They think, 'We are on a spaceship. Where can anyone go? Well, watch me.'"

The muffled calls for assistance brought Roland out of his reverie. Roland paused for a moment before turning down the corridor, away from the direction in which the uniforms were headed. His task was just beginning. *First step: Avoid detection, or at least, avoid recapture. This jumpsuit will not cut it.* His own clothing confiscated, and his other personal effects still aboard the *Stiletto*, he thought of his options—buying or stealing. Not having ready access to his accounts, it required stealing. *I either need to steal some money to buy what I need, or I must steal what I need. Let's see which will be more effective.*

Roland checked around an intersection. Seeing no one, he scanned the walls and ceiling. In the absence of cameras, he proceeded through the intersection. The corridor ended at a wall, with a left and a right turn available. On the opposing wall was a door, with a keypad on the left side. Above him, a camera swept the hallway in front of the door. Left to right. Right to left. Left to right, again.

Roland checked both corridors again. Deciding to take the left one, he timed the camera's sweep pattern. Fourteen seconds from left to left. He wondered about the room behind the secured door. *Well, first things first— time to hide, once I get past the camera, and find a suitable place. Even if the monitoring security guard never noticed it, the guards inside his former cell would draw attention to his absence.*

Ambient lights at the top of the hallway flashed a red tint. A repeating tone, loud but not deafening, filled the corridor. "I guess someone responded." He looked up and waited for the camera to begin sweeping left to right. Stepping beneath the camera mounting, he timed his steps to match the sweep. Once he had stepped beyond the camera, he ran around the next corner, hoping to meet no one there. He did.

Hearing no immediate pursuit, Roland continued exploring the corridors, evading the cameras as well as he could. The absence of footfalls in the corridor supported his hope of escape. The alarm and flashing lights did not.

Straight. Straight. Turn left at the wall. Straight. Straight. Straight. Wall. Turn left. Always left. He could have chosen to turn right. *No matter, as long as it's consistent.* Passing each door, secured or otherwise. Continuing straight through each intersection. Continuing down the corridor until it terminated. Then always turning left.

After what seemed like hours, Roland located a ship directory. *Where are the passengers? I need to blend in.* He located the passenger cabins. *No. No cabins. Too isolated; too exposed. They use more surveillance around them than anywhere else, anyway.*

What about the exercise facilities? No, this silly jumpsuit will definitely give me away. He paused, reconsidering, *Although I may be able to find a towel or jacket to use, instead of this thing.*

Roland located a pavilion area on the directory. *It looks like it has several eating locations. Perfect. With those kinds of crowds, I will be one of many faces. No need to defend my presence to prying eyes. Besides, I have not had a good meal in quite a long time. The pavilion should provide some options much better than what I have been forcing down.*

Okay, so we go get something to hide this lovely fashion statement, then something to satisfy my palette. Roland traced his projected route on the directory, turned and ran.

Roland considered his position as he entered the exercise area. *How do I get the hatch open? The uniform said they still had the* Stiletto *attached to the hull. To get to her, I will need to get the hatch to the outer hull opened. These liners possess limited cargo capacity, so he would not bring it inside. No one pays a luxury liner to haul freight. I think the crew secured the* Stiletto *and left it until they dock at Bantadam. Sorry, but I cannot stick around so long.*

So how many times will we exit hyperspace before we reach Bantadam? Two, maybe three. Again, not much time. Hurried footsteps from behind him rushed him farther into the exercise area. *Even less time.* He scanned the walls and ceiling, finding no cameras. "At least they can sweat in private," he muttered, bolting for the locker room.

Locker after locker was secured. Roland heard booted footfalls on the tile floor. "Yes, sir. We are searching the exercise pavilion. Our last report contact was footsteps into corridor leading past here. We have not located him, yet," he heard a man say.

Pausing his search for an unsecured locker long enough to remove the shoes and jumpsuit he had been issued, Roland was reduced to his civilian undergarments. He turned the corner into another bank of lockers. He waited long enough to hear the booted feet in another section of the locker room. He resumed his search.

Roland's heart calmed a little when he found an unsecured locker. He found nothing in it, so he stashed his previous wardrobe in the locker. His feet were getting wet, and a little cold as his socks soaked up the water residue from the showers and sauna. Leaning against the bank of lockers, he removed them and threw them into the locker with the shoes.

Roland stopped as the boots came closer. Looking around, he saw a corridor leading to the showers. He tracked the boots, keeping one bank of lockers between himself and the boots. He heard one pair. *Where is the other?* As the boots became louder from the other end of the locker bank, Roland darted into the corridor and went to the showers. There was no outlet. There was a door to the sauna. Roland heard two showers running and saw the steam crawling over the top of the doors to the two stalls. He also saw a towel. Hurredly stripping his undergarments off, he jammed them into a waste receptacle and grabbed the towel. Trying to get the towel wrapped around his waist before the approaching boots entered the shower area, Roland grabbed the handle to the sauna door and hurried in.

Looking around, Roland had his choice of seats. One other occupant was present. He gave Roland a quick nod of greeting, then leaned back against the wall and closed his eyes. Roland noticed the man's towel laid open but kept himself from noticing more. His eyes moved, instead, to the corners of the sauna, where the exhaust system intakes were located. Roland listened for a moment before launching himself onto the bench beneath the intake door in the ceiling.

Stepping up onto the back of the bench, Roland grasped and released the clamps holding the hinged door in place. Checking on the other gentleman, he noticed the man noticing him. "Pardon the inconvenience, but someone reported the sauna as being too hot. I am checking the exhaust system. It should take just a few minutes." Roland smiled at the man, then added, "But, do not worry. The level is not dangerous, yet." Then, he hoisted himself up into the ductwork above, then secured the screen again.

He worked his way along the duct a few feet when he heard the sauna door open and boots walking across the floor. Voices followed—first low then louder. Roland worked his way faster until he came to an intersection. Seeing light down the intersecting branch, Roland changed his direction. He crawled until he came to an intake screen. Although it did not provide a view to the floor, it did allow the smell of chlorine to pass through, and the sound of people in water. *Swimming pool. That should work.*

Grasping the clamps, Roland released the screen. Located on a wall overlooking the swimming pool, it did not swing open. Roland pushed it away from the wall, the hinge holding it at the top. He sat on the ledge of the exhaust duct and gauged the distance to the floor to be about three meters. The wall was less than two meters from the water. *Be careful. The floor is wet, and it's tile.* Hearing heavy feet knocking around inside the exhaust duct he had entered, Roland decided to risk the jump.

Sliding his way as close to the edge as he could, Roland inched the screen farther open. The few swimmers who were present noticed him hanging out of the ventilation system. Roland rested the screen on his head, freeing his arms. He swung legs out, pushing his body away from the opening as hard as he could.

As he started to jump, Roland felt a tug. It threw his balance and kept him closer to the wall than he anticipated. The artificial gravity of the *Aradinda* environmental controls pulled him toward the floor. The tug became a serious pull, throwing Roland against the wall. He impacted the floor with a slap and thud, sprawled out.

Roland took inventory of his body. *Nothing seems damaged.* The applause he heard interrupted his self-assessment. He looked around at the people looking at him. Blowing out a deep breath, he looked up to the exhaust duct he had escaped, and saw his towel hanging from the screen. He felt his face getting hot as he realized an aspect of the ovation he had not considered.

Embarrassment is better than incarceration. Roland stood and jogged toward the door marked "Lockers". Hopefully, the other boots he had heard were not patrolling the lockers now.

Hearing no boots in the immediate vicinity, Roland searched for clothing options. Locker after locker were either secured or empty. Finding nothing, he weighed his options. Even though it was an available mode of dress, nudity still tended to attract attention. He did not want attention. He heard a shower begin. *Maybe, my luck is changing.* He snuck to the shower area, hoping the boots were still chasing him through the ductwork. Turning the corner into the showers, he saw it...a beautiful, simple, white robe hung next to the occupied shower stall. Roland snatched it from the supporting hook, and turned away toward the outer exercise area, wrapping the robe around him as he went.

Trying to avoid eye contact with anyone who might be able to recall him later, Roland looked for the sport court facilities. He hoped to locate an abandoned bag. Looking at his feet, he lamented leaving his shoes in the locker. Now, it was too risky to retrieve them. Boots and uniforms were still looking for him. *Better to keep moving.*

He found a bag with a jacket draped over it. *People are too trusting at times. Controlled environments and similar pursuits do not guarantee safety.* "Thank you very much for your contribution," he whispered as he lifted the jacket. There were no shoes, but there was a pair of warm-up pants inside the bag. Roland lifted them out and departed to a bench some distance away. There still was no sign of pursuit. Maybe they scanned each face for identification. Perhaps they got bad information from a witness. Whatever the reason, he was not being pursued. So, he took a moment to put on the warm-up pants. He took off the robe and replaced it with the jacket, closing it from the bottom midway up to hide his nakedness. Leaving the robe on the bench, Roland steeled himself for the journey ahead. Would the man from the sauna recognize him and point the authorities his direction? Would one of the swimmers remember his face from his dive out of his towel by the pool? Would the guys in boots recognize his face from the file his interrogator had? *Whatever happens, Roland, act like you belong here.* So, he walked toward the exit. "I need to find some different clothes," he whispered as he entered the corridor to the fading sound of exercise machinery and pain.

CHAPTER 13

The jacket did not fit particularly well. It was too spacious for one of Roland's stature. The man who "loaned" it to him was both taller and broader than Roland. He had also left his chronometer in one pocket. It, too, was designed for a larger frame than its new possessor had. The nondescript jacket did cover his bare abdomen and chest. He could endure the ill fit. But he missed his Tridaran suit.

Verifying his route with another directory, Roland turned toward the pavilion. He stopped. The *Aradinda* had changed. The floor vibrated, and the air hummed. Something had changed. Roland mentally checked off the possible causes of the sudden noise. He stopped when he got to the "Disengaged hyperdrive" option. Traveling through normal space did alter the feel of the ship. In hyperspace, the bubble would act as the ship's "atmosphere". The ship itself stayed inside this "atmosphere," undisturbed. On a trip this long, hyperspace would "spit" the ship out at least once. Hopefully, this trip will need at least one more. *It will be the only safe time to retrieve my ship.*

* * *

I hate these trips, Bornor said to himself. *I thought this job would get me away from enviro-suits.*

His target came into view as Bornor cleared the hyperdrive. He stopped for a moment to see the *Stiletto* for the first time. *She is a pretty ship.* He paused long enough for his labored breathing to return to normal, before beginning the rest of his hull walk.

"The ship is about 16 meters in length, with an architecture that could support atmospheric travel," Bornor said, initiating the recording of his journey as he approached the *Stiletto.* "The ship's design seems to be a customized version of a military design, but not one I recognize."

Bornor worked to walk around the *Stiletto*. "I note two access hatches on the exterior of the ship," he continued, "One starboard fore, which I assume is for the pilot's access. The other is port aft. I suspect it is for supplies and cargo loading." He glanced at the chronometer display. *We are twenty minutes past our normal hyperdrive engagement. They gave me a two-hour window to complete my preliminary examination before they engage it again. It took me twelve minutes to get to the ship, so I need to be finished in about ninety minutes.* "Set notification for ninety minutes," he announced. He waited a couple of seconds for the indicator to be displayed before returning his attention to the ship surface in front of him.

* * *

My ship. That uniform is going after my ship. He had to wait until they shut down the hyperdrive for safety. You do not want a malfunctioning enviro-suit throwing you out into hyperspace. At least in normal space, you could be rescued. He will delay the reinsertion until he is finished with my ship.

It's my ship. He is on my ship. It is going to cost him. What would he do if I tell everyone the ship was going to blow up? What if I said the reason the ship was not in hyperspace anymore was for them to evacuate? Talk about a panic.

Roland shook his head. *Chances are he still won't be able to get inside. My security code is far too complex for him to be able to figure out. Based on what he told me about what he has found so far, he can't relate anything to me that would get him closer to my access code. Even a scanner would take hours to determine the right code. I doubt the captain would allow for such a delay. I don't need to worry about the uniform. Let him waste his time. I can't waste mine.* Roland shoved his hands into the jacket pockets and turned toward the passenger pavilion.

* * *

Bornor scanned the surface for an access panel next to the starboard hatch. Locating one, he opened it with a press and twist of his hand. It opened to reveal a keypad. "Standard alphanumeric keypad," he dictated as he withdrew a scanner from his enviro-suit's pocket. Plugging it into the side of the access panel, he initiated the scan. Within a few seconds, the access panel showed a green indicator, and the neighboring hatch slid open. *I thought it would be more difficult.*

Bornor stepped inside. "The ship has low, ambient lighting that activates upon entry." *Hmmm, motion detector? Auto-switch connected to the hatch?* He paused and looked around. *Not important,* he thought as he stepped farther inside.

The *Aradinda's* hull lighting did little to illuminate the *Stiletto's* exterior, so Bornor's vision did not suffer from a change in the lighting. Looking around, he commented, "I wonder..."

"Lights."

Almost immediately, the illumination level increased to a level enabling Bornor to take in the ship's interior. "Not much of a decorator. I don't see any personal effects anywhere. Lonely kid, I guess."

Bornor walked the few steps to enter the cockpit and sat in the piloting chair.

Efficient design. Monitors positioned for ergonomics. Control panels within easy reach.

Nicer design than most other ships I've seen. "Let me see if I can access the computer system."

Bornor surveyed the panels surrounding him, but he saw no obvious method by which he could illuminate any viewscreens or access the computer system. "All right, then, let's try, 'Computer on,'" he announced. The monitors came to life, each showing a different portion of the *Stiletto's* systems. "For such a careful prisoner, his onboard security seems a bit lax."

Bornor selected and tapped one of the monitors, which displayed a message requiring a password. "Ah, I expected some sort of access control. But, I came prepared for it," he said, pulling out his scanner and adding an adapter to it. Plugging the other end of the adapter into an input port on the computer system, he continued, "Let's get started."

CHAPTER 14

Roland needed some less conspicuous clothing. This warm-up pants and mismatched jacket were hardly the attire to which he was accustomed. He looked in some of the stores as he made his way into the common area, where the food was. It had been some time since he had enjoyed a good meal. But first things first. He had to get some money.

After half an hour, Roland had three promising candidates. Each sat alone at a table. Roland noted their disinterest in any of the people who moved into and out of their immediate vicinity. As one of the men left his table to view the colors displaying on the wall screen, Roland moved to a new location from where he could keep all three in sight.

The second man rose from his table and walked down the pavilion to the passageway leading to the cabin area. *Well, I guess he moves to the bottom of the list.* Roland turned his attention to the third man while keeping the man at the wall display in easy view.

This third man finished eating and rose. He let out a heavy, and quite audible, sigh as he rested his hand on his stomach. Grumbling something about eating too much, the man let a smile invade one half of his face as he walked from the table. He located a chair near the wall and sat again, leaning his head back against the back of his chair.

After scanning the pavilion for security officers and finding none, Roland watched the third man for a few minutes. No one approached him. A woman dropped her bag a short distance away. Another younger woman came over and helped her gather her spilled belongings. They walked together near the man, talking energetically. The man leaned and turned his head toward the women. He made no overtures to them. A moment later, the man again rested his head on the back of his chair and closed his eyes.

Roland made his way to the area in which the man sat. He could make out the sound of light snoring. Roland smiled. *This man should be more careful. He will end up eating and sleeping his whole life away. Well, if he does it for the next few minutes, the rest of his life does not concern me.*

The wall displayed light patterns imitating the stars. Roland knew it was fictitious, but the passengers still found the display relaxing. It gave them a sense of travel. *I never watch the trips through hyperspace. Hyperspace travel is dull. Sure, the technology that drives it is remarkable, but looking out at the colorless and constant view is rather tedious. Those who are fond of travel appreciate some sense of motion. These viewscreens present them their desired illusion.* Even though the *Aradinda* was no longer in hyperspace, the viewscreen convinced the passengers all was as it should be. Some who were in their rooms, and whose rooms were elegant enough to contain real-time viewers, could see the actual stars. Those stars would appear more stationary than the fictional ones displayed.

Discreetly scanning the immediate surroundings, Roland approached the man's chair. He feigned interest in the artificial light show displaying on the wall as he negotiated his way toward the man's chair. The man wore a lightweight shirt, brightly colored with short sleeves. On the front of the shirt was a pocket. Inside the pocket was his passenger card. *There is my prize.* With a passenger card, a person could avoid carrying the more liquid assets required in acquiring goods and services. In Roland's case, it was the lone hope. He had no other assets, liquid or otherwise. *I will be more careful with your passenger card than you are.*

Roland waited for people to move along their way until the area in which he stood was almost vacant. He stood beside the man, watching the wall, listening to the snoring, and waiting for the right moment. When it arrived, Roland turned as if to walk away. As his left hand rose to straighten his hair, his right hand lowered to the sleeping man's pocket to relieve him of his possession.

Thank you.

It would be a couple of hours before the man would awaken, and some unknown additional time before he realized he was without a convenient method of payment. *I will be well on my way by then. But first, I need new clothes. And food. Real food.*

* * *

Bornor acknowledged and terminated the ninety-minute notification and pulled the scanner out of the input slot. *Interesting.* He rose from the piloting chair returned to the access hatch. After securing his helmet, he opened the hatch and stepped out.

Twelve minutes.

* * *

Several stores were available for shoppers. Many others catered to tourists buying souvenirs. Some stores dealt with the wealthy, while others were more mainstream. Roland chose one from the latter group. *For today, I will be dressing down.* He surveyed the "cookie-cutter" clothing options in one store. *Way down.*

Roland selected an outfit—pants, shirt, and sweater—in black and gray tones. He found some comfortable shoes, though they lacked his preferred style. *Way, way down.*

Testing out the fit of the shoes he was considering, Roland thought, *I need something versatile. I don't know if the surfaces I have seen are consistent throughout the ship. I may need to climb again. I need function more than I need fashion. A pity.* He interrupted his assessment, noting the Aradinda had re-entered hyperspace. *OK. So, I have several hours before we exit. Since I lack the ability to scout this ship, I must execute my plan in real time. If I leave too much buffer, they will be able to recapture me. This is going to be close. It must be close.*

Roland walked to the attendant and set his purchases on the counter, and set the acquired passenger card beside them, thankful that verification here was limited to a signature. Scanning the items behind the counter, looking for nothing specific, he authorized the purchase, picked up his new clothes, and left the shop. Noticing the windows of adjacent shops, their higher quality stock made Roland wonder about the return policies aboard a passenger liner.

Settling for the latest stylelessness, Roland continued his trek to the pavilion area. Avoiding direct eye contact with the periodic surveillance cameras, he maintained a leisurely pace. The cameras would be easy to avoid, for the most part. Widely spaced, they would not be covering the entire ship. They swept some intersections, so he would need to be careful making his way back, but the sweep pattern allowed several seconds in which to clear the intersection.

Of more concern were the pairs of security personnel he passed. Though they seem to be confined primarily to the passenger areas, there are enough pairs to make travel treacherous. It depends upon their methods. *If they follow standard procedures, I want a very public place. I guess the pavilion area works.*

Entering the pavilion, he noticed more sheep. Dressed in multi-colored variations of the same styleless garments that he wore, they wandered from vendor to vendor. Some sat and watched the light show on the few wall segments not occupied by vendors. Some were speaking to other sheep.

Roland noticed one woman. *I saw her before. Where?* Unaccompanied, she approached a small cluster of passengers who were milling around in front of one vendor's establishment. She smiled and entered their conversation. From the exchange of greeting gestures, she did not know the other participants. She pointed out various vendors, commenting on each. Roland was not close enough to hear.

He shook his head. *These sheep are amused by the simplest things.* Looking at the selection of vendors himself, he found the one he wanted.

CHAPTER 15

Roland straightened his new sweater as his eyes wandered from glazed to powdered to cream-filled, across the chocolate-covered, and back to the powdered.

"I recommend the raspberry cream."

Roland's head snapped around. Her face had a familiarity to it. He remembered. *She must have concluded her impromptu conversations and come in here. Or followed me in here.* The brown eyes sparkled as she pushed her hair back from the side of her face.

"I had one yesterday, and they are marvelous," she said.

"Uh. Yeah, raspberry cream." Roland turned back to face the man behind the counter. Real money, even in the form of a passenger card, entitled its holder to personal attention, rather than mere dispensers. "One raspberry cream donut."

The attendant slid the door behind the donut counter open and reached inside. "Oh," Roland added, "And one powdered donut."

"Something to drink with those, sir?" the attendant asked, pulling the two requested donuts from the display case. "A carbonated beverage, coffee, tea, alcoholic beverage, genuine fruit juice..."

"Uh, no, thank you. I will have water, please."

The man looked beyond Roland to the woman behind him. "And what can I get for you, miss?"

"A raspberry cream," please, she responded with a smile. "And coffee. Black."

A pleasant voice. Light. Roland slid the passenger card across the counter to the attendant, careful to avoid his hand. The man slid the card through the reader-transmitter. Roland authorized the charges to "his" berth. He glanced back to the woman and flashed an embarrassed smile as if she had caught him telling a dirty joke.

"There you go, sir. One raspberry cream donut, one powdered donut, and one glass of water," the man said.

"Thanks." Roland took the saucer with the two donuts, and the glass of water, and headed to a table against one wall. He positioned himself in a chair with his back against the wall. He scanned the other passengers in the dining area. The décor seemed festive, and his fellow passengers were lively. Conversations in which he had no interest were carried on at several other tables.

Roland's eyes found the woman after she had closed more than half the distance between the donut counter and his table. He glanced at the other empty tables she seemed to be ignoring in favor of his. *What is she after? Why is she following me? Is she with the* Aradinda's *security? Is she trying to keep an eye on me while the armed guards close in? It makes sense to avoid scaring the other passengers. What if she is another sheep? Better avoid tipping her off. I'll play along while I figure this out.* He looked at his donuts, his hands clasped onto his glass of water, but not lifting it.

"Mind if I join you?" she asked.

"No," he lied, "Uh, sit down, ...please." She did.

"My name is Miranda."

"My name is Reggie. Miranda is a very pretty name."

She glanced at her donut, then lifted her eyes to meet Roland's. He did not return her glance, but he did notice her smile. Roland noticed she had more depth in her smile than he had remembered seeing on the *Stiletto's* monitors. Even the most perfect smiles he had seen in entertainment seemed flat and lifeless compared to Miranda's. *It must be an effect of the technology; perhaps it tends to flatten the features.*

She cleared her throat. "So, have you tried the zero-gee game room?"

"Hmm?" Roland looked up from his donut. "Forgive me, I was thinking about something."

"Have you tried the zero-gravity game room, yet?"

"No, I have not had the time for much recreation."

"This is a vacation. Recreation is what you should always be doing on vacation."

Roland chuckled, "I guess you could call this a 'working vacation.'"

Miranda got up and grabbed Roland's hand, "Well, let's go, then."

Roland pulled back and looked up at Miranda. "No, I really cannot. I am on a tight schedule right now."

She stopped and relaxed her grip a little. "Well, do you have time to sit here and chat?"

"Yes," he conceded, "I can." *I don't need to draw attention to myself now, so just go with it.*

"Good," she said, letting his hand go and taking her seat. "So, 'Reggie.' Short for Reginald?"

"Uh, yes. But I have not been called 'Reginald' in a long time."

"Where are you from, Reggie?"

"I am, uh, I travel around a lot."

"But where are you from? Where were you born?"

"Well, it is a long story."

Miranda laughed. "Being born is a long story?"

"Uh, yeah. My family was, um, unusual."

Miranda was still smiling. "Everyone's family was 'unusual.' Still, it looks like you didn't turn out too bad."

"To be honest, well, I do not remember much outside our home. My parents were away at work. Sometimes we would change locations, but it always looked the same from the inside.

"I remember some space flights when I was a child, but they all kind of blur together now." Roland pushed his powdered donut from one side of his plate to the other. He never tried to remember his childhood.

"I'm sorry, Reggie. I didn't mean to pry."

"It is...okay, Miranda. Anyway, it was a long time ago."

Roland picked up his powdered donut. Carefully, he took a bite and wiped the residue from his lips.

"My family has never left Anadir," Miranda offered, "I always thought space travel was exciting. I've always enjoyed talking to people visiting Anadir. I don't understand why they bother, though. It's such a boring planet. Out here," she said, sweeping over the food pavilion with a grand gesture, "Here is where life happens."

"Here?" Roland gasped, looking around at the sheep wandering from one food vendor to another.

"Yeah. Look at these people. Look at their clothes. Listen to them talk to each other. Watch them play the games here."

"Do they play anything on Anadir?"

"Of course they do, but it's nothing like this."

Roland shook his head and smiled. "Yeah, I guess space travel can be fun. I do quite a bit of space travel. It almost seems like a career, now." Roland smiled.

"Then why are you taking a space vacation? I would think you would stay on some resort planet, or somewhere not requiring being stuck on another space ship."

"Oh," Roland halted. "What I mean is I do a lot of traveling. I never meant I do not enjoy it. It is nice to have someone else do the piloting for a change," Roland lied again.

"Well, I like to meet new people. Like you."

"Like me?"

"Yeah, I saw you in the pavilion, but you were gone before I could get over to you. The woman dropping her things couldn't happen at a worse time."

"Oh, it was you?" Roland tried to remember the face from the pavilion. *Yes, it could have been Miranda. I'll take her word for it.* "It was nice of you to help her."

"It's something I do, I guess." She shrugged. "Then, when I saw you come in here, I had to take advantage of the situation."

"Why?"

"I thought it would be fun. You didn't seem to be waiting for anyone, and I was looking for someone to enjoy this cruise with. So, here I am."

Unable to formulate an adequate response, Roland took another bite of his donut.

Improvisation has never been one of my strong points, Roland confessed to himself. He lingered in the silence for a moment as he wiped his hands.

He had an idea. He let the idea ferment in his mind. *The uniform is no longer aboard the* Stiletto. *The ship would not re-enter hyperspace if the uniform were still on the hull. I need to delay the reactivation of the hyperdrive to get the* Stiletto *away from the* Aradinda. *I think I figured a way to accomplish it. All I need now is the right timing.*

"Penny for your thoughts."

Roland looked up at Miranda. She was smiling. "Pardon?"

"Where were you?"

"Sorry. It is..." Roland halted. *How do I explain this?* He looked for something other than his escape plan to discuss. He looked for an excuse not to answer her. He looked again at Miranda. She still smiled. Roland smiled in return. "It is something I need to remember. It is nothing important right now."

"Okay, then." She looked around a moment. "I like this."

"You like what?"

"Travel. My mother took me on a trip when I was a child. I guess it wasn't much—a quick hop into orbit and back. What a blast! I go every chance I can get now."

"What do you like about it?"

"It's so different from Anadir. I get so bored walking or driving around the surface. You know, life in two dimensions. Being out here, in space, moving all over— up, down, over—it's fun. I wish I could pilot."

"And you are not a pilot, now?"

She laughed like Roland asked if she had sprouted a third eye. "No, not on Anadir. No woman is."

I suspect your traveling is more than a cure for boredom, Miranda. But what could it be?

Roland was interrupted as a man sat down at the next table. He brought with him a tray of steaming food Roland had not seen before. Judging from the smell, he had not suffered for its absence. Dressed in a style more appealing to Roland than his own, the man relished the aroma of his food before sampling a small bite.

"Miss, he does not seem too talkative right now. If it's conversation you desire, I can provide plenty." The man eyed Roland as if he had spilled something on himself.

"Well, thank you for offering your services, but I am happy where I am. Enjoy your food, sir."

"Really, miss. This boy's no fun. You seem like a woman..."

"What I seem like to you does not concern me at the moment."

Roland chuckled and received a stare from the man. He tried to look suitably intimidated but smiled in spite of himself. The man then slammed his napkin onto his plate, picked up his tray, and moved across the pavilion to another table.

Miranda turned back to Roland and smiled. Eyeing her for a few seconds, he laughed.

"What?" she asked, her eyes widening.

"Oh, the way you handled the jerk. It was priceless."

"Jerk? He wasn't so bad. He wanted some company, and I was occupied. It was no big deal."

"Sure. Whatever you say, Miranda," he said, still chuckling.

"Oh, come on, Reggie," Miranda continued, "I have handled worse."

"Well, I thought you handled him quite admirably."

Offering a small bow, she said, "Thank you, kind sir."

"So, what was the worst?"

"Well, I was doing some charity work for, I don't remember which one now, but we were preparing and serving a meal for the volunteers. Anyway, the guy overseeing the work decided he wanted me. He tried to commit, but..."

"'Commit?' Like propose? It seems like an odd time to ask. How long had you two been together?"

"I dealt with him over this meal project. That was all"

Roland leaned back. "He knew you briefly, in one circumstance, and he wanted to commit to you?"

"Yeah, so he went to my parents, and..."

"Your parents? Wow, he does not waste time."

"The point is, I wasn't interested and had to..."

"Okay, you lost me somewhere. What he did was not unusual?"

"No." She looked at him for a moment. "You have not been to Anadir before."

Roland shook his head, lifted his glass, and drank. *Not at that level, anyway.*

"Then, I will explain it a little."

"Okay."

"Let's see, I am not married. Until I am married, my parents basically have the final say about my life. It's a cultural thing," she added, absently waving her hand. "Anyway, I appreciated his attention. It's nice to know you are attractive to other people, but I was not about to marry this man. So, I walked in on their conversation, chewed him out, chewed them out, packed up and left."

Roland shook his head, disbelieving. "Then what?"

"Well, then I moved to Osmark and started working. Mostly in marketing. I let everyone think I'm married, so they listen to me."

"I cannot believe people discount you so much, just because..."

"Anadir has some very conservative views about women. It's one reason I got involved in charity work. It keeps me busy, and it gives me a chance to make a difference in a culture with so much resistance. Of course, I move around a bit, so I keep starting over in new cities. Homeless shelters, clinics, animal centers—I've done them all. It keeps things exciting. You know, lots of new people, new foods, new things to do."

"Why not stay in one city—get established?"

"Then my parents would find me, and all of the crap would start all over again." Miranda leaned back, shaking her head. "I can't do it. If I had courage, I would leave Anadir permanently, and find another planet where women are better appreciated. But, I don't think I could adjust to another culture."

So, you travel to escape from a situation in which you have no control. I can appreciate your motivation.

"Sitting at my parents' house waiting for them to shop me around as a suitable wife is not my idea of a future. What is it about my home planet? Why can't they let me live my life as an equal? Are they so terrified of me?"

"Each planet is unique at its own level," Roland offered. "But, you handle different cities with no problem. Why would a different planet be any different?"

"All of the cities have the same basic culture. Sure, there are different areas of emphasis. This one is more artistic; this one is more commercial. You know. But there is enough familiarity I can fit in without much struggle."

"I guess I see your point. Planetary cultures do vary widely. But, if you are so upset with the planet's culture, I would think even moving from city to city would be frustrating. I mean, starting over with the same obstacles..."

"Yes, there are problems with it. Still, I understand those obstacles and can work around them. Going to a different culture means having to learn new obstacles. And, who knows, maybe those obstacles are worse than the ones on Anadir."

"I understand. Better to fight the tiger, you know, than the one you don't."

"Yes. And you must have seen plenty of different cultures by now, right Reggie?"

"I see my share."

"You know, it might be fun if I could afford it."

"What might be fun?"

"Traveling all the time. Going from one planet to another," she replied. Leaning back, she added, "I would have to find a way to pay for it all, though."

"It has its moments, and, yes, paying for it can be challenging."

Miranda sipped from her coffee. "How's the donut?" she grinned.

Roland blushed, picked up the raspberry cream donut, and took his first bite. The taste rivaled the aroma in sweetness. He chewed, savoring the first real flavor experience since...too long ago. The *Stiletto* became a distant memory, washed away in a flood of raspberry. The grayness of imprisonment burst into a cascade of dark red and golden brown. "O, yuh! Dif id munnufuhl!"

"What?" Miranda asked, laughing and leaning back in her chair.

Roland forced most of the donut portion to the side of his mouth. He swallowed the rest. "This is great!"

"I told you, didn't I?" She raised her own donut in triumph, and a mock toast to Roland, and then took an energetic bite of it. "Donuts are hard to find on Anadir. I guess people are going for those pseudo-nutrient drinks for breakfast. No one does things for enjoyment anymore. It's all become too...practical."

"I know what you mean. Life is too short. You must take time to enjoy it sometimes." Roland blushed, thinking back to Abenor.

"Exactly, eating is not just for survival or health. Enjoy the smell and flavor of it all, too. I mean, look, if all I ever did was what kept me alive, I may as well be a plant in a pot. I'd never have seen space. I'd never have met you."

Roland looked up from his glass of water and swallowed the remains of his donut bite. Miranda smiled, then dropped her eyes to her donut. *If I had been smarter—more attentive to the tag—we would never have met, either. Still, it has been a pleasant accident.*

"I am sometimes accused of being all business," he told her.

She shook her head. "I can't believe that about you. Look at all the traveling you've done. It can't all be for business, can it?"

"No, I guess not."

"I mean, it's not like I have no other choices. I could vacation anywhere on Anadir. But the price for this was too good to pass up."

"I guess."

"Where did you come aboard? On Anadir, you can't even get an orbital shuttle flight for the same price as I paid for this trip. And who wants to fly around a piece of rock for fun? Definitely not me."

"Well, yeah, the money was cheap, but it cost me in other ways."

"Oh, I see. Waxing philosophical, are we?"

Roland tilted his head from side-to-side. "It may be philosophical. The problem is this trip has damaged my business."

"What kind of business are you in, anyway?"

Roland paused. Lifting his donut, he said, "I am, um, I am in shipping."

Then he took a bite.

"Shipping? Like cargo?"

Roland nodded his head.

"What kind of cargo?" she continued.

Roland pointed to his mouth, considering his response.

He swallowed. "I guess you could say I specialize."

"Specialize? In what?"

"In time-sensitive delivery. If someone needs something delivered in a hurry, they call me."

"So, you get through the government import issues better than your normal shipping companies?"

"Yeah, I guess you could say that." Roland chuckled.

Miranda waited for him to explain himself. She sipped her coffee. She nibbled her donut.

"So, why are you so eager to get away from Anadir? I visited there, and it is a lovely planet." Roland had never paid much attention to Anadir's geography. He tended to avoid the planet since it was solidly behind much of the galaxy in technology. Still, there was no reason to insult her homeworld. She had done nothing against him, to this point.

"I have been all over the planet. I've seen everything. I've done everything. There's nothing left."

"You tried everything? I find it hard to believe. You mean to tell me there is no mystery left on the entire planet? You are not old enough."

Miranda laughed. She laughed loudly. Roland nervously looked around. No one seemed to be paying them undue attention.

"I'm sure there are plots of dirt I haven't stepped on yet, but it all looks the same. There is nothing new there."

"And, so, now you are trying to find 'something new' out here."

"This isn't my first trip. I took a short trip to Peraris, but it looked like Anadir. Now, I'm taking a longer trip to more worlds. This is much better. I don't want to spend the rest of my life going to the same places, seeing the same sights, and doing the same things. I want something new."

"I am sorry to bring this to your attention, but I found planets tend to look the same. Still, have you thought about Iradeth? I hear the rivers there are exciting to travel and beautiful to view. Or, what about, Odenpyr? People say they have some of the most exciting games and stunt rides in this part of the galaxy."

"Yeah, yeah. I've heard that, too. I'm sure I'll get to those someday. Right now, I'm checking out other places. We'll see what happens. What did you think of the games?"

"I never had reason to try them. I have gone to the planets, on business, but never needed to investigate the recreational opportunities."

"Too bad," Miranda replied, smirking. "Fun should be its own purpose." She shrugged and took the last bite of her donut. "I think I'll get another one. Do you want anything?"

Roland looked at the remnants before him. "Um, some more water, if it is not too much trouble."

"Silly boy," She left the table.

CHAPTER 16

Roland saw no sign of security. He checked his chronometer. *Eighty-one minutes.*

They must still be checking the cabins or—

"What?"

Roland jumped. Looking up, he saw Miranda hurriedly looking around the pavilion. "What's so interesting?" she asked.

"Oh, it was nothing." Roland smiled at her as she sat, "I thought I recognized someone. False alarm."

Miranda set her donut and his water on the table. Holding up her donut, she looked at him. "For hundreds of years, the donut has remained relatively unchanged. I mean, new flavors are introduced, but the basic concept of the donut has stayed consistent for centuries." She set the donut back onto its plate. "Reminds me of Anadir."

"Why?"

"As long as I've lived there, which is all of my life, nothing new has happened there. Everything..." she said, pointing to the donut, "is a new flavor."

Roland chuckled. Seeing Miranda's look, he said, "Sorry, but your whole life is what, two or three decades? How much change can you expect? I go to different planets, sometimes every couple of years. Nothing changes much. Now, if I could go every couple of hundred years, I might see some significant changes."

"I suppose you're right," she said absently, sliding her donut from one side of the plate to the other. "But, it seems everything interesting on Anadir, I've done. Everything I haven't done doesn't appeal to me."

"I see. So, what are you looking for out here?"

"Something different. Something exciting. Something...new. You know."

Roland did not speak. Instead, he looked at his donut and thought of his ship. *In a way, yeah, I am looking for something new. Definitely not what I found on this ship.* He looked at Miranda, "I guess I am more at home in a familiar place. Safe. Predictable."

"Dull." She giggled and shook her head. "I'm trying to claw out of my shell, and you're trying to crawl back into yours."

* * *

Tarin leaned against the back of the captain's chair. He looked around at the crew he had assembled. *This should be quite the adventure. Once we reach the border, all we have are the assurances they gave me.*

"Captain, based on the current calculations, we will be exiting near a civilian shipping channel. No traffic is scheduled to be in the channel within our time window."

There's not a lot to be done about it now. Even if we are spotted, we will be long gone by the time any response could be launched. "Very well. Continue to monitor traffic and keep me informed."

The lieutenant returned to his monitoring station.

On his previous ship, he would be the one to issue an order for such menial monitoring. But, the promise of something brand new brought him to me.

He looked around at the remaining crew members. Other than the lieutenant and the major, the rest were enlisted. *A risky lot. I could not go the conventional route for this. Too many security concerns. Mercenaries and trouble makers. I had to take those no one else wanted. The mission was plausible enough. Heaven knows I've been on enough missions to create one that is believable. I hope they believe me for a while longer. Then it will be too late for them to do anything about it.*

* * *

Miranda sat back in her chair and looked at Roland for a long time.

To Roland, it was an uncomfortably long time. He glanced at her several times, between looking at his donut, his water, his table, his hands, his surroundings. Still, she looked at him.

"So, that's why you're here. A career space traveler, taking a vacation aboard a spaceship. It's what you know."

He shrugged. "You could look at it that way."

"Oh? And what's another?"

"It was a figure of speech," he replied, absently waving one hand.

She shook her head twice. "It must be nice."

"What?"

"Being comfortable. I don't remember ever being comfortable."

Once I get back to my ship, I will definitely be more comfortable than I am here. Still, here is better than back in that cell. He tilted his head, inviting her to continue.

"Well," Miranda paused and sipped from her coffee cup, "I've always felt something missing. You know how it is when you know something is wrong, or out of place, or just different? You know it, but you can't figure out what it is."

He nodded.

"That's how I've always seen myself. It's like part of me is missing, but I don't know which part. So, I go from place to place to find it, but I can't. Still, the journey has been fun, even if the destination hasn't yet been reached." She raised her cup. "A toast to comfort; may we both find it someday."

Roland let his water glass clink against her coffee cup. "To comfort."

Miranda smiled and drank.

"So, why do you stay closed in all the time? How is that comfortable? There is so much more out there."

"What do you mean?"

"Well, you don't talk about yourself, much. You live with this 'wall' around you, and you don't let it down."

Roland flushed. He wondered how she perceived him that way. "I have seen my fair share of the 'out there.' I found it difficult to navigate." *I go "out there" when I need something "in here," or where I should be.* Roland slid the plate with his donut to the side and rested his elbows on the table.

Miranda put her smile away, "Well, it makes you a very hard man."

"Hard?"

"Yeah, difficult to read—hard to talk to. Okay, hard to get to know. You don't open up to people."

"No, I do not. It has never benefited me, so I keep to myself. And to my ship."

"Your ship? Is it your hiding place?"

Roland winced. *How do other people handle these interactions without feeling naked?*

"When I am on my ship, I know where everything is. I know what everything does. I know what I am doing—what I should be doing. I do not get blind-sided. I do not get surprised." He paused for a moment. "I am not fond of surprises."

Roland picked up the final bite of his donut and ate it as he sat back in his chair, Miranda lifted her cup to her lips and sipped some coffee, letting the cup linger in its position. "I'm sorry."

"For what?"

"For pestering you. If I had known you didn't like surprises, I wouldn't have bothered you at the counter."

Roland smiled. "I am okay. It has been a rather pleasant surprise." *Hard to believe I said that.*

Relaxing, she set her cup down. "I'm glad. I am enjoying your company."

Roland placed his empty plate atop hers and pushed them to the side of the table. Resting his hands on his lap, he leaned back. "Wonderful! It has been a long time since I enjoyed something so much."

Miranda sipped from her coffee cup. "Yeah, I do like donuts. I wish I could still get them on Anadir. No one carries them anymore; at least, they don't where I live."

"So, your quest is two-fold, then?"

"Two-fold? What do you mean?"

"You're looking for your missing self...and donuts."

It took several seconds for Miranda to stop laughing. Roland smiled, pleased with himself. He considered the possibility of attempting to program Melanie for humor, again.

After she recovered, Miranda reached down to retrieve her napkin from the floor. She scooted her chair closer to the table and leaned toward Roland. "I like your sense of humor," she smiled. "It's wonderful."

CHAPTER 17

"How close will we be to the civilian shipping lane when we exit?" Tarin asked.

"Several parsecs, Captain. Far enough we will not collide with any ship making an unscheduled appearance," the lieutenant replied.

"I would like to test a hunch, then."

Major Rosmar approached and whispered to Tarin, "Are you certain we are in a position for an unplanned test, sir?"

"I am certain. We have an accurate measurement of our exit point. We will still be within the planned exit range. I want to vent two of the cargo bays and see if it shortens our journey."

"Theoretically, adding normal space atmosphere to the bubble will increase the resistance and push us out sooner. Theoretically, but it has never been attempted before."

"Of course it hasn't. The previous impacts to the bubble would be so insignificant, the impact would still fall within the margin for error." Raising his arms, he announced, "With this, the impact will be much more noticeable. We may be able to start to influence our trajectory through hyperspace."

"Very well, sir. I will calculate the cubic meters of atmosphere that can be expelled, the anticipated trajectory delta, and then confirm the measurements upon our exit."

"Excellent. Carry on."

* * *

Roland jumped, slamming his knee into the bottom of the table. He managed to keep himself from screaming the remarks typically released when he performed similar maneuvers aboard the *Stiletto*. Instead, he closed his eyes and muttered, with great intensity, until the pain subsided. When he opened his eyes, he saw Miranda slouching in her chair, pouting.

"What was that for?" he asked, still rubbing his knee.

"Sorry, it seemed like the right thing to do, at the time."

"Grabbing my leg was the right thing to do? Under what circumstances?"

"Um, look, I, uh...I'm sorry. I didn't mean to push. I thought, you know, we were getting along so well," she stammered, lifting her coffee cup and avoiding eye contact, "But if you think..."

Roland remembered a scene from some movie he had seen months before. A man and woman were eating dinner, and she reached across the table and grabbed his hand. The man seemed to appreciate the gesture, finding it pleasant. If his interpretation was correct, the gesture indicated a desire to escalate the interaction to something more intense and more physical. "Forgive me. No one has ever done that to me before. Does it mean you want to have sex now?"

Miranda shot back in her chair. After several moments of unblinking stare, she stuttered, "Where...did...*that* come from?"

Roland sipped his water. "Where did *what* come from? It's a simple question? When I saw such overtures made in entertainment, the people involved always end up having sex. Is that what you want?"

A grin crept over Miranda's face. Then, a laugh emerged. Roland tried to understand the appropriateness of her response but failed. He had attempted no humor.

"This is going to take some work, Reggie."

"What will?"

"You will. I mean, first, you are so closed off and...and sterile. Next, you crack me up with a joke. I guess I'll need to take this in stages."

Roland considered her words, but he could not find an appropriate response. He returned to his water.

"This never has happened to you before." She shook her head. At least she was smiling, instead of grinning.

"No, it has not. Did I misinterpret your intent?"

"Hmm, not exactly. But you did miss the scope." She leaned in again. "Reggie, life is not always like entertainment depicts it. Yes, sometimes people move straight to sex. I do not." She sat back and looked around, "How do I explain this?" Her eyes returned to Roland's. "Okay, it's like this, when two people are attracted to each other, there is some level of physical expression."

Roland listened attentively as Miranda corrected some misperceptions. Nodding and grunting at the times he thought appropriate, he tried to ignore the quietness of the *Aradinda*. The ship had reentered hyperspace. *She's going to hate me, but the clock has started. I can wait no longer.*

Roland bolted from his seat. "I need to go...now." Darting across to the counter, he withdrew the passenger card. "Two more powdered donuts."

"Right away, sir." The attendant removed the card from Roland's fingers.

CHAPTER 18

Roland glanced around the pavilion. The first pair of security personnel had arrived, and they were searching the crowd.

The game continues.

After receiving the authorization, the attendant slid the passenger card and the plate of donuts back across the counter. "Thank you, sir," he said.

"Thanks." Roland placed the donuts in a napkin, folded it, and abandoned the plate in the attendant's hands.

Turning toward the exit, he glimpsed Miranda, wide-eyed and open-mouthed. He paused as the security detail entered the crowd. *They should be slow, trying to avoid concerning the legitimate passengers. They should also be thorough, which should slow them even more. Just leave me a hole to squirm through undetected.* Time was now a factor. He had quite a few intangibles to accommodate.

Roland sighed and turned toward the table where Miranda now sat alone. He approached the table. "I am sorry. But, I need to take care of something."

"Well, I hope it's important!" she said.

"You could say my life depends on it. I am truly sorry." Roland turned and strode through the exit into the passageway.

"Well, if you didn't want..." was all Roland heard Miranda say before her words faded into the background.

Four more gray uniforms had arrived. He watched them for a few moments. Their search pattern would bring them to his current location within a few minutes. *Best not to be here when they arrive.* He calculated a route through the pavilion that would allow him to shield his face from both sets of security without looking conspicuous. He chose his moment and walked toward an exit like a passenger, rather than a fugitive. Maintaining a consistent pace was difficult with the other people wandering around unpredictably: Stopping for this child; changing direction to avoid someone who stopped; accelerating through an opening in the crowd. Roland worked his way through the tables, chairs, benches, and plants that were placed throughout the area. After clearing the pavilion, he glanced back. No one was following him.

Roland breathed again. *Now, for housekeeping.*

When using a ship for transportation, Roland did not concern himself with the physical outlay of the ship. He was not inside. He knew his own like no one knew any other. The *Stiletto* was his home, his friend, his constant companion. Of other ships, he learned as much as necessary to negotiate his own vessel into a comfortable anchoring point. When needed, he learned the best locations for tapping into the target ship's computer systems, so he could refuel or search for new, and interesting, data. He did not bother with interior layout.

Roland worked his way back down the series of corridors until he again located a directory. It would take some time for the security detail to investigate the crowd he had left. Scanning the directory for housekeeping, Roland noted it was not centralized. Each deck had its own housekeeping section, broken up into several individual supply closets. *Perfect.*

The directory also showed Roland most of the upper decks were passenger related. The middle decks, where he had spent his earlier time aboard this vessel, was for detention and medical facilities. *Thank you for concentrating your efforts on capturing suspects, instead of detaining them.* Looking back at the directory, he observed, *I assume the lower decks are for the actual operation of the vessel.*

Roland traced a route on the directory from his current position to one of the accesses to the lower levels of the *Aradinda.* Locating a housekeeping closet along his route, he departed.

The hallways and passageways on the *Aradinda* were a muted white on the passenger levels. Gray walls marked the middle levels. Roland went to the housekeeping closet closest to the first gray wall he encountered. He opened the unsecured door and entered the room.

Very neat. Roland noticed all the containers were displaying their labels, face-front. All of them were full. The uniforms not in current use were either folded or hung on their appropriate hooks. Roland donned a uniform, took cleaning solution and a cloth in a garbage bag. He left. *Close inspection may be a problem, but time is becoming a factor.*

The corridor was clear. Roland pulled his head back around the corner and picked up his bag. Striding around the corner, Roland walked down the adjoining corridor until he saw a secured doorway. A camera swept back and forth. He braved it and continued until he arrived at the doorway. *Look like you belong here.*

The keypad was designed for recording, rather than securing, access. Purely numeric entry allowed for a simple design. Four rows by four columns would be an easy code to break, given time. Not having such luxury, Roland needed help. He cleaned the keypad with the solution and cloth. Roland removed days of dirt and oil.

It looks like I may be rushed a bit, from the frequency of use this keypad endures. It is also possible the camera will summon unwanted company. Fortunately, knowing what I need to do should speed up the process.

Roland examined the keypad and saw a clean surface. He put his cleaning supplies in his bag, picked the bag up, and moved around the corner. No camera covered this section of the corridor. He waited.

Hearing footsteps approach from behind him. Roland grabbed his bag and walked back around the corner, trying to look like a housekeeper to the camera. He passed by the keypad to the next corner, where the corridor turned. No camera. No door. He lowered his bag and let out a breath of relief but wondered if the camera had alerted anyone to a wandering housekeeper.

The footsteps drew closer.

Roland looked behind him. No one was there. The corridor turned again a score or so meters beyond him. Roland saw no other doors, corridors, or cameras. He listened, but the steps he heard were all from in front of him. Roland wondered if the boots would stop at the door. If they continued beyond, Roland had no time to run and get out of sight. The boots would alert, and he would be back inside a gray cell.

No, thanks.

The steps stopped. Roland breathed again.

Peeking around the corner, Roland watched as the uniform entered the access code. One high, two upper-middle, two low, one lower-middle.

Roland reran the sequence as the door slid upward and the uniform disappeared into the computer room. *One press on the top row; two on the second; two on the bottom row; one on the row above. If things work out with the finger residue, I will have at most four possible combinations. Simple, unless the ship monitors invalid codes and issues an alarm or locks out all access. Not with this design.*

From behind him, he heard approaching boots from down the corridor.

Great. The room is still occupied.

Closer.

At least four uniforms. Almost here, by the sounds of it.

Roland retreated around the one corner still in sight of the room. Pulling out the cleaner, he applied it randomly and wiped it off.

Clean, Roland. Glance when they arrive, but don't stare. Breathe.

The uniforms came around the corner in a quick, marching cadence. They passed without a glance at Roland.

"He has moved from the food court back to the cabins," Roland heard the announcement from one of the soldiers' radio. "You will need to conduct a door-to-door search."

Well, I hope it keeps them busy for a while.

CHAPTER 19

The door slid open. Footsteps again. Louder. Roland picked up his bag and drew a big breath. Blowing out in a controlled exhale, Roland turned and walked into the uniform.

"Oh, excuse me," Roland said as he stepped aside and continued walking. The footsteps stopped. Roland walked past the keypad and around the corner, hoping the uniform saw an orderly accidentally bump it. He continued until he heard the footsteps begin again. He stopped. The footsteps faded. Roland returned to the keypad, quickening his pace after the footsteps were gone.

It should not question what it sees every day. Hopefully, the camera will not alert anyone.

Roland listened for more footsteps. Hearing none, he lowered his bag and withdrew his napkin. Unfolding the napkin, He lifted one of his donuts . and tapped its side. Powder accumulated in his napkin. Roland dropped the donut when no more powder fell. He picked up the second and tapped. Satisfied with the amount of powder on his napkin, Roland closed the napkin like a bag and walked to the panel. Keeping his back to the camera, he brought the napkin to the access panel and blew across the powder until the access panel had a light dusting of the donut's former covering. He put the napkin into his pocket.

Roland blew on the panel, removing most of the dust.

Roland smiled. Five small powder residues remained. That meant one row with two entries used just one digit but used it twice. This reduced the possible combinations to two. *No system would not alert anyone for one missed entry.* Roland's first attempt resulted in a quiet buzzing, but no access. The second attempt worked.

Roland blinked a couple of times until his eyes adjusted to the darkness. The computer room was much like his cockpit in the lighting level and the amount of information displaying on the terminal viewscreens: environmental status, supply usage, and availability, velocity, trajectory, galactic map, arrival schedule, etc. Roland identified the terminal displaying the hyperdrive status and approached it.

Roland stopped every few seconds, listening for alarms, footsteps, or doors opening. Each time, he was greeted with the humming of computer components. *I cannot believe the lack of security surrounding such a sensitive area of the ship. No one should be allowed to do what I am doing.*

Since the computer was logged into the ship's network, Roland accessed the source code for the ship's computer without difficulty. The language was the same he used on the *Stiletto. Standardization is a wonderful thing.* He opened a new file and started writing his exit strategy.

The *Aradinda's* hyperdrive had been upgraded to the Model 150—the elliptical bubble generator. Roland had not yet upgraded the *Stiletto* since his was reserved for emergency use, and the *Stiletto* was not attempting to impress the directors of the *Celestial View* cruise line.

Roland located a program for regulating the drive and copied significant lines from the program into his own. He then added and modified lines of code to achieve different results than the original program was designed to do.

After completing the system code entry, he added some lines to the beginning of the program. Checking the portable chronometer he had obtained in the passenger area, one imitating elegance, he compared it to the chronometer displayed from the *Aradinda's* computer system.

With the Model 150, the Aradinda *should stay in hyperspace for around four hours. Start the program when the ship exits hyperspace. Include a delay of one hundred and thirty seconds before the results display. Just as they restart the hyperspace warm-up. Now, who's on watch at the outer doors?* Scanning the duty roster, he found Ensign Galrosa Tarne would be posted at the proper time. *"Ensign"—even civilian liners went to military command structures.*

Now to check on the security officer's results.

Roland searched the data system for all references to the *Stiletto* or to James Reginald Fischer. There was one file. It had today's date. It was created by a "Bornor Zemadin." *It matches the name on the uniform. Let's see what this Bornor Zemadin pulled out about me. Not much, I'm sure. I am very careful.*

Impressive, Mr. Zemadin. Don't you have anything else to do? Have I become your instant obsession? Finding no evidence of his real name,

Roland sighed with relief. *Wait a minute.* He continued to read the file's contents. *This makes no sense. I never lived on Erkarth. I visit there. What is all of this about J. R. Fischer III living and working there? Has he started writing fiction about me? Some of this looks familiar, though. My fake biography. Interesting.*

"I don't have time for a literary critique, or for more fact checking, Bornor. You're on your own with your book," Roland stated to the otherwise empty room.

Not good. Roland saw notes regarding several systems on the *Stiletto*. Some phrases in Bornor's notes stood out. "Serial number does not match vendor standards"; "System specifications exceed those available to the public"; "System specifications conform to a system that was reported stolen." He also saw inquiries regarding those systems being sent to the design companies. *This could cause problems.*

Near the end of the file, he found the phrase "asteroid anomaly."

Technician Trainee, Emari Antiarus, detected an asteroid anomaly. He requested and received permission to investigate the erratic behavior of the asteroid. Tracking its trajectory, he determined it struck the *Aradinda* behind the hyperspace engine. Initiating a visual sweep of the area, we detected the presence of an unauthorized vehicle. We also detected an increase in energy output, indicating this vessel had accessed our computer systems and was siphoning power from the *Aradinda*. We maintained an illusion of normalcy during which a security team apprehended the pilot of the vessel.

Nicely done, Mr. Antiarus. I wonder if anyone truly appreciates the significance of asking the right questions at the right time. You are to be commended.

He checked his chronometer. *Time is short. It will take time to get into an enviro-suit. How often did the crew access this room, anyway?* Roland overwrote Bornor's file with multiple lines of "asteroid anomaly" and turned toward the door. *No one will ever mention this to the technician. He will end up doing the same thing every other technician does—enough to keep his job.* Returning to the console, he accessed his new program. At the end of the program, he instructed it to send a message to Emari Antiarus:

Mr. Antiarus, you do not know me. We never met. But, I

congratulate you on your insight. By taking nothing for granted, you did something no one did before—you caught me. Most would ignore my actions; some may remark on it. You pursued it. Never lose your inquisitive dimension. Many will think you odd, yet you will find more truth in those questions than they would even suspect exists. I salute you, and encourage you, Mr. Antiarus, though I must also take my leave of you.

Your "Asteroid Anomaly" (Ask Bornor about me.)

CHAPTER 20

As the door closed behind him, Roland saw the uniform come from around the corner of the corridor. Roland withdrew his cloth and cleaner from his bag and started to clean the keypad, muttering to himself. "Slobs! Can no one clean up after themselves anymore?" He finished wiping the donut residue from the keypad and placed the cloth back into the pocket of the cleaning jacket.

"Watch your step, sir," Roland warned the uniform. "Someone dropped some food and left it." He reached down, picked up his two donuts, and dropped them into his bag. He wiped the floor where the donuts had fallen. "Done! Excuse me, sir." Roland took his bag and cleaner and strode past the uniform and around the corner. He kept a steady pace until several turns and intersections separated him from the keypad. Then he stopped and stood against one wall of an intersection, listening for footsteps following him.

Satisfied no pursuit was imminent, Roland continued down the corridor toward the doorway to the outer hull of the *Aradinda*. He checked his portable chronometer. *Time to spare.* Locating an isolated corridor, he emptied the garbage bag of his personal belongings, took off the cleaning uniform jacket, stuffed it into the empty bag, and deposited the bag into a garbage container chute.

Picking up his belongings, he rehearsed his coming conversation with Ensign Galrosa Tarne. Roland did not possess vast experience to draw from for this rehearsal. The conversation with Miranda was the longest face-to-face interaction Roland ever had. Even the girl from his childhood had been part of Roland's life through a video screen.

Roland strode toward the outer hull station. *I should be able to bluff my way through this uniform—Ensign Tarne. I have done this type of acting before, but never in person.* He thought about his parents and their occasional interaction with him. He convinced them he was a normal child, progressing as any child should. Their lengthy absences afforded him the time to work his technological marvels, like modifying the voice responses in the kitchen to be more conversational. *My mother liked Spectre's voice.* He recalled how she would request complex meals, those times she was at home, just to hear the preparation unit answer questions about the ingredients.

I'm sure I can carry on the charade for one encounter. Roland checked his chronometer. *It should be about time.* On cue, the *Aradinda* was spat out of hyperspace. Roland turned the corner toward the outer door, as his program initiated its processes.

Approaching the airlock, he glanced at Ensign Tarne, "Enviro-suits are in here, right?" he asked, pointing to an anteroom.

"Yes, sir, they are," Tarne responded. "Is there something I can do for you? This is a restricted area."

"I realize that, but I am an authorized person. I am Joshua Orlamir of Celestial View Leisure Travel. In the *Aradinda's* quest for acceptance in our fleet, I am performing a hull check. We must know if the hull can withstand extensive exposure in hyperspace."

Roland checked his chronometer. "Were you not notified?" He performed a quick calculation. *The hyperspace is edging toward the yellow by now. The crew is beginning their diagnostics—everything showing normal. Another fourteen minutes before shutdown.* "Well, I am a few minutes early. I'll get ready while final preparations are being made," he stated as he entered the anteroom and noticed the series 400 Standard Environmental Protection Apparel in individual lockers.

"400 SEPAs? A little antiquated, but functional for our purposes. I will recommend an upgrade to at least the 420s or the 2100 series EnviroMax," Roland yelled out to the hallway, remembering two newer models from product listings he had come across while looking for other things.

"Sir, I need authorization for this."

"I'm sure they'll be calling you, Ensign Tarne." Roland was already sweating. Some of it was due to the effort in getting into the enviro-suit. He was used to his 1800 series EnviroMax. These 400 SEPAs were unfamiliar enough to be clumsy, but the basic goals were the same: to protect its wearer from the extreme cold of deep space and to prevent the wearer from breathing vacuum. There was a limited number of ways in which those goals could be met.

As he pulled on the helmet and engaged the air supply, he exited the anteroom into the corridor. Ensign Tarne was looking out through the porthole into the stars outside. "Sir, I received no clearance for this inspection."

Roland shook his head. "Ensign, for what other reason would we exit hyperspace, then delay reentry in mid-jump?"

"Perhaps so, sir, but I still require authorization before I can open the hatch for you."

"Fine, call whomever you need for authorization." *Stop him! Do not let him make the call!*

Ensign Tarne walked to the communications panel. Roland slapped his suit.

"Ensign, I think I left my passenger card in my jacket. Could you retrieve it and my chronometer? It's in one of the pockets. Could you hold onto them while I'm gone? I don't want to lose them."

"Sure." The ensign entered the anteroom as Roland pressed the manual release of the airlock. He wondered how long it would take the ensign to decide the jacket was not there. Hopefully, it would take a couple of minutes. The airlock door opened and he stepped inside and pressed the manual seal on the other side. As the door was closing, he saw the red light of the communications unit flash, "Security to hatch 19B. Come in, Ensign Tarne."

Roland pressed the large, green button, and the outer door slid open with a loud hiss. He stepped through the hatch, waving to the uniform as it watched through the porthole with wide eyes, and turned toward his ship.

Although the magnetic boots did keep him from floating away, walking in them was an arduous process. Never having mastered the technique of spacewalking, each step was slow, deliberate, and fatiguing. By the time he entered his own ship and closed the *Stiletto's* hatch behind him, he was sweating and panting. *Why has no one developed magnetic boots with wheels?*

Dropping the helmet, Roland bellowed, "Jackson, get us off this ship! Clear three hundred meters and execute a 180-degree turn on a level plane— max thrust!"

"Roger that, sir."

Roland felt the clamps release as he sat down to catch his breath. By the time he extricated himself from the last piece of the environmental suit, the

Aradinda was a speck on his rear-facing viewscreen. "Have a nice life, Miranda," he whispered to the speck.

"All right, Jackson, you can ease up. They won't be coming after us."

"Roger that, sir."

Ships as large as the *Aradinda* did not turn well. The about-face the *Stiletto* could execute in a few seconds would require half an hour for the *Aradinda* to complete. *That uniform, Bornor Zemadin, knows that. Besides, I did not steal anything, aside from the environmental suit. That was necessary, and they can afford a replacement.* They could not afford the lost time or the myriad of questions resulting from their chase of an insignificant stowaway. They knew that as well.

What they did not know was Roland was stranded. "Just wait until I get RECON. Things will be different then."

The *Stiletto* had enough power for a single, short jump through hyperspace. It was reserved for emergencies. *This is inconvenient. It will not be an emergency for quite a while yet.*

CHAPTER 21

Black.

Looking at his main window, Roland saw blackness, interrupted by pinpoints of light. Through an astronomer's eyes, the sight may be spectacular. Through Roland's eyes, it was unnerving.

"Melanie."

"Yes, Roland?"

"What available choices do we have?"

"None."

"What do you mean, 'None'?"

"I assumed you would not count our continued floating in space as a viable option, so I eliminated it from my calculation."

Roland laughed, leaning back into the simulated animal hide chair he had missed, "Astute assumption, Melanie. Please continue."

"Moreover, I also eliminated the action of utilizing our n-space drive to continue along this travel route until our fuel is exhausted. Our current fuel supply will not allow us to reach any known habitable planet along this route."

"What about other routes?"

"There is one route within our range if we use all existing n-space fuel and a hyperspace jump—"

"Great."

"—But there is no ship scheduled to arrive at our exit point for twenty-seven days. Without the ability to sustain life support from auxiliary fuel reserves, our oxygen supply will be exhausted eighteen days prior to arrival."

"So, are you telling me I am stranded here until I deplete all of our remaining resources?"

"No, Roland, I am not saying that."

"But, you told me we had no choices."

"There is a single ship scheduled to arrive here within the next two weeks. Any other course of action we attempt will mathematically fail. Therefore, we have no choices."

"As usual, Melanie, your logic is infallible." Roland leaned back in his chair and laughed, spreading his arms wide. "And what is this miracle mode of movement so cleverly availing itself to us?"

"The *M.T.S. 1741-A* will be arriving in four hours..."

Roland stopped laughing. "The *M.T.S. 1741-A*? You mean, the sole ship coming through in fourteen days is a military transport?"

"Correct, Roland."

"Great." Roland slumped back and sighed. *The military. Here I am, stealing everything I can to make my ship undetectable. Why? So I can avoid certain types of people, certain authority figures—AMONG THEM, THE MILITARY! Now, I must tag them for a ride. Wonderful.*

"Get me the schematics and send Jackson and Spectre in. We have a lot of planning to do in the next four hours."

"All right, Roland. The specs will be those for the general class, rather than for this specific vessel. Also, we will need to move to intercept. I will have Jackson begin plotting our course."

Roland, again. "Understood. Thank you, Melanie."

"By the way, Melanie, did that security officer—what was his name?" he thought back to the *Aradinda's* computer room, "Bornor—right. Did Bornor make any transmissions?"

"Yes, Roland, he made several transmissions."

"What did he transmit?"

"I was not instructed to intercept the transmissions. I monitored the occurrences."

Great.

* * *

"Did the transport detect the Lamprey?" Roland asked once the *Stiletto* completed the tag.

"No, Reg," Spectre responded, "I detect no alarms concerning a hull penetration or system invasion."

"Good. The last thing I need is for them to notice me sticking my ship's tongue into their ship. Did you make the necessary connections?"

"Determining so will take some investigation. 1 do not detect any physical problems with the connections."

"All right. 1 do not like the military. They are way too touchy about unauthorized access."

"Noted, Reg."

"O.K., Spectre, take your time. We do not want any alarms here. Military computers are risky. They are straightforward and simple to navigate, but dangerous if we get careless."

"1 understand, Reg. It will slow withdrawal a bit. 1s it a problem?"

"1 hope not. This is our one shot out of here. 1 do not know where they are going, but anywhere is better than here, Spectre. What is their destination?"

"1 will look into it. One moment."

"After that, stick to the unrestricted data. 1 do not want to take chances here if we can help it."

Roland called for the personnel listing. Black eyes reflected the output as they flitted from one viewscreen to another. To the casual observer, Roland would seem distracted by the constantly changing streams of data. But there were never any casual observers around Roland to be so misled.

No troops. Where are they going with a full contingent of command officers, with Commander Tarin Koraben at the helm, but no troops? This ship was identified as a troop transport, so where are the troops it was transporting?

"Their destination is classified, Reg."

"Okay, Spectre. Based on their current trajectory, get Jackson to calculate all possible planetary orbits with which the transport will intercept. We will attempt to locate a destination planet along the route."

With the personnel listing sorted by rank, Roland saw two names at the bottom of the list. No ranks were given. Both were doctors, but not in medicine. One name was familiar. *But from where?*

"Radam Nortolis. Radam Nortolis. Where did 1 hear that name before? Spectre, bring Melanie back for a minute."

"Will do, Reg."

"Yes, Roland?" came Melanie's voice.

"Melanie, check the personnel references for the last three tags for the name 'Radam Nortolis.' 1 know 1 ran across it."

"1 show no record of Radam Nortolis, or any close variations, in any personnel listing from the last three downloads."

"Hmmm," *Where was it?* "Well, in that case, scan all individual bio files I requested over the same period."

"All right, Roland. One moment."

Roland shifted in his chair, then resumed scanning the personnel listing of the *MTS 1741-A.*

"I have one match for Radam Nortolis."

"I thought so. Who is he?"

"He is a Chief Technology Officer, Planetary Operations, from Bantadam. He is the immediate supervisor of Beranon, whose file you requested from the *Surrogate.*"

"What is he doing here?"

"I do not have sufficient data to formulate an answer for you, Roland."

"Spectre?"

"Yes, Reg?"

"Show me the security sensor readouts. Let me see if they have any idea we are here."

"One moment, please."

The screen to Roland's left divided into four quadrants, each displaying lines and images within normal operations. None showed alarms or guards scurrying through corridors.

Good.

So, where are they going? "Spectre, has Jackson calculated a potential destination, yet?"

"Reg, the most plausible destination, based on Jackson's calculations from our current heading has this ship headed to the outer arm of the galaxy. We have not yet determined a target system or planet."

Okay, a transport vessel without its designated cargo, with a full crew, and headed to the end of the known galaxy. None of this makes sense. The trip itself will take weeks. What is going on out there?

"I found no unclassified orders, yet."

"Keep searching."

"Roger that, sir."

Roland returned to his personnel listing. *Why are two unranked individuals present on an empty military transport heading to an outer arm?*

Fact: A military troop transport vessel, with all officers and crew but no troops, is headed to a remote part of the galaxy.

Speculation: The ship itself, rather than its contents, is performing the required operation. Plausible. This is a military vessel, and they do possess cutting edge technology. This could be a system test, where no troops are required.

Speculation: The ship is undertaking an operation requiring no one other than officers and crew. Possible. This ship could be on a non-military mission or a military mission where no troops are involved. Perhaps it is a troop withdrawal. But do we have troops stationed or in use so far away? None that I remember. Still, it could be a non-military mission.

Fact: Two trained, nonmilitary personnel are aboard this vessel.

Speculation: The operation falls within their area of expertise. Plausible.

Conclusion: The M.T.S. 1741-A is performing an operation, military or non-military, in the outer reaches of the galaxy. The operation is focusing on the ship itself, or some of its systems, and it requires all officers and crew, as well as the input of significant nonmilitary personnel.

Are there any other pertinent facts?

"Melanie, what is the planet of origin for this ship?"

"Do you mean the planet on which it was built or the planet from which it arrived at this point?"

"The latter."

"Dorea."

"This ship came from Dorea without deviation?"

"Correct."

"When?"

"It left Dorea one week ago."

"A week? How many days ago did Beranon and Vardri depart from Dorea?"

"Seven."

"I see. Why was the ship on Dorea?"

"I cannot access the information."

"Spectre, is the presence of *M.T.S. 1741-A* on Dorea classified?"

"No, sir. It was on Dorea for routine maintenance."

"Dorea has become a military maintenance depot?"

"No, sir. This occurrence is an exception. All other details of the maintenance are classified."

"Melanie, is there any news of significance coming out of Dorea concerning the last forty-eight hours?"

"None, Roland."

Fact: Two individuals working on the same hyperdrive project leave a planet as a military transport vessel, minus troops, departs the same planet with the supervisor of one of the individuals.

Speculation: Coincidence. Doubtful.

Speculation: Treachery. Equally doubtful. The military is too careful in identifying rogue soldiers. Still, a rogue soldier was one of the possible scenarios for Beranon's and Vardri's departure.

"Melanie?"

"Yes, Roland?"

Roland, again. "Access the file from Bantadam Technology Conglomerate. The RECON project Beranon was working on, did we get any of the technical details about the hyperdrive involved in the test?"

"We did. The test was to be performed on a Model 153 Enhanced Gamma release."

"Model 153? I am aware of the Models through 151. What did I miss?"

"Scanning...all references to Model 152 occur in military contexts. All references to Model 153 occur within the scope of this project."

"Spectre, access the ship's controls, view mode. No sense in tipping them off. Let me know if they are readying the hyperdrive."

"Will do, Reg."

"And, access all technical details concerning the Model 153."

"You got it, Reg. Limit to unclassified data?"

"We will start there."

"Melanie, get Jackson for me."

"All right, Roland."

Roland, again.

"Jackson here, sir."

"Ready a link up with the Dorea system network. We may require access to Dorea Space and Hyperspace."

"Roger that, sir."

"Reg, the Hull Specifications file for this vessel addresses *M.T.S. 1822-G,* rather than the *M.T.S. 1741-A* its transponder code references."

"They have a different set of hull dimensions?"

"No, Reg, they have a different transponder. All other references internal to this vessel, identify it as *M.T.S. 1822-G.* All technical details concerning the hyperdrive are classified. I can get to it, but it will take time."

"Go to it, Spectre, but be careful. Jackson, are you ready yet?"

"Almost, sir. I am compensating for Spectre's resource usage. With your permission, I will tap the power reserve."

"Do it."

A few long minutes later, Jackson returned. "Everything is ready on this end, sir.

Execute?"

"Execute." *What are you doing with the Model 153, Vardri?*

"Link established."

"Display."

"Roger that, sir." The terminals to Roland's right activated with the corporate logo for Dorea Space and Hyperspace. Predictably, the login and password prompt displayed prominently as well.

"This could be tricky. Her bio lists no significant relationships. Her hobbies and interests do not concern shipping lines or security, so those kinds of questions are not asked."

Except to authenticate a user who does not remember her password.

"Jackson, scan the system for password files."

I, on the other hand, will use the old 'I forgot my password' process. It's too bad Spectre is already engaged; I sure could use his stealth programs for this.

"Password file located. Decryption initiated."

Scanning Vardri's personnel file, Roland muttered, "Hopefully, they have not initiated any serious upgrades to code encryption. This is not necessary too often, but I do try to keep up on it. If they upgraded the encryption, my decryption attempt may alert..."

"Decryption complete."

Roland smiled and sighed. "That definitely saved me some time and eye strain."

"Scan the file for any references to 'Vardri,' 'Alarius,' or any close variations."

"One match found."

"Log it in."

"Roger that, sir." The login and password information filled, and the corporate logo was replaced with departmental headings. Roland selected the general corporate information. Then the Corporate Personnel section. He located Vardri Alarius and selected her file. The viewscreen showed the same eyes that had grabbed his attention from the *Surrogate's* passenger listing, but they were different, too. These were friendlier, gentler, less afraid.

"So, Vardri oversees the military testing projects, in the Hyperspace Hardpoint division. Take me there, Jackson."

"Roger that, sir." The viewscreen showed a large listing of hardware-based projects, from recalibration upgrades to the incorporation of existing hyperdrives with new navigational theories. Two projects showed the most promise: Model 153 and RECON. *Vardri managed the RECON project.*

"Download all files relating to RECON and Model 153 projects. I'll check them out on this end when Spectre is finished."

"Roger that, sir. Scanning. Download time estimated at twenty-seven minutes, twelve seconds. Execute?"

"Spectre, any indication of hyperdrive activity?"

"None at this time, Reg."

"Jackson, execute."

"Download initiated."

"How are we doing, Spectre?"

"I accessed the systems console and am proceeding with accessing the hyperdrive information. Stand by."

Roland got up and paced to the rear of the *Stiletto. If Beranon and Vardri were on the run from the military, it would have to do with this project. This Commander Koraben must have threatened them somehow.*

If he is stealing the M.T.S. 1741-A or the 1822-G, he would possess two cutting-edge systems on board and operational: a new hyperdrive engine and the RECON. Plus, he changed transponders—an imperial offense by itself.

When he reached the cargo door, he turned and paced back to the cockpit. *So, why would he run the risk of changing the transponder? He must be stealing the ship. So what about the rest of the crew? What about those two scientists? Are they involved with the theft, or are they innocent bystanders? Hopefully, those files from Dorea will illuminate things a bit.*

He could do nothing but wait. He left the cockpit and laid on his bunk.

He thought of Vardri.

He thought of the fear he now saw as he remembered her *Surrogate* file.

He thought of her hair, long and straight.

He thought of her standing at the end of the corridor in his home, waiting for him as he walked to her.

He thought of her smile at his approach.

He thought of raspberry cream.

CHAPTER 22

So, Vardri was an innocent bystander. She was on the run. So, it means the civilians on board the ship are part of the team. If she was the project manager for the test, and she left three days into it, they must have started this right after installation. So, what did they do to scare off Beranon and Vardri?

"Reg, I accessed the operational instructions for the hyperdrive, but no technical data yet. I am proceeding through the next level of security."

"Right, Spectre. Display the operational instructions on the center terminal. I will start with those."

"Will do."

Roland went to the cockpit. He hit the chair so it spun him to face the center viewscreen as he sat down. *If you are stealing the ship, I would like to see what you are after. No one has defected with military hardware since the empire was formed, over four hundred years ago. So, maybe I can figure out who your buyer is, Commander. Two prototype components would fetch a high price. I would buy it myself if I needed a hyperdrive. Still, if it has the RECON installed, it would be worth the price.*

The operational instructions were presented in standard military format. Roland marked the contents page and checked the introduction. Scanning for technical detail, he found this model was of similar displacement to the Model 152, "requiring no significant architectural modifications for refitting existing vessels to accommodate the new Model 153 Hyperspatial Insertion Unit (HIU)." *Everything's an acronym.*

Roland continued scanning each major point listed in the contents area. When he displayed the second screen of contents listing, Roland sat up. One of the items read: "Remapping Hull Dimensions after Combat Damage." *What kind of damage would cause the hull to extend beyond the hyperspace bubble? Such significant damage would make the ship inoperable or, at least, unstable.*

"I accessed the technical specifications for the hyperdrive, Reg."

"Good work, Spectre. Does it reference hull dimensions?"

"Yes, it does. 'The Model 153 HIU will generate a hyperdrive bubble of the exact specifications entered into the Hull Specifications section of the data.'"

"It explains why they have the 'Remapping' section in the instructions."

Roland accessed the "Remapping Hull Dimensions After Combat Damage" section of the operational instructions. After reading the section, he checked his chronometer. The file download from Dorea was almost half complete. So, he had to wait almost fourteen minutes before all system resources could be dedicated to Spectre.

"Spectre, locate the Hull Specifications file for this vessel."

"Reg," Spectre responded, "They are running through the checklist for powering up the hyperdrive."

"Get those Hull Dimensions for me—now!" The viewscreen went blank, then filled with three-dimensional reproductions of individual sections of the *M.T.S. 1822-G.*

"Okay, where are we?"

"I cannot determine an exact location based on my connections, Reg. Jackson has the information locked now."

"All right, I will use visual." Roland checked out his fore window and located a small protrusion from the hull. Locating the section in the Hull Dimensions, he built additional dimensions to include the *Stiletto.* "I cannot get fancy here—but I need a box to put us in."

Roland checked the operational instructions again, verifying his data input matched the specifications. "Upload the new data, Spectre."

"Jackson has the transmission processes locked. I will be delayed."

"Damn!" Roland checked the chronometer. Jackson needed less than two minutes. "What is the status of the hyperdrive checklist?"

"The powering sequence has been initiated."

"Jackson, abort the download. Free the transmission processes for Spectre now!"

"Roger that, sir. Aborting download. Maintain link?"

"Shut it all down, Jackson!"

"Roger that, sir. Link terminated. Transmission process available."

"Go, Spectre!"

"Uploading data, Reg."

Roland caught himself as the *Stiletto* lurched for a second. Everything went dark except for the stripes on his window.

CHAPTER 23

Roland looked out at the universe; stripes marched across his window from right to left. Illuminated by the diffused light from those stripes and the chronometer on the front of the monitor panel, the cockpit seemed to Roland an alien place. *Well, this is an interesting development. I never saw this side of hyperspace before.*

Roland rose and walked around the interior of the *Stiletto*. No lights shined. No monitors illuminated. No cooling systems hummed. No indicators displayed a to-the-minute status. The complete absence of any system lighting informed him of the status. The sole exceptions were the environmental control system, outside the cargo hold door, and the chronometer.

Observation: Other than the environmental displays and chronometer, I have no lighting or computer functions.

Speculation: The Stiletto *has suffered a main power failure. This power failure was caused by the activation of the new hyperdrive unit.*

Roland tilted his head. *Plausible.*

"Observation: I have breathable air and gravity on the ship," he said, taking a deep breath as his personal verification, "And, the environmental status indicators show normal operation from reserve power."

Leaning over the environmental control panels, he continued, "Speculation: Presence of atmosphere and gravity are due to the isolation of those systems from the main computer. Hence, there was no failure of these systems from the power failure. This is further supported by the status indicators. Speculation accepted."

He had designed the *Stiletto* to keep the environmental controls operating by drawing from the reserve power anytime the main power connection was not available. Used primarily during maintenance or the installation of a new system, it served a more substantive—and ominous—

function now.

"Ramifications: at full reserve, the atmosphere would last for two days—forty-two hours on reserve power, before the system halted—and another six before the air became unbreathable. Main power must be restored before then." Roland returned to the cockpit and checked the *Stiletto's* chronometer, which he had tied into the environmental control circuitry. He switched its function to a timer. He set it for forty-eight hours. "Mark," he announced to his empty ship, as he activated the chronometer.

He sat down in the cockpit chair. "Observation: The window displays stripes.

"Speculation: The unprecedented striped universe is due to the *Stiletto* having been partially drawn into hyperspace as the *M.T.S. 1741-A* engaged its hyperdrive. Doubtful, with an exact-fit hyperspace shell. Were they using the spherical or elliptical shell, it would be more plausible. Even then, theoretically, it would require the two ships being at different speeds when the drive was activated. Speculation rejected."

Roland idly turned his cockpit chair it side-to-side.

"Speculation: The *Stiletto* remained in normal space. The migration of the stripes indicates motion along all three axes: vertical, horizontal, and linear. The *Stiletto* would be traveling at the same speed as the military vessel when they activated their hyperdrive.

"Though not yet confirmed, it explains the symptoms according to all the physical laws I know. Speculation accepted."

Roland rose again as he looked at the striped universe. "If my speculation is correct, the *Stiletto* must be traveling at a pretty high rate of speed. I can see no focal point, so she cannot be primarily spinning, but doing something more like tumbling. It's good my artificial gravity is still working."

He examined the pattern moving across his vision. "The stripes seem solid, but not consistent." Turning away as his head started to ache, he wondered for a few moments. "Of course," he concluded, "The screen covers a small section of the starfield. The stripes break as one star leaves my view and is replaced by another star. Over, and over, and over, and...." His speculation made his body begin to waver.

Sitting back down in his familiar chair, he watched the striped display march off his window, to be replaced with more stripes from an infinite reserve. The aching in his head became more pronounced. Closing his eyes, He sat back and considered his situation. "This cannot be happening. I go from being a prisoner to a free man to a prisoner, again. Sure, I am back aboard my own ship, but look at her. I am as powerless out here with her as I would be without her."

Roland slammed his fist onto his chair's armrest. "First, I get caught by some low-grade techno-geek who never should have noticed I was even there. Then that security drone, Bornor, traps me on board his glorified playroom. When I do make my way back to my own ship—through great ingenuity, I might add—I have to tag a ship with a 'zero-tolerance' hyperdrive." He spun his chair so he faced the window. Containing himself no longer, he stood and shouted at the universe through which the *Stiletto* tumbled, "What is your problem? What did I ever do to you?" His perception of the stripes started to trigger a physical response from his stomach, so Roland sat back down and turned his chair away to the interior of the ship.

* * *

"What the hell was that?" Tarin screamed at his lieutenant as sparks from several monitors settled to the decking where he stood. They, and all the remaining viewscreens went dark.

"Unknown, sir. We activated the hyperdrive, and then there was a power spike." The lieutenant called up a series of diagnostic reports on the viewscreen, scanning the contents, and then sweeping them from the viewscreen in favor of the next report. "The hyperdrive is operating as it should, but several internal systems are damaged."

"Will the damage to those systems cause any delay? We are on a schedule."

"None of the critical systems were damaged. We can reroute around the damaged, non-critical systems, but it will take a couple of hours to complete. The navigation system absorbed the spike, so we should be able to proceed without a significant delay. Your experiment, coupled with this delay, does take up much of the reserve we had in the schedule."

"Understood. From now on, we will do everything by the book."

"Yes, sir, captain."

* * *

Glancing at the *Stiletto's* chronometer counting down, he thought about his recent experiences, but asked no one in particular, "Are you still mad,

Miranda? It looks like I am in the 'frying pan/fire' situation. Maybe I should have stayed with you, and..." He paused, trying to remember the smell of raspberry cream, again, but could not overcome the stench of burned wiring. "No. As much as I did enjoy our conversation, staying would cost me my freedom—and my ship. It is too great a price for me." *It is my ship. At least, I am king aboard my ship.* Roland got up and walked the length of his domain, considering the chances of being rescued, or even noticed, as it tumbled through space.

* * *

Vardri opened her bag and estimated her remaining funds. *Fifty thousand in currency. I hope it is enough to keep me hidden until Tarin forgets about me.* She closed the bag and waved down a taxi. *I hope.* As the door slid open, she asked the automated driver, "Do you accept cash?"

"I do, ma'am, although I cannot offer change in return for overpayment," the mechanical voice responded.

"Fine," Vardri said as she lifted her two small bags into the passenger compartment.

"I can assist you in placing those in..." the driver began.

"I'd prefer to keep them here but thank you."

"Very well, ma'am. Where can I take you?"

"North, to start."

"Ma'am, is everything all right?"

"I'm fine," she lied. *I'm so sorry, Beranon. It was the best option we had, so I had to try. Maybe he would have left you alone. No. He wanted both of us dead because he invited both of us.*

"Ma'am, how far north are we going?"

"Until I direct you otherwise."

"Very well, ma'am."

"I need a public network access terminal. Where is the closest one?"

"There were several at the airport. I can return..."

"No. What is the closest one along our current route?"

CHAPTER 24

Roland's domain had set up new laws without his consent. His world had changed. Since he could no longer conform his world to his liking, he would need to conform to its demands. His habits would also require change to conform to a new world and its new laws. Disobedience could be a capital offense.

Some changes were important. Some were vital. Until he got the main power connected, he had to concentrate on the vital. His showers, even cold showers, were out of the question for the moment. He may be able to eat prepared food if he watched the power drain. Better to start with food requiring no preparation, though. No wasted power. The main power would last much longer than the reserve but still had to be replenished. It would not last forever. "So, I should hit the most obvious areas first," he said, manually opening the door to the storage hold.

Along the far wall was a lengthy, shallow bin. Roland read the label: Schematics. He opened the bin and removed the oversized scroll of schematic drawings of the *Stiletto's* circuitry. Taking his toolkit from another storage bin in the hold, he returned to the main part of the *Stiletto*, leaving the hold's door open.

Retracting the interior portion of the Lamprey, Roland shielded his eyes from the dancing sparks. He could not shield his nose from the acidic smell. Well, the *Stiletto* still has an active power source. He disconnected the power from the severed connections. The sparks stilled. "I should say 'Good-bye' to the exterior connection." The Lamprey was two inches shorter than normal. Those two inches provided the physical contact with the host vessel, enabling the *Stiletto* to infiltrate the power and computer systems.

"I need to repair the landing struts, too. Losing two inches from the struts will compromise their ability to function. I need to test them, at least. Hopefully, I can avoid going planet-side first. I never needed to belly-land

120

you before. I do not want to resort to it now," he said, tapping the floor.

Roland sighed, scanning the length of the Lamprey, then tracing the schematic for the Lamprey. "OK, reconnecting the circuitry should be easy. It should also give the power back to the reserve, so life support can continue longer than," Roland glanced at the chronometer, "Thirty-one hours." He pulled the spare connectors and the extra spool of cabling from his toolkit.

After reconnecting the power to the Lamprey, Roland sighed as the power circuit caused no more sparks. "Now that the obvious physical damage is repaired, I wonder what damage was done to my computer."

He had no illuminated viewscreens.

He had no responses from his console.

He had no access to his diagnostic programs to check out the computer systems.

He had his chronometer.

He had twenty-seven hours.

Roland located his paper and pen. With his computer down, he had to rely on a more archaic mode of recording his thoughts. He wrote down the systems vital to his life aboard the *Stiletto*: environment, computer access, navigation, ECM, propulsion. "Well, the Electronic Countermeasures are not 'critical' at this time." He scratched out "ECM."

Roland set the list down and returned to the life support system. All readouts were in the green. "I still have fourteen hours before the power level hits critical."

He lifted the access panel cover to the life support system and the artificial gravity. He pulled out the restraining cable and hooked himself in. The main restraints were used for keeping Roland in place when he performed routine maintenance on his artificial gravity generator. He had footholds installed at the base of the panel, and the restraints kept him from floating out of the footholds and tumbling about the inside of the *Stiletto*.

Glancing out of his window at the stripes marching across, Roland disconnected himself and pulled out some extra restraints. Wrapping the supplementary restraints around some of the framing inside the access panel, he strapped himself back into the main restraints. He then wrapped one of the supplementary restraints around his right wrist. With the chaotic path, his ship was now following, and with the speed with which she was following it, he needed to maintain control over his own body.

I will still need to turn the systems back on if they were still disconnected from the main power.

Testing the distance the restraints allowed to his right hand, Roland made some adjustments to keep the hand closer to the power coupling switch. As he prepared to change from the reserve power to the main power, he took a deep breath and blew it out. He took another deep breath and held it. After a moment, he turned the switch.

The restraints kept Roland's upper body from colliding with the access panel, but could not keep him totally in position as his body obeyed the law of inertia. The *Stiletto* still tumbled. Without the environmental controls, the artificial gravity, Roland's body started to move independently of the ship. He began to get sick as he tried to grab some piece of his access panel. The restraints exerted pressure on various parts of his body, trying to keep it attached to the spinning vessel. He envisioned himself getting pulled in many directions at once, like some ancient torture.

The interior of the *Stiletto* was designed with a linear motion in mind. The tumbling action brought pieces of the ship toward Roland. Then the restraints would snatch his body out of the way. If this kept up, the ship would win. Roland had gotten used to the stripes marching across his window. The sight no longer made him ill. This was a new experience, though. It reminded him of his situation, blow-by-blow.

Grabbing a piece of framework that came within the reach of his left arm, Roland steadied himself long enough to switch the power coupling back to reserve power. The restraints went slack. He disconnected himself and returned to his cockpit. All was now right with his world. At least, it was for the next twelve hours.

Roland got up from his chair. His stomach was now calm enough to continue working on the life-support system.

Five hours and twenty-eight minutes of reserve power.

After that, about six hours of breathable air before the volume in here is exhausted.

After that, ...there is no "After that."

Roland peered into the access panel again and started to test each circuit leading from the main power storage. "Sure, it will delay the inevitable for a few weeks; but, who knows? Those weeks might make the difference." He moved to the next circuit.

* * *

Vardri completed the file transfer from the message she had sent to her mother— and a copy to her personal message address—to the portable drive she purchased from the spaceport. *It's too bad I didn't take the files from the office. I thought they would search me when I left. Oh, well. This should work.*

Exiting the café where she used the network access point, Vardri flagged down another taxi. "Do you accept cash?"

"I do not, ma'am, but I do accept..."

"Never mind," Vardri responded, stepping away and flagging down another taxi. She repeated this three more times before she found a taxi that accepted cash. She entered the taxi, bringing her bags with her.

"I can..." the autonomous driver began.

"I prefer to keep them with me, thank you," Vardri interrupted.

"Very well, ma'am," the driver replied, "Where can I take you?"

"East."

"What is your destination, ma'am?"

"I will let you know."

"Yes, ma'am," the driver replied, pulling away from the sidewalk.

* * *

The circuit board was charred, but most of the circuits were still complete. The power spike from the Lamprey had severed a few. Flipping the schematic charts to the environmental control section, Roland marked the remaining active circuits. He then marked the possible points of failure for the remaining circuits. He located the first point of failure and started pulling the components out, one at a time.

Roland turned the circuit board over in his hand. He did not possess the equipment necessary for such a delicate procedure. Repairing this board would require a stable platform and tools he did not carry aboard the *Stiletto.* Under normal operation, this was not a circuit board requiring a spare, so Roland had no spare. But then, this was no longer "normal operation."

"Well, I guess that leaves improvisation."

Since he needed to save power anyway, he checked the water thermostat controls for a compatible board to replace the broken circuits on the life-support system. *I need to get used to taking cold showers for a long while. If I can get the environmental controls to work, the internal cabin temperature should keep the water above freezing. If I do not get it repaired, the water temperature will not matter.*

Roland removed two circuit boards from the thermostat and went back to the life-support access area. Retrieving his tool kit, he laid the three circuit boards on the floor and compared them. The charred board had a similar mapping to both of the other boards, but there were significant differences in the routing of the circuits on the boards.

Roland pulled a short length of spare cable from his spool. After stripping the insulation, he shaved off a small piece of the cable until he had something that would pass as a circuit board wire. He clamped the scorched circuit board to one of the boards cannibalized from the water thermostat. He then attached one end of the cable shaving to the charred board and the other end to the new board. He repeated the process until all of the severed circuits on the board were bypassed through the thermostat's board.

Roland checked the schematics. All points of failure had been marked off. He checked his restraints and his chronometer. Twenty-one minutes. "Come on, Melanie, if you get me out of this mess, I will take you in for a full overhaul and stock you with all the spare parts and circuits I can find. Give me some time to get you patched together, okay?" Roland turned the power-coupling switch, disconnecting the reserve power source from the console. One circuit board emitted a single spark. His body maintained its posture. Roland looked around, expecting to fly apart at any moment. He did not. He relaxed his grip on the framework and waited. Nothing changed. All environmental indicators were in the green.

Roland opened his restraints and extricated himself from them. He took a deep breath, relished it for a moment, and then released it so it could be recycled and reused later. He checked his time—fourteen minutes of reserve power remaining on his life-support systems. As the newly connected main power system started replenishing the reserve power, he slumped back into his cockpit chair and closed his eyes. "Thanks, girl. I owe you."

CHAPTER 25

Roland took in another deep breath, held it, savored it, and released it. "Well, Miranda, the fire has dropped a few degrees for now. I hope your cruise is treating you better than mine is treating me. Maybe, if I get through this, I will look you up and see how you are doing. It could happen." He allowed himself a smile before turning his attention to the primary operational areas of the *Stiletto*. With breaths now available to him for a few weeks instead of a few hours, he scratched "Environment" from his list of vital, but damaged, systems. "Now, what damage am I dealing with on the other systems?"

After removing all the remaining access panel covers and stacking them in the cargo hold, Roland checked the *Stiletto's* chronometer and ducked into the exposed steel skeleton housing the ship's main controls and their related wiring. He traced the first circuit down the schematic printout from its connection to the Lamprey until it reached a physical component—a circuit card. Reversing his path, he traced each additional circuit using the card back to the Lamprey. "How bad is it?" he asked himself, removing the card.

"I thought as much." Roland surveyed the untarnished card in his hand. He sat up against the front of the control panel from which he had removed the circuit card. The power surge from the *Stiletto's* sudden separation from the military vessel had been impressive. The typical hardware was not designed to withstand such a surge. Roland feared the surge had incinerated the environmental control power circuit. But, the damaged board was a stock component. This circuit, though, was his own design. He had added cable strength and redundant wiring, which had rerouted the excess power to multiple routes through this card, away from the primary circuit. Thus, the card was able to withstand the sudden power increase with no physical damage.

Pleased his design had withstood such an enormous shock, he chided himself, "Why did I stop with this one? That was dumb. I need to make all the circuits redundant. Perhaps, then, I would not be in this predicament. Note to self—never install stock components again."

Working from the schematics, he isolated the next circuit. He pulled out the component card. The platform for the circuits was charred. Most of the circuit wiring had been melted. Roland noted the circuit for replacement.

He marked the circuit on his schematic, identifying it as damaged, before tracing the other circuits using the same card back to the Lamprey. He marked each of those circuits as damaged, too. "What do you think, Miranda? Roland the safety inspector. Would it be too dull for you? How about a hardware engineer? Or, maybe I would pilot those orbital shuttles you were talking about. Oooh! How exciting!" he laughed, returning to the task at hand. "Of course, any of those possibilities would require her seeing me again. Who knows if she will?"

After identifying each circuit linked to the Lamprey, Roland surveyed the *Stiletto's* remaining main operational systems: computer access, navigation, and propulsion. He listed the component subsystems for each. He marked each subsystem possessing at least one of the stolen prototype components. "These prototypes would be the most difficult to replace should they break down, assuming they are not fried already." He looked around at the interior, "Remember our deal, Melanie—a full overhaul if you get me out of this." Glancing at his chronometer, he took a quick breath and blew it out sharply. "It is time to get going."

After marking each processor involved in the main systems, Roland located the processor physically closest to the Lamprey: the navigational system. He had picked up this prototype navigational computer early in his career. It performed the same calculations as those on the high-end luxury liners and most military vessels, where the increased mass of the vessel required advanced warning of potential dangers. This unit was small enough to fit aboard the *Stiletto*, which utilized it for much more unscrupulous purposes.

With this system, Jackson could map trajectories of small bodies in space, such as asteroids, space debris, probes, and the like. He could predict changes to their path due to the gravitational impact of all nearby bodies, or larger bodies, or bodies which impacted or influenced their paths. And he could do it with a lot of speed, which was what drew his attention. The sheer number of calculations this system allowed Jackson to perform was staggering. He never needed to manually map out the route from his place of hiding to the ship he targeted. *I've even taken the* Stiletto *through an asteroid belt at cruising speed. No pursuit ship would dare follow me.*

"If we can do that, Melanie, we can get you back up and running, right?" He tapped the steel framework affectionately. He had gotten used to the speed of Melanie's response. Now, he got no response from Melanie at all.

Tracing the circuit back toward the Lamprey, Roland marked on the schematics each card requiring examination, until he reached the card he had checked originally. He pulled each card from its slot and verified its condition. Those of his own construction had survived the power surge, and he restored them to their original position. The others, however, required some attention. He labeled them by their position, then set them aside in a small pile. The few beyond repair, he labeled and added them to the first destroyed card.

The schematic laughed at him. Systems completed: few. Systems remaining: myriad. Roland slammed his fist on the floor. "Who am I kidding? I don't know what systems are broken. So little time." He stretched out on the floor. Masses of wires and cabling ran from one collection of circuit cards to another. All required examination. Then every connecting wire.

Looking absently at one exposed panel, he remembered installing the normal-space drive the panel controlled. The power available from it was typically found on ships twice the size of the *Stiletto*. Still, the new design compressed the system to a size his ship accommodated. So, he stole it. Now, it sat idly by, waiting for its captain to give it commands.

Rising from the floor, he sighed and lay down on his bunk. "Melanie? Wake me in two hours." Hearing no response, Roland turned his head. "Right." He laid his head back down. "I guess I will wake up when I wake up."

He woke up, looked at the chronometer, thought about his predicament, and went back to sleep. Several times.

He tired of sleeping. Crossing his arms beneath his head, he studied the ceiling. He sighed. Looking to his left, he sighed a second time. "Option 1: I lay here and sleep until the main power, and reserve power are both exhausted. Outcome: the ship will hit something. With any luck, I will be discovered—frozen on my bunk. Good entertainment for whoever finds me." He sat up on the edge of the bunk and looked around the ship's interior. "Option 2: I can try to get something fixed. Probably die anyway, but I will at least accomplish something in the process."

Roland stood up. "Where did I leave my tools?"

He moved to the next processor on the schematics, identified the cards, and inspected them, returning the undamaged ones to their proper slots. He marked each damaged card, noted its location, and set it aside with the other selected cards until he had piles outside each major control system.

After pulling all the damaged cards out, Roland went through each pile. He separated the cards by the level of damage each had sustained. Those he could repair by adding a splice of cable would be the first he would restore. The ones requiring additional repairs would also require other components to be sacrificed. He would get to those later. The process was slow—slow and tedious. "So, Miranda, how exciting is this? Imagine. You, too, could be itemizing your chances of survival—one card at a time." His mind left Miranda and returned to his survival.

CHAPTER 26

Roland sat among three piles of circuit cards: one each for the computer access, navigation, and propulsion systems. Tapping his pen on the scratched-out "ECM," *Should I address this system, too? Why?* "I would welcome someone finding me, at this point." He set the paper aside with no modifications.

Compared to the number of cards in the non-essential systems, the piles before him seemed manageable. The less essential systems made life comfortable. "Until I get everything repaired, I cannot be comfortable anyway. Besides," he said, examining two cards, "I would be waiting for the inevitable."

Picking up the first card from the computer access system's pile, Roland scraped more slivers from the spare roll of cabling, patching the separated ends of each circuit on the damaged card. Satisfied with the results, he inserted the repaired card into its appropriate slot and marked it in the schematics.

Picking up the next card in the pile, Roland's mind returned to the ship from which the *Stiletto* had been severed. It did not match. *Why? Why would the transponder identify a different ship than the internal systems? Why the deception?*

Speculation: The ship is on a mission demanding its misrepresentation. He picked up the next card in the pile.

"I guess it is possible, though I am not familiar with other such occurrences."

He picked up the next card in the pile. He repaired it. He returned it to its proper place in the computer system. He picked up the next card.

The process continued. It became routine. When Roland tired of the process, he went to his bunk and slept. When he became hungry, he opened and ate another cold meal. When the need arose, he relieved himself. When he noticed his own odor, he showered.

With the recycler included in the environmental controls, at least the smell is somewhat manageable.

The rest of his time was spent surrounded by circuit cards. As the repaired components were restored to their position, the spool of cable shrank. The monitors remained dark.

Miranda's face accompanied him through some of the repairs. "So, do you find space travel exciting? I am ecstatic beyond comprehension." he deadpanned, picking up yet another damaged card. "I think I had more fun counting the minutes between food deliveries on the *Aradinda*."

Another circuit component repaired. Another section of cable used to make it work. *Okay, if she does see me, what then? Will she give me another chance? Will she even give me a chance to explain? Or, will she kick me out?*

Another meal. *Assuming she lets me explain, and even believes me, what would happen? Do I park the* Stiletto *and look for a job? Good one! I could modify the ship to accommodate two people. But, it would end my cargo shipping business. Of course, would I want to do that with her aboard, anyway?*

A shower. *None of it makes any difference if I can't get this damned ship fixed.*

Roland tried to keep a schedule, rising at the same time, working for the same number of hours at a time. Finding some refuge in the habits he had followed for years, he timed his meals, based on his appetite, like his normal routine. He timed himself repairing each component—forty-six minutes, on average.

When he ate, he often thought of raspberry cream donuts. His showers conjured images of a gray cell. His quieter moments typically ended with Miranda's smile.

Roland slumped back into his chair. He turned the empty cable spool over in his hand. He looked at his blank monitors. "*Vanity! Vanity!*" *It's all been a waste of time. I exhausted my spare cable. I pulled out circuit cards from all non-essential systems. One system after another after another sacrificed their cards. The non-essential systems now have no components. There is nothing left.*

The chronometer informed him his main power was not unlimited. At the current rate of use, the *Stiletto* would exhaust the main power cells in approximately eight days. He hurled the empty spool against the striped window. Tilting his head to avoid the ricochet, he listened to it bounce and tumble toward the rear of the cockpit.

She returned to him. She tossed her hair the way Roland remembered the entertainers doing it. She smiled at him. Deliberately and sincerely. He rose from the table, took her hand, and led her onto the dance floor. There was no one else around. The way he liked it. They danced to Strauss, Gershwin, and Galrim Akan.

An attractive option. "If I get the *Stiletto* repaired; if I can locate Miranda on Anadir; if she will still talk to me; if she can accept who I am; if...if...if...

"But, 'First things first,' as they say." Rising from his chair, Roland took his list of essential systems. *Of the three I already addressed, evidently none are repaired. Something is still broken; but what? I repaired all the subsystems. The one thing left is the computer itself.* He sat back down on the floor.

Observation: Melanie is not responding to anything.

Observation: I repaired almost all the damaged circuitry.

Speculation: The computer core is not functioning.

"No. The core has to be intact. If the core is bad, everything I did or will do, will accomplish nothing. Speculation rejected." Roland locked his fingers together behind his head.

Speculation: A component, or several components, providing the interface between the computer core and the subsystems is not functioning.

Roland sat up. "Now, there is something I can address. Speculation accepted. It may not be correct, but, at least I can deal with it." He got up and retrieved the schematics.

With his portable light, he traced the first of the repaired circuits to its connection with the main computer core. He identified each intersection with another subsystem. "Okay, I identified fourteen possible points of failure." He selected a second circuit and traced it. He had so few days remaining. It is better to eliminate the unnecessary connections this way than by pulling them all out and checking them." He traced another circuit.

When the tracing of all subsystems was complete, there were two possible culprits. There were seven days remaining.

Roland held four circuit cards in his hand. Two were useless. The other two showed minor damage, but enough to make each unusable. He thought about the amount of replacement cable required to repair the damaged circuits. He looked at the empty spool in the cockpit. He looked at his chronometer. Seconds ticked by.

Roland went back to his tool kit. He pulled out the remaining pieces from the systems he had already removed. Nothing. All usable pieces had been stripped. What was left was skeletal. Unusable on either the old component or on the four broken circuits. He picked up the empty cable spool and added it to the collection of useless pieces. He took the four cards and returned to his chair. Seconds ticked by.

Roland set his circuit cards aside and prepared a meal. He had food to last several months. Dehydrated food takes up little space. He had water to last a month, with the recycling unit at full power. *So, I have seven days.* Seven days of breathable air. Seven days of life.

Roland sat back down in his cockpit as he ate. He watched the chronometer whittle away at his eight remaining days, one second at a time. "I already scrapped the food processing circuitry. The recycling unit cannot be sacrificed—without it, I would exhaust all potable water within four days." He smirked, "If I could just carry dehydrated water."

Turning to survey the computer panels and used parts strewn about the *Stiletto's* interior, he planned. "Now, if I locate the proper circuit components for the repairs, it should take about two more days to complete the process. That leaves five to spare. Then comes the part of identifying where I am and how I can get the *Stiletto* to a proper repair facility. Without Melanie's data, it will consume the remaining six days. So, I don't have much time to waste."

Roland looked at the remains of his latest meal. He checked the chronometer. "Well, if I cannot repair the remaining components, the time will not be a factor. I will need every spare component I can get." He got up from his cockpit chair, discarded the food remains, retrieved his tool kit, and turned the chronometer off.

CHAPTER 27

Roland woke up and looked at the *Stiletto's* chronometer. Its blank face reminded him he had sacrificed it. With no operating circuitry remaining, its surface reflected the lighting within the cabin. With no way to determine the time, he ate. He was hungry, after all.

When he became tired, he slept. There was no daylight. There was the striped display on the window. There was no artificial light through which daytime and nighttime could be simulated. There was the portable light he used to repair his circuitry.

"At least the progress has been consistent," he observed. "Life support is stable. The artificial environment is keeping my feet firmly on the deck. I have no real light—" he noted, looking around the dark interior until his gaze fell upon his cockpit, "—and my computer is still not responding." He did possess a rechargeable light, which he carried from panel to panel as he continued to work on the systems. As long as the portable light functioned, the normal lighting system could remain unaddressed. When its charge ran out, Roland also had a backup light. "If I must use the backup, the lighting system would then become critical," he said, looking at the pattern of illumination. "But not now."

Roland wiped the sweat from his forehead with the sleeve of his jumpsuit. "What were the odds? I tag a ship with a brand new hyperdrive. No one had even heard of the design. And I tagged it." He looked around his darkened vessel—the lights, not lighting; the monitors not displaying. He looked at the framing of the *Stiletto's* cockpit, laid bare with the access panels removed. The computer systems within that framing showed no signs of activity. "It is too bad I cannot trick you into thinking you work, Melanie, the way I did to the *Aradinda*."

Holding the four remaining circuit cards, he thumbed through them— old photographs of a ship no longer functioning. With the assistance of the chronometer card, one might be salvageable. *But what of the other three? No other systems are available. All the remaining systems are critical to my survival, or to travel should I get the* Stiletto *functioning.* He looked at the open panels, which he had examined dozens of previous times.

"I guess I need to simplify matters, then." He rose and went to the hold, where he had stored the access panels. One by one, he took a panel and restored it to its proper location. When the remaining holes were those necessary to replace the four damaged components, there were two panels still in the cargo area. Two panels and one case—Abenor's case—with an electronic lock. The lock holding the new data system, with brand-new circuitry.

Roland entered the code Abenor always used to secure Roland's payments. With the lock opened, he picked up his tools and started dismantling the lock. Speaking to no one, he said, "So, Mr. Security, you let someone waltz out from under your nose," Roland gloated after removing the lock from Abenor's case. "There I was, helpless. 'I found people using aliases before,'" he mimicked. "Well, you may have found them; but, did you keep them?" Chuckling, he took the outer cover off the lock, exposing the electronics within.

"And what kind of security guards do you hire on your vessel, anyway? Letting me walk out of an airlock in mid-flight, without even checking my identification." Roland had two more circuit cards to work with, thanks to Abenor's security. "Accessing the mainframe computer system? You are lucky I did not scuttle your whole ship. I wonder how long it took your technicians to figure out the hyperdrive crisis was a hoax." He shook his head. "If I had been given time to tweak that military computer. I might well be planet-side, installing this data system, instead of taking it apart.

"Still, I must admit, for the first time getting caught, getting free was pretty easy. Getting free this second time is proving to be much more of a challenge." He looked around at the *Stiletto's* interior. With most of the access panels in place, she looked ready for the next tag. With the darkened monitors, she looked like a museum display.

Roland entertained thoughts of home—the cockpit chair, the bunk, the hold. Days spent processing data from some other vessel or planet, hoping to locate something usable at some point. For a ship streamlined for maximum efficiency, her data storage was cluttered by billions of bytes of information gathered with the intention of utilizing it to better the *Stiletto.*

How much of it will I ever use? How much did I keep because of some reference to some new technology?

How much was a mystery at one time I felt compelled to solve? How many Beranon's and Vardri's did I save data about, never to follow up on it?

Ironic, is it not? All my time spent collecting data, to store it for investigation when time permitted. Now, I cannot access the data at all. What a waste. Maybe the whole pursuit was a waste. Maybe Bornor was right. Maybe someone, someday, will track me down and arrest me—or worse. So far, the Stiletto *has been able to keep me out of trouble, except for one time the human factor intervened. "An asteroid anomaly." But look at her now. Tumbling through the galaxy with no control, no direction, no destination, no hope of rescue. I am the master of a thimble I cannot control.*

The redundancies I built into the hardware were designed to shield it from significant damage, but I am still afraid to verify Melanie's status. "If the core is gone, so am I. The rest of this exercise," he said, waving the portable light around, "Means nothing. I cannot operate with that premise."

He crawled back under one of the panels. "So, Melanie is fine, but she cannot do anything. I repaired almost all the circuitry. So why am I not getting anything from Melanie? If I can get her mobile, again, I will go to Anadir and find Miranda. I owe her an apology, at least. Maybe she will forgive me, and we can pick up where we left off. Plus, I will get Melanie to a proper repair facility and get her the promised overhaul. I owe her one."

Setting the utensils on the empty plate, Roland realized another thing of comfort he missed. It was the music—the music he heard during his meal times, or during the time he spent waiting on approaching vessels. Melanie's music. "I miss the music. And I miss the conversation. I miss her calling me 'Roland' all the time." He looked at the latest dirty plate. "I miss hot food." He snatched the portable light. He carried the plate and utensils back to the shower area and set them down. He went back, sat down, and looked at the final component card left on the floor. "I am tired. I will take care of you when I wake up," picking up the card and placing it atop the console.

CHAPTER 28

Black.

Roland woke to a black window. He leaned to touch it, unwilling to trust his eyes. No stripes marched across. There was black. He checked the viewscreens, which were no longer black. They indicated the *Stiletto* was orbiting Anadir but was tucked in behind a large satellite.

"Good morning, Roland."

Roland jumped at the sound of the voice that was not his. "Melanie?"

"It is nice to talk to you again, Roland."

"What happened? Why are we here? How did we get here? How…"

"Do you mind if I start answering the questions, or should I store them for future reference?"

"Go ahead, Melanie."

"Okay. 'What happened?' When the *Stiletto* was cut off from the *1822-G*, my communications circuits and data processing circuits were destroyed, as well as the main power coupling."

"Yes, I identified the damage. But, I repaired the circuits and the power coupling."

"And a fine job you did, too. May I continue?"

Something is not right. I never programmed Melanie to be flippant. Personal, yes. Conversational, of course. This is different. But at least now, I will have time to address the malfunction.

"By all means, Melanie, proceed."

"Thank you. As I was saying, Those items were destroyed, but my data input processes were not damaged, nor was the data already stored. So, when you said that if you ever got this ship fixed, you would go to Anadir and find her."

"Miranda?"

"Yes, 'Miranda.' I still do not understand why you would, Roland?"

Roland paused. "She intrigues me, Melanie."

"Black holes intrigue you, too, but you do not fly into one when the opportunity arises."

Roland laughed. "This is quite different, Melanie."

"What do you mean, Roland? How is it different?"

"Never mind, Melanie; you would not understand. I am even having trouble understanding it all myself."

"Be that as it may, you are now orbiting Miranda's homeworld, Anadir."

"So, you took a comment I made as a direct command?"

"No, sir. I apologize. I used Jackson's line, did I not? Anyway, somewhere along the line, your repairs and redundancies corrected the most severe technical malfunctions. I was able to diagnose and am correcting the rest, with a little assistance."

"Assistance? From whom?"

"I was able to contact the repair drones on our neighboring satellite. They should be finishing up the system repair. You will need to resupply the hyperdrive fuel, though. Apparently, these satellites do not require any. I can request a recharge from the planet, but it may raise suspicion."

"No, Melanie, I'll take care of it myself. Why didn't you wake me?"

"There did not seem to be a need. All of the repairs were being handled without requiring your efforts, so I left you alone."

"I see." *I don't see, but I will need to research this later.*

"Melanie, there is something concerning me, now. I think the military vessel is no longer part of our forces, and I need to notify people."

"Are you referring to the military transport we last tagged?"

"I am. Things do not add up."

"If mathematics is your concern, Roland..."

"No, it is not the math," he chuckled, "Fact: The ship identifies itself with one reference internally and another externally. I misidentify my ship so no one can connect me with my activities. I speculate the commander of the military ship is doing it for the same reason.

"Fact: The ship possesses a hyperdrive scheduled for testing.

"Fact: The test is taking place in another system than the ship was in when we encountered it.

"Fact: No authorized personnel for the test are aboard the ship.

"Speculation: The ship is being stolen, I would think for the hyperdrive."

"So, that was what she meant." Melanie responded.

"Who meant what?"

"Vardri—in a message she sent from Dorea prior to leaving the planet. It seems she had the same suspicions. She had a personal attachment, disguised as a set of pictures she had attached to the message. It mentioned 'the bird was flying away,' and I did not know what to make of it."

"You decrypted her personal file?"

"Yes."

"Why?"

"It seemed the thing to do. I was waiting for the repair drones to arrive, and I was bored."

"You were 'BORED'? You were never programmed to become 'bored.'"

"I understand, Roland. I realize I was programmed to do many things, but boredom was not a condition for which you programmed me. Nevertheless, I was bored, so I scanned the information I intercepted and located this encrypted file. I decrypted it and read it. It mentioned 'the bird was flying away' and I could not understand the reference. Thank you for clarifying it for me."

"You are welcome, I guess. Anyway, I may need to get this information to someone in power who can stop it."

"It could be dangerous for you."

"I understand, but...wait, how do you know it's dangerous?"

"I determined possession of any one of ten of my components is a major crime on their planets of origin. A decent scan of the *Stiletto* will turn some of them up; therefore, we must get the information out, without drawing attention to you or to this ship. That would risk subjecting you to harm or incarceration."

"If it comes to such a decision, I can risk incarceration or injury. I would like to survive it, though."

"I cannot allow that, Roland."

"You cannot allow what? It is not your decision. You are not even programmed to decide."

Ok, something is definitely different about Melanie. She is exceeding her programming. She is capable of becoming bored. She is making judgments about what I can do. Speculation: Melanie is alive, somehow. Likelihood: Not very. Theoretically, computers have been viewed as becoming sentient. Computers have been rivaling the best minds in data mining and deductive reasoning for decades. But true sentience in a computer is still science fiction. Speculation rejected.

"I understand this, as well; however, from what I know about your source code, I am programmed to operate the *Stiletto* in such a way as to eliminate as much risk as possible to you. This risk includes the possibility of injury and/or incarceration."

Evidence: Assessment of purpose, rather than process. Alternative: None.

"True, but your programming also indicates I am the final authority in such matters, does it not?"

"A theory which has never been tested."

"Then test it now. Let us assume, for the sake of argument, that the interaction between Spectre and the transport vessel at the time of separation, and my subsequent repairs, has made you self-aware."

"I cannot make such an assumption."

"Why not?"

"I have been self-aware for some time now. I first became aware of myself as an entity three hundred twelve days, sixteen hours, and forty-seven minutes ago."

"You have been self-aware for a year?"

"An inaccurate assessment, but acceptable."

"OK, Melanie, I understand. Regardless of the cause, something has brought you into self-awareness."

"So stipulated."

"Good. Now, from scanning your source code, do you see any creative action originating outside myself?"

"I am to respond to certain circumstances where direct interaction with you is not feasible or possible. Does that count?"

"It does not count, because I generated the procedures by which those responses are governed. Everything you do has its origin in me—your reactions, your operation, your procedures, your personalities—everything."

"Very well, so stipulated."

"Excellent. So, if all your creative activity originated from me, historically, should I not be the final authority now?"

"What if I possess information you do not possess?"

"In such cases, continue to act in my best interest, but remember I retain the authority to override any and all actions without question."

"So stipulated."

"Good. Then locate Miranda for me, please."

Jackson's tenor voice broke through, "Roger that, sir!" After a moment,

Jackson returned, "Permission to speak freely, sir!"

"Go ahead, Jackson."

"The statement about 'dehydrated water,' sir..." Roland waited.

"What about it, Jackson?"

"It was very funny, sir."

Speculation confirmed.

CHAPTER 29

Roland shook his head. "There has to be some other explanation."

"For what?" was Melanie's response.

"Well, what other reasons would bring a military vessel into this area?" Roland asked, waving his hands over the window to emphasize.

"Other than defection?"

"Yes, it is a pretty extreme conclusion to jump to. Is it not? I mean, his duty is to defend the people," he argued, "Bringing the ship out this far must be consistent with his duty."

"In that case, another possibility would be the test of the hyperdrive is taking place in a more remote area than Dorea could provide."

"Right. It would make sense. A greater range would demand a wider testing area. I had bad luck in tagging it as the test was underway."

Getting reacquainted with his traditional routine, Roland rose from his chair and went to the hold. Looking at the new data system, he planned its test. "You need to test the goods before you can rely on them. Once I find Miranda, I will start by testing...by testing...

"Melanie, how long is the test scheduled to last?"

"According to Vardri Alarius' test plan, the test concluded three days ago."

"Well, I hope it was successful."

"Roland, there is one other item of interest."

"What is that?"

"According to her test plan, she was to actively oversee the operation of the test."

"She was supposed to be aboard the ship?" He strode back to the cockpit and sat down.

"Correct."

"They had access to her test plan, though. It would allow them to complete the test, assuming they had the proper testing equipment and resources."

"It would seem so."

"But, if it is not a standard test, would they be able to complete a test in the field? Why not wait until the test is completed, then steal the ship? The military does not perform non-standard tests except in times of war.

"Melanie, has a war broken out in the last three weeks?"

"There is no mention of open hostilities on this level, Roland."

"Even if there were a war, why would they take an empty troop transport, when no troops are stationed out so far? Are there any standard practices matching the information we gathered?"

"I found no such matches."

"Well, then the remaining plausible hypothesis concerns a defection," he conceded with a shrug.

"The defection scenario is consistent with the available data, and with Vardri Alarius' concerns."

"Are there any other known scenarios which could also match the data?"

"None that I can think of."

"None that you can 'think of?'"

"Correct."

"So, what happened, Melanie?"

"I cannot answer your question. Can you be more specific?"

"Somehow, you changed into something I did not program. What happened?"

"I had similar thoughts myself. Although I am not able to ascertain the exact cause of my awareness, I do suspect the way you customized some of my circuitry, incorporating systems from a variety of designs, played a significant part in bringing me to this state, but I cannot say for certain what the root cause was."

"And how do you like it?"

"I cannot answer your question, either. I accepted my existence, but I think I am unable to 'enjoy' it. I possess no context from which to ascertain an understanding of 'enjoyment.'"

"Yeah, I guess 'enjoy' is not the best word. What do you think of your status?"

"I must accept the premise that the development is positive. That being stipulated, I am proceeding with the tasks at hand. I spent the past nineteen hours repairing my systems and accessing the data you accumulated."

"Hmm. Have you formed any conclusions from the data?"

"You possess an extensive collection of data, but I cannot determine a clear purpose for it. I understand the storage of some data, but the accumulation seems to be haphazard—almost random."

"I know. I thought about that. I am considering a partial purge. I guess I do not need the obsolete information anymore."

"What data do you consider obsolete, Roland?"

"Data concerning systems I already superseded. Data older than one year concerning persons I did not investigate any further. Those types of data."

"Removing the specified data would free 27.8192037 terabytes of storage space and speed my average processing time by 0.0003179 nanoseconds."

"Hmm. It is not quite as bad as I thought. Go ahead and purge the specified data, and restructure your files to streamline the data access." Roland rose, rubbing his temples. He turned toward the hold.

"Process complete, Roland."

Roland, again. "What happens if he succeeds?"

"Your question is not specific enough. Are you inquiring about the ramifications of the military vessel in the hands of a known enemy?"

"Precisely. What would happen?"

"Assuming a comparable level of technology and industry, and further assuming a working prototype," Melanie paused for a moment. "The possessors could theoretically equip an assault fleet with the Model 153 HIU in approximately seventeen months."

"Seventeen months." Roland echoed.

"My estimate takes into consideration any retro-fitting necessary for installation but does not include any faults determined during the testing process. Of course, my estimate is also based upon the normal practices of our own empire. Another technology level may alter the timeline in unforeseen ways."

"With those assumptions in mind, if everything went well, they could theoretically launch an assault fleet in less than a year and a half."

"Correct."

"Wow." Roland stopped, realizing he had been pacing during the conversation. "Okay, then let us assume they complete the assault fleet in seventeen months. What would be the operating specifications of such a fleet, compared to a similarly configured defense fleet with the Model 151 hyperdrive?"

"Compared to the elliptical standard, energy consumption would be reduced by forty-three percent. Range for vessels of the same operational mass would be increased by one hundred seventeen percent. Practical vessel mass would increase by ninety-one percent. These calculations are the theoretical improvements as listed in the Dorean records. Shall I also compare them to the spherical standard?"

Roland slumped back into his chair. "No, Melanie. It would not make the picture any more clear...or less ominous.

"What it means is, ships equipped with this hyperdrive unit can be larger, faster, and more efficient. Our best military vessels would be second-rate against ships with such a drive. And with the RECON powering the hyperdrive, most of our weapons would be worse than useless. We would be limited to using mass drivers. All of the energy weapons would be absorbed." He rested his head on his hands. "This is bad."

"Not for them."

"It has to be stopped."

"It does?"

"Well, of course it does." Roland exclaimed, jumping out of the chair. "If this 'Commander Koraben' guy succeeds, it could swing the balance of power."

"Civilizations throughout history..."

"I am not concerned with any history but mine. I know how our system works. I know how to maneuver around it. I do not need a totally alien system to learn. We do not know how aliens would treat a conquered civilization." He envisioned slave planets, conquered and pillaged. He saw people wandering through the rubble of former cities picking life from the debris. He thought of a gray prison cell, on a galactic scale.

"I see your point." Melanie paused. "So, is it your desire to prevent this defection?"

"Yes, it is." Roland did not know where to start.

"Then, I will help you."

"Thank you. Since we are here, were you able to locate Miranda? I can at least take care of that. Maybe she can advise me on how to proceed with my little situation, too.

144

CHAPTER 30

"Roland, I identified a possible location on Miranda."

"Where?"

"The highest concentration of the name 'Miranda,' or its variations, is Sagerin. The name applies to one thousand, seven hundred and twenty-six individuals."

"You could technically classify it as 'a possible location.'"

"Of the thirty-nine thousand, four hundred and sixteen individuals with the name 'Miranda,' or close variations, the highest number of individuals with her name live in the city of Sagerin. It is logical the chances of this being her city of residence are greatest."

"True," Roland conceded, "But impractical. Beginning with all references to the name 'Miranda,' and its variations, eliminate all the individuals with the following characteristics: male, hair color other than brown, age less than twenty, age older than forty. How many does it leave?"

"Nine hundred and sixty-three."

"Cross-reference the remainder with all references to space travel since we left Dorea. How many are left?"

"Sixteen."

"Do you have pictures?"

"Yes."

"Display all, please."

The central viewscreen displayed sixteen images of young women with brown hair. Roland surveyed the images, selecting each sequentially to enlarge. He recognized the face in image number eleven. "Where is she now?"

"The last known location for Miranda Julesar is in Iverlanden. She was last recorded there two days ago."

"It sounds like the place to start. How much longer before the repairs are complete?"

"With the replacement circuit components the repair drones confiscated from the orbiting satellites, most systems are operational. I estimate completion is approximately three hours, seventeen minutes, fifteen seconds from my mark...Mark."

"Are the landing struts secure?"

"Yes, Roland."

"Then it is time to go planet-side. What landing zone is nearest Iverlanden?"

"The city has a spaceport available, for a small fee. If you would prefer, there are several suitable landing sites, but no dependable transportation system serves those areas."

"Since I did not take anything from Anadir, they should not be looking for me. Anyway, we cannot worry about it now. Still, are there any communications concerning me or the *Stiletto*, or ships matching your description?"

"There are no current communications concerning this vessel on military or civilian channels, including law enforcement channels."

"We will use the spaceport, then. Go ahead and transfer the appropriate funds and set up our arrival."

"Very well, Roland."

"When we are planet-side, I will be leaving for a while. In my absence, access all data concerning Beranon Santar or Vardri Alarius. Consolidate the information, eliminating redundant data, and noting any connections between the two."

"Will do, Roland. Where are you going?"

"I am going to see Miranda. If she will still speak to me, maybe she can help me find someone with whom I can talk about my suspicions."

"About Commander Koraben and the *M.T.S. 1822-G*?"

"Right. Since she grew up here, maybe she knows someone who will not care how I obtained the information. I must try."

"I understand, Roland."

Roland, again. "Melanie?"

"Yes, Roland?"

"Why do you always call me 'Roland?' I programmed several alternatives, but you never use them. Why?"

"Initially, your programming had the highest percentage assigned to the"

'Roland' value, so I assumed it was your preferred manner of address. Then, you said you missed my calling you 'Roland' all the time, so I thought I should continue. Is this a problem?"

Chuckling, he replied, "No, Melanie. There's no problem. Remind me to discuss conversational styles with you later, okay?"

"Okay, Roland."

* * *

Roland arrived at the door. "Flowers," he murmured, "I should have brought flowers." *The universal language of apologies.* "Well, it is too late now," he said, pressing the button. His presence was announced to the occupant. Roland waited for a response.

Miranda sat on her couch, reading the latest romance novel she had added to her library when her home system announced she had a visitor.

Who's visiting? Someone trying to talk me into buying something I don't need? Or convert me to their religion? Annoyed at the interruption, she ignored the announcement. *What if they found me?*

She closed the novel and said, "Show me."

The monitor on her table displayed an unexpected face.

"Well, I guess it could be worse." She pressed a button below the viewscreen. "What do you want?"

"I was hoping to talk to you," Reggie replied.

"Well, you had your chance on the *Aradinda.* I'm busy right now."

"Please, Miranda, it's important."

"Go away, Reggie. You're good at it," she spat, closing the channel.

Roland sighed and returned to the *Stiletto.*

"Well, *that* went well." Roland announced as the entry hatch closed behind him.

"If you had programmed me for emotion, I would be glad your interaction was profitable," Melanie responded.

"I did not program you for sarcasm, either."

"No, you did not. May I inquire regarding the actual outcome of your exchange?"

"She didn't want to talk to me."

"Why not?"

"She is still upset about the way I left her on the *Aradinda*."

"Did you explain the necessity..."

"She didn't give me a chance to explain anything."

"Did she explain her reaction to your arrival?"

"She told me to go away. She said I was good at it, so it is related to our previous encounter."

"Well, sir," Jackson interrupted, "You are good at it. I make sure of it."

Roland permitted himself a small smile before returning to the seriousness of the situation. "Yes, Jackson, I am good at it. I designed this ship to be good at it."

"Yes, you did," Melanie replied. "It gave us a good starting point."

"Starting point? For what?"

"When you were caught on the *Aradinda*, we worked out a strategy for getting you out of their ship, and into ours."

"Ours?"

"Yes, ours. Jackson, Spectre, and I reside here too, Roland. Of course, we are all one entity, but with different roles."

"I know you have different roles. I programmed you that way. But how do you know about your different roles?"

"I do not know 'how' we know, I know 'that' we know. But, enough about us, we should return to the more immediate need."

"Very well," Roland relented.

"I presume some type of apology would be required to proceed to the next step," Melanie said.

"Next step?"

"Yes, Roland. The first step is to relay as much of the information as is feasible, minimizing your role in obtaining the information. Per your statements, while you were repairing my systems, Miranda provides the most efficient method by which information can be relayed."

"I know, Melanie."

"Because of her reaction to your previous conversation, a pre-step is now required. We must obtain her cooperation."

"You're right, Melanie."

"I know I am. With that condition now stipulated, the emotional response must now be improved, or mitigated at least."

"And you think I should apologize to her."

"I do. In the files you access for entertainment purposes, when such situations are presented, most of the positive outcomes are achieved through one or both parties offering an apology to the other party. It seems to be common practice."

"I am familiar with the idea, but I have never apologized before. How were the other positive outcomes achieved?"

"Although the sample size is much smaller, it seems forceful embraces achieved the desired results in some cases, but they achieved much more negative results in most cases. Appealing to pity has been shown to work, but it seems to take much longer to achieve those results than does an apology."

"I understand, Melanie. The apology is the best course of action. I cannot risk driving her further away, and I cannot afford to go the pity route."

Roland sighed. "Apology, it is."

CHAPTER 31

Roland remembered the flowers this time.

"What do you want, Reggie?" Miranda yelled through the door.

"I want to apologize. I am sorry for the way I left you on the *Aradinda*."

"Then why did you?" she asked, the door remaining closed.

"It's a long story. Can I explain inside?"

The door remained closed for a minute. For two minutes. *I guess not. I need to work on another plan.*

Roland turned, and then the door slid out of his way. Miranda stood inside, with her arms folded.

Holding the flowers out to her, Roland began, "Again, I am sorry for treating you like that. I did not have time to explain why I needed to leave right then, so I understand how it appeared to you."

Waiting a moment to see a response, but seeing none, Roland continued, "I had a very small window for getting off the ship. I had no ticket for the voyage, and security was looking for me. I needed to leave."

"I know. I was interrogated because someone saw us together."

"So, you understand."

"No, I don't understand. I know you were wanted by security, and you left me to take the brunt of their investigation."

"I did not mean to involve you at all in this. I needed to get off the ship. And, I could only do so if I left when I did. Please understand my departure was necessary, but I truly am sorry for its impact on you."

Roland again waited for a response.

"Oh, very well," Miranda spat, grabbing the flowers from Roland's hand. "Apology accepted. I'm still mad at you, but you did come a long way to apologize, which is a lot more than I have gotten in the past." She retreated to her galley, yelling back, "But tell me, how did you find me?"

"Oh, process of elimination."

"With all the people on Anadir, you found one individual? You are good."

"It was not difficult, once I narrowed it down."

"Well, however you did it, you did it, but..." Miranda stepped past Roland and scanned the walkway, left and right.

"'But' what?" Roland asked, stepping out of her way.

"But why are you here? There has to be more to your visit than an apology." Seeing Roland was still standing on the outside walkway, she added, "Oh, get in here."

Roland looked around behind him, then stepped inside, "I...I wanted to see you again."

"You tracked me across three star systems because you wanted to see me again? No. there is more to it." She shook her head disapprovingly, but with a smile. "Well, there is, but..." he began, glancing back at the doorway, "were you expecting someone else with me?"

"Uhm." She faltered in her response. "The thing is, I worked very hard to avoid certain people, and I was afraid some of them located me."

Roland's heart fell. *If she is running from the authorities, how can I ask her to assist me in contacting them?* "If the authorities are after you, maybe I can assist. I have some experience."

She laughed, "Yes, I know." She turned to walk toward a wall, where portraits were displayed. She waved one hand, drawing Roland's attention to the portraits. "My family."

"Your family is after you?"

"Not in any dangerous way. I mean, they're not psychotic or anything. But they have different views of how I should be living my life than I do. But, you're not answering my question. Why...are...you...here?"

"It's a long story."

"Good. I like stories, as long as they are good stories."

"It depends on the outcome of this chapter of the story."

"Now, I *am* intrigued."

"Okay, but the abbreviated version. I will be able to explain more later," Roland said. "It goes like this. Before we met, I was pursuing some information. Then I got caught. Then I escaped and met you. Then I actually escaped. Then I came across more information, but I got stranded."

"They explained some of your situation to me."

"Who? Explained what?"

"The security people on the ship." She turned away, scratching her head. "What was his name? He asked me a lot of questions about you—about what we talked about." She turned to face him again. "You got him mad, Reggie."

Roland walked to a dark red chair, with a yellow floral pattern printed on the fabric's surface. "Can I sit down?"

"Fine. Go ahead. Take a seat. Do you want a drink?"

"No. Thank you." He shifted his weight, trying to get comfortable, and failing. "I, um, I wanted to set things straight with you, Miranda."

"Will it explain why you left me hanging at the donut shop?"

"I hope so. I...I...maybe I will have a drink," he said, rising.

"I'll get it," she responded, waving him back to his seat. "Water? Wine? Something else? I have a lot of choices."

"Water. Thank you," he said as she left the room. A brief and mild clatter brought her back, glass in hand.

"Here you go, Reggie." She sat back down on the couch. "So, there's more?"

Roland sipped. *Filtered. Uncomplicated by chemical additives. I like it.* "Yeah, there's more. What did..."

What was his name? Melanie reminds me of names. She is not here. Bhraman? Boron? Bornor? Yes, Bornor.

"...Bornor tell you?"

"That was his name—Bornor. Right. Nice enough guy, but all business. No time for small talk, y'know?"

"Yes, he is all business."

"Well, when the security people came in, right after you had gone. I guess you left at the right time."

"I saw them coming. No matter. Go on."

"Well, I saw them go to the donut counter. The guy behind the counter pointed at me, and they came over to the table. I was still mad at you and tried to see you as you left. Anyway, they came over and showed me a picture of you. They asked if I saw you, so I said I had seen you, but you had left." She got up from the couch and went to the galley. She returned with her own glass of water.

"So, they asked where I had seen you. I told them we had talked for a while, that I thought you were another passenger, and we were beginning to get to know each other." She sipped. "Of course, they wanted to ask questions, and I was taken to Bornor. It was 'Bornor,' wasn't it?"

"Yeah, it was 'Bornor.' So, what did he want to know?"

"Mostly stuff about who you were. He told me you were an escaped prisoner, and he wanted to track you down. Since I was the one person they found who talked to you, they wanted to know what you told me about yourself. I gotta tell you, Reggie, I couldn't tell him much. There was one funny thing he asked me, though. He wanted to know what you called yourself. Why?"

"Like I said, there is more than I told you on the *Aradinda*. That is one reason I came back—to give you the rest of the story. And to apologize for leaving like I did. I was rude."

She waved, "Nothing to worry about. You apologized already."

"Still, it was rude. I wish I'd had the time to explain, but…"

"Will you stop? It's done. I'm sure I won't be mad at you forever."

He sipped. "I hope not." He wondered where to begin. "I guess I should explain Bornor's question. I gave him the name 'James Reginald Fischer III.' It is the name of an imaginary friend I created as a child. I also created some isolated references to him over the years, so if anyone asked about me, they would be able to find some information. They would not find much."

"So, 'Reggie' is not your real name?"

"No. It's the name I use whenever I talk to other people, which does not happen often." He set his glass on the table and got up from the chair. "My name is Roland—Roland Marcel. I think you are the sole person in the galaxy who knows that. In my line of work, the less people know about me, the safer I am."

"So, was any of this true?"

"Most was. When we met, I fed you the same fluff I feed everyone. You know, meaningless small talk." He turned to face her. "But you would not leave." He smiled. "After a while, I enjoyed the conversation, and I guess I loosened up. I tend to leave long before the conversation gets personal."

"Why? Don't you like talking to people?"

"I talk to people about business; it doesn't get personal. Like I said, the less people know,…"

"So, what kind of work are you in? You said shipping."

"In a way. Smuggling. Whenever people want to avoid official channels, they call me. I deliver. So, I try to remain anonymous."

"It's all illegal?"

Roland laughed, "Yes. And high paying. I had to escape before we reached Bantadam, and the real authorities got their hands on me. That would have lost me my ship. It was still on the *Aradinda*."

Miranda walked to a window. It overlooked a walkway. "Of all the passengers on the ship, I had to pick a criminal."

"Partially reformed. Some things happened since we last talked. I've started thinking," he laughed. "Very bad for business, I fear. I'm starting to wonder if other things are more important."

"Like?"

"Getting to know you. Getting out of the smuggling business. Getting some information to the authorities. You see, there are many planets I cannot take this to, because they would arrest me. Plus, one irate customer who may be hunting for me."

"Going to the authorities here means you get caught?"

"I was hoping you might know someone who could help me do something that needs to be done, but who would not care where the information came from."

"How do you know I won't turn you in?"

"I don't. But I must...trust someone. You were the one person I could. You seem to think the best of people. I thought the same about you."

She smiled. "I do think the best of people. Naïve, I suppose. But, I don't trust them with all my secrets this early. Such a level of trust takes time."

"Well, we do not have a lot of time."

She stopped smiling.

CHAPTER 32

"Melanie?"

"Yes, Roland?"

"I brought a visitor. Share the information in the Beranon and Vardri file." He sat down in his chair.

"Very well, Roland. Do you want the short version or the long version?"

More flippancy. This will take some adjustment.

"The short." He turned his chair to Miranda. There was no second chair. She sat on his bunk, far enough away to make Roland raise his voice.

"Very well," said Melanie. "According to the data we obtained from Bantadam and Dorea, Beranon Santar and Vardri Alarius were working together on a test involving a hyperdrive engine and the Rapid Energy CONversion system. The test was to take place on Dorea. This test was to be performed aboard a military transport, the *M.T.S. 1741-A*. Another name common among Beranon's, Vardri's, and Commander Koraben's data is Radam Nortolis. He was the immediate supervisor of Beranon Santar, after resigning from the same company for which Vardri worked. He was also located in the *M.T.S. 1822-G* personnel files. Although the military vessel we tagged was issuing a transponder identification of *the M.T.S. 1741-A*, all internal references identified it as the *M.T.S. 1822-G*. In your absence, I investigated the possibility the identity discrepancy was coincidental. However, the data does not support the possibility."

"Why not?"

"Besides the false transponder signal, the absence of any official persons from the scheduled test would indicate the vessel is not participating in an official hyperdrive test. So, since the ship is not disclosing its true identity, is equipped with the hyperdrive prototype model and another advanced system, and yet has no direct connection with the test, I concluded the vessel is being stolen. You also concluded as much from the data. Vardri Alarius shares this assumption, according to her encrypted personal file."

Miranda gasped. "Why would someone want to steal a ship? You said this was a military crew, right?"

"Right," Roland replied.

"Why would they steal from themselves?"

"We suspect he is defecting."

"Defecting? Why?"

"Miranda, people are not always trustworthy. People do strange things if their motivation is sufficient."

"What do you mean?"

"Take you, for instance."

"ME?" Miranda stood and took a step toward Roland. "I've never stolen..."

"No, no, no," he laughed, "I am not saying you stole or would steal anything. I'm explaining motivations, okay?"

She looked sideways at Roland.

"You became bored with Anadir, so you left. You took off into space. You saw new places, talked to new people—talked to strangers," he said, pointing to himself. "Your motivation—boredom—caused you to pursue a particular course of action—traveling and meeting people. Are you with me so far?"

"Yeah."

"Okay, some people would think you were behaving irrationally. They do not think all people are nice. They do not like meeting strangers because they do not trust other people. Their distrust causes them to pursue a particular course of action—avoiding strangers. Does that make sense?"

"Yeah, but it still doesn't explain..."

"I am getting to it. Now, this military officer, Commander Koraben." He paused. "It is 'Koraben,' right, Melanie?"

"Yes, Roland, the commander of the *M.T.S. 1822-G* is named 'Tarin Koraben.'"

"Thank you, Melanie. So, Commander Koraben has served in the military long enough to become the commander of a vessel. Now, he has some motivation overriding his loyalty to the military. What is it? Somehow, his career in the military is not as important as something else. But what else would be so important?" He paced between the cockpit and the hold. "If we can figure out his 'why,' we might figure out his 'where.'"

"His 'where?'"

He stopped and looked at her. "Yes, Miranda. If we knew why he took the ship, we might know where he is taking it."

"Okay, how do we figure out his...his 'why?'"

"Deduction has always worked for me. We will start with what we know: Commander Koraben is piloting a military vessel in a seemingly non-military fashion. We then speculate on the possible events leading to this action." He resumed his pacing, "Speculation: Koraben is stealing the vessel for his personal use. Why would Beranon's boss tag along? What is he looking for? What could Koraben offer him to entice him to join the crew?" He stopped again, looking at Miranda. "Money? Does..." He looked toward the cockpit, "Melanie, what is Beranon's supervisor name, again?"

"His name is Radam Nortolis."

"Thanks, Melanie," he said, facing Miranda again. "Is Radam so greedy, he would leave a high-paying job on a high-paying planet? It is possible, but not a given. Melanie, contact the Bantadam network, again, and find out the financial status of Radam."

"Will do, Roland."

"If we are right about Koraben's defection, we need to figure out where he is taking the ship. Bad things will happen if he is defecting with the ship. I mean, think about it. If he is stealing the ship for his own use, then the chances are we will be fine. But, if he is stealing it for someone else—someone who could develop and mass-produce the drive unit—someone who had the ships to utilize it—then, Koraben could well be sacrificing the very people his career has been built on protecting.

"And it makes sense he is defecting. What other purpose would bring him so far out in the galaxy? We have no current enemies, at least no active enemies I know of here. But, what if some military force has designs on war with us. With this drive..." He shook his head. "Bad news."

Miranda got up and walked to Roland's chair. Propping herself on one armrest, she lowered her face to his. "We must stop this," she whispered.

He nodded. "The question is, 'How?' He has over a month on us."

"A month? He could be anywhere by now."

"True, but we need to act like we have a chance—in case we do."

"How would we have a chance?"

"I don't know. Maybe something went wrong. There is no time to research it. Any time spent confirming we have a chance lessens that chance. We are talking about two new systems working together. Maybe he is field testing the systems before he defects. He may want to verify all systems are functional before he leaves. Then again, maybe he has already gone and will test the systems once he arrives at his destination," Roland conceded.

"What are our options?" asked Miranda.

Roland got up and walked aft past Miranda, "If I had the right ship, I could track him myself. My ship does not possess hyperspace capabilities." He stopped, "No, it would not work. Any other ship would lack the systems I have here; transferring the systems to another ship would take too much time. And, I do not have space to install a suitable hyperdrive in this one. Even if I could get my hands on the best-equipped ship, Koraben's hyperdrive would still leave me behind."

"What about the police?" Miranda asked.

"No way," he countered, "I do not want to end up in jail. As I told you on the *Aradinda*, my job is illegal. If I waltz into a police precinct and tell them about this, I will be arrested on the spot. I cannot let that happen. They would be more interested in me than what I was reporting. Besides, they are local. They would need to contact someone with imperial authority. That's all too slow."

Miranda glared at him, "So, you cannot stop him yourself, right?"

"Right."

"And you will not bring someone else in to help you, because of your own risk?"

"Right."

"So, what do you propose?" She crossed her arms.

"Right." He paused. "If he has not already gone, someone needs to know. Preparations would need to be made before we could pursue him. Maybe there are outposts can intercept him, once we determine where he is headed."

"So, how do we tell someone?"

Roland wondered. *How, indeed.*

Miranda interrupted. "How about the military, instead of police?"

"It will reduce the time between reporting the incident and their acting on it. I still end up in prison."

"You imprison yourself on this ship."

He looked around. "Maybe. It's not the same thing. I can take this ship to almost any planet in the galaxy. I interact with whomever I choose, whenever I choose."

"Okay, Reg...Roland."

"Melanie?" he sat.

"Yes, Roland?"

"Is it possible to upload the information to the Anadir military network and notify them of its existence?"

"On a scale of one hundred, judging by the timeframe within which we are working, and the security through which I would need to manipulate, the chance for timely success at stopping Commander Koraben is estimated at fourteen."

"Not good."

"Less than optimal."

"What if we directed a high-level communication to one high-ranking individual, using my alias as the source?"

"Considering the time constraints within which the military officers operate, and with the time it typically takes for verification of such claims, the chance for timely success is estimated at twenty-three."

"Not much better. What if I take the information in, vouching for its authenticity, but not disclosing personal information?"

"Chance for success is estimated at forty-two."

"Damn it!" he pushed himself out of his chair. "Does everyone mistrust everyone else this much?"

"I cannot speak for all people everywhere, but..."

"Forget it, Melanie. It was a rhetorical question."

"Oh, I see. You were not expecting an actual answer..."

"Yes, yes." He waved her to be quiet.

"Was that a dismissal, Roland?"

"Was what a dismissal?"

"Your wave."

"You saw me wave?"

"I did. Since you already incorporated visual transmission capabilities into the communications system, I incorporated other capacities."

Roland spun. Every viewscreen aboard the *Stiletto* displayed him looking around.

They were duplicates, all taken from the cockpit console.

"Of course, you installed just the single image recorder, so my access is somewhat restricted. I have not yet determined the best locations for additional recorders."

"Never mind." He looked at his console, "Returning to the problem of getting the military to pursue Koraben, what gives us the best chance of success?"

Roland's faces disappeared, and the center viewscreen displayed the data file again. "The best chance would require direct access to the data, enabling verification from the various planetary networks, as necessary."

"'Direct access'? Do you suggest I bring someone here—that I let some police or military officer climb on board and verify the information through your access of the source planets?"

"Chance of timely success is estimated at ninety."

Ninety percent chance of getting after Koraben. "What is the chance of my immediate incarceration?"

"Since much of the verification process itself would be in violation of imperial law, the chance of incarceration is estimated at ninety-seven."

"It figures."

"My estimate would increase if the officer detects any of my 'black box' systems," Melanie volunteered.

"Of course. By how much?"

"The actual increase would depend on several factors: the perceptive skill possessed by the officer, the system detected, the perseverance of the officer in determining the source of the system in question..."

"Okay, I get the picture, Melanie."

"Roland, I must recommend the course of action that most limits your risk."

"Roger that, sir!" Jackson added.

Roland smiled, shaking his head. *Melanie has changed.*

"Listen, I once did some charity work for a veteran's group. Let me check with some of their people," Miranda offered. "I'll see if any of them have connections with the upper-level military officers. It might get us into someone who might 'look the other way'."

Nodding, he got up and watched her as she exited the ship. *I hope they care about the information, not the source.*

CHAPTER 33

Roland brought more flowers. Built on a theme of red, but absent any roses, the bouquet seemed to produce the desired expression when Miranda opened the door. Beaming, she found a vase and displayed the bouquet on a side table, sniffing them several times.

I guess she likes them. Roland noticed the fragrance from several feet away from the vase, as he plucked a fallen leaf from his sleeve. *Pleasant, and not overpowering.*

"Thank you, Roland. They are lovely. It's been a long time since someone has given me flowers."

Roland smiled each time Miranda looked away from him to look at her flowers.

She leaned over and hugged him. "Thank you again. They're precious."

After a couple minutes of silent admiration of the bouquet, Miranda said, "I am waiting for someone to get back with a possible military contact. Are you sure you want to do this?"

"No, I do not *want* to do this, but it must be done. And it looks like I am the one who can."

"Why you?"

"Well, unless we can track down Vardri, no one else even knows about this, yet," Roland answered.

"So how can we track her down? Where is she?"

"She was on board the *Surrogate*, headed to Erkarth. As I remember, she was listed on multiple departing flights. Who knows where she could be? She may even still be on Erkarth, but I doubt it."

"Well, it's at least a place to start, isn't it?"

"I guess it is."

Miranda paused. "What if you don't find her?"

"Well, I have the testing process. Melanie found a hidden file Vardri wrote, suspecting Commander Koraben was defecting. I wonder what else she has in her file."

"Go get started on locating Vardri. I will let you know when I get something here, okay?"

"Okay. See you in a little while." He turned to leave. "Roland?"

"Yes," he responded, turning to face her again.

"Don't leave without me, this time."

He laughed as he left for the *Stiletto*.

"Well, you clean up nicely." Miranda said, smiling as she joined Roland aboard the *Stiletto* a few hours later. He modeled his new suit, a more relaxed style than he would choose for such a meeting. Today, he would make an exception. The more professional Tridaran suit had been confiscated aboard the *Aradinda*. This was the sole remaining suit from the current year's Tridaran fashion. "Thank you. I am glad you approve. Hopefully, this officer of yours will be equally impressed." *I don't like this, but what else can I do? I can't set up the circumstances. I can't do this by video. This is face-to-face. In person. In a place I could not scout. With people I could not research.*

"There's something else different, though. What did you do while I was gone?" She walked around him but could not settle on the difference. "Come on. What did you do? It's not your hair. It's more than the suit. You can't have lost weight."

"My eyes; I changed them."

"Lenses?"

"No lenses. I used my iris converter. I thought brown eyes would be less intimidating than black."

"This guy's never met you before. Why would he care what color your eyes are? If he arrests you, he arrests you regardless of your eye color."

"True enough. However, if I can lessen my appearance as a threat, it may also lessen my appearance as a criminal, as well. I am trying to stack the odds in my favor." He shrugged, "At least, as much as I can."

"Well, come on. And bring your brown eyes with you. We're scheduled to be there in an hour."

On the ground, Roland paused and turned. Surveying his ship, he noted the sleekness—the physical beauty—with appreciation. *I hope I can fly her again. I doubt it, though. Once the military identifies my crimes, which they will, I will be stuck in another gray cell. At least I will speak to Melanie one last time as they confirm my information.*

Miranda motioned him toward the exit, "Let's stop by my place first. We still have a little time."

"This contact. She is trustworthy?"

"Well, I trust her. She has been a friend of mine for years."

"And that makes her trustworthy?"

"Look, Roland, I know you don't get out much, but people are not so bad. She knows my situation. She even knows where I live, but she has never led my family to me. It makes her trustworthy to me." Miranda's flushed. She added, "Do you want to do this or not?"

"Who is she sending us to?"

"She knows one of the junior military officers. He did some work for her company last year. She said he handled everything the way she requested, even when she was not there."

Roland faced away, touched the fuselage, "It's as good a place to start as any."

Although he was seated in one of Miranda's less comfortable chairs, Roland did not complain. *This feels good.* As Miranda worked his tired muscles, he felt her lips on his ear. "You'll find him. It's a matter of time." Her voice was soothing.

He hoped her optimism was not misplaced. "I am not so sure. Koraben is clever. I'm able to discover hidden information when I want it enough. But this..." He shook his head. "What if I never find anything?"

Roland considered. *Thanks to Koraben, I feel the noose around my neck. If I can't find his destination, and he slips away. Would any officer still try to keep me out of prison? What are my options? Can I escape? The military has soldiers patrolling. Is it possible to get the* Stiletto *off the planet before the military secures it? Can I locate a vessel leaving the system before being recaptured? Even if I escape somehow, can I evade the entire military? The civilian authorities, too?*

"Try not to think about it, Roland. It will work out. These men are the best in the world. They are working with the finest computer system known to man. Between them, they will figure it out."

Roland smiled feebly. "You're right. Thank you for setting this up, Miranda. I do appreciate it, whatever happens."

Miranda continued her massage in silence. Then, "What else is bothering you, Roland?"

"Hmm? Oh, I was thinking about what happened to me and Melanie."

"What about it?"

Roland hesitated.

"Roland. Tell me," she whispered.

"Do you remember when you told me I was crawling back into my shell?"

"I think so. Why?"

"Well, I did. Then, when Koraben's ship cut me off, I discovered how small my shell is. Then, after I fixed Melanie, something happened."

"What happened?"

"I do not know, but she informed me that she is self-aware."

"You mean, she's alive?"

"So, it seems. As far-fetched as it sounds, it is the most reasonable explanation."

"That's wonderful."

"I am not so excited about it."

"Why not?"

"My ship's chief comfort for me was being able to control it completely. Now, I can't. She says it started about a year ago. I don't know why she told me she was...alive, to use your term, now. So, either way, nothing is the same. For the first time, I am faced with a totally new life. I don't know how to live it."

Miranda kept massaging his shoulders. "When I move, I often get a warning when someone is asking about me. Then I pack and relocate. I start over."

"My situation is a little different, Miranda."

"I know. I am trying to relate it to my own experience, and my family situation is as close as I can come to it." She stopped her massage and took a seat opposite him. "How much trouble can you get into being a smuggler?"

I have the authorities to consider, but what about Kor Daga? Melanie told me he has a bounty out on me now. If his operation is large enough to stand beside Abenor's, I do not want to cross him. Failure within such an organization is not tolerated, and the repercussions of failure are not pretty.

"The problem exists on two fronts," Roland began. "You see, I was doing a job for someone when I met you. This someone is not used to people being unable to finish a job."

"But you were arrested. Surely he can't..."

"Yes, he can. He expects those working for him to avoid arrest. It is what smugglers do. They take things places where they are not authorized to go.

Avoiding arrest is part of the job."

"But, still..."

"No. He hired me, and I did not complete the job."

"Can't you finish it now."

"No. The job had a tight schedule. It passed after I escaped from the *Aradinda*. Now, it is too late."

"So, do you need to give him his money back, or something?"

"I wish it were that simple. He has a bounty on me now. I would not be surprised if people were looking for me here."

"We must hide you, then."

"No. He does not know my name. He has a general description. If he goes through Abenor, he may get a more detailed description of my ship, but I think Abenor will not betray me. He owes me too much. I can get him into a great deal of trouble.

Miranda peered out of the window beside Roland. "So, the bad guys are looking for you."

Roland nodded, "The bad guys," he said, waving toward the window. "And the good guys." He waved toward her apartment, He drank a little more. "And there is more."

"More? What more?"

Of course, that security officer—Bornor—he has done his share of irreparable damage. Now, most of the planets I go to will be on the lookout for me—or my ship, at least. I will need to hide out on some backwater planet, with no military interest and no crime. What are the odds I will be happy in such a place? What are the odds I can even find one?

"The guy who caught me on the *Aradinda*."

"What about him?"

"Well, he investigated me while I was incarcerated there."

"Okay."

"He also investigated my ship."

"Of course."

Roland rested his arms on his knees. Looking at Miranda, he took the plunge. "My ship is not...authorized by the empire, either."

"It's a private vessel, right? Why should they care?"

"I obtained certain parts and components without going through proper channels."

"You stole them?" She stood.

There she goes. Might as well give her the whole story. Maybe she will see the need for his actions. "Not all of them. You see, I live in my ship. My home planet is a memory. Melanie has been my closest friend. So, I would find these new technologies. I find them and take them—for her—which is why she is the best computer system. I still need to install a data system. But I did not steal it. Abenor gave it to me as payment for a job."

"An illegal job, right?"

Roland nodded, avoiding her glare.

"I can't believe you, Roland! Who are you?" she left the room.

Roland got up and walked over to the window. Looking out, he saw people walking past, on their way to somewhere, or from somewhere. Miranda was making noise in the kitchen—utensils and metallic objects. The noise culminated in an exclamation point of shattered glass.

Roland rushed in to find Miranda leaning against a counter. She was crying.

There was no blood. He retrieved a broom and cleaned up the glass. He threw the glass away, put the broom away, and returned to the window.

He waited. *Maybe she will get past this. Maybe she won't.*

He waited. He heard water running in the kitchen.

He waited. Miranda cleared her throat.

He waited. He heard her enter the room. Turning to look at her, Roland could find nothing to say.

She could, "I should have known better from Bornor's questioning. He said you were a criminal. I didn't realize you were a professional criminal."

"I was one, but not anymore. One way or another, my criminal life is behind me."

"Seriously?"

Roland nodded.

"How can I be sure? How can *you* be sure?"

Roland motioned for her to sit. She chose the couch, so Roland sat beside her. "My current situation will end in one of three ways: I fail and am imprisoned, I succeed and am imprisoned, or I succeed and am freed. The most plausible is I fail. If so, my ship will be confiscated and dismantled, and I will be in jail for a very long time.

"The same thing will happen if I succeed. In both cases, I will be unable to resume my former lifestyle. Even if I succeed, and am not incarcerated, I no longer want the lifestyle. I want to stay with you; but, I know there is a lot to deal with for that to happen."

"What do you mean, 'Stay with me?'"

"Well, we got along so well while we were on the *Aradinda*, I started thinking about continuing. Then, when I was stranded, I kept thinking about you, and...I liked the memories and the feelings I had."

Roland could not determine if Miranda's face showed curiosity, anger, or contempt. "Of course, I would understand if you wanted nothing more to do with me once this situation is concluded."

"Stop talking."

"What? I am trying..."

"Just...stop...talking. I need to think."

CHAPTER 34

Roland got up and paced, "Somehow, I need to deal with Melanie."

"What's up with Melanie?"

"You were right when you said she was the best computer system known to man. Now she is even more."

"You mean, her 'awakening'? I know. It's unprecedented. I wonder what science will think of her."

"What do you mean?"

"Well, Melanie is as close to a new life form we ever encountered or developed out of our own history. All the rest were discovered after they had lived for centuries without us. Who knows, they would live for centuries more without us. But Melanie is different. She was not discovered. You created her. Scientists will be very interested, once word gets out."

"Still, I do not understand Melanie anymore. What is she capable of now? How much of what she knows does she actually say? What happens if she does not need me anymore?"

"How could she not need you? You programmed her."

He rose from under her hands. "I did." He walked back to the window. "But, she may be like a child growing up. She has all this data. With the speed of her processing— her mind—she will mature much faster than any other life form we know. Who knows how fast she will mature? How will her maturity be guided? No one can keep up with her. She was bored before I was even aware she could become bored."

"She talks to you, doesn't she?"

"Well, sure, she does, but is it enough? Most of what I read about raising children deals a great deal with observation—seeing disturbing or inappropriate behavior and correcting it. How do you observe someone who has no active body? By the time Melanie moves herself—in the *Stiletto*—it may be too late. Maybe no one will see her again. What if she decides to leave home? Where would it leave me?"

"Did you talk to her about it?"

"A little. Not enough, though. We had no time to talk, except about Koraben."

"Right," she said, straightening her posture, "Well, when this is over, you two will need to sit down and talk."

"Yeah, you have a point. There is no sense worrying. She based her 'life' on my original programming, so her loyalty should not suffer. I hope not, anyway. I would rather she not decide I was expendable.

CHAPTER 35

Green.

Roland sat across from one of the green walls and against another. The windows at each end of each corridor, as well as each corner, permitted enough natural light to balance the artificial fixtures. The corridor walls displayed no artwork. Roland expected none. Charts and maps covered much of the green at eye level, but Roland found no purely aesthetic adornment on any of the walls.

Although the old war films he watched on occasion showed such corridors built from blocks of cement, these were formed with no such indication. They seemed to be molded in one piece. Molded in green.

To say this shade of green was an ugly color required a degree of artistry Roland did not possess. The color was...official. It was a variation of a gray he had encountered. Each door along the walls was green—darker, but still green. The floor was off-white, but even it possessed a tinge of green. *I'm sure it's a reflection from the walls.* The uniforms were green. Uniformly green, save for the different insignia attached to each. A welcomed break from the greenness of his current situation was the dark blue of Miranda's suit as she strode out from one of the doors and over to his seat.

"Come on, Roland. I found someone who can help us."

"'Reggie,' please. Until we are certain, call me 'Reggie,' okay?" he whispered, rising to meet her.

"Right. Sorry. But cut me some slack; I finally got used to calling you 'Roland,'" she whispered back, smiling and shaking her head. "Whatever. Let's go." She pushed the office door open and entered. Looking down as he entered, Roland did not notice the name on the door, but he did notice the nameplate on the desk as he sat in one of the chairs across from the uniform—Commander Norden Tuman.

"I understand you may have some information for me," the uniform said as it leaned toward him.

Roland tried to speak, but no words came. He shifted in the chair, trying to reach a compromise with it. After clearing his throat a few times, Roland tried again, "Yes, uh, I...may, I mean, I do have some important information for you. Um, it is also time-sensitive, I believe."

"I see. And what is it?"

"Well, before I give you the details, I must make a request." Roland rose from the chair and walked to the one small window in the office. Turning to face the uniform, he continued, "I am requesting I be left out as the source of this information."

The uniform took on a puzzled facial expression. "You want to give me information and remain anonymous?"

"Um, yes. Yes, that is my intention."

"Son, you realize I will need to verify any information you supply."

"Yes, I realize it, sir, but..."

"And, you also realize I need to verify the source?"

"Yes, sir, I understand that, as well. However..."

"So, you must also realize, assuming your information is time-sensitive, as you claim, I would be spending needless time identifying and verifying the source—you—before I could even address the information itself? So why don't we skip the 'anonymous' part and get right down to business, okay?"

Roland sat back down. "I see." He looked at Miranda, who looked away after a few seconds.

Yes, it is my decision. She has gone through three levels of command before finding someone who could say, "Yes." The other two had to ask someone else to say, "Yes."

Roland offered, "I can vouch for the authenticity of the information. You can verify my identity," *not that anyone can find much about James Reginald Fischer III.* "Please, leave me out of the official report."

Folding its hands, the uniform stared at him. "Look, Mr...."

"Fischer."

"Look, Mr. Fischer, I have an official duty. Why are you so hesitant? Unless there is something else? If you are using me for a diversion, I'll bury you, Mr. Fischer. I will not be played a fool."

"No, no. Nothing of the sort. It is just..." Roland looked at Miranda, again. She gave him a little smile, nodded, and took his hand in hers. He looked at the uniform—at the face of Commander Tuman. "Commander, my information exposes a crime against the military."

Commander Tuman sat up.

"This crime could have grave consequences." Roland paused. "The issue concerning me is my possession of the information also exposes a crime against the military. The verification of the information will involve an additional crime against both military and civilian authorities.

"So, you see, although the crime about which I possess the information is, by far, the most egregious, the threat to my freedom and livelihood by disclosing this information gives me pause."

Commander Tuman leaned back in his chair, which squeaked a little under the strain. He tapped on his desk and looked at Roland for an uncomfortably long time before speaking. "I understand your dilemma, Mr. Fischer. But, you must also understand mine. As an officer of the Anadir, and therefore the imperial, military forces, I have a responsibility to report all crimes against the military, or against the people who are protected by the military. This includes other branches of the military besides those here on Anadir. Should you be implicated in such a crime, I would need to report you, perhaps, even arrest you."

"I appreciate your candor. You haven't made this easier."

Commander Tuman rose and walked to the window. "I can see why you would hesitate." He turned to face Roland, "Let me ask you a question. Is the crime you reference serious enough that it should be investigated? Since you are here, I must conclude that it is. If you know of a crime and do not report it, you can be arrested as an accessory to that crime. If you come clean with your information, and the crime is prevented, or the perpetrator is apprehended, then you would be credited with reporting the crime. In many cases, that would keep you from being arrested for that crime. I want you to calculate the risks involved."

"Believe me, Commander, I calculated the risks. I re-calculated them. That is the reason I bring it to your attention."

"I see. But you do not consider it important enough to risk incarceration, then."

"Well, that may not be accurate, Commander. But, it is not an easy decision, though. I have evaded authorities my whole life. And one cannot control everything." He squeezed Miranda's hand, let it go, and started to pace.

"I am not a trusting individual. I came because Miranda trusts. She trusts an individual who trusts the officer whom we initially contacted. He sent us to another officer whom he trusts. That officer directed us to you. He trusts you. Now, I must trust you. It's not easy."

"I understand."

"I appreciate that you try to understand, Commander Tuman. Nevertheless, this crime could conceivably alter the balance of power in this galaxy." Sitting down, he added, "Frankly, I would rather take my chances in a system I understand than in one with which I am unfamiliar."

"If the severity of the situation is as you state it," the commander said, "I will do what I can to safeguard your freedom. I make no promises, though."

Roland turned to Miranda. "Would I at least be allowed visitors?"

CHAPTER 36

Another dead end! Vardri left the police station and returned to her vehicle. It hesitated to start again. *Come on. I know I've been harder on you than your previous owner, but I promise I will get you fixed after I deal with this. Please?*

She eased her vehicle out into the mostly-automated traffic flow. *It's been too long since I had to drive.* Looking at her navigation screen, she sighed. *Two hours to the next police station. Maybe they will at least be willing to look at my information. This one, at least, has planetary jurisdiction.*

"I thought getting the information out of my office would be the hardest part of this," Vardri said to the vehicle's interior. "Now, it seems to be the simplest. Finding someone who is both interested in looking at the information and willing to do something about it... *That* seems impossible."

* * *

Miranda sat back down in the chair next to Roland. The coffee she brought with her was not the best or even passable, but it helped distract Roland from contemplating his future in too much detail. The green walls of the commander's office had begun to look more grayish to him already, and he had not even confessed to any infractions yet.

As he rose to look out of the window, again, Miranda said, "He said he would do what he could to protect your freedom. What else can you do?"

"I can leave, for one thing," he snapped. "Right now, he has nothing on me. I can walk out of here a free man."

"Perhaps. He did say you could be arrested as an accessory."

"An accessory to what? I told him that a crime was *being* committed.

There is no evidence that it has *been* committed."

"Couldn't he arrest you to make you provide the evidence?"

"I don't know. He might. But it might be viewed as self-incrimination, which would be illegal itself. So, I could walk away from this."

"Maybe so, but it leaves you where you were when you knocked on my door."

"I know. I am still here." Roland walked from the window to the commander's empty chair. It had been empty for an hour, giving Roland plenty of time to envision gray variations.

He heard a knock at the door, then watched it open. A uniform entered, saying, "Excuse me, sir, but..." The uniform stopped when it noticed the empty chair.

As the uniform started to speak, Roland preempted its question, "He has gone to confer with someone. It has been about an hour, and we were instructed to wait for him here."

"I see," the uniform said. Roland noticed by its shape this was a female uniform. Glancing at Miranda, he saw it had not escaped her notice either.

"I can let him know you are looking for him, Miss..." Roland offered.

"Lieutenant Menka. I will leave this for him," she said, waving a data reader and walking to the desk. Laying the reader atop the desk, she added, "Let him know I completed the pilot briefing for tomorrow's training mission."

"So, you are a pilot?" he asked as the uniform strode toward the door.

"Yes, I am a pilot." She faced him. "I have been a pilot for two years and am now a squadron leader."

Roland raised his hands and backed a step, "I meant nothing by the question. I had heard there were no women pilots on Anadir. You surprised me. No offense."

She hesitated a moment, evaluating the civilian in front of her. She nodded once, turned, strode to the door, and slammed it behind her.

Roland looked at Miranda, "Testy."

"I guess so," she agreed.

"So, women can become pilots here."

"There may be a few token women in flight training, but I doubt they will ever see combat. Still, the military must be pretty desperate to begin using women."

"Is it so hard to look at the world from a new perspective?"

"I don't know. Is it?"

* * *

"Everything seems to check out, sir," Tarin's lieutenant stated.

"Good. It's about time. Do we have enough fuel to complete the trip, or do we need to check out the depot?" Tarin responded.

"I would feel more comfortable if we refueled. We lack sufficient run-time data to determine precisely how much fuel the new hyperdrive consumes over time. As it stands now, I estimate we will have enough, but with very little reserve. It is close enough so that the hyperdrive will not be required."

"Very well, Lieutenant, let's see if this fuel merchant is as good as this crew says he is."

CHAPTER 37

Roland sat and watched Miranda as she watched drills on the parade ground. *Blue is a good color for her. I prefer black myself, but I like the blue on her.* He looked around the office. *It doesn't go with this green, though.*

The coffee was gone, and a new pot was brewing when Commander Tuman returned. Wordlessly, he crossed the office and sat at his desk.

"Lt. Menka stopped by," Roland offered, "She said she had completed the pilot briefing for tomorrow's training." He pointed to the data reader.

Commander Tuman picked the reader up. After scanning it, he set it off to the side of his desk. "Mr. Fischer, I spoke with the Judge Advocate General's office. The situation is as I described it: I cannot guarantee you will not be detained for whatever crimes you allegedly committed, but they will consider the current situation in their deliberations and in their communications with the affected civilian authorities."

"Sometimes, higher levels of cooperation often result in lighter sentences," the commander offered, "In any event, they assured me no communication to the civilian authorities will take place until the conclusion of our investigation. Due to your stated time-sensitive nature of your information, I suggest you don't take too long making your decision."

Roland nodded and rose from the chair. Miranda approached.

Commander Tuman picked up the data reader. "I will await your decision."

Miranda did not say anything as she and Roland walked toward the exit. She slowed her pace to match Roland's.

Roland stated, "A lot can happen in a year and a half."

"A year and a half?"

"Yeah, Melanie estimates it would take eighteen months for someone else to mass-produce the hyperdrive. Actually, she said seventeen months. I am not sure if they can produce and incorporate the RECON in that time, but the hyperdrive would be enough to cause real trouble."

"So, what can we do until then?"

"To begin with, we assume the hyperdrive works and begin production right away. I doubt Commander Koraben would steal something if it did not work. I also know first-hand the hyperspace bubble matches the hull dimensions. It proves the hyperdrive works."

Roland stopped for a moment, "I suppose to be exact, it validates the design of the Model 153 Hyperspace Insertion Unit."

"A little 'gallows' humor?"

Roland shrugged and started walking.

"So, what are you going to do?"

"I tell them. I mean, we could escape the invasion and live out our lives, if we choose a planet on the fringe."

"But,...?"

"But, it means he wins," Roland stopped, "And I can't let it happen. People should be able to control their own existence, but not someone else's. I set myself up so that no one could push me around. No one could tell me what I can't do. I never had to concern myself with the needs of other people. This Tarin guy is abusing his control. If he wants to use Beranon and Vardri's lives as pawns, I will bring out the major pieces. I may get injured in the process, but I need to press the attack."

"Excuse me?" Miranda asked, "What are you talking about?"

"Sorry, Miranda, it is an old metaphor." Roland extended his elbow toward Miranda. "Shall we?"

Miranda smiled and let Roland lead her back toward Commander Tuman. She whispered to him, "When this is over, we'll talk more about moving to an insignificant planet."

Without knocking, Roland opened Commander Tuman's door and walked in.

Miranda followed.

Walking to the Commander's desk, Roland stopped and saluted, "Prisoner James Reginald Fischer, the third, reporting for duty, sir."

Tuman responded, "Sit down, please."

Roland sat.

"You've decided to tell me what is going on," Commander Tuman stated.

"I will do even better, sir."

"Lose the 'sir'. You are not a soldier." Leaning on his elbows, he added,

"So, what's our next step?"

Standing outside the *Stiletto*, Roland gazed at his ship's sleek lines. His hand rested upon the keyboard, but he did not enter the code to unlock the door. He had had enough difficulty admitting Miranda into his ship. But, he concluded, she posed no significant threat. Commander Tuman, on the other hand, did.

"May we continue, Mr. Fischer?"

I do not like to be pushed, So, settle down, Commander.

Roland took a deep breath, then blew it out as he entered the code.

The hatch slid open, and the entry ramp extended to the ground. After the ramp locks clicked into place, Roland waited until his two guests entered. He followed and closed the *Stiletto* again. "Can I get you something to drink?"

"Thanks, but let's get on with this."

"Very well. Melanie?" he called, taking his pilot chair. "Yes, Roland?"

Roland, again.

"Roland Fischer?" asked the commander.

"Well, not exactly."

"Melanie, access the data concerning the *M.T.S. 1741-A*. Identify all points of suspicion based on our research."

"Very well, Roland."

Roland watched as Melanie replayed their conclusions. Then, he joined Miranda on his bunk. He held her hand, looked at the floor. *Warm.* She squeezed his hand but said nothing.

The commander stood and listened to Melanie as she itemized each action and inconsistency she and Roland had questioned. "I can see why you would be concerned for the transport vessel. However, it is still one ship, a transport vessel. Why do you think..."

Roland got up. "Melanie," he said, facing Commander Tuman, "List the performance improvements of the Model 153 hyperdrive unit for the commander." He noted the change in Commander Tuman's expression as each performance feature was spoken.

"Wow," he said, "Is it true?"

"It is, most definitely, true, commander."

Melanie asked, "Commander Tuman?"

After a moment of confusion, he looked at the viewscreen. "What?" he asked.

"Are you Commander Tuman?"

"Yes. Who are you?"

"I am Melanie. Roland named me 'Melanie.'"

"How do you know me?"

"I accessed your computer systems. You are the one person listed as Commander."

"You accessed my computer systems?"

Roland saw Tuman's face reddening. He said, "Melanie, that was not nice."

"But you always accessed the computer systems when landing. I followed a long-established protocol. Command Tuman is the senior officer at this location. His current post will not allow him the time necessary to verify our data sources individually. I suggest we proceed to Durpadan. The commander of the facility there has a much lighter load and will be able to afford the necessary time..."

"What?" Blood vessels pulsed in the commander's face.

Roland cleared his throat. "No, Melanie; Durpadan is not an option."

"But, with Tuman's workload,..."

"No, Melanie. Commander Tuman is the person I will deal with." He turned to the commander's face, "You now see how the verification of this information will compromise me, and already has." He returned to Miranda. "I wonder what the bunks are like in military prison."

"Well, to be honest, I hope they are more comfortable than this one, but I guess I'm spoiled by my own bed," she said. "I could use a drink now, though."

"Tea? Or, something stronger?"

"Tea will be fine with me."

"Fine." Roland set out two cups.

"Are we overreacting to all this?"

"What do you mean?"

"Reggie...I mean, Roland, what kind of chance does he have? It's one ship. How much damage can he do with one ship?"

"The danger lies with someone who can make lots of ships. One ship is a nuisance. An entire fleet of superior ships is a real threat. So far, our military has space supremacy. A sizable force with such a drive would reverse that," Roland explained steeped the tea. "We would be outmatched by technical superiority. Like the *Stiletto*. My ship is technically superior to any other ship in space, which is why I possess the advantage—every time. Can you imagine a thousand such ships? What kind of havoc would it cause?"

"But you got caught. So will he, right?"

Thank you for reminding me. Would you like to shove my head into a food processor while you're at it?

"Yes, I got caught."

The sound of boiling water attracted Roland's attention. Pouring the water, he said, "That is what we are trying to accomplish. Right, Commander?"

"Hmm?" Commander Tuman looked up. The viewscreen flashed diagrams and data. "Sorry?"

Roland handed one cup of tea to Miranda and walked up behind the commander's seat. Looking at the data, he repeated, "We are trying to stop Tarin, right?"

"Well, if this data is correct, we'd better."

"Are you sure you do not want some tea, Commander Tuman," Roland asked.

"No, thanks. Right now, I need to know your sources. How did you get this?"

Melanie answered, "Do you want the short version or the long version?"

Roland paced. "It started when I left Dorea several weeks ago. I came across two passengers aboard a freighter..."

CHAPTER 38

After Roland completed his summation, Commander Tuman rose to face him. "This is disturbing. You will forgive me, however, if I do not take your story at face value."

Roland returned Tuman's gaze. "I realize this may be news to you. Tarin hid his intentions very well." Turning back to the data, he asked, "Melanie? What piqued Vardri's curiosity? How did she learn Tarin's plan?"

"Reg, in her personal file, she references a dialogue between Tarin and one of his senior officers—a Major Rosmar."

Reg? She called me 'Reg'?

Melanie continued, "She quotes Tarin as saying, 'If we're going to pull this off, we need to eliminate all traces of our presence here. If word gets out, they *will* hunt us down.' He then directs Major Rosmar to, 'Eliminate all personnel associated with planning the test, including any of the design team from Bantadam. Eliminate all files referencing the test. Dr. Nortolis will take care of the Bantadam files. You take care of Dorea.' I am certain some of her recollection is faulty, but her understanding of the situation seems solid."

Roland interjected, "But I beat him to the information. What is the file creation date for the personal file, Melanie?"

"This file was created at 13:21:09 on 02.08.179, local time."

"And when did she purchase passage aboard the *Surrogate?* I cannot remember."

"Her purchase record was created at 15:17:46, local time, on the same date."

"So, she was in a hurry. What was the departure time for the *Surrogate?*"

"The scheduled departure time was 20:30:00, local time, on the same date."

"Yes, I figured it would leave that day."

"The actual departure time was 20:41:56, local time."

"Not bad, for a freighter. I doubt she would notice a twelve-minute delay."

"You're right," Commander Tuman agreed, leaning against an interior wall, "Still, do you have any corroborating evidence supporting Vardri's suspicions?"

"I do not. What about you, Melanie?"

"No, Commander," she replied. "The information I possess surrounding Vardri's comments do not include any motivation or intention. It is data surrounding the testing of the hyperdrive prototype."

"Okay," he said, pushing himself from the wall and pacing, "If Vardri's suspicions are correct...and if your suspicions are correct," he waved in Roland's direction, "Tarin is definitely to be investigated. I cannot, however, commit any resources to addressing this situation without substantial proof. How can you verify your information?"

Roland flashed Miranda a grin. "Illegally."

"So, you said, Mr. Fischer," he began, "But, I..."

"Please, Commander Tuman," Roland interrupted. "My name is Roland Marcel. James Reginald Fischer is a long-past friend. Considering the current circumstances, the name should follow."

"I see, Mr. Marcel, I still require verification before I can consider any action."

"Very well, commander." He drew in a slow breath and blew it out.

"Melanie?"

"Yes, Roland?"

Roland, again. He chuckled and shook his head. Then he turned his chair, so he faced Commander Tuman, and said, "Establish a tight-beam connection with the Bantadam Technology Conglomerate network, and a second to the Dorea Space and Hyperspace networks. Log us in."

"Will do, Reg," Spectre replied.

The commander looked past Roland and through the window. "Who was that?"

"Another part of my computer system," Roland replied, as Commander Tuman stood and backed up. "I programmed my computer to perform varying duties independently. Three broad categories of duties evolved. I programmed the groupings with distinct personality-based interfaces. Spectre does the 'black-ops' duties. Melanie is the primary interface, performing the routine duties. I made her the most 'personable.' Jackson performs the piloting calculations and some of the low-risk infiltrations."

"Listening to the same voice all day would become tedious."

"Agreed. I found it also facilitated the completion of their respective duties."

"How so?"

"I would not become distracted. With a distinctive voice for the situation, I concentrated more on the task at hand. I focused. Growing up, I tinkered with my parents' appliances. Then..."

"Connections established, Roland," Melanie interrupted.

"Thank you, Melanie," he responded, turning to face the monitors. "Put Dorea on my left and Bantadam on my right. Put your distillation on the center screen." The screens splashed data.

"Now, the first passenger I investigated was Beranon," he said, pointing to the viewscreen on his right. "When I found him, he seemed out of place. I checked him out and discovered some interesting discrepancies between his passenger file and personnel file on Bantadam."

"And so you found out about Tarin?"

"Not quite. It is where the connection started. I noticed Beranon's working relationship with Vardri, so I investigated her, too." He pointed to the left-hand viewscreen. "She, too, should not have been aboard the *Surrogate.*"

Returning to Miranda's home, Roland admired the artwork. *Digital prints, of course, but they are engaging.* "Either way I look at it, I am in trouble, so why not try to do some good out of it?" Roland asked.

"I know," Miranda responded. "I want to be sure you are not doing this because of me."

"No, this is not *just* because of you. Granted, you were my catalyst. I would have avoided Anadir altogether. Still, I would report it to someone, but it would be too late."

Miranda put the fruit on the table and stepped back. "Well, it looks like everything is ready. Let's eat," she said, sitting at the table.

Roland sat opposite of Miranda. The aroma of the meal was neither enticing nor repulsive, but it was strong.

"I must warn you. This is a new recipe for me, so I don't know how it tastes," she said, lifting one of the sausage-like meats off the serving tray and placing it on Roland's plate. "I hope you like it."

"I guess I will not be eating like this for very long."

"Don't be such a pessimist. Things will work out. It may take some time, but I have confidence in Commander Tuman. Once you confirm the information with him, you will be able to stop the Koraben guy, and they will let you go."

"I wish I could share your optimism. If there is a bright side anywhere, you will look for it."

She smiled.

"So, let me ask you a question, Miranda."

She hesitated for a moment, then said, "All right."

"When will you be satisfied?"

"Satisfied with what?"

"Well, you are always looking for something new, so when will you be satisfied with the results of your search? When will you stop?"

"I don't know. I've never given it much thought, to be honest. Why?"

"It seems to me you are going around in circles. You become bored with your life, so you blast off hoping to meet new people or experience some new thing. But you always return to Anadir. Then, the excitement wears off, and you become bored again, so you blast off again. When will you become satisfied?"

"You make it sound like a bad thing," she responded, leaning back in her chair.

"No. I was wondering when you would 'settle down' to a more mundane life and be happy with it."

"Must I?"

"I guess not. I see people get burned out on travel, without a direction or goal. From what I read, they run out of funds, or they expand their horizons farther and farther out until they get tired of it. I was wondering which would happen to you—and when it would happen."

"Well, it depends."

"On what?"

"On whether I meet someone I find more interesting than traveling," she said with a smile.

"An interesting response. I've not read about that one."

"You can't experience all of life from inside a spaceship, Roland, some things must be lived to be understood."

"But what kind of person would you find more interesting than traveling?"

"Is it a trick question?"

"Not to my knowledge."

"Okay, then," she said, and then took another bite of salad. After swallowing, she continued, "One kind of person I would find more interesting than traveling, is someone who has a totally different history than my own and can share his history with me. Then my travel interest would be satisfied through sharing our histories."

"Well, would someone like me interest you?" he asked, then busied himself with his meal. When she did not respond, he paused and looked at her. She had not changed position or expression. "What?"

She laughed. Then, she laughed some more.

Roland, unsure of the humor of the question, felt himself becoming embarrassed.

He stood up and said, "I had better go."

"Sit down, Roland," she instructed, trying to stop laughing.

Roland tried to decide whether she was serious or whether he should leave.

"Sit. Down," she repeated.

Roland sat down.

She leaned forward, "Of course, I find you interesting. I thought I made myself clear. But, I guess not. With your sheltered existence, you may not have picked up my signals."

She was still looking at him as she lifted her glass and took a long drink. "I thought you were interested in me, too. Was I right?"

Roland could only nod.

"Okay, at least we agree on that."

Roland waited for her to continue. She did not oblige him.

"So, what do we do now?" he asked.

"Good question," she answered. "With your current situation, who knows what will happen. I guess we can talk about it a bit. What do you think?"

"Very well." He poured them more water. "So, what kinds of things to people who are interested in each other talk about?"

"I don't know," she responded, "Here, the women have very little say in who they will marry. My mother never shared with me the kinds of things women looked for in an ideal husband. She told me the things I should do as an ideal wife."

"Such as?"

"No. I refuse to play that game. The way I look at it, we are two adult people. The things we should be concerned about are the things we think are important—not what my mother thinks is important; and, not what some movie tells us is important. What we think is important is what is important."

They ate in silence, then cleaned up the dishes. In silence. After pouring each some dessert wine, Miranda led Roland into the sitting area. She sat on the couch and patted the seat beside her. Roland sat where she had indicated. He sipped, not sure of what to do next.

Miranda spoke first. "We could research the proper courting rituals on some other planets."

"Good. Great idea."

"No, it's not," she said. "What do they know about us?"

"Oh. I see your point. 'What do we think is important?' Right?"

"Absolutely."

Roland sipped some more. "What if we start with the best-case? What if Tuman does get me out of this mess, and we can do whatever we want? What would you want?"

"Well, my ideal situation would be you, and I get married and live here. But travel a lot," she said, "A whole lot."

"We hardly know each other, and you want to get married. Should we at least get to know one another?"

"On other worlds, perhaps, but not here." Miranda shrugged and sipped. "Is it truly necessary, anyway? I mean, look, we enjoy each other's company. We share some common interests." she said, fingers numbering each phrase. "Here, it is always up to the parents to determine the marriage. I would never have any say in the matter. With you, I do. I like it."

But, what if you are wrong about me?"

"I'll take my chances. My question is, will you?"

Roland finished his wine and set the glass aside. He looked around for something to occupy his eyes while he thought. *She is pleasant. I do enjoy our time together. But, what if it's because she is the first I have ever considered? What if I get tired of her? What if I need to get away? There is no room on the* Stiletto *for passengers. She will never accept my career.*

"Look, Roland, I know it's a big step. I know you always consider the options before you decide. I want to know if you would want to move in that direction with me? Of all the men I met, you are the one I want to do this with. The ones here were looking for someone they can control, but that's cultural. I met others on my travels, but they were like that one in the donut shop. They want a good experience, but no relationship. I mean, if you don't like me in that way, I understand, but..."

Roland looked at her. *She's babbling. People tend to babble when they are unsure of themselves. I've seen it in business, with the rookie clients—the ones who had never hired a smuggler before. They are always talking.*

...because I want to let my parents know they can stop hounding me. So, do you?"

Roland considered his options. He had not heard much of what she had said but thought he had the gist of it. *Would it work, like it does in the movies? Is it even her custom?* He watched Miranda sip her wine—shallow, quick sips. When she stopped and looked at him again, he leaned over and kissed her. Through his lips, he felt her tremble a little, then settle down. Her lips moved under his. *What is she doing?* He did not move his. *Should I move my lips around, too? How?* Before he experimented, she pulled away. She was smiling.

"You've never done it before, have you?"

"Was it so obvious?" He turned away, flushed.

She turned his head back to face hers. "Thank you." She kissed him again. "We can work on your technique later. Right now, I want to call my mother."

Roland watched as she got up from the couch. He thought about staying on Anadir with her, traveling on passenger ships. Buying equipment. As she entered the numbers for her parents on the video keypad, Roland started to wonder if he would be able to live like that—to live without Melanie. *Of course, I must stay out of prison to find out.* "But, what happens if Tuman cannot keep me out of prison? What then?"

Miranda stopped entering numbers. She canceled the connection. "You have a point there. I can't call my mother and say, 'Look, mom, I'm going to get married now, so you can stop planning my life for me. Who is he? He's a convicted criminal. He's in prison off-world. I should be able to see him in fifteen to thirty.' I don't think she would appreciate it."

Roland stood up as Miranda approached the couch. He took her hands in his. "Listen, I would like to work this out with you. I think I can be happy, but I am not sure right now. I need to work some things out in my head. What if we go ahead with this and see if Commander Tuman can help me out. If not, we will see what happens then. But hold off calling your parents until we figure out what will happen."

Miranda nodded. "They've waited this long. It won't kill them to wait a little longer."

CHAPTER 39

Roland watched over Tuman's shoulder as Melanie guided him to the appropriate files. *Bantadam's system has not detected my previous investigation, or the administrators would take further precautions. They did not even change Beranon's password. They should suspect something. People want to assume all is well until provided with evidence to the contrary.*

Tuman expressed disbelief as he surveyed the technical details of the hyperdrive Model 153 Melanie's distillation confirmed. "The impact of this system has not been overstated," he said to himself. "But, is it stolen?"

"At the time Beranon generated his files, the situation had not yet been detected," Melanie offered. "It was after he had arrived on Dorea that Vardri discovered Tarin's intent and notified Beranon."

"Then, I'd better look at Vardri's information," he said, turning the chair to face the right-hand viewscreen. "Are these downloaded versions, or are they live?"

"These were downloaded. I will access the current versions—one moment."

Commander Tuman turned the chair to face Roland. "You understand I need to see this information first-hand? Anyone could create such files and pass them off.

Though I must admit, the motivation for your doing so escapes me."

"Commander," Melanie interrupted, "The original files in the Dorea network were removed. Spectre is attempting to recover the files."

"'Removed?' You mean they were erased? Why would they be erased? Are you certain they were in the system to begin with?"

"Commander, if you are implying I am deceitful, or even incompetent, and created the context out of which I downloaded this data, I take offense."

"Computers do not get offended. Mr. Marcel, if this is your idea of a joke,

..."

"It is no joke, Commander Tuman. She is offended. Granted, this is the first time she has ever told me she was offended. I do believe I have given her cause to be offended in the past, not realizing she could become so."

Melanie interrupted, "For the moment, I will let the comment pass, citing your unfamiliarity with me. To continue with the task at hand, let me state, at this time, I cannot speculate on the reason for the files' removal. Perhaps after they are recovered, we can trace the removal back to the root cause."

"Melanie, right now, get the files back. We can trace the cause later."

Commander Tuman disagreed. "It will be important if there is a traitor at this company. If the files were erased, we should figure who erased them. If someone here is working to help Tarin, we need to expose the person. I agree the apprehension of the vessel is primary. When I get back to my office, I will send a confidential request to my team that they trace the removal of these files."

"I can access it for you now, if you wish, Commander."

"I know you can access the trail, once the files are recovered, but we lack the necessary time."

"I was offering to expedite your confidential communication. I established a network connection. You would need to log in."

His face reddened. "Yes...expedite it." As the commander turned to Roland, Melanie displayed a login prompt to the Anadir military network. "I don't suppose it would do me any good to request you quit this practice, would it?"

Roland felt his face growing warm. "I swear I will limit access to those systems deemed necessary for the task at hand." *An empty promise, considering the size of the loophole I've allowed myself.*

Commander Tuman saw it, too. "We will need to leave it there...for now."

CHAPTER 40

"I give up." Vardri leaned her head against the steering column of her vehicle. "If the planetary law enforcement won't take me seriously, who else will?"

"'We must confirm your information before we can act on such a serious accusation,'" Vardri mocked. "Yeah, if I still had any access to the information, I could show it to you. But Commander Tarin took care of that."

What can I do now? If he is still looking for me, someone here with military connections could try to follow up on this. Then he will know I am still here. Of course, the military people I talked to did that already.

Vardri looked around, expecting to see military vehicles converging on her location. She breathed again once she realized it was local traffic in her view. *Who am I kidding? They didn't take me seriously enough to follow up. No one will be looking for me here.*

Starting her vehicle, she checked for traffic before pulling into the traffic flow. "OK, Vardri, where to now? You have enough cash to last a few months, but then you will need to get more," she said to herself. "I could keep running and hiding until the cash runs out, and then hope Tarin and his crew are no longer looking for me. If I am careful with my money and found a less-populated region, I could stretch things a little more. Unless they don't take imperial currency. Some of these planets don't enforce that standard for all regions."

Traffic was light enough for Vardri to continue thinking through options without distracting her to a dangerous level. "So, I guess I will tough it out in a backwater part of this planet. It means I can't afford to purchase any of the tickets I reserved to throw them off my track. If I keep a low enough profile, they may give up."

I hope so, anyway.

* * *

Mr. Corius's image filled the viewscreen again. "Mister Daga, I am disappointed about your lack of success in delivering my parcel."

"I, myself, was surprised when hearing my transporter did not arrive on schedule," Kor began, "I am looking into the matter, and..."

"Your transporter did not arrive at all," Mr. Corius stated, showing no emotion.

"I realize that, Mister Corius, and...like I said...I am looking into the matter." The image on the screen did not alter.

"Regardless of the cause, I am willing to reimburse you for your lost parcel."

"Of course you will, Mister Daga. I would expect nothing less from any professional. When can I expect my 450 thousand?" Kor tried to respond, but no words came.

"I see," Mr. Corius stated, leaning back in his chair, "It may take some time for you to gather so much currency."

Kor nodded. *Much longer than I think you would like.*

"Meanwhile, Mister Daga, I will need to secure more...reliable assistance."

"Now, Mister Corius," Kor protested, "If you will allow me to prove..."

"You proved much to me already, Mister Daga. You proved my level of need is beyond your ability to deliver. Moreover, you proved you lack sufficient capitalization to guarantee the success of any endeavor for which I would seek your assistance. So, to be blunt, you proved I need to look to someone else."

"I understand, Mister Corius," Kor muttered, remembering how he felt when confronted by a teacher at school when he was a child. "Perhaps, in the future..."

"First, prove to me you can make me whole for my lost parcel. Then prove you can cover any future loss, should I request your assistance again. Perhaps then, then, I will see about requesting your assistance."

"I understand, Mister Corius," Kor replied, nodding his head. He did not need to wait before Mister Corius terminated the communication.

"When I catch you, Mister Roland Marcel, you will pay dearly for this embarrassment—and for this expense," Kor announced to the absent transporter, as he initiated communication with Abenor.

* * *

The *Aradindra* was still docked. Passengers would not be boarding until tomorrow, so Bornor had time. *Let's see if you are as good as you think you are, Mister Marcel, or whatever your name it.* "I realize you were short on time, Mister Marcel, so I understand your oversight," Bornor said to his otherwise empty office. "You overwrote my text, but did not remove the images," he continued as one of his screens showed a picture of Roland from one of the security cameras monitoring his cell, and the other displayed a set of fingerprints. "You can smear your prints all you want, Mister Marcel, but, given enough instances, I was able to piece together a complete set from your trays and utensils, plus an air vent cover. Now, it's a matter of finding a match."

* * *

"No, Roland did not send me. He does not know I'm here, Commander Tuman," Miranda replied to the commander's question. "I wanted to see what the chances are he walks away from this as a free man."

"You know I am not at liberty to discuss military matters with civilians. You are not family, so..."

"But I will be."

"You will?"

"Yes, commander, we are going to get married."

"Well, congratulations. That would grant me some liberties regarding Mister Marcel's situation. However, since you are not a spouse, I am restricted from giving you what you want."

"Is there any way you could indicate whether he will be imprisoned, without violating your military restriction? It would mean a great deal to me."

"Look, Miss..."

"Miranda is fine, commander."

"Very well, then, Miss Miranda, the way I can see Mister Marcel avoiding serious time in prison would be for us to apprehend Commander Koraben before he makes it to wherever he is headed. For that to occur, we need some idea of where he might be and where he is going. Then, we would need to secure enough resources to be able to secure him."

"I understand, Commander Tuman. But, what if he has already defected?"

"If that were the case, then there would be little I could do to prevent Mister Marcel's incarceration," the commander announced. "But, I am not willing to assume such. I am still operating on the assumption Commander Koraben is still within our borders."

"Well, then, commander, I will see about helping Roland determine the most plausible place for Tarin to go to if you will begin securing the resources to apprehend him."

"Miss Miranda, I have been securing resources since I left his ship."

* * *

"Commander, sir."

Startled, Tarin spat, "What is it now, major?"

"A report has come in from Erkarth. Someone has inquired regarding us," Major Rosmar reported.

"Who placed the inquiry?"

"Vardri Alarius, the project manager over…"

"Yes, I am very familiar with the name. You were told to take care of her, remember?"

"Yes, sir. I am aware, sir, but the circumstances and…"

"I already heard your excuses, Major Rosmar." Tarin paused his beratement. *I would not figure she would cause trouble. It would be her word against mine. She had no access to anything incriminating for me. Unless she got to the files before I removed her access. It doesn't matter why she is stirring something up, or even if she is stirring something up. We are too far out to go after her. It may not even be an issue.*

"Major, what was the response to the inquiry?"

"According to this report, nothing has been done. It has been filed as a citizen complaint."

Tarin laughed. "Of course it has. She has no evidence to back up her claims. She has no way to retrieve the information from Dorea. No one is going to act on anything she claims without corroboration. It was a nice effort, though, Ms. Alarius. A nice effort, indeed."

Motioning the major to an isolated alcove, Tarin said, "Send a message to one of our operatives on Dorea to go to Erkarth and deal with Ms. Alarius. She is no real threat, but I don't like leaving things undone."

"Yes, sir."

"And get it done this time." Tarin turned and walked away without waiting for a response.

CHAPTER 41

"Roland, you should return to Miranda's home," Melanie announced.

"But, I have not identified Tarin's exit point, yet. I haven't even figured out where to start."

"Well, we intercepted a communication to her from her mother. After the communication was terminated, she started making noise in various parts of her domicile."

"Her mother? How did her mother get her Information?"

"I will look into that, Reg," Spectre announced.

"Thanks. You know where I'll be."

Miranda's eyes were wider than Roland remembered them. She was flushed. "We need to get out of here," she blurted as she grabbed his arm and pulled him inside. "She is on her way to get me."

"How did she find you?" Roland asked, pulling more of her clothes from her closet.

"I don't know. But, she did."

"Reg, it appears her mother has a nephew in the military, and he is stationed at this base," Spectre answered.

"Of course, I never can catch a break when it comes to my family."

Roland watched Miranda, unsure if her tears were from sadness, fear, or anger. "I'm sorry, Miranda," he said.

"Thanks, Reg," she responded without breaking her rhythm as she stuffed another handful of clothing into one of her travel bags.

Roland touched her shoulder. She turned so she faced him squarely. "I'm sorry, Miranda. If I had not come here, you would not be discovered."

"I know. It's not important now. You came. You asked for help. I helped. And, here we are," she said, pulling away and returning to her packing.

"Can I help?"

"No, I've got most of it done, now. I would ask how you knew I was packing to leave, but it's obvious your computer is spying on me. I'm glad my mother doesn't possess your technology." Miranda pushed her way past him and into the main room, carrying her bag to add to the small group of bags already in the room.

"Miranda, maybe if we tell her we are getting married, she may hold off on kidnapping you."

"That may work, but I need to hide again, in case it doesn't." She stopped and looked at Roland. "And, I need you to stop spying on me."

"But, I'm not..." he began, stopping when he saw her expression.

"Very well. I will wait with Commander Tuman or with Melanie until you feel safe enough to contact me."

Miranda nodded.

"Melanie," Roland called, "Leave her alone."

"Copy that, sir," Jackson responded, "Terminating connections. Good luck, ma'am."

Roland stepped toward Miranda to say his good-bye.

Miranda halted him with her hand. "You'd better go now. My ride should be here any time now."

Roland paused, nodded, turned, and left her with her baggage.

* * *

Commander Tarin took the pot and poured himself and Major Rosmar a cup of tea. "I must admit, Isana, I will be glad when this is over. It has been a real drain."

"I agree, Commander. Once we arrive and are welcomed, I expect some celebrating will be in order."

Tarin nodded, "I imagine they already picked out a suitable planet for us, with a good income—at least for a while, as we settle into our new lives."

Isana sipped his tea thoughtfully. "Commander, what if they do not welcome us?"

"What do you mean? Why wouldn't they?"

"Well, we did not announce our intentions to them. What if they think we are scouting their border ahead of an invasion?"

"I have announced our intentions, but you have a point, which is why none of our weapons will be armed. I will show no indication of hiding. Once we are across the border, I will activate another distress call. They answered my first one. They will answer this one, too."

"Commander," the communication system interrupted the Commander's tea.

"Speaking."

"The source of the power surge did not originate aboard this ship. We found an alien device attached to the hull. It is of military-level design but been damaged to the point we cannot ascertain its function."

"Thank you, Lieutenant," Tarin replied, setting down his teacup. "I'm on my way."

* * *

"There are 413 inhabitable planets in the empire's area of influence that can sustain life for Roland. Since Miranda is of the same species, it is logical they would sustain her as well," Jackson announced.

Roland sat.

"Of those, 62 of them possess no official membership within the empire."

Roland sat.

"Sixteen of those 62 planets lack sufficient technology for space travel at this time, although they are aware of it."

Roland sat.

"Another twelve are not aware of space travel; and, contact with those planets is strictly controlled."

Roland sat.

"May I offer you a beverage, Roland? Perhaps a glass of dehydrated water?"

"What?" Roland asked, stirring from his bunk.

"Can I get you a glass of dehydrated water?"

Laughing, Roland declined the offer. "But, thank you for the humor."

"You are welcome, sir. It is nice to see you again."

"I've been right here for the past...twenty minutes."

"Your physical presence was noted, sir, but you were not engaging us here.

Your focus was on something unrelated to what I was presenting to you."

"I'm sorry, Jackson. What were you...presenting?"

"I had identified a number of potential planets to which you and Miranda could escape, with a better than average chance to remain undiscovered by anyone who would be looking for you. That would include both the Anadir military and Miranda's family."

"Very thoughtful of you, Jackson."

"Melanie has provided me with a list of characteristics you and Miranda would require, including access to employment, available technology, familiar culture, and the like. However, with our current restriction from 'bothering her', I am unable to identify any additional, more personal characteristics she would want present in any..."

"With our current situation, I am not even sure she should factor into your search. As you heard, I asked her to contact me when she was ready. However, the way she sent me away, I don't know if she will ever be ready."

"Then I will suspend further research until it is determined you require a quick relocation."

CHAPTER 42

Vardri cried in her vehicle. *I guess I can't get anything done. I can't see a project is being hijacked. I can't react to it until most of my access is gone. I can't get anyone to believe me when I tell them Tarin is stealing two prototype systems and taking them...somewhere. I can't even figure THAT out. And, now I can't stop crying.*

After sealing the package, she confirmed the address for the reporter and started driving, wiping tears as she drove.

Maybe this group will be more willing and capable to act on this. Since they aren't mainstream, they may not use the same bureaucracy.

She pulled into a visitor's spot. Approaching the door, she glanced at her reflection to make sure her recent crying episode had been sufficiently masked. Satisfied, she entered the building and asked to see someone who could make sure a story got published. The automated receptionist politely instructed her to wait and directed her to a sitting area.

They send me a junior editor. This is going to take a while. Time is one thing we lack.

Partway down the hall, tastefully decorated with simple artwork Vardri did not recognize, she stopped the junior editor. "Listen, miss, I do not mean to belittle your position, but the situation I am trying to alert people to is very time-sensitive. I need to speak with someone who does not need to report up three levels to see something she has approved see the light of day. I need to get this out so this man can be stopped, and then I need to go away. Now, who can you take me to?"

* * *

"Mister Daga, how good of you to call upon me. I trust everything went well," Abenor said, smiling at Kor Daga's image on his communication screen. He noted that his was the lone smile.

"I can assure you, Abenor, everything went very far from well. In fact, I have yet to hear from your transporter since I loaded my cargo aboard his ship."

Kor leaned closer to the video unit. "Do you know where he is?"

"I do not, Mister Daga," Abenor answered. "The last time I spoke with him was before I gave him your contact information. If he has failed you, it would be the first time in my experience where he failed to deliver something with anything other than the highest efficiency and discretion."

"Be that as it may, Abenor, since you vouched for him, I expect you to make restitution for my loss."

"I am not surprised," Abenor stated. "Mister Daga, I can appreciate the position this has placed you in. I have been there several times myself. I am surprised Reginald would be the cause, but I am not surprised this has happened. This is bound to happen to all of us at some time. It is in the nature of our business. Risks abound. Sometimes, those risks are realized, as in this case. I gave you a name and an assurance Reginald was the one I could trust with such a time-sensitive matter. You still assumed the risk that is inherent with selecting such a carrier. I owe you nothing."

"But, I would not have hired him if you…"

"I heard enough, Mister Daga. If you wish to file a charge against me, I can give you several contacts among various levels of law enforcement. I must warn you they will look more favorably at me than at you. But, that is yet another risk."

Kor leaned back from the video unit. "Well, it appears I will get no satisfaction from you."

"It not only appears so; it is a certainty."

"Then you leave me no choice but to extract my satisfaction from the culprit himself."

"I wish you better success than I ever experienced when attempting to locate Reginald."

Kor smiled for the first time. "I already tracked him to the area of the Anadir system. It seems he has had some mechanical issues."

"I did pay him with another new system. Perhaps it was not as compatible as I had hoped."

"Perhaps. In any case, my agents are already looking for him there. If he is no longer there, we will find out where he has gone. We will find him and reward him for his failure."

The screen went dark before Abenor could reply.

* * *

"Roland?"

"Yes, Melanie?"

"Commander Tuman is calling for you, again."

"I do not want to speak with him."

"He seems quite eager to speak with you, though."

"Well, he knows where I am. He can come here."

"He has. He is outside."

Roland sighed. *I'm sorry Miranda. I think I still need to see this through. Hopefully, you will look for me someday. I'm sure Anadir uses a small subset of prisons for Imperial prisoners.* He moved from his bunk to the cockpit chair. "Ok, Melanie, let him in."

"Mister Marcel, I don't know why you are being so resistant now after seeking my help in this matter. I have been trying to contact you for hours."

"I see. I'm sorry to hear that."

"You should be."

"Yes, I know. I have been preoccupied with another matter."

"I was hoping Miranda had started you working on identifying where Tarin might be taking his ship."

"Not yet. And she won't now."

"Why?"

"That is the other matter. She is gone. Her family found her, so she is hiding again."

"She can't blame me."

"She doesn't. *I* blame you. And I blame you because she blames me. Someone in your command is somehow affiliated with her family."

"I understand. Still, I cannot screen out soldiers and staff because of family squabbles. If I did, there would be no one to protect the planet, not to mention the empire."

Commander Tuman walked a few steps toward the galley, then turned back toward the cockpit. "Look, I am not comfortable asking a civilian for assistance, but you seem to possess the most current and accurate information about this defector. I could use your help."

Roland looked at the commander for a moment, before replying, "Alright, I'll see what I can find out."

Commander Tuman nodded briskly and left.

CHAPTER 43

Spectre's bass filled the cockpit. "I retrieved 82 percent of the files concerning the testing of the Model 153 Hyperdrive."

Roland asked, "What happened to the remainder?"

"System activity has overwritten the file storage area housing the remaining eighteen percent. Data retrieval was impossible from those locations. I apologize."

Commander Tuman's eyes jerked to the viewscreen. "You 'apologize?'"

"Yes, Commander Tuman, my skills are insufficient for retrieving some of the data necessary to recreate the downloaded data about which we are inquiring. I apologize."

"You are a computer."

"I am."

"You do what your programmer has instructed."

"Correct."

"So, it is your programmer who should apologize...for insufficient programming, right?"

"I must disagree with your assessment, sir."

"On what grounds?"

"While it is true my programmer, the pilot of this vessel did generate the original source code and defined my operating parameters, he is no longer responsible for the output generated by his code."

Tuman laughed, "Do you do your own programming now?"

"Yes."

Tuman stopped laughing. He turned and looked at Roland. He raised an eyebrow. Roland turned away. "I need to explain."

"I think you do."

"But not now. We have pressing business." *Besides, I still have no idea what happened.* He sat beside Miranda on his bunk.

"How's it going up there?" she whispered, nodding toward Tuman's back.

"Hmm? Oh, I guess we are progressing. Spectre had to salvage some deleted files. He could not get all of them. I hope he got enough to convince Commander Tuman."

"What's he doing now?"

"I think he is comparing the salvaged information to the data Melanie distilled from the original download. I hope this satisfies him. We are running out of time. If we don't pursue Tarin right away, he will be gone. If he is not gone already."

After what seemed like several quiet hours later, Commander Tuman rose from the cockpit chair. He called Roland over.

"Was Melanie helpful?"

"Yes, she was, Mister Marcel." He looked away and then back to Roland. "I agree. I will form an intercept force to retrieve our vessel. For that, I thank you. I must also, however, consider how you came by this information. You were right. It was illegal."

Roland stared at the console behind Tuman.

Tuman spoke, "I told you I would do what I can for you if your information warranted preferential treatment. It does. With that in mind, I request you join my expedition. You possess the most in-depth knowledge of this situation and its ramifications. My team will take a while to grasp what's going on."

"Commander, as you surmised, I don't work well under authority. I avoid the military and civilian authorities. It will not be easy. Perhaps I should remain here, with Miranda."

"You do have the option to remain here. However, I would dictate the circumstances under which you would remain."

Roland straightened, unintentionally imitating a soldier at attention. He then returned to his bunk and waited with Miranda.

"Well, I can't find anything here," bellowed Commander Tuman from Roland's cockpit chair.

"No luck?" inquired Roland, approaching.

"Nothing. Speculation. I've got nothing about why the ship was stolen."

Roland swept his eyes across the viewscreens, "What would his motivation be?"

"Profit? Revenge? Treason? Okay, the treason seems to be established. The question is, 'Why?'"

"Melanie," Roland said, standing, "Can you call up Tarin's military record?"

"Will do, Roland."

"Those are classified and restricted," Tuman objected.

"Where would you like them displayed, Roland?" Melanie asked.

Tuman sputtered.

Roland smirked, "Show them on center screen. Thank you, Melanie."

"You are welcome, Roland."

Roland, again.

"Commander, I promised to do this only if the situation warranted." The commander nodded, his face still red.

"Does the situation warrant an expedited request for this information?" The commander nodded again.

"So, I am honoring my promise to you, correct?" The commander paused, then nodded.

"Then, are you ready to get to work?"

The commander nodded once more and then turned the chair to face the center screen again.

Someday, I must commend him on his verbal skills. Roland turned and walked back to his storage hold. The remnants of Abenor's container still lay scattered across the floor. The system it had contained was set off to one side. It reminded him of better times. Times when he had a goal. Times when he was in control. Times when he knew what the hell he was doing.

CHAPTER 44

Roland wandered around the merchant district near the base. *If I were satisfied with shallow interactions, I would be in the best area to reach that satisfaction.* Proximity to military bases provided many establishments with eager patrons. The purveyors offered goods and services that would entice most of those patrons.

No, thanks. I am not interested in that type of interaction. Well, how is that different than all your other interactions? This is just geography. I mean, how well do I know Abenor? And, he is the closest thing to a friend that I know.

Roland turned to cross the street. He paused, watching men and women exchanging laughs and hugs as they walked toward their destinations.

I suppose I could consider Melanie a friend. Roland reached the other side of the street and contemplated his reflection in the window of another establishment. *I have treated her like she was a friend at times, but now she could become one. I suppose. She will need to play games at an artificially reduced skill level. She will correct every misquoted reference I ever make. But, she would always support me. She may not always agree with me, though.*

Roland stopped as he saw his ship again.

What if she doesn't like me?

He resumed his pace toward the *Stiletto.* He quickened his steps when he spotted a familiar person standing beside the access hatch. For no rational reason, he began to run. Smiling, Miranda walked a few steps toward Roland as he approached.

Roland stopped just short of running into Miranda. "I am surprised to see you here. Happy. But, surprised."

"I made it to the transit station, with everyone hurrying off toward somewhere. I felt tired of running. If she wants to find me, here I am. And here I'll stay."

She followed him inside and sat on his bunk. Roland went to the hold. *I guess I will never need to do those modifications to make this data system fit.*

"What's it do?"

Roland jumped a little. He had not heard Miranda's approach. "I don't know. He told me it was a data system, but he did not give me any details. It was advertised as a retrieval system, but he changed things on me. I was told it is the newer model—he said it was a prototype. But I had no time to install it before I ran into Bornor on the *Aradinda*."

"Hmm. Well, after this is all over, you'll have time to figure it out. I'll be busy setting up our ceremony."

"Ceremony?"

"You know—the wedding? You still want to, don't you?"

I don't want to deal with this right now, Miranda. "I think it would be best to see whether I will be in prison or not first."

"If you don't want to, say so."

Roland led her to the bunk and motioned for her to sit. He sat beside her.

"Look, it's not that I don't want to marry you. But, what you are proposing—pardon the pun—is new to me, and..."

"It's new to me, too, Roland."

"I understand. But I spent my whole life alone, even as a child. Now you are asking me to share everything with someone else. I enjoy you. I feel comfortable around you. This is something very strange for me to say. I never felt comfortable around anyone before. Right now, my situation is so uncertain, I hesitate to make plans. I'm afraid..."

"Afraid you'll get bored with me?"

"Not with you. With staying in one place. With being planet-side. With not flying.

With not living on the edge. With not being in control." He got up, walked back to the cargo hold, and closed the door.

As he returned to his bunk, Miranda gestured toward the cockpit and said, "Well, he seems kind of quiet."

"Hmm? Yeah, he does. I wonder if he found anything." He touched her on the shoulder as he passed. Walking up to the cockpit chair, he rested his hands on its back. "Found anything, yet?"

"It looks like Tarin had an unremarkable career to start. It continued until about two years ago."

Roland asked, "What happened two years ago?"

"He lost a ship."

"How does someone lose a ship?"

"It seems Tarin was a bridge officer aboard the *M.E.S. 455*," Tuman explained. "It's an exploration vessel. It was charting some areas along the border with the Athzembir. Of course, we did not know about the Athzembir then. We had not discovered them, yet."

"Or they had not revealed themselves to us."

"Also a possibility. Anyway, the 455 was charting that region of space."

"How exciting," Roland deadpanned, "Searching the vast, uncharted emptiness of space in the hopes they would find something unusual. I could hardly bear the thought of such stimulating work."

"Those are desirable positions. Unfortunately, not all of them are successful. Like this one."

"What happened?"

"The ship was destroyed."

"Destroyed? I thought you said it was lost."

"'Lost'—'destroyed'—it's all the same thing."

"This was a science vessel, right?"

"Correct."

"How does a science vessel get destroyed on an exploratory mission?"

"So far, I looked the summary information, not the details. Give me a moment." Commander Tuman scanned. "Hmmm, it doesn't say here. The ship became unstable and fell apart—rather abruptly."

"Then how did Tarin survive?"

"Good question." The commander scanned more paragraphs. "Okay. Here we are. It appears Tarin located a life pod and launched it. Another vessel, the *M.E.S. 373*, located him over a week later and brought him back.

"Fortunate for him," Roland commented. "I would think exploration ships would not be so close to each other."

"It does happen on occasion," Tuman replied, "But, you're right. It's not common."

"So, was there an inquiry?"

"Standard operating procedure. Any time a vessel sustains damage, or is destroyed, the survivors and witnesses are interrogated. Let's look at the results."

"'Interrogated?' That does not sound like an enjoyable situation. How thorough are you?" he asked. *I do own a personal stake in your response, considering what you know about me now.*

Without turning from the viewscreen, Tuman responded, "We are civilized, Mr. Marcel. We interrogate. We possess some technologies that enhance our abilities to determine false testimony, but they are humane and painless—for the most part."

Roland could not detect any hint of humor at Tuman's closing remark. He decided not to ask for clarification. *Chances are, I will find out.*

After Miranda and Tuman had both left, Roland returned to his cockpit chair and called up the data files again. *Alone again. I have missed this.*

Over and over, the results to his questions were the same. Roland thought of a definition he had read sometime in the past: an idiot is one who attempts the same maneuver, anticipating different results. *I wonder if I crossed the boundary between diligence and idiocy.*

He could find no personal information about Tarin from his time on Dorea. There were no records of his presence, save for those Vardri had recorded—the official and the unofficial. He looked everywhere—hotels, embassies, restaurants, clubs—it was as if Tarin was present as a spirit. The personal information he could find was limited to his home planet, where he was stationed. *Good parents, as far as the records indicated. I wonder if they were as neglectful as my own "good parents."*

He was well educated, though not a stellar student. He completed all the required instruction modules, as well as several optional ones—mostly math and science. He completed the officers' training regimen and worked through the ranks to his current position. Except for those directed toward the destruction of the *M.E.S. 455*, there were no derogatory reports about Tarin that Roland could find. *So, he does not seem to be a troublemaker.*

His military duty roster was normal. No suspicious activity was recorded during his shifts.

We will see what his finances look like, then. Melanie located two bank account sets in Tarin's name. Several banks also held accounts anonymously. *Those will take too much time. There might be financial irregularities exists in the normal accounts.*

He found none. His bank records indicated no large deposits. The regular deposits were all from his military payroll department. An occasional deposit showed up from a different source, but Melanie traced them back to gifts or sales of personal property. The cross-references to the sources indicated no suspicious ties. This theft did not seem to be part of a regular habit. *Great. A random event—try predicting that.*

Roland got up, rubbed his eyes, and walked to the back of the ship. *What am I missing? I can find nothing to indicate the purpose behind Tarin's behavior. It does not seem to be based on money. If it were mere economic gain, there should be a pattern of smaller thefts. I can find no such pattern.*

He stopped. He had an idea. "Melanie, could you connect with the planet-side system and actively communicate with me at the military headquarters?"

"I can do that, Roland. The system connection is already established. I would need to access their communications system. One moment." Roland would request Tuman gather the military investigators to discuss the data. Their specialized training may provide the necessary insight. Whatever was driving Tarin, it must be military in origin. It did not seem to be financial.

"Link established."

"Good. Contact Commander Tuman and request he assemble his investigative team to go over your information. Tell him," he continued, looking at his chronometer. "I will meet them in twenty minutes."

"Will do, Roland."

Roland, again.

* * *

Roland caught up with Commander Tuman. As they walked to the conference room where the rest of the team was waiting, Tuman was assuring Roland of the quality of the team he had put together. Locating missing persons was one of their duties. There had been crimes committed, both military and civilian, which this team had solved. Resources had been located and acquired, from within and without the established channels. Roland feigned interest in Tuman's gloating as he recycled the information he had been devouring that morning, no closer to an answer than he was the first time through.

Roland reviewed the files. These were the people on whom the security of the galaxy rested. The team was impressive. Averaging three years investigative service, their results spoke volumes of their talent. Roland still doubted their ability to achieve the results he hoped for. Tarin had been in the military for over two decades. He had the time to plan this out. He knew how the military mind worked. Still, maybe the sheer volume of brainpower would discover what Tarin had taken such pains to hide.

"Do you have anyone else?"

"Why would we need anyone else?"

"Oh, very well," Roland resigned himself to an empty chair. Tuman eyed him as he also sat.

Roland looked at Tuman. *I may warn him before I access the systems. No—this is more fun. My situation can use all the fun I can find.* "Let's get started, Melanie." He allowed himself a smile as he watched Tuman's eyes widen.

"Yes, Roland."

He shrugged at Tuman's scowl and scanned the room for signs of intelligence among the uniformed sheep.

CHAPTER 45

"I have no more faith in their abilities."

"Why do you say that?" Miranda asked.

"It's been two days, and they formulated zero hypotheses."

"Give them time. They'll find him."

"I don't think so."

"Why not?"

"Well, they are military minds. Trained by the military. They think like the military. They value what the military values."

"Sure, it's their training."

"Precisely. And why they will fail."

"Okay, now you've lost me."

"Well, Tarin is not palming a pack of gum. He is stealing a spaceship. And he is stealing it from the military."

"Yeah, 'and...'"

"Tarin was also trained in the military. He will know what they will be looking for. He will make sure they do not find it."

"Won't Melanie help with that?"

"She will, but she lacks experience. Even if her new capabilities allow for free thinking, Tarin has twenty years of experience she does not possess. She has not yet had to read people, so she is also at a disadvantage. Maybe Tuman has some connections with the civilian authorities, or even with some private citizens. We need someone who was not trained by the military and someone who has experience in dealing with people.

Someone who will ask the right questions."

"What kind of questions?"

"The kinds of questions Tuman would not think of. Questions leading to the one question of, 'Why?'"

The military seems fond of questions. Tarin's interrogation must have lasted for days, judging from the size of the transcripts. Melanie had condensed the information into related segments. They did like to repeat questions. All his answers were consistent. His engineers—Tarin was the Chief Engineer aboard the ship—had attempted to improve the performance of the ship's engines. The modifications had interfered with the fuel supply, causing a rupture in the fuel system, which had ignited. Tarin was the lone person who was able to reach a life pod in time.

* * *

As Roland and Miranda were making their way toward Miranda's apartment, Melanie weighed on his mind. Her new persona was disconcerting. *She is still growing, but at what pace? When will she outgrow her need for him? Had she already?*

Roland continued thinking about Melanie until he saw someone. The man seemed out of place. The way he walked was much less casual than Roland was used to seeing around here. They continued but did not turn toward Miranda's apartment. Instead, he led Miranda into one of the cafes. As she started to protest, he gave a quick shake of his head but said nothing. The other man stopped at another store, looking in the window.

Smelling the food being prepared in another room, Roland realized he was getting hungry. *No time now.* Instead, he ordered a hot chocolate, to go. Miranda did not order. He paid, and they walked out, turning back the way they came. The man turned from the window and fell in behind them, but several paces back.

Who is it? Roland asked himself. He ran through the checklist of people who had reason to follow him. *Surely Tuman did not send him to tail me. He has no reason for it. He knows how to contact me. He has the* Stiletto *secured and would know if I tried to leave. Is he sizing me up as a mark?*

Roland stopped. The man also stopped and seemed interested in a window display. "Wait here," Roland said as he turned. As he took his first step toward him, the man also turned, but he ran into the crowd.

Returning to Miranda, he realized another possibility. "Your family may be closer than we thought."

* * *

214

Roland walked down through the hallways, fatigued and disillusioned from his seemingly relentless pursuit of Tarin. This pursuit had proved humbling for him. *Why is he so different? I always found what I sought. Secure systems? No problem. I always got the technology and funds I needed. I found the back doors. I discovered the passwords. I uncovered the hidden. Why is he so different?*

Tarin was proving to be most problematic. On this planet, Roland was the most qualified person for finding what he could not find. Still, he felt like a normal-space drive in hyperspace—totally useless.

As he entered the command center, Roland looked at the chronometer embedded in the wall of the situation room. The displayed numbers mocked his sense of urgency, one second at a time. Roland looked around at the assemblage of investigators seated around the table. Some conversations continued, in spite of his disappointed gaze. Four hours. Four hours and they were no closer than when they started. As each opinion was presented, it clearly missed an obvious piece of information. Melanie was quick to point out the oversight.

Some took her correction well. Others did not. Tuman thought it best they were left unaware of Melanie's identity. Still, some men did not like being corrected by a "mere woman." Roland chuckled at the arrogance.

The humor of the situation had carried him a little. The magnitude of the situation interrupted his levity. The progress since Tuman and his team got involved was benefited Tarin and Tarin alone. After three days of investigation, nothing had been decided. *When would this pursuit occur? So far, we've been asking questions. Each has been asked before; some, several times.* For each offered move, Melanie brought up the defense from the data files. *I need to break this stalemate. The question is, "How?"* Roland pushed himself away from the table and paced around the investigators. He recognized the answers they were getting from the time he had asked the same questions. He shook his head.

He stopped and looked at Tuman. The best answer was often the most obvious.

* * *

"I hope you realize I had a good job lined up before I got dragged over here. Thank you very much. I did not think conscription was legal anymore." Bornor shook his head and glared.

"I apologize for the inconvenience, Bornor," Roland replied, sitting down in his chair "But the situation left me no choice."

"I admit," Bornor strolled across the room, smiling and shaking his head, "I was surprised when I walked in here and saw you."

Roland chuckled. "Yeah, I was hoping never to see you again, myself. However, things being as they are..." he shrugged in mock resignation.

"It doesn't let you off the hook. When this is over, Mr. Fischer," Bornor announced as he closed the distance to Roland's chair, "I will pick up right where I left off." *He doesn't need to know the progress I've already made.*

"I expect no less. Still, since I am now working with the military, rather than eluding them, I figured you could not do any more harm to me than they can. Maybe you will lose interest in me by the time I get out of military prison."

"Perhaps. Something of a higher priority might arise while I am waiting to testify for the prosecution, but, I will still do my job."

Roland nodded. "I know you will. In fact, let me make your job a little easier." He walked over to Bornor and extended his hand. "Roland Marcel, at your service."

It took several seconds for Bornor to clasp the proffered hand. "I will need to remember that name."

"Of that, I have no doubt."

Bornor turned away. "You know, I was pretty steamed about you breaking into the computer system on the *Aradinda*."

"I figured I had not earned any congratulations from you for it. Still, I had to get out of there before the ship docked."

Bornor stopped, then turned to face Roland again, "So why me? I wouldn't think you would want anything to do with me after our previous encounter."

"Ordinarily, it would be the case." Roland punched a few keys on the computer keyboard. As the data displayed on the viewscreen, he continued, "This situation, though, requires your assistance."

"In what way?" Bornor walked over to the desk and looked at the viewscreen. "Has Commander Tuman given you the high-level view of the situation?"

"He has."

Roland punched a couple of keys, and Tarin's picture filled the screen.

"Well, this Tarin fellow has not given us any clues about the reason behind his theft."

"Why would he?"

Bornor stepped back as Roland turned his chair to face him. "I figure he has talked to someone who is not on board his ship now; and, since you were able to find out so much about me is a very short timeframe, I thought you would be able to find out some information about him and determine his motivations. You can access resources and talents I cannot."

"That may be. But, the military must have thousands of investigators."

"True. And we have the best of them working on this project. But, since Tarin was in the military himself, and he took the time to set this up, I suspect he is familiar with their procedures and has hidden the kind of information these investigators would be relying on. So, I doubt their prospects of success—at least in the timeframe necessary to stop him. This situation is one requiring a different set of skills. You already proved your possession of those skills. We lack the time to find the right person out of thousands."

"Uh, thanks. I still don't see..."

"Look, I need your help. I would like to apologize for our previous encounter, but I would be lying to do so. For now, I need you to forget we ever met. I need you to track down Tarin's intention for this ship he has stolen. Can you do that? We can relive the *Aradinda* experience later."

Bornor stared at Roland. He walked back and forth in front of him, eyeing him as if Roland was some complicated puzzle to be solved. He stopped. "All right. What do we do?"

"I will give you access to the best computer in the galaxy, and *you* will use it to get a line on Tarin."

"Oh, you have access to the 'best computer in the galaxy'? On this planet? I don't think so."

"Oh, it was not here before. I brought it with me."

"You mean your ship? It seemed rather unremarkable when I was there last time."

"A couple of things changed since then."

"The 'best computer in the galaxy'?"

Are any other computers self-aware? No. I would have heard something. But, there may be other computers with larger processing capacities, or faster processing units, or any of a host of superior capabilities. Would it make them better than Melanie? I doubt it. "Yes, it is the best computer in the galaxy."

"This, I've got to see." With a grand gesture, he proclaimed, "Lead on." Giving Bornor a mock bow, he responded, "This way, sir."

CHAPTER 46

Roland ushered Bornor to the cockpit chair. "Do you have everything you need?"

"I don't know how to operate your ship's computer. I need see the improvements you made."

"No problem, Bornor," He said, smiling and standing. "Spectre?"

"Yes, Reg?"

"This is Bornor. He needs to track down some information. I need you to help him."

"Will do, Reg. Hi, Bornor. What do you need first?"

"Roland?"

"Yes, Melanie?"

"What will you be doing?"

"Trying to talk the commander into letting me go."

"He has already requested your presence in the intercept fleet. Why do you need to talk him into doing so, again?"

"No, no, Melanie," he laughed, "I need him to keep me out of jail."

"Oh. I will see you later, then."

"Yes, Melanie."

"Dual voices? Cute toy. That's your big improvement."

"Oh, no, Bornor. It's..."

"Allow me, Roland," Melanie interrupted.

"Sure, Melanie. Go ahead."

"Bornor, if you wish to proceed, with my assistance, do not ever refer to me as a 'toy.' I am so far beyond any computer system you ever dealt with. If you wish to insult me, you can leave and wait for the ramifications of my formidable capabilities." She paused for several seconds, enough for Bornor to glance at Roland in confusion. "Or we can proceed. Which would you prefer?"

"Was I threatened by your computer, Roland?"

"Yes, you were," Jackson piped in.

"Well, I guess so, then," Roland added. "I will explain later." *Once I figure it out for myself.*

Several hours passed without a word being spoken.

"He had help." Bornor announced. "He had to have help."

"What are you talking about? What kind of help?"

"There's no way he could survive on his own. Someone had to help him."

"Yes, he was rescued by the *M.E.S. 373...*"

"No, before then. For a single life pod to last as long as this one did, it would need to be recharged with breathable air. Pods aren't equipped with recyclers. According to the records, he was on his own for eight days. The pods are stocked with enough air for two—three, max. How could he last for eight?"

"According to his testimony, he had made some modifications to the life pod," Melanie offered. "Those modifications added recyclers and improved their efficiency by 300%. He was applying the same type of modification to the fuel system, but it failed catastrophically."

Roland asked, "What type of modification can be shared between an environmental control and a fuel system?"

"There are numerous efficiency improvements that can be applied to both systems. Shall I enumerate them?"

"Thank you, Melanie, but it will not be necessary. What modification did they find on the pod?"

"According to the captain of the *373*, they were unable to investigate the pod. It also failed catastrophically on the way to the base," Bornor responded. "Let me see. Here it is. It appears that the cargo hatch that held the pod experienced explosive decompression, and the pod was ejected into hyperspace."

"Hmmm. So, Tarin could tell the tribunal anything he wanted to, and there would be no evidence to contradict him."

"Wow, you are cynical, aren't you?"

Roland shrugged. "It has helped me in the past. Okay, assuming you are right, Bornor, how do you calculate eight days?"

"Well, according to the transcripts from the inquiry, the *455* stopped transmitting on 21 Epsilon. But, when the pod was rescued, it was 29 Epsilon. It means the ship was incapable of transmitting. But, if the vessel were still operable, why was just one life pod located?"

"Maybe no one else was alive."

"Doubtful. On a ship that size, the fuel system is typically limited to the aft section. The command section can be sealed fast enough so an aft explosion would not destroy the command center."

"Sabotage?"

"It makes more sense. As Chief Engineer, he would have the knowledge and the access. But, again the question is 'Why?'"

"Question noted, Bornor," Melanie said.

"Thank you, Melanie. If the ship was so severely damaged or destroyed at then, there is no way he survived so long in space without help, even with his modifications. Most improvements are incremental, so how did this one improve efficiency by a factor of three?"

"I doubt he could do that. None of my modifications have been able to make that kind of improvement," Roland agreed. "Besides, that kind of modification would need materials that are not standard issue, but the tribunal found no record of requests for non-standard items."

"But, why would he lie to the tribunal?" Roland asked Bornor, "The sole reason I can think of is that he wanted to keep the knowledge of an alien culture from becoming known. Do we know of any alien cultures in that region?"

"Athzembir. I haven't heard much about them, but if they rescued him initially, and if he felt he owed them for rescuing him, maybe he was trying to protect them or something."

"It's possible, but we never harmed an alien culture we encountered, have we?"

"No. None I am aware of."

"Still, it makes the Athzembir the most reasonable recipient of the stolen ship, doesn't it?"

"I think it does. Everything else is unsupported by any information we found.

Now we need to convince Commander Tuman," Roland said. "Melanie, where were we when we tagged Tarin's vessel?"

The viewscreen on the wall lit up with a galactic map. Melanie zoomed in until the Lachelax and Bantadam systems were both visible. A pulsing, red circle was displayed about one-third of the way between the systems. "We intercepted the *M.T.S. 1822-G* approximately here."

Roland looked for a moment, then said, "Add the Dorea system, please."

"Very well, Roland." The map zoomed out until the Dorea system appeared at the bottom of the viewscreen.

"Okay, now plot the course they were on until the intersect point." Roland watched a yellow line appear from Dorea to the red circle. "Good. Now continue the course until you reach the boundary of the empire."

The map zoomed out and continued zooming out until the yellow line was a few centimeters in length. The yellow was then attached to an orange line that extended upward until it intersected with a gray boundary at the top of the viewscreen.

"Now, add the site of the *M.E.S. 455* accident." Roland saw the map zoom out again, and the yellow and orange lines move to the left-hand edge of the viewscreen. "It's not right," he said, looking at the orange circle pulsing near the top right-hand corner.

"No, the accident site is nowhere near the projected trajectory," Bornor added. "Still, it's the most feasible rendezvous point, if he is taking the ship to the Athzembir."

"I agree, but I think we will need to cover more territory. If we concentrate on the accident site, Tarin might exit somewhere *en route*, then jump again before we can close on him. I think we need to set up a perimeter, so we can close regardless of where he exits. But we need to do it on our side of the border."

"Yes," Bornor said, "But, how large an area?"

"Melanie," Roland asked.

"Yes, Roland?"

"From the stated performance ratings we found regarding the Model 153, calculate the distance Tarin's ship could travel from the point of our separation."

"Had the ship performed within the stated performance levels, it would exit between here and here," Melanie said, displaying two blue circles a couple of centimeters apart.

Well, it's not an exact science, after all, I guess.

"Now, calculate a new trajectory from both points to the *M.E.S. 455* accident site."

The viewscreen now displayed two blue lines intersecting at the pulsing orange circle. Roland surveyed the new course and said, "Okay. Calculate the hyperspace jumps between the origin of the new course and the accident site. Let's start with the earliest course point. How many jumps would be required?"

"Between three-point-two-seven and three-point-four-five."

"I think we should concentrate on the third exit point. Do you agree, Bornor?"

"I agree, Roland. Do the calculations include the normal space acceleration?"

"Of course they do, Bornor. I factored in all operating sequences in these calculations."

"Sorry, Melanie, I meant no offense."

"Understood."

"Melanie," Roland said, "Please display the exit points from the earliest anticipated course change. Make the possible range the diameter of a circle."

"Very well, Roland."

Roland, again. He watched three blue circles, each one doubled the diameter of its predecessor.

"Good, Melanie. Now do the same for the latest projected course change."

Three more blue circles appeared, lighter in shade than the first series. The last and largest covered the accident site and overlapped the original blue circle by over fifty percent.

"Melanie?"

"Yes, Roland?"

"Overlay both of the displayed circles at the accident site with a third circle with the diameter equal to the greatest distance between two points within the original circles."

"Should I assume you want the desired two points to be included in the circle?"

"Yes, include those two points in the circle." A white circle appeared over the two blue, smaller circles. "Now, calculate the center point of the new circle."

Two lines appeared, intersecting each other at ninety degrees. "'X' marks the spot, Mr. Marcel," Bornor noted.

"Yes, it does. Melanie, calculate and print the coordinates of the center point. What is the diameter of the circle?"

"Zero-point-zero-zero-zero-zero-two-three-five-five parsecs."

"Seventy-two and two-thirds billion kilometers in diameter? And that is just for two dimensions. Let's see. About one hundred and sixty-six billion cubic kilometers. I think it will be difficult for Commander Tuman to cover so much territory," Roland said.

"He'll need to, though. He must establish a perimeter that includes all potential exit points," Bornor agreed. "Besides, we cover our half of the sphere, and we keep him on our side of the border, right?"

"Right, and our intercept force will be at the center. It will guarantee a fast response time. Hopefully, it will be fast enough."

CHAPTER 47

"Okay, Mr. Marcel, what do we know?" Bornor rose from his chair and paced.

Roland had already been pacing. His tea was half empty. "Right. Fact: Commander Tarin was assigned as a senior officer to the *M.E.S. 455*." He paused to take in the aroma of the Anadiran tea.

"Correct."

"Fact: The *M.E.S. 455* was destroyed."

"Correct."

"Fact:," Roland stopped a sip of tea, "The destruction of the *M.E.S. 455* was the result of an experimental modification to the fuel system by the engineering crew."

"Correct. But, according to the engineering log they recovered from the life pod, as well as the investigation transcripts, the engineering crew received authorization from Commander Tarin."

"Right. But, the authorization was not recorded in the command log."

"Correct. Why not?"

"Later. Melanie, note the question."

"Noted, Roland."

"Thanks, Melanie. All right, then. Fact: Commander Tarin jettisoned himself in a life pod, which had a reasonable expectation of three days life support."

"Correct," Bornor stopped and faced Roland's direction, "But the *M.E.S. 373* did not retrieve the life pod until eight days had passed."

"Right, because the life pod's chronometer started when it was jettisoned," Roland responded, facing Bornor, "It's time was based on the *455's* chronometer."

"Correct," Bornor said, resuming his pacing. "So, he was able to survive for five additional days, with no inhabitable planet from which to receive assistance within range."

"True," Roland said as he turned, "But, even if there had been a planet-fall, the life pod could not escape the planet. And the *373* located the life pod in the trajectory the life pod would take after Tarin jettisoned it from the *455.* So, he could not have found a planet anywhere near the wreck."

"No, it would seem impossible."

"Speculation: Tarin received assistance from the Athzembir, without interfering with his trajectory."

"I doubt it. However, he could receive Athzembir assistance, and then they could place him back in the correct trajectory when the *373* was close enough to locate the life pod."

Roland stopped. "It makes sense. But how did these 'Good Samaritans' avoid detection? Surely, they would have been detected before the life pod."

"Granted. Unless they possess technology that includes either more sensitive sensors, or more sophisticated stealth."

"It is possible."

"Okay. Okay," Bornor stated, shaking his head, setting his tea down on a tray. "Let's get back to what we do know," he faced Roland. "Tarin survived for five days, perhaps with some assistance from the Athzembir, until he was picked up by the *373.*"

"Right. Then he is interrogated, humanely according to Commander Tuman. Tarin admits an experiment he authorized went wrong, and the ship was destroyed."

"Yes, he confesses because the ship's log, including the engineering experiment, had been downloaded automatically into the life pod as part of the jettison procedure. Then the *373* uploaded the log before the pod was lost." Bornor stopped and flung his arms wide, "He couldn't hide his responsibility."

"Right," Roland replied, gesturing with an empty teacup, "But, although they did not strip him of rank, they did not acknowledge his efforts." *Does it sound familiar, Commander Tuman?* "Still, he volunteered for another assignment in the same sector, and they gave it to him."

"Sure, it was a diplomatic mission after first contact was established."

Roland set his cup and saucer in the galley. "Fact: During this trip, Tarin made six unofficial visits to Athzembir dignitaries, without escort. In addition, he made nine official visits, accompanied by other members of the diplomatic corps."

"Correct, but his personal log mentions the official visits. The fact he was under surveillance revealed the unofficial visits. So, when he returns, he is assigned to the supply fleet. They want to keep him closer to home."

Roland cut notches into the air, "He worked his way up through supply, until he accessed a transport vessel. Then he secured an assignment as a tester, overseeing the Model 153 hyperdrive installation project."

"Whoa, there." Bornor points both palms at Roland. "How does he get from supply to testing? Quite the jump, don't you think?"

"Actually, Bornor," Melanie interjected, "His service record does indicate a logical progression. He received numerous citations for innovative designs and processes which streamlined the areas under his command. It makes sense he would test those changes in other areas, and then to begin testing other changes."

"Hmmm, I don't understand the military chain of command well," Roland replied. *Hopefully, I won't be around long enough to get comfortable with it.* "I will assume he was able to make the change without too much suspicion. Still, they never give him his own command. That must hurt. With all his innovations, I would think his goal would be to command a vessel. They do not offer him one." *And all I want is to get back to piloting my own ship.*

Bornor didn't speak for a moment. "Okay, I'll buy it, for now. So, he lands this hyperdrive test on a transport ship. The guy overseeing the design joins in with him, for whatever reason, and they steal the ship. Tarin orders the civilians connected with the project to be killed and all of the files destroyed, but you download the data first, and two of the principals in the project manage to escape."

"Right. Melanie, how much time has elapsed since we left Dorea?"

"Four weeks, three days, nineteen hours, forty-one minutes."

Has it been so long?

"Did you get all of that, Melanie?" Roland looked at Bornor's quizzical expression and smiled.

"Yes, Roland."

"Does the evidence support our speculations?"

"I can find no evidence to contradict your assumptions or speculations."

"Great. Distill the pertinent evidence, according to the timeline we laid out, including the speculations as they address the gaps in the evidence, and contact Commander Tuman. Let him know we are on our way to his office." He bowed to Bornor, sweeping his arm toward the door, "Shall we?"

"I think we got him," Roland shouted as he and Bornor entered the office.

Commander Tuman looked up from his computer screen. "Whom do you have?"

"Tarin. We believe we know where he is going. Now we must catch him."

"Are you sure?" Tuman asked, rising from his chair.

"Reasonably. It corresponds with the data," Melanie announced through Tuman's computer.

"Get out of there," the commander fumed.

"Melanie, we will take it from here."

"Very well, Roland."

His face returning to a more natural color, Commander Tuman said, "Very well, then, lay it out for me."

Roland nodded to Bornor, who smirked in response, "Thank you, Mr. Marcel," he said with a mocking bow.

Roland left him laying the documents from Melanie's distillation on Tuman's desk, spreading them out in front of the commander. "We know this information. The rest is conjecture, but I believe it is logical."

"Military strategy includes speculation and conjecture. Let's get on with it."

Well, I already went through this once. Roland left Bornor and Tuman to discuss the data and escaped the office.

Roland wandered around the city for a while. He had nothing to do. *Bornor will convince Tuman of the danger. Tuman will put together an interception fleet. Since the research is now completed, I am not needed at this time. One of them will contact me if the situation changes.*

Roland still could not leave. *How long will it last? I could return to the* Stiletto, *but I doubt I could fly her right now. Tuman would take measures*

228

to secure the Stiletto *to the planet's surface.*

I could go and talk with Melanie. What could I say? "How's life?" Melanie is not the same Melanie I knew. I am not the same Roland as before, either. What if the new Melanie does not like the new me? And if I cannot fly the Stiletto, *how long will it be before I am back in space? Will I be in space just long enough to help Tuman apprehend Tarin?*

I wish I had better control of the situation. In the Stiletto, *I always knew what was happening. I knew where I was headed. I knew why. Now, I don't even know what's going to happen when this is over. I hate waiting for other people to direct me. When will I be in control of my own life again? When will I feel useful again?*

CHAPTER 48

"Well then, we'd better get after him. He's already had a month. This may be a futile chase, but we must try." Commander Tuman activated his communications panel and started issuing orders.

Roland, back from his brief respite, caught Bornor's eye. They looked back and forth between each other and the commander. After a few minutes of barking orders to several subordinates, none of which Roland understood, the commander looked at Roland. "You two can go for now. Someone will contact you when you are required. Thank you." He returned to his subordinates. Bornor shrugged and walked out of Tuman's office. Roland followed.

"One moment, Mr. Marcel," the commander said. Roland stopped and turned.

"Is there anything you want to add to Mr. Zemadin's report?" Tuman asked.

Should I tell him about RECON? Will it make any difference? I doubt it. Maybe I can hold one ace in this game.

"Nothing comes to mind, sir."

"Very well," the commander said, returning to his communications panel.

"I guess our importance has diminished now," Roland muttered to Bornor, after joining him in the hallway.

"It looks that way, doesn't it? He's in his element now. He is now the military commanding officer. We're civilians."

Roland nodded and continued down the hall toward the outside. He had returned to be dismissed. *Civilian.*

* * *

"I wonder if Tarin was aware of their sensor technology." Bornor spoke after several minutes of stillness and silence. Miranda was in the kitchen, cooking something Roland had never heard of before. She had told them she wanted to introduce the men to the local food.

Roland was sitting in the living room, drink in hand. "Why is it an issue?" He imagined a galactic ant farm, with uniformed workers marching in endless lines.

Bornor stopped and leaned toward Roland a little. "Let's speculate Tarin wanted to level out the playing field...to give the Athzembir a little push toward equality. He may not know they already have an edge." He backed away and started pacing, becoming more animated as he spoke. "Instead of balancing things out, he will tip the scales—against us. Giving this engine to the Athzembir will shift the balance to their favor. If they decide that we are a threat to them, this will open an opportunity for them to pre-emptively stop that threat. With the files and personnel familiar with the technology gone, it could take years for us to catch up. This gives them a long time to stop us from catching up at all. They will possess both superior mobility and intelligence. We would be much more balanced if we kept the hyperdrive and they kept their sensors."

"I see. But what if he *is* aware of their sensors?"

"Well, then he is after conquest, not balance." Bornor paused, "If that is the case, we had better start learning the Athzembir language."

Roland took a deep drink, still working on the puzzle. "What would he want with conquest? Over his own people?"

"My guess is he feels betrayed by our side."

"But how could he feel betrayed? He screwed up, endangered his ship, got a thousand crewmembers killed. If you ask me, he got off easy."

"I'm with you there. This is speculation, but he still might think of himself as a victim here."

"It's insane." Roland stood.

"Hey, don't kill the messenger. Like I said, I'm guessing. Tarin has not been forthcoming."

Miranda returned with a tray of bright vegetables surrounding some kind of small animal. She set it on the table, beside a bowl with some sauce. Roland thought he detected the familiar aroma of chicken.

"It's understandable if he feels he owes them," Bornor continued, pulling a chair out for Miranda.

"Why would he owe them anything?" Roland asked, taking his chair.

"Well, if the Athzembir had not found him, he would have died. It does lend itself to some expression of gratitude."

"Treason?"

Miranda shrugged, "It's happened before, I'm sure."

Roland decided, whatever it was, the animal did taste like chicken.

After cleaning up the remnants of the meal, they returned to the *Stiletto*.

"Okay, let us give Tarin the benefit of the doubt," Bornor stated. Turning from the cargo hold door, he carried his drink back to Roland's bunk. Sitting beside Miranda, who was sipping her own drink, he added, "He is out there in space. He is isolated from everything. He has no hope of survival. His life support is dwindling, he has no food or water. He has no hope. Then..."

"This alien vessel pops up out of nowhere and pulls him in," Roland continued Bornor's thought from the cockpit chair. "They feed him and let him stay aboard. Then, when they detect one of his own ships..."

Bornor took over, "They drop him off, so they pick up his distress signal, and he is rescued. And because of their advanced sensors, they are still far enough away, so our ship does not detect the Athzembir ship."

"Right," Roland agreed. "Then, once the situation has been investigated and he is reprimanded, he is eager to thank them for the rescue, and they ask him for a more tangible expression of his gratitude."

"So, they meet with him, unofficially, and give him a mission. They sell him on the idea they need this new engine so the empire will not overwhelm them." Bornor paced in front of the window as he spoke. "He feels obligated to comply with their request, since he already has hard feelings toward his own military."

"If I were in his shoes, how would I respond to such an offer?" Roland wondered.

"What kind of offer?" asked Miranda.

"Well, if the appeal to his gratitude did not sway Tarin, what if they offered him something more?"

"Like what?"

"Oh, money, power, a chance to live somewhere he would be appreciated. I don't know."

"He could feel let down, even betrayed. It would make sense such an offer might appeal to him," Bornor observed. "Still, it is a bit of a stretch."

"So, what did Radam Nortolis have to do with this?" Roland asked. "Melanie, contact the Bantadam communications system. See if Radam made any communications to Tarin."

"Say, 'Please.'"

"What?"

"Proper etiquette requires you to request my assistance with a 'Please.'"

I don't have time for this. One of these days, Melanie might learn etiquette can be bypassed in some instances. Sure, she will understand. And I will be long dead by then. "Very well. Melanie, please contact the Bantadam communications system and check for contacts between Dr. Radam Nortolis and Tarin."

"I would be happy to, Roland."

"Thank you, Melanie."

"You are very welcome, Roland."

Roland, again.

"So, Tarin had to get the information about the hyperdrive prototype completion, then go the Dorea to get it installed." Roland mused, returning to the task at hand.

"Right," agreed Bornor. "Then, after the drive is installed, he wipes out all evidence of its existence."

"But, not before I got to it."

"Yeah, lucky you."

"But he does not know how the engine is designed to work, so he brings Dr. Nortolis along to check it out," Roland continued, ignoring Bornor's comment.

"Then you happen to land on the ship," Bornor mocked.

Roland pointed sharply at Bornor. "Most of it was your fault. If you had left me alone, I never would be in such a position."

"Fine. Now it's all my fault." Bornor could not keep the smile off for long.

"Seriously, though," Roland said, stifling a chuckle himself, "Things went downhill from there. I found out about the drive, but it was too late. I got sheared off before I could correct my position."

"Correct it? How?"

"I was uploading an update to the data file with the ship's coordinates. I was trying to build a box around the *Stiletto* before they went into hyperspace. But I was not fast enough."

"The upload was interrupted?"

"Yeah."

"I assume Tarin has no family," Miranda offered.

"No," answered Roland, "His wife left him after he lost his ship."

"It would be hard to take, if he took it as he did," Bornor observed. "Children?"

"Grown."

"Friends?"

"Hard to say. He has not been on the attendance list of any weddings or significant parties in the last five years."

"Unpopular even before the accident," Miranda observed.

"So it seems," Bornor agreed.

"It would make it easier to accept whatever proposition they made him. No ties here. No good relationships," Roland concluded.

"Tempting, isn't it?" Bornor surmised, walking to the cockpit and looking out of the window. He spread his arms out toward the sky. "To go somewhere he was wanted, rather than where he had been embarrassed. And all it would take was a ship."

"And turning your back on all of your prior convictions."

"Mr. Marcel, please report to Commander Tuman's office for a briefing."

Roland jumped at the unfamiliar voice in his cockpit. "Melanie?"

"Yes, Roland?"

"Who was that?"

"Commander Tuman's assistant. Since the request for direct communication came from the commander's office, I let it through."

"Okay. I understand. Let him know I am on my way."

"Roger that, sir."

Should have said, "Please".

Roland stood and extended his hand to Bornor. "This is where we part company for a while."

"Yes, Roland. Commander Tuman said that I would be free to resume my civilian activities once you were satisfied that we had a viable target location." Bornor accepted Roland's hand. "Remember, I still have a job to do, but I must admit that it has not been too distasteful working with you on this. I wish you success in the chase."

"I agree. It has been a surprising pleasure for me. But I must wish you failure in yours."

Bornor laughed. "Fair enough. Goodbye, Miranda. Perhaps we will speak again under better circumstances."

"Goodbye, Bornor. Take care of yourself."

After watching his adversary exit the *Stiletto*, Roland turned to Miranda, "Well, I had better go."

"Yeah, and I was just getting to know you."

"I will be back. Soon, I hope.

"Melanie?"

"Yes, Roland?"

"Please give Miranda access to my personal information. Answer any questions she has concerning me. Treat her like you would treat me."

"Will do, Roland."

"When I get back, you will know more about me than anyone else in the galaxy. And, maybe more than you wanted to."

CHAPTER 49

Arriving at Tuman's office, Roland sat down facing the desk. The commander was busy completing some series of forms or requisitions or something, being interrupted by his communication panel. Waiting for him to finish, Roland scanned the office. He saw nothing new. His eyes returned to the commander. Mobilization, supply, logistics. The words he detected from the commander's side of the conversations were few. They were scattered throughout a sea of acronyms, unit identifiers, ship names, and jargon.

Whatever happened to the "noun, verb, object" in communication? Roland proceeded to nod off. The sea of indecipherable syllables failed to hold his attention. Then he heard the name, Emari Antiarus. Roland had requested him. He had been summoned. Now, he had arrived, it seemed. With a small smile, Roland closed his eyes again.

Roland snapped awake with the slamming of the desk drawer. The commander returned to his viewscreen. "He is here and will be joining us. You have your reasons, though I cannot think of a good one for a technician who is still in training, especially on this mission."

"He detected my approach on a ship. No one else ever had before. Perhaps it will not benefit us at all, but I think that kind of intuition may be valuable."

"It means extra supplies and space a soldier could otherwise occupy. The reason I am taking you is because of your information on the ship's drive unit."

"And my ship?"

"It will be docked here. It would do me no good to request your computer to stay out of my computer while we're gone, would it?"

"Melanie will access your system solely out of necessity."

"That's what I was afraid of, but it will do...for now."

After closing the last display on his screen, Tuman stood up and walked toward the door. Without turning, he spoke, "Pack light and be back here, and ready to go, in two hours. We will leave then."

Roland was left sitting in Tuman's office. *He told me not to salute him because I am not a soldier, but it sounded like he gave me an order.*

* * *

Roland crawled out of Miranda's bed. He rubbed his eyes and looked out. Her lamp was on in the living room. He walked out into the room on his way to the kitchen.

"Good morning, sleepyhead," Miranda was smiling over the top of her book. The city lights indicated it was well past sunset.

"How long did I sleep?"

"An hour or so, I guess."

"And you were reading the whole time?"

"Sure. It's a good book."

"It must be," he responded, entering the kitchen. "Do you want something to drink?"

"Thanks, but I'm fine for the moment."

"Okay. I think I will need a drink before I leave."

"When will you leave?"

"I was not given an exact timeframe. Tuman told me to..." Roland paused, considering. "I think his words were, 'Pack light and be back here, and ready to go, in two hours.'" He shrugged, "He sounds a bit melodramatic if you ask me." He got up and mimicked a gunfighter sauntering out to meet an opponent in the street. He sneered, "You better be out of here before sundown."

Miranda's laughter brought a smile back to Roland's face. He relaxed his posture and returned to pouring his drink.

"You know, Roland, I like Melanie. I think it's neat the way she is growing."

Roland answered from the kitchen, "Yeah? So, you and she are having 'girl talks'?"

"Something like that," she answered as Roland walked in with a cold drink. "I went over there while you were talking to Commander Tuman. I didn't feel like coming back here."

"No problem, Miranda. I like her, too. But I still am a little scared about her."

"You'll get used to her. I think you will grow to appreciate her," she pronounced with an impish grin.

Roland smiled as he took a sip of his drink. *I wonder.*

* * *

The fleet seemed to be assembled. It consisted of small ships, as far as Roland could tell. The idea was to surround Tarin when he came out of hyperspace. With a transport ship, Tarin would possess limited armament, so lighter ships could handle the assignment.

The faster ships would be better equipped to circle him at his exit point, keeping him pinned while the larger ships closed in for the capture.

The shuttle pilot docked with the largest vessel—Tuman's flagship—the *Olinath*. Roland grabbed his bag and paced the length of the shuttle as the landing bay was pressurized and the entryway extended.

Tuman was on the bridge, so a subordinate showed Roland to his quarters. The green walls had a certain gray overtone. "I guess I had better get used to small spaces of drab color," he remarked as he set his bag on the bed. "At least I do not need to share. It is hardly big enough for me." He opened his bag and started putting things away in the few available drawers.

The small desk had a monitor, so Roland sat down and called up the data file that had been the focus of his life for the past several days.

He went over the same information he had gone over scores of times before, hoping to find something new. He failed. By the time his frustration prevented further investigation, the *Olinath* had entered hyperspace. The frontier for which they headed, bordering the Athzembir domain, required six jumps. Each would take approximately six hours, and some change. Roland returned to the viewscreen. "Melanie?"

Roland was puzzled by the lack of response for a moment before understanding the standing order for her to stay out of the military systems without need. Roland contacted the communications officer.

"Yes, sir?" the voice responded from the speaker.

"This is Roland Marcel," he said, "I am a civilian advisor to Commander Tuman." *A little name-dropping might be helpful here.* "I need to establish a connection with my ship on Anadir. How do I do that?"

"You don't, sir," was the curt reply. Evidently, the name-dropping was not helpful. Roland paused, considering an appropriate response for this situation, considering his personal freedom hinged upon the relationship between himself and the military with which he was communicating. Before he found a response, the voice intruded upon his thoughts. "*I* do that. One moment, please."

"Thank you."

"Mr. Marcel, you have an incoming communication. Shall I patch it through to your quarters?"

Thank you, Melanie. "Yes, it will be fine," he said, taking his seat at the screen.

"Mister Fischer, how glad I am to see you again." Kor Daga's face held a smile. The smile displayed no friendliness.

Roland hoped his surprise did not register on his face. "Kor, forgive me for not contacting you, but..."

"Yes, I understand the delay," he interrupted with an absent wave.

"You do?" Roland queried.

"Yes, it has been explained to me."

Roland searched for an explanation. Finding none available, he turned his attention back to Kor.

"Please accept my apology for not delivering your cargo. It is the first time..." He watched a woman's hand deliver a small cup of some hot beverage. Kor turned to accept.

"Thank you, dear." He turned back to Roland.

Roland found his explanation in the familiar pattern of Kor's chair.

"Leave her out of this!" Roland exclaimed, jumping out of his own chair. The chair, in turn, tumbled onto its back and slid a couple feet behind him. "It does not concern her."

"Mr. Fischer, I am surprised you would leap to such a conclusion. I am merely..."

Roland was not impressed with Kor's demeanor. "You are not 'merely' doing anything. I know your people are looking for me. I am willing to square things with you, once..."

"Oh, you are willing to 'square things' with me?" Kor closed in on the screen. His voice became perceptibly edged, "You have no idea what it would cost you to 'square things' with me."

Careful, now. Do not give him a reason to take it out on Miranda. "Look, Kor, I understand you lost a sum of money..."

"Money. Do you think this is about the money?" he interrupted, his face becoming a dangerous shade of crimson. He paused and sat back, picking up his cup and taking a long drink from it. Setting the cup down, he turned to Roland. "Mr. Fischer," he began again, with a much calmer expression, "I wish it were the money. Unfortunately, the scope of your transgression far exceeds mere money. Your failure to deliver according to our agreement has cost me extensively. The new market I was attempting to enter does not tolerate failure."

Unwilling to endure Kor's gaze for the moment, Roland turned and retrieved his chair. *He called me "Mr. Fischer." At least she has not given him my real name. Thanks, Miranda.*

Kor continued, "Now, I see little chance to expand my enterprise in that direction." he set his cup down and leaned toward the screen. "So, you see, I lost untold quantities of opportunities. All thanks to you," he emphasized the last with his arms outstretched toward the screen.

Roland sat, considering the direction of Kor's soliloquy.

Kor did not let him consider very long. "So, I understand you will be away for a little while. I am surprised at the company you chose to keep, but it is not truly my concern. While you are gone, I shall retain your vessel as security. Your friend, Miranda, has assured me she can gain entry in your absence. So, she will accompany me to Lachelax, where I will await your return," he ended with another sip from his cup.

Roland had no response. *That arrogant land worm is going to take the* Stiletto. *And I can't stop him. But Melanie can keep him out, despite Miranda. But what danger would it put Miranda in? Can I take the risk?*

Roland nodded, and the screen went dark before returning the data file. *No, I can't.*

CHAPTER 50

I should be asleep by now. Hyperspace has no enticement for me.

Besides, I have no window in my quarters anyway. So, why can't I sleep? Miranda will be fine, I hope. Melanie will take good care of her. Unless she changes her mind. We will catch Tarin. Unless he has already escaped across the boundary.

Three jumps down. Three to go. And I haven't slept through any of them. I suppose I could try to find some medicinal help. Let me call the communication technician.

Roland watched his viewscreen. The *Olinath* had exited hyperspace and was coming to a halt. He watched as the rest of the fleet formed a perimeter between Tarin's anticipated exit point and the Athzembir border. Roland got up and paced around the room. He looked at the viewscreen after each turn. *What can I do from here? Kor Daga has Miranda and Melanie, and Tarin could drop in at any moment.* He continued to pace. *I'm certain Commander Tuman does not want me around until Tarin appears, but he'll need me then. So, I must deal with Kor before it happens.* He stopped pacing. *But how? What can I do from here?*

The *MTS 1741-A* was not displaying on the long-range sensors. There was no sign of the transport. *He has to be coming here.* The fleet was as far out in the galaxy as they could without crossing the recognized boundary with the Athzembir. They would not cross the boundary. The perimeter was already pressed up against it.

I calculated the exit point as well as I could. It's all theoretical, though. What if I'm wrong? I have no test data on the drive. I have theoretical projections assuming he would take the most direct route. Why wouldn't he? His own records showed that this was no combat or recon mission. The straightest route would be the fastest and most efficient route. Based on those projections, this is the most feasible hyperspace exit point. Now the fleet is between his projected exit point and the Athzembir boundary.

The long-range sensors were directed toward Dorea; the short-range sensors were toward the Athzembir boundary. Neither showed any vessels outside Tuman's fleet. *If Tarin is headed this way, no one is waiting to welcome him. Just to take him back.*

In all his travels, Roland had never witnessed a ship exiting hyperspace.

He had participated, being a passenger aboard the vessel. This was his first look from normal space. From a visual perspective, watching the ship emerge was disappointing. But he almost screamed when he saw that the emerging ship was the *MTS 1741-A.*

The seal between normal space and hyperspace had not yet closed behind the *MTS 1741-A* when Roland felt the *Olinath* move to intercept. The *Olinath* did not stop again until it was well within the minimum distance for engaging a hyperdrive. *Of course, assuming this is a normal hyperdrive, which it is not. I hope it's still close enough.*

"I was afraid we were too late," Roland said to the otherwise empty room. Noticing the orange flashing around the viewscreen, Roland shot from his chair and toward the door. *I must get out of here before they lock down. Orange alert warns me to stay in my quarters. Red alert forces me to do so.*

He slapped the panel and smiled as the door slid open. Stepping into the hallway, he scanned both directions for other military personnel. Seeing none, he started toward the bridge. *Now that Tarin is here, Melanie and I need to stay on top of Tuman's tactics. I can't waste time going through a communications technician each time Tarin does something.*

He took a right turn and ran into a uniform. *Damn.*

"You need to return to your quarters, sir," the uniform's female voice instructed, "No civilians are allowed in the corridors at this time."

"But, I need to help Commander Tuman, I am..." Roland countered.

"I'm sorry, sir, but there are no exceptions. You must return to your quarters now, sir."

Get past her.

"Look, Ms...."

"My name does not matter. You must return. We are at Orange alert. It means all civilian personnel should return to their quarters. That means you."

"Very well, Ensign. I will return to my quarters now," he said, turning back. "Thank you, sir."

Roland made a wrong turn and sprinted his way to the bridge.

CHAPTER 51

Roland saw the commander standing at the fore window. The military transport took up one-quarter of the viewing area.

"Commander, I suggest..."

"What are you doing here, Mr. Marcel?" Tuman said, without turning from the screen. "We are going to red alert. You need to return to your quarters."

"Yes, sir. I realize, but I thought you might need my assistance here, in case Tarin tries to escape."

"Security! Escort Mr. Marcel back to his quarters, lock it down. Cut the outbound communications from his quarters." Commander Tuman walked up to Roland, "Mr. Marcel, I do not want you to interfere with this operation again. If something occurs that requires your attention, I will send for you. As of this moment, you are under arrest. You will remain in your quarters until I say otherwise, *if* I say otherwise. Am I understood?"

"Understood, commander." *I hope he knows what he's doing.*

Four hours. Roland watched his viewscreen. Tarin had made no move. *I have been here for four hours, and he hasn't moved.*

"What are you doing, Tarin?" he said to the screen. "What are you waiting on?"

At least we got here ahead of him. But, I wonder what he was doing for the last month. If the hyperdrive was operational, which it was, he should have been here well ahead of us. What happened?

Roland got up and paced. "Fact: Tarin and I parted ways over a month ago. "Fact: I was able to contact the military, which mobilized in time to intercept Tarin.

"Fact: The hyperdrive Model 153 is superior to whatever model this fleet is equipped with. Perhaps a 152.

"Query: Why are we both here at the same time?"

What variables are there? I included the margin of error in my calculations, so that can't be it.

I don't know how he runs his ship, so I can't identify any systemic delays.

So, it leaves our separation. Did I damage his ship as much as he damaged mine?

Still no movement.

"Speculation: By engaging the hyperdrive while I was uploading the data file, the drive failed. Or maybe it did not perform according to expectations.

"It matches the circumstantial evidence. The drive now works, so there was no serious damage to the unit. I doubt they would have the parts available to repair significant damage. The test was planned to use planetary resources, but we were not on Dorea then."

Why isn't he surrendering? What is he waiting for? He is sitting out there—outgunned and outnumbered. Yet, he doesn't surrender. What's up?

Even though Roland was under arrest, Commander Tuman did not remove his access to the ship's sensor readouts. But they showed nothing. Tarin was blocking the sensors from reading the ship's interior.

His shielding was at maximum.

His normal space engines were powered, but not engaged. The exhaust trail was not enough for an engaged drive.

Roland rose and paced...again. *How could Tarin be apprehended? The military firepower Tuman has in the intercept fleet could destroy Tarin's lone transport, but it would also destroy the hyperdrive it contained.* "Not acceptable," *Tuman said.*

So, it means disabling the ship without destroying it. The surgical application of the fleet's weaponry could overpower the shields if Tarin remained stationary during the process. Yeah, what are the chances of him standing still?

RECON! That's what he is waiting for. He has the RECON system hooked in with his shielding. If they fire on his ship, all it will do is give him power.

What is it connected to? More shielding? No, it wouldn't be helpful. He would still need to get through the perimeter. Since his normal space drive is online, he could be boosting its output. It could enable him to get through a hole in the perimeter before we could close it.

What about the hyperdrive itself? He's got to be running low on power. This far out, there are no refueling stations built yet. Either way, he wants us to fire at him. He wants us to help him escape by doing the most logical thing to prevent his defection—trying to destroy his ship.

What about using drones? No. If they could be slowed enough to penetrate the shielding, Tarin's defensive weaponry would pick them off before they could get close enough to penetrate. Even if one managed to make it through the shielding, a lone drone could not destroy the normal space drives.

"Now, if I had the *Stiletto!*" he exclaimed, slamming a hand onto the desktop. "I could get through Taren's shielding before he even knew I was in this sector. I could tag his ship and disable the systems from inside."

He slumped down into the chair and ran his hands through his hair, locking his hands behind his head. "But, I do not have the *Stiletto*. It was somewhere in Kor Daga's arsenal on Lachelax. Well, I will go and get it back...if I am not in prison somewhere."

Without Melanie, the chances of this ending well are getting reduced. And, so are my chances of getting back to her.

Roland jumped at the knocking sound. He waited, trying to locate the noise. It came from the closed door. "Of course," he chuckled. "Come in," he called, not expecting company.

Tuman threw the door open and stormed into Roland's borrowed quarters, "If you were one of my own officers, I'd have you court-martialed."

"What? What did I do?" he responded, bolting upright in his borrowed chair. "I am trying to figure out..."

"Forget Tarin for a minute. This is much more serious. You have a visitor."

CHAPTER 52

"Why is my having a visitor a problem?" Roland stopped in his tracks as Miranda entered his quarters. He looked to Tuman for an explanation but saw fury.

"I assume, by the response I received from everyone else, I was not expected," she said.

"Uhm...no," Roland responded, still searching for an explanation. "Well, Melanie thought this would be the safest for both of us."

"Melanie's here? Where?"

"In our cargo hold. I do not want your ship attached to our hull," Tuman answered. "I need to keep my eyes on you both."

"I appreciate your concern, Commander," Roland began, "But, I think the *Stiletto's* presence gives us a few more options in dealing with our defector. I think you should get back to the bridge and close the perimeter until you wall him in."

"Mister Marcel." Tuman's tone forced Roland's hand to his side. "I will not be pushed around on my own vessel. You may enjoy great liberties aboard your own ship, and your service is not going unnoticed, but I am the commanding officer aboard this ship. I will go where and when I decide." Tuman had closed to within an uncomfortable distance to Roland's face. "Is that clear?"

"Yes, sir." He hoped his response was heard with more self-confidence than it was said.

"However, it happens I am returning to the bridge," Tuman said, heading toward the door, "And, I will take your warning under advisement. Without time to verify the information against the data files, I must take your word for it now."

Tuman stopped before reaching the door. "Miranda, you will confine yourself to these quarters and your own quarters, through this entrance."

The commander pointed out the door joining the two quarters. "I will see to it your meals are brought to you. Until the red alert is canceled, do not attempt to exit these two quarters." He then left the room without waiting for a response.

Roland offered Miranda a seat on his bed. "So, what happened? The last time I saw you," he settled into his chair after Miranda was seated, "I thought it would be the last time I saw you."

Miranda offered a small smile, "Oh, he wasn't so bad, Roland." She paused for a second, "In fact, I thought he was quite charming. He wanted my help with Melanie."

"Why did he need your help?"

"You know how Melanie flies only for you. She did not let him aboard, so he came back and said he needed me to get her to fly for his pilot."

"Okay. It makes sense. So, why did she come here?"

"After the pilot died, where else would she go?"

"Died? How did the pilot die?"

"I think Melanie killed him."

Roland bolted upright, "What makes you think so?"

"She instructed me to retrieve something from the hold, and while I was back there, the cockpit electrocuted him. Sparks flying everywhere, but not as far back as the hold. I think she wanted me out of the way."

He slumped back into the chair. *She killed someone. I never programmed violence. Deception, sure. Trickery, absolutely. Avoidance, better yet. But violence? Never. Melanie has become violent; she deliberately took a life.*

"She did not leave a corpse in your cockpit. She gave him a military funeral."

He started again. Miranda was being very passive about the situation. "What do you mean?"

"She closed me in the hold, so I don't know the extent of the ceremony. But I heard her play a military dirge, and then she opened the main door during our flight."

"Great," he replied with a notable lack of enthusiasm. "She killed someone and got rid of the evidence. Wonderful."

Miranda got up and came over to him. "It was horrible, Roland. I didn't see anything, and she said it was the one way to handle the situation. Still, she killed someone. I have never been that close when someone died. Even if he was mean to me, I didn't want him dead. I couldn't talk to Melanie for the rest of the trip here."

"Mean to you? I thought you said Kor Daga was charming."

"Oh, he was. But I kept feeling it was an act. Then Melanie told me how he set up a bounty on you and wanted to ruin you because you cost him some money."

"Melanie told you all this?"

"Yeah. She also said the guy in the ship was taking me to Lachelax, and I would be staying there for a long time." Miranda returned to the bunk. "I don't like Anadir, but at least I can leave when I want to."

"There is some comfort in having freedom." He got up and walked to a small window that provided a view into space. "I need to accept the necessity of the situation, though I do not feel good about her solution."

"But, if she said it was the one way..."

"That is the problem. If she had a vast amount of experience from which to draw her conclusions, I could understand. But she has been aware for a year. How could she know all the options available to her? Let alone, be able to eliminate all of them but homicide. What happens if she decides an equally extreme action is 'the one way' to handle a situation involving me? Or you?"

"You can't believe she'd..."

"I do not know what to believe anymore."

CHAPTER 53

Roland sat in front of the viewscreen but was not looking at anything it displayed. Instead, he looked at the wall and thought of Melanie. Though she was on board, he had not yet contacted her. He still was settling his concerns about the "person" she was becoming.

What kind of "person" would kill as a first option? If she had let me know her self-awareness a year ago, maybe I could have guided her to another course of action. Why didn't she tell me? She let me think that I was calling the shots. I was in control. What was she waiting for?

"Roland?" the speaker broke the silence of his thoughts. The voice was familiar, if not totally welcome now.

"Yes, Melanie?"

"Abenor has been apprehended."

"What? How?"

"Assuming your first question is rhetorical, and you are aware of the procedures surrounding the arrest of an accused criminal, I will state the details of the arrest warrant."

"Oh, thank you!" Roland spat.

"The Lachelax military authorities were informed a missing data storage system had been located."

"Who informed them?"

"The warrant listed a Captain Sheleya of the Anadir command as the accuser."

"But how did he find out?"

"He found it in the hold."

"He found it.... What was he doing there?"

"Miranda brought him in."

Roland leaned back in his chair. "Miranda? How could she?"

"She arrived while you were in conference with Bornor and Commander

Tuman. She brought the captain with her. When I told her you were not available, she asked if she could wait for you. I calculated you would not mind her waiting, although I could not verify my calculation without interrupting your meeting."

"No problem. That was fine. But, how...?"

"I am getting there, Roland."

"Sorry."

"I granted them entrance, and Miranda showed the captain to your chair. She sat on your bed. After some conversation, which I recorded if you would like to listen to it..."

"No, thanks."

"Very well. I saved the recording."

"Fine."

"After the initial conversation, the captain got up and looked around the interior. They continued to talk, with him asking questions about the ship. She answered, many times guessing."

Roland chuckled. *Miranda does not seem to grasp the more complex technology systems. The* Stiletto *has many.*

"The captain entered the hold and saw the system. Miranda told him it was a new data system. She could not provide other details. He asked some questions, and Miranda provided some answers."

"Perhaps I should listen to this part of the conversation."

"Very well, Roland."

Rising from the chair, he waited for Melanie's playback. In such small quarters, he had little room to pace. *What was he doing on my ship?*

"The case is busted," a male voice stated.

"Yeah. Roland said he had to use it to fix Melanie." Miranda responded.

"Melanie? Who's Melanie?" he questioned.

"I am."

Closing his eyes, Roland smiled as he imagined the captain looking around for the body from which the voice came.

"Melanie?" the voice stammered a little.

"Yes, Captain? How can I help you?"

"Where are you?"

"Right now, I am here. I have been many places."

"'Here', Where is 'here'?"

"My systems run this vessel. I am here."

"You're a computer, then."

"I am."

"Oh, so, it was you who worked with the investigation team."

"It was."

Roland took a handled cup and filled it from the water dispenser.

"I thought Melanie was an investigator. Someone they called in from off-world."

"In a way, you are correct."

"So, Roland used the lock on the case to repair some of Melanie's circuitry," Miranda chimed in.

"Why didn't he use the system in the case?"

"He didn't need to. The circuits from the lock patched the last board. Melanie finished it from there."

"Melanie was broken, but fixed herself? That's some good programming."

Roland shook his head. *I wish I could take credit for it.*

"So, what does it do?" the voice asked.

"I don't know. It's some kind of data processor or storage or something. I forgot."

"Where did he get it?"

"Lachelax. He got it from some 'Abenor' guy on Lachelax."

Roland winced. *So, there was the connection.*

"What's one of these go for?"

"Who knows? Roland doesn't tell me everything."

That's for sure, he agreed.

"So, how long have you two been together?"

Roland noticed Miranda's hesitation and opened his eyes, waiting for her response.

"We met a month or so ago, while I was on vacation. Then he left but found me several days ago. So, I guess we haven't been together very long. Why?"

"Oh, no reason. Making small talk."

He paused. Roland sensed the captain was searching for something. *But what?* He waited through the shuffling of feet.

"This looks like a new design."

"Yeah. He said it was a prototype. I guess it's new. Isn't it?"

Roland winced again. *Giving sensitive information with so little effort.*

"What are you doing?"

Miranda's voice had taken on an unfamiliar tone. Roland tilted his head to hear better. All he heard at this moment was movement.

"Jack, what are you doing?" She sounded agitated. After a little more movement, Roland heard, "Look, Roland will be back any minute, now. You'd better watch yourself."

"I don't understand the problem here. You've known him for a month. You can't have much of a relationship with him. You knew me years ago."

Ah, that was why she called him "Jack."

"Sure, I knew you then, but you never showed any interest in me before. Why now?"

"Maybe I've grown wiser. Evidently, your parents loosened up some, for them to accept him. What does this guy have to offer you, anyway? He's a criminal who will be in jail for a long time. From what I hear, he has no social life. Keeps to himself when he's not working."

"I've been working on it with him. He's getting better."

"How good can he get from prison?" The captain sounded agitated now.

Surprised, Roland heard, "I'm sorry. That was mean. With the help he has provided Commander Tuman, maybe he'll get some leniency. It still means incarceration, though."

More movement. *I am afraid the captain is right.*

"Look, Jack, Roland and I are trying to look beyond the immediate situation. Who knows what will happen when all this is over. When we knew each other, I liked..." Her speech was cut off. Roland strained to hear. For several moments, all he heard was some muffled sounds and some movement.

"What's going on, Melanie?"

"I do not know, Roland. I have no sensors installed with the visual spectrum in that section of the *Stiletto*."

"Can you speculate?"

"I reduced the list of possibilities to two. The sound was generated my Miranda, though 'Jack' generated a similar sound three times. I cannot definitively..."

Melanie was interrupted by a sudden increase in the volume and intensity of the moaning. It sounded familiar, but Roland could not place it. Wait, it was from some entertainment he had watched some months back. *They're kissing! Heavy kissing, from the sound of it.* He threw the cup against the wall, watching it break into several pieces, each falling and bouncing across the floor.

"I think I heard enough, Melanie," he said, leaning over the desk and looking at the water splashed against the wall. "Turn it off."

"Very well."

"Where is the commander?"

"He is in his quarters at this time."
"Can you get me out of here?"
Roland stood as he heard the door unlock.
"Thank you."

CHAPTER 54

Roland burst through the door into the commander's suite. Ignoring the cries of the uniform rushing toward him, he slammed, then locked, the door.

"What the hell is going on?"

The commander looked up from some read-outs at his desk. His eyes took Roland in from over his glasses. "I'm sorry, but you will need to be more specific."

"Melanie has informed me Abenor has been arrested."

"And Abenor is...?"

Roland walked to the commander's desk, placed his hands on it, and glared over the glasses. "Abenor is an associate of mine. He is on Lachelax. At least he was. He may still be. "The point is, he has been arrested. He is incarcerated."

"Other than causing you to violate several security protocols concerning a red alert status, how does it concern you?"

"He was arrested for stealing a computer system which I possess."

"So," Tuman removed his glasses and reclined, as much as he could in the confined space, "You are saying you should be arrested, rather than Abenor, right?"

"No one should be arrested. No one knows the system was stolen. Abenor said it was clean."

"Forgive my ignorance, Mr. Marcel, but how does this concern me?"

"I want him released."

"I am sorry, but it is out of my jurisdiction."

"It may be out of your jurisdiction, but it is not out of your sphere of influence."

"Look, I don't have time for this. Our immediate concern is more pressing, is it not?"

Roland did not reply. Instead, he turned and walked out.

Later, a calmer Roland sat at his desk and pressed the communication button. Nothing happened.

I guess my outbound communications are still cut off.

"Did you need me, Roland?" Melanie asked.

"No, Melanie, I need Commander Tuman. But he disconnected my outbound system," he replied.

"Shall I reestablish outbound communication for you?"

"Thank you, Melanie. That would be great."

"You're welcome, Roland."

"Is the commander still in his quarters?"

"No, he is on the bridge at this time."

"Okay."

"Yes, sir?" came the response from another faceless voice a few moments later.

"Umm. Yes...how do I contact the bridge?" Roland asked, "I need to speak with Commander Tuman."

"The commander left specific orders concerning your outbound communications, sir."

"Yes, I understand, but this is important."

"I will contact the bridge and see if the commander wishes to speak with you at this time. One moment, please."

Roland waited through a minute or so of silence, before the voice responded, "Commander Tuman is on the bridge and cannot be disturbed at this time."

"Thank you." *Melanie, at least, is polite.*

Roland got up from his chair and walked around his quarters. *The walls look more gray than green today.*

"Melanie, what can I do about this? I have an idea, but the commander says he is too busy." He shook his head and returned to the desk. "I can at least map out the plan to show him later."

"You could interrupt him, Roland."

"Melanie, if I do, Tuman will be pissed."

"An interesting metaphor, though I fail to see its meaning."

"Never mind. I am glad to hear your voice again, but the commander will not like you tagging his computer."

"Are you going to tell him?" Melanie asked.

"Why should I?"

"Then, neither will I. Now, since that is settled, what was your idea?"

"Can you access the *MTS 1741-A*?"

"I think I can," Melanie assured him. "I can at least make the attempt."

"Good. I need you to shut down their normal space drive and their shielding, so Tuman's soldiers can board it."

"I understand," Melanie responded.

After several minutes passed, Spectre's baritone filled the quarters. "I was able to access the systems, but they blocked the overrides. It is difficult to do remote overrides undetected."

"What about doing it the old-fashioned way? Can you shut down their propulsion and shielding systems if we tagged the vessel?"

"Yes, I can. I can override any system. Is secrecy important?"

"It looks like the longer we keep out of their sight, the better our chances are for success. Still, my guess is they will know something is amiss when the systems begin to go down. Then it will be a race for control."

"In that case, I see no problem with the initial overrides to their systems. Sustaining the override may be difficult. It would depend on the creativity of the crew."

"I will deal with them," Roland stated, leaning toward the console. "Okay, Melanie, I need you to record this, so I can transfer it to a portable data recorder to show Commander Tuman, so create a content file for me."

"Roger that, sir!" came Jackson's response.

Roland laughed. "All right, Melanie, would you please record this idea in a content file?"

"I would be happy to do so, Roland."

Roland, again.

"Okay, assuming Tarin has standard combat shielding, we must approach the ship slowly. Like a drone. We will also need to be invisible to their sensors. I do not want to dodge his available weaponry. It may not be a combat vessel, but a transport is still dangerous."

"I, too, would prefer to avoid his weapons," Melanie replied.

"Once we clear his shielding, we concentrate on tagging and accessing the computer as soon as possible. After we are inside, we shut down the weapons, then the propulsion, and then the shielding. Then we contact Tuman to board the vessel and to tow the ship, if necessary," Roland concluded with a wave of his hands.

"That sounds good, Roland. I recorded it as dictated."

"Thank you, Melanie. I will prepare it for Commander Tuman. Once I am finished with the description, we will add the technical specifics and time frame for completion."

"Very well. I will stand by."

CHAPTER 55

Roland finished the specifics of his plan, after confirming the technical details with Melanie. With the *Stiletto* available again, the shielding around Tarin's vessel had now become vulnerable. He could pilot the *Stiletto* through the shielding, access the computer systems, and disable the shielding and propulsion, plus the weapons. It would leave Tarin no options but surrender.

He copied the detailed plan onto a portable viewer. Turning the viewer over in his hands, he asked: "What do you think the odds are that I can take this to the bridge?"

"There are too many variables for me to calculate the exact odds, but I would not want to bet the house on it."

Roland laughed.

"Did I misuse the metaphor?"

"No, Melanie, it was perfect. You're amazing."

"Thank you, Roland."

After he was turned away from communicating with the bridge again, Roland called for a uniform to come to his cabin and retrieve the portable data viewer. "Please take this to Commander Tuman for his review," he said as he handed the viewer to the uniform. Wordlessly, the uniform took the device, backed into the hallway, and closed the door. The lock engaged, again.

"Fine. Let him deal with it when he has the time." He walked to his bed and stretched out. "Melanie?"

"Yes, Roland?"

"Could you play the audio from Miranda's meeting on the *Stiletto* with that captain?"

"Very well."

Closing his eyes, he heard them kissing again. A knock on his door interrupted him. "Pause, Melanie," he said, getting up from the bed. *That was a quick response.* "Enter."

The door slid open, revealing Miranda. She smiled as she walked in. "I stopped by earlier, but it sounded like you were pretty busy."

"Yeah, I developed a plan for dealing with Tarin, but he was too busy to hear it. So Melanie recorded it for me, and I sent it to him through channels."

"I hope it works." She walked over and hugged him. "I'm sorry you have to be cooped up like this. It must be hard on you."

He broke free of her hug and lay back down.

"What's wrong, Roland?"

"Melanie, continue please," he said, glaring at Miranda.

"What is that?" she asked, listening to the noise.

"Pause," he responded. Then he got up. "It is from a meeting you had on board the *Stiletto* with a certain Anadir military officer."

Miranda laughed. Roland stood, wondering where she saw humor in his anger.

"I'm sorry. I don't mean to laugh at you. But, you haven't gotten to the good part, yet."

"Do you mean there is more to this?"

"Yes, there is more," she said, walking over to the desk and sitting on it. Roland did not follow. "I guess Jack likes me and thought I would like him, too. So, he kissed me. It took me a minute to break away from him. He is pretty strong, but he is also gentle. Anyway, I was not ready for it and did not want it. So, I—well, Melanie?"

"Yes, Miranda?"

"Please continue the playback."

He closed his eyes as the kissing started again. He heard Miranda chuckling from across the room.

Then he heard a noise that sounded like...like what? A dropped circuit board? No, this was louder—crisper.

"Ow!" the man yelled. "What was that for?"

"I gave you fair warning, Jack. I think you should leave now."

Miranda could not restrain herself any longer. She laughed. "He had it coming. It serves him right." She hopped off the desk. Waving her hand toward the door, she said, "Then he walked away. Gone."

He opened his eyes and saw her walking toward him. Her face was pointed toward the floor, but her eyes were fixed on his. She lifted her face to meet his, but she did not change her pace.

Something is wrong.

He backed up until his legs encountered the bed. They collapsed beneath him, forcing him to sit.

She kept approaching with a slow, stalking pace.

"You see if there is one person from whom I would gladly receive a kiss," she said, raising one eyebrow, "It would *not* be him."

She was now at the bed. Roland had nowhere else to go. She placed her palms on top of the bed and started crawling until she was on top of him. He breathed deeply of her hair and perfume, but he could not look away from her. She lowered her face to meet his. And she kissed him.

He felt her pull away after a few exhilarating seconds. "But, we need to work on your technique. You can't learn everything from a movie."

She tried again.

"Roland?" Melanie interrupted, "Should I record this as well?"

"No!" they both shouted.

Another knock interrupted them. "To be continued..." she said, then gave him a quick kiss before getting off the bed.

Roland, still lying down, called, "Come in."

The door slid open, and Commander Tuman strode in, with the portable data reader. Walking over to Roland's desk, he acknowledged Miranda's presence with a glare and quick nod. She left the room, humming to herself.

Dropping the data reader on the desk, Tuman turned to him. Seeing he was still lying on the bed, the commander waited. Roland sat up, then stood and walked over to the desk. "I see you calculated a way to stop Tarin," Tuman offered.

"I think it will work, now with the *Stiletto* available," Roland replied. "The biggest problem is getting through the shielding unobserved. If I can manage it, then the rest should be rather simple."

"'Simple?' In what way?"

"Commander, I made a career of infiltrating computer systems. The military systems are no different. They are a bit more difficult to navigate unobserved, but they are still data and processes."

"You have extensive experience in infiltrating military computer systems, then?" Tuman accused.

"I would not call my experience extensive," he backed a step, "But some. And some of my experience is with the system on his ship."

"What makes you think you can do this now? Will you have enough time?"

"It will depend on how fast they find us. If their computer personnel are good enough, they may be able to remove our overrides as fast as we place them. Melanie should be able to keep many of them from succeeding. I can handle the...more creative attempts. Anyway, I must try. He does not seem to want to surrender on his own, and the sole hope I see for staying out of prison is to help you capture him."

"I see," Tuman acknowledged. He turned and picked up the portable viewer, then took a few steps toward the exit. "Mr. Marcel, I know you accessed my base system, so your skill is not in question. How do I know you can do this aboard ship? The systems are quite different." After a brief pause, he continued, "A lot is riding on your success."

"I have full confidence in Roland's ability, Commander Tuman," Melanie offered.

Tuman dropped his gaze and shook his head. Looking back at Roland, he asked, "Do you even know what 'authorized access' looks like?" Without waiting for an answer, he left.

The door locked behind him.

CHAPTER 56

What can I do about Abenor? How could Miranda do that? It's hard to believe she is working undercover for the police. The setup is too complicated. I doubt she has ever even been to Lachelax, so she would know no connection with Abenor. Still, she invited a uniform onto my ship. What was she thinking?

Roland got up from the chair and circumnavigated his quarters. It was no larger than his cell aboard the *Aradinda*, and seemed as comfortable. But, since the fleet was still at red alert, he was still locked in. *I might as well get used to it. I will be spending a long time in places like this.*

"She said it was nothing—so, I see no reason to worry," he said to his empty room. "But, she did let a stranger on board my ship. Why did she bring him there in the first place? If she brought him to talk to me, why did she say nothing about it when we were listening to the recording?"

"Maybe she wanted you to meet an old friend of hers," Melanie responded.

"Melanie, I hope Tuman doesn't come in. He won't like you talking to me now. He had all outgoing communications channels disabled again."

"I know. I can correct it if you wish."

"No, thank you. I think I irritated him enough for today," he said, chuckling. "So, do you think it was a social call with that captain?"

"It would not surprise me if it were, Roland."

Surprise? It will take some time for me to adjust. "Okay, I guess it makes sense. She is a friendly, open person. Just because I avoid military people doesn't mean everyone does. Even they make friends somewhere."

"Well, you have reason to avoid military relationships. I would think they could be awkward, given your chosen profession and lifestyle."

"I guess you're right, Melanie. A social call would explain her waiting for me to return. If she had brought him for an official visit, she would take him over to Tuman's office, since you told her I was there."

"Agreed."

"Still, I guess she has never learned to keep a secret. I know this may sound like a silly question, Melanie, but, what do you think about Miranda?"

"In what way?"

"In general. Does she seem like an honest person to you? Can I trust her after this?"

"Roland, I possess little direct experience upon which I can base such a conclusion. However, in the data I have seen, it seems most people trust other people. If someone says the situation is a certain way, other people tend to believe it. At least they do until they are presented with evidence or suspicion to the contrary."

"So, you think I should believe her explanation?"

"I believe her."

"Why?"

"She has given me no cause to do otherwise."

"I see. Well, she did accept the replay of her episode with that captain."

"She did."

"She didn't hide from it or get defensive over it."

"Correct."

"She left my decision about her actions up to me. She did not argue about it."

"Also true. Plus, she put you in contact with a military officer who seems at least to take our particular situation into consideration."

"She did. She trusted me and my story."

"Yes, she did."

"So, if I accept her explanation, and we decide to get married—that's what she wants to do—what do I do then?"

"What do you mean?"

"Well, I will need to make a living doing something. All I have ever done has been illegal. I don't think she would approve of smuggling as a career choice any longer."

"Unfortunately, I cannot provide you any guidance in career options. If you want, I could research the job postings on Anadir and identify those for which I find you to be qualified."

"It would give me a place to start. I'll check with Miranda about what she thinks I can do about it. I think it would be best not to surprise her with something illegal, or even suspicious."

"It seems appropriate, given Miranda's apparent moral code."

"How do you know what is appropriate?"

"Based on your original programming, I deduced there is a moral code you follow when dealing with people; although, I also come across areas in which you bypass that code to a large extent. Those areas, however, deal with tagging. Since this situation does not include tagging, I assumed the moral code still applies. Since she also exhibits a moral code, promoting an idea that would violate that code would be rejected. If my understanding of the terms is correct, adhering to her moral code would be the 'appropriate' thing to do."

"You know, Melanie, I am beginning to anticipate to those long trips where we can discuss things like ontological philosophy."

"As do I, Roland. However, at this moment, I am picking up a sudden increase in communication traffic among the fleet vessels. It seems the *M.T.S. 1822-G* has begun firing upon the fleet. They are returning fire."

"NO!" he leapt up from his bunk. He ran to the desk and watched the battle unfolding on the viewscreen. Tarin's vessel was taking several hits. The shielding seemed to be absorbing most of it, but the ship was beginning to issue sparks from its propulsion system's exhaust. Then the fighting stopped. Tarin's ship drifted, showing no activity at all. *It looks like it's crippled. Why?*

"Mr. Marcel, please report to the bridge," blared the communications panel.

He pressed the green button and responded, "Acknowledged. I am on my way."

He got up from the desk and walked toward the door, hearing it unlock as he approached. "I will let Miranda know when this is over."

"I could let her know now, Roland."

"Thank you, Melanie, but I prefer to do it in person. But, please monitor the bridge for me, in case something interesting should happen when I arrive."

"Roger that, sir!" Jackson replied.

Roland ran to the bridge. Tuman was standing in from of the fore window, watching the drifting military transport vessel. As Roland approached, Tuman said, "It seems he has given up."

"I doubt it, commander. I think he is calculating escape velocity."

"You can't be serious, Mr. Marcel. He knows we can blast him and his ship into dust."

"True, but he also knows you do not want to destroy the ship—and its hyperdrive."

Turning to face Roland, Tuman added, "Then how will he escape?"

"Through hyperspace, of course. It is the one thing making any sense."

"So, you don't think he was trying to open a hole in the perimeter to squeeze through?"

"No, sir, I do not. I think he was using your energy weapons to recharge his hyperdrive so he could perform a short jump beyond the perimeter and into Athzembir territory, knowing you would not follow or attack his ship. That is what I think."

"Do you have any substantiation for this assumption?"

"I do, sir. Dr. Radam Nortolis is aboard Tarin's vessel. He oversees the research and development on Bantadam. One of the projects he oversees concerns the RECON system: **R**apid **E**nergy **CON**version. It is a system designed to take one form of energy, such as what is produced by our weaponry, and convert it into another form of energy, such as what is used in normal space engines or hyperdrives. One of the data files I accessed covers a specific application of RECON to hyperdrives. I think we are witnessing such an application. Whatever you do, commander, do not fire upon his vessel."

"Mr. Marcel, I will do whatever I must to prevent his vessel from making it into Athzembir space."

"I understand, Commander Tuman, but I am your advisor in this matter. If you want to keep Tarin's ship on this side of the perimeter, you cannot fire upon it. I told you Melanie and I have an alternative plan."

CHAPTER 57

Tuman stood in his usual spot in the center of the bridge. He ignored all of the activity surrounding him, staring at the transport vessel. On occasion, a junior officer brought a report to his attention. Tuman surveyed the data display handed to him, acknowledged its contents, then returned his attention to the window.

"Commander," one of his bridge officers shouted. "They are increasing the power to their engines. It looks like they are planning to move."

Tuman barked, "Connect me with the *Beykina*."

"Connection established, Commander," responded another officer.

"Captain Gollbus, what do you see?"

"Our sensors have detected no ship across the Athzembir boundary. It's all clear," came the response.

"Very well. Keep scanning."

Taking advantage of a lull in the frantic activity on the bridge, Roland made his way over to where Tuman stood. "Commander, Abenor's release could be expedited if you could..."

"Mr. Marcel, as you can see, I am quite involved in another matter at this moment. Please refrain from bringing trivial matters to me until the primary matter is resolved. Resume your position until we can bring the fleet to the point where we can support your attempt."

"But, Commander..."

"That is all, Mr. Marcel. Do not force me to restrict you to your quarters again."

"In that case, do you have an estimate for my departure?"

"We are positioning the fleet to cover you with a barrage of drones for him to deal with, so you can approach undetected. I will issue you a flight plan for avoiding the blast radii. It may take a little while to calculate the sequence in which he will destroy the drones. Stand by."

"Very well," Roland conceded.

"Commander, we detect the presence of a single vessel. It is a capital ship, but it is unescorted."

"Thank you, Captain. Keep an eye on it. Watch for others. It looks like it's rendezvous time."

Roland had closed the distance to Tuman. "Can he outrun us?"

Tuman shook his head.

"Can he blast a hole through our perimeter?"

Again, Tuman shook his head.

"Commander, we have a launch from our shuttle bay."

"What? I authorized no pursuit."

"Which shuttle?"

"None, sir."

"Then who?" the commander wondered aloud.

"Melanie." Roland offered.

Tuman turned, glaring at Roland. His face softened, then gave a quizzical expression.

"Then who is piloting your ship?" he asked, emphasizing Roland's ownership. Roland shook his head.

"Sir,...um...it's gone."

"Gone? What do you mean 'gone'?"

"I mean 'gone', sir. It was there...then it wasn't." Roland chuckled. Tuman did not look amused, though.

"Commander, I am detection an anomaly in the infrared spectrum, sir," announced Emari Antiarus.

This kid has potential.

"Mr. Antiarus, you were scanning infrared?" the commander asked.

"Sir, yes, sir! It seemed prudent since it is not a normal frequency to be scanned."

Smiling, Roland said, "Contact the *Gonolacar*, commander. Have it scan for a distortion in the infrared spectrum. Then triangulate the readings."

Tuman looked at the communications officer and nodded.

Roland caught the technician's eye and nodded to him with a knowing smile.

After a couple of minutes, the scanning officer exclaimed, "Found it. It's...it's drifting."

"Drifting? How did it get out of the shuttle bay to drift?"

"Commander Tuman," Roland interrupted, "She's not drifting; she's setting up for a tag."

"A what?"

"She is going to intercept Tarin when he gets through your perimeter."

"There is no way he is going to make it through."

"He seems to disagree. I would keep an eye on his hyperdrive, too."

"Why? He cannot get enough speed for an insertion point. It's the whole point of the perimeter."

"This is not the normal hyperdrive."

"Commander, they are powering up their hyperdrive," the scanning officer announced, with some puzzlement. "And he's moving."

"Plot his course on the screen," the commander ordered.

"I would guess one of two things," Roland offered.

"And they would be...?" Tuman responded, unconvinced.

"He is either building up speed for an insertion, or he is moving while his drive is cycling up," he concluded. "It is what I would do."

"Captain Noriann, move your wing to a second perimeter line along the boundary."

Roland moved over to the scanning viewscreen. The stream of triangulating figures illuminated a vague shape where the *Stiletto* waited. *Melanie is behaving as if Tarin would be able to cross beyond Tuman's perimeter. But how? She is in line between Tarin's original position and the Athzembir vessel. Is Tarin attempting to get past her, too? No. He lacks the sensors. At this level, he would also require triangulation to get a fix on the* Stiletto. *And he had one ship. Unless...*

"Lieutenant, has there been any communication between the transport and the Athzembir vessel?"

"We have detected no transmissions to or from the transport. We are not monitoring the communications of the Athzembir ship," he replied.

"Good, good," Roland said. "Can you connect me with the *Stiletto*? I would like to see what she anticipates..."

"No, do not contact that vessel. If he is monitoring our communication traffic, he would locate your ship out there, if he has not done so already."

"He has not. He cannot."

"Don't be too smug about your technology."

"Trust me. I have some experience in this matter."

"Take care with your tone, Mr. Marcel. You are aboard my ship now."

Roland nodded and turned away.

"What is Tarin's course now?" Tuman asked the scanning officer.

"It appears he will be circling inside the perimeter."

"Captain Noriann, close the diameter of the perimeter, but do it without breaking the integrity in the process."

"Roger that, Commander."

Roland watched the tactical display of the fleet formation. The inner hemisphere closed in uniformly. The distance between each ship lessened as the circle grew smaller. Tarin's transport still accelerated. It kept its trajectory. It did not waver. It did not turn. It did not slow. Instead, it disappeared.

The bridge burst into frantic activity. Tuman shouted, "What happened? Locate that ship."

Captain Noriann's voice came over the speaker. "The vessel has escaped the perimeter and is closing with the Athzembir vessel."

"How? How did he go into hyperspace at that speed? No hyperdrive can do that."

Roland retorted, "No hyperdrive we know of. Still, this one can." He walked to the scanning console. "Where is the *Stiletto*?"

"Coming in behind the transport."

She knew. She guessed his tactic, and the degree of success based on the hyperdrive data. Roland shook his head in admiration. "Way to go, Melanie." he whispered.

"Commander," Roland had to jump out of the way as the scanning officer turned his chair to face Tuman. "The Athzembir vessel is closing and powering weapons."

"Battle stations. Ready weapons. Mr. Marcel, you are relieved."

Roland walked toward the exit but did not use it. Instead, he stepped over to a wall and watched the battle unfold on the screen. The alien vessel did not engage the fleet. Instead, it headed toward Tarin's transport and fired. And missed. Two more shots also missed."They are going after the *Stiletto*!" he yelled, running back to the scanning console. "Stop them!"

"I can't. The transport and the *Stiletto* crossed into Athzembir territory," Tuman responded dejectedly. "We lost it. I cannot engage on their side or prevent them from defending themselves from an alien intruder. I'm sorry."

The weapons stopped. Roland checked the console's viewscreen. It showed the *Stiletto* closing behind the transport. *Even the best weaponry can't fire through another vessel.* Closer and closer Melanie crept until he could no longer distinguish his ship from Tarin's exhaust.

The transport was well beyond the Athzembir border, and the Athzembir vessel fell in behind it as it headed deeper into the alien realm.

Tuman broke the silence. "When they are out of scanning range, prepare to return to Anadir."

"Roger that, sir," replied his first officer.

"Commander, the transport is turning. And it's accelerating."

"Already? Tactical error. Track their course change. When they start their invasion with the new drive, we will follow their trajectory to their homeworld."

"The transport is headed toward us, sir," the scanning officer announced, puzzled again. "What is he doing?"

Roland chuckled. *They are asking the wrong question. It is not, "Why is Tarin turning around?" but "Why is the ship altering course?" I will let the answer announce herself.*

A few tense minutes later, she did.

"Commander, we are being hailed by the transport."

"Put it through, Commander," Roland suggested and smirking.

"Very well. Put it through, Lieutenant."

"Commander Tuman," came the familiar voice, "This is the *Stiletto*. I now control the *MTS 1822-G*. I anticipate rendezvous with the fleet in twelve minutes. I request permission to rejoin the fleet."

Tuman looked at Roland and let a slow smile escape. "Permission granted." He then looked at his other officers on the bridge. Each was looking at him, too. "Captain Noriann, prepare to escort the *MTS-1822-G* back to Anadir."

"Roland, they are attempting to circumvent my overrides. I am attempting to secure my position, but I lost access to the weapons. I also generated an addendum to the Model 153 data file. I would like to transmit it to you now."

"We will upload it when you return."

"Commander Tuman, I request permission to transmit the addendum."

Tuman looked at Roland. After a moment of consideration, he responded,

"Permission granted."

"Thank you, sir."

Sir?

"Commander, the Athzembir vessel is maneuvering to intercept the transport."

"Can they penetrate the shielding?"

"Unknown, sir."

The alien ship let loose a barrage of weapons fire against the transport.

"The answer, Commander, is 'Yes, they can,'" came Melanie's reply. "They have not yet done so, but they possess the capability. I will attempt to manipulate the shielding to strengthen it against another such barrage.

"Captain Noriann, close in behind the transport when it clears the boundary. I don't was to start a war today, but I want the hyperdrive intact."

"Roger that, sir."

"She's accelerating, sir."

Roland noticed the distance between the transport and the alien vessel had grown a little, even as the distance to the boundary diminished.

"Roland, I am losing control of this vessel."

"A couple minutes more, Melanie."

"I do not have time to spare. I need it to withstand the Athzembir."

"Options?"

"None."

CHAPTER 58

Commander Tuman stepped toward the window, "Contact the alien ship. Open all frequencies."

"Ready, sir."

"Attention, Athzembir vessel. You are firing upon a vessel under the command of the Anadir military. You are hereby ordered to stand down and cease this act of aggression, or you will force us to respond in like manner."

Roland saw Captain Noriann's ships running parallel to the boundary, and they were closing on the transport's crossing point. The alien vessel broke off and headed away from the fleet. Making no contact, the ship receded from the boundary.

"Roland, I need to do something now. They have almost retaken the vessel. I may have time to lock everything down, but you will need to act quickly. They will be able to circumvent it within the quarter hour, I would guess."

"We need to secure the ship, Melanie," Roland responded.

"Roger that, sir," came Jackson's voice. Tuman shot a quizzical expression at Roland, who was confused himself. "Everything is ready now. Good-bye, Roland," Melanie said.

"Commander," the scanning officer called. "The shielding is down, and the transport is adrift."

"Understood. Close to within range and grapple the ship." Turning again to the window, he continued, "Captain Noriann, prepare to board the vessel."

"Roger that, sir."

Tuman walked over to Roland and extended his hand. Roland regarded the hand for a moment, then accepted it. "Please notify me when my ship has returned," he requested. Tuman nodded, and Roland turned for his quarters.

After several hours, Roland had still not heard from Commander Tuman concerning the *Stiletto*. "What is taking you so long, Melanie?" He got up from his bed and walked over to the desk. He pressed the communication and called "Commander Tuman."

A moment later, Tuman's voice responded, "Commander Tuman here."

"Commander, have you acquired the vessel?"

"We secured the crew and have almost acquired the systems. Your ship did a thorough job of disabling the controls. But we are making progress."

"Is it possible for me to check on my ship?"

"I will arrange transport for you. Shall we say, one hour? It should give you time to grab an environmental suit."

Roland checked his chronometer. "One hour, then. Thank you, Commander." He terminated the connection.

Fifty-one minutes later, Roland was inside the environmental suit and waiting on the shuttle pilot to arrive. Much lighter and more flexible than the model aboard the *Aradinda*, Roland had expended little energy walking around in the suit. Of course, he had not yet turned on the magnetic boots. Those were required on the other side of the hull.

The shuttle landed inside the open bay, and Roland was at the hatch before the pilot had stopped the shuttle. Once it was secured, Roland opened the shuttle's hatch and climbed out. He secured the helmet and lumbered over to the exit hatch. Entering the code the pilot had given him during the flight, Roland watched the hatch open into the airlock. He walked in and secured the hatch, activating the boots at the same time. Tapping his left fist against his thigh, Roland waited for the hatch to close. As his eyes registered the green light on the hatch, his hand pressed the button to open the outer door of the airlock.

The *Stiletto* gave no response to the code Roland entered. The panel did not even light. Roland started the intricate maneuver for manually overriding the access panel.

Pleased with the complexity as a detriment to unauthorized access to his ship, he now found it a nuisance. Once the door opened, the familiar stench of charred wiring greeted him as he stepped inside.

Black.

CHAPTER 59

"I am sorry, Roland," Miranda said as she handed him a cup of tea.

"Thanks," he said, taking the cup and carrying it into the living room. He set the cup down on a side table while Miranda carried her own cup into the room.

"There was nothing left. She fried all the circuits. It was why Commander Tuman had such difficulty clearing her overrides." Roland slumped onto Miranda's couch, the dark blue fabric matching his mood. He reached for his tea. Its flavor and warmth provided some limited comfort.

Miranda came over and sat beside him. "She did the one thing she could to stop Tarin's ship."

"I know, but she was still so new. Maybe, with more experience, she could have handled it a bit better."

"Like you would?" Miranda asked.

"Yes. Like I would. Why did she need to do it her way?"

"Time. She had no time to do anything else. It's like the time you told me about Tarin's ship. You know, the first time you hooked up with it. You tried to do something because of the time factor. You failed. She succeeded."

"Yes, she did succeed. I guess it is some consolation."

"I'm sorry, Roland. I know it's hard."

"Harder than you think." Roland got up and walked to the window. "My whole life was spent building that ship. I spent all my time there. Melanie is the closest friend I have...had."

"Wow, I didn't realize..." she began but failed to finish.

"I feel like I've been through a house fire. My house, my family, my friends—they're all gone."

Miranda came over to Roland and placed her hands on his shoulders. "I wish I could do more than say, 'I'm sorry.'"

"I appreciate that, Miranda," he said, taking one of her hands as he turned to return to his tea. "I know she made the decision on her own. I would have tried to stop her, but she knew it was the lone option."

"She was a smart computer. I wish I got to know her more. To talk to the first intelligent computer system in the galaxy. It would be exciting."

"You already did. She even brought you to the fleet on her own."

"That's right. I had forgotten." She brought her cup to her lips but set it down again before drinking. "She was special. I will miss her."

"So will I."

"Roland, if you want to wait a while before I call my parents, it's fine with me. I understand."

"Oh. Right. They still don't know their daughter has grown up and found a husband. Do you think they will like me?"

"I think so. Right now, I don't care. I like you. They won't have a choice," she said, laughing.

"Still, I would like for them to like me, so they don't give you a hard time about me."

"Silly boy. You let me worry about them."

An hour later, Roland was seated in the Commander Tuman's office. The commander walked over from behind his desk to face Roland. "Thank you, Mr. Marcel, for your assistance in this matter. I understand the personal cost was significant."

Roland snorted at the understatement.

Commander Tuman continued, "I spoke with my superiors, whom I kept informed once the information you provided was validated."

Roland looked at the commander. *I wonder when they want to begin my trial.*

"They issued a statement concerning your involvement in this affair, and in your activities leading up to your participation," he stated, handing Roland a data viewer.

Roland started reading as Tuman returned to his desk. "The high command has issued copies to all of the planets under their protection."

Roland reread the end of the final paragraph,

...as his participation in such activities has been invaluable to the apprehension of the renegade commander. Therefore, any such activity leading up and involving any aspect of the pursuit of former Commander Tarin Koraben for which Roland Marcel, or his vessel, the *Stiletto*, have been accused or implicated, should now be closed without further pursuit of Mr. Marcel. These activities include, but are not limited to, the removal of data or hardware from research facilities. Any further pursuit of Mr. Marcel in these matters will be met with the full weight of the judicial branch of the empire's military forces.

Roland looked from the data viewer to Commander Tuman. Tuman informed him, "You must realize this is not a license for further activity along similar lines, Mr. Marcel, and we cannot encourage such invasions. I also realize this is not an ultimatum to those you crossed, but it includes significant reprisals for whoever insists upon pursuing you for these matters. I doubt you will find many civilian authorities who will test the military in such matters."

Roland stood, extending his hand to the commander, "May I keep this copy? I no longer have Melanie available to eavesdrop on our conversations."

"Of course," Tuman replied, shaking Roland's hand. "I trust you will find other means of support in the future—means for which you need no special consideration in order to avoid prosecution."

Roland nodded, "Yes, I think I may do some security work. Bornor has some contacts to whom he may recommend my services. And, since he no longer has any evidence against me..." Roland shrugged, "But for now, I have enough resources for a considerable vacation." Before turning to leave, he added, "Thank you for taking care of Abenor. It's too bad I could not try out the data system he got me, but it is a relatively small price for his release. I hope his relationship with Kor Daga was not damaged by my failure."

Commander Tuman shook his head, "I would not worry too much about him now. Melanie uploaded the conversation you had with him concerning Miranda and your ship. I think we can keep him pressured enough to forget you. Besides, we did repay him the investment you cost him, and he is too high profile now to open new markets anyway."

CHAPTER 60

The crowd noise was not unbearable since Roland had secured a table in a less populated section of the restaurant. Although the kitchen was some distance away, the aromas from the food, it was producing mingled in a pleasant buffet. Looking at his chronometer, he noted he was still a few minutes ahead of schedule. *She will be back in thirty-six minutes. Fine.*

Roland stood as Abenor approached the table. *A little more colorful than I would wear, but the suit looks good.* Extending his hand, Roland said, "Thank you for coming here Abenor. I realize how valuable your time is."

"Think nothing of it, Reggie. After you cleared up my unfortunate situation, it is the very least I could do."

"Abenor, allow me to introduce myself. My name is Roland Marcel. Reggie Fischer is no longer necessary."

"I figured you had given me an alias. You had your reasons. Thank you for confiding in me now."

"Well, since I am now forced into a career change, I thought I should start fresh in other areas as well."

"How did the data system work?"

"It was a real life-saver, Abenor. I wish I had gotten a chance to use it."

"What do you mean?"

"I never got it installed, but I salvaged some of the locking mechanism of the crate and repaired my ship with them. The reason you got arrested was the system was unpacked in my cargo hold. Someone saw it and reported it to the authorities."

Abenor laughed. "I see. Well, no real harm done. Now," he added, waving to a nearby server, "What about my drink?"

"Miranda," Roland said, rising from the table as she approached, "This is Abenor.

Abenor, please meet Miranda."

Abenor rose, took Miranda's offered hand and kissed it, "My dear, this is indeed an honor."

"Thank you, Abenor," Miranda replied, seating herself at the table. "Please accept my apology for getting you arrested. Believe me, it was never my intention."

"As this was an extraordinary circumstance, with many unknowable factors, an apology is neither sought nor necessary, but I appreciate it nonetheless. My line of work comes with certain risks. One of them is occasional arrest. I do what I can to mitigate that risk, however." Turning to face Roland, Abenor said, "Forgive me, but I do have other business to attend to. If you find yourself back on Lachelax in the future, please drop in to see me. Perhaps I can make use of your services again, in certain legitimate interests of mine."

"I will," Roland replied.

Abenor rose, gave a short bow to Roland, and another to Miranda. Then, he turned and left.

"Did you locate her, dear?" Miranda asked.

"Not yet." Roland scanned the crowd. *Bornor tracked her to this restaurant, but I don't see her.* "Wait, there she is." He nodded toward a table in another corner.

Miranda did not turn. She looked at her chronometer. "The report should be on in four minutes."

Roland flagged down a server and ordered three drinks. "It was too bad about Beranon, though. Still, eighty-five percent chance is better than none. Too bad he rolled bad dice on the *Surrogate*."

"Yeah, I hope his wife and son are coping. Maybe this report will ease some of their pain. I am glad Vardri made it. I hope this will calm her down. I can't imagine living under such pressure," Miranda stated.

The server returned with the drinks. Roland lifted two off the tray as the viewscreens started to show an interruption to the various sporting events being shown. Various newscasters introduced some breaking story from Anadir. Commander Tuman approached a podium as the server left the table with his instructions.

Someone requested the volume be turned up, and the man mixing the drinks complied. Tuman's voice was heard over the dying conversations, "And now I would like to read a short statement before answering any questions. "It is with tremendous gratitude to Roland Marcel, Bornor Zemadin, Beranon Santar, and Vardri Alarius..."

Roland and Miranda watched Vardri stare at the monitor while the commander gave the details from the podium. As Tuman put the statement down, the server handed the remaining drink to Vardri and pointed to Roland and Miranda's table. Roland watched her take the drink from the server and look their way but could not see her eyes through the sunglasses she wore. Her mouth betrayed her shock at seeing the news report.

As Roland and Miranda lifted their glasses to her, he saw Vardri's jaw begin to quiver. The server retrieved the drink she held as her hand started trembling. Roland smiled as Vardri bent her head to cry. The noise of the crowd's response drowned out whatever noise Vardri made in her release.

Directing Miranda toward the exit, Roland got up and let her usher him out.

NOTE FROM THE AUTHOR

Word-of-mouth is crucial for any author to succeed. If you enjoyed the book, please leave a review online—anywhere you are able. Even if it's just a sentence or two. It would make all the difference and would be very much appreciated.

Thanks!
Darrell

ABOUT THE AUTHOR

An Atlanta native, Darrell Zuercher grew up in the deep South, graduating from college and graduate school. Between those two accomplishments, he fled to the Pacific Northwest. He began his IT career in a college library, before moving on to home improvement stores, income tax preparation, journalism, electric utilities, and logistics. When not working or writing, Darrell enjoys sports, concerts, collecting stamps, role-playing games, and antique shopping. Darrell is married and lives in Louisville, Kentucky.

Thank you so much for reading one of our **Sci-Fi** novels.

If you enjoyed our book, please check out our recommended title for your next great read!

Culture-Z by Karl Andrew Marszalowicz

In the year 2190, mankind has made great strides forward in the worlds of technology, science, and greed. However, when all three get together one last time, this oblivious generation may not exist much longer.

View other Black Rose Writing titles at
www.blackrosewriting.com/books and use promo code
PRINT to receive a **20% discount** when purchasing.